P9-DNR-983

Praise for
The Phantom Hollow Series
by Kathy Herman

"A masterfully woven mystery involving flawed people struggling in a flawed world, where grace and forgiveness are major players in *The Grand Scheme*. Herman's vivid characters and their conflicts kept me reading well into the night, in the end reminding me of the one hope of mankind—our Savior's unconditional love."

> —LINDA WINDSOR, author of *For Pete's Sake* and *Wedding Bell Blues*

"Kathy Herman rivets the reader with her trademark blend of family saga and suspense story in *The Grand Scheme*. The three-dimensional characters leap from the page as Herman weaves a dark tangle of deceit, betrayal, and jealousy into a magnificent tapestry of redemption and forgiveness."

> —JILL ELIZABETH NELSON, author of the To Catch a Thief series

"*The Grand Scheme* won't disappoint Kathy Herman fans, who have come to expect strong characters, clever plot twists, and plenty of heart. Herman gives us a story we'll need to stay up all night reading and characters we'll want to mull over and live with long after the book is closed."

> —DANDI DALEY MACKALL, author of *Maggie's Story, Crazy in Love,* and *Love Rules*

"Kathy Herman's talent is in getting the reader immersed in her story. I stepped into Jewel's Café on the first page. I cheered for the good guys and scratched my head as they tried to puzzle out the twists and turns of their summer calamities. This is the right book for those readers who like to be a part of the characters' lives on the pages."

> —DONITA K. PAUL, author of the best-selling DragonKeeper series

"*Never Look Back* picks up speed, racing around twists and turns, so you have to hang on tight until the end. Now I need to read the next book in the series."

—LAURAINE SNELLING, best-selling author of *The Brushstroke Legacy,* the Red River of the North series, and the Dakota Treasures series

"Once again, Kathy Herman creates a world full of intrigue and suspense, full of characters easy to love, with poignant emotional and spiritual threads that transcend story and touch hearts. I cheered for Ivy and Montana and their story of hope and second chances. Don't miss *Never Look Back!*"

—SUSAN MAY WARREN, award-winning author of *In Sheep's Clothing*

"Kathy Herman just keeps getting better. The deep characters, heartfelt storyline, and escalating drama in *Never Look Back* left me wanting more. Congratulations, Kathy!"

—CRESTON MAPES, author of *Nobody*

"Kathy Herman is a master at weaving heart-racing mystery and biblical precept into unforgettable narrative. Not only will the twists and turns in *Ever Present Danger* keep the pages turning, her characters will inhabit the soul."

—DEIDRE POOL, author of *Loving Jesus Anyway*

THE
GRAND
SCHEME

PHANTOM
HOLLOW

BOOK THREE

THE
GRAND
SCHEME

KATHY
HERMAN

MULTNOMAH
BOOKS

THE GRAND SCHEME
PUBLISHED BY MULTNOMAH BOOKS
12265 Oracle Boulevard, Suite 200
Colorado Springs, Colorado 80921
A division of Random House Inc.

All Scripture quotations are taken from the Holy Bible, New International Version®. NIV®. Copyright © 1973, 1978, 1984 by International Bible Society. Used by permission of Zondervan Publishing House. All rights reserved.

The characters and events in this book are fictional, and any resemblance to actual persons or events is coincidental.

ISBN 978-1-59052-923-2

Copyright © 2008 by Kathy Herman

Published in association with the literary agency of Alive Communications Inc., 7680 Goddard Street, Suite 200, Colorado Springs, CO 80920, www.alive communications.com.

All rights reserved. No part of this book may be reproduced or transmitted in any form or by any means, electronic or mechanical, including photocopying and record-ing, or by any information storage and retrieval system, without permission in writing from the publisher.

MULTNOMAH is a trademark of Multnomah Books and is registered in the U.S. Patent and Trademark Office. The colophon is a trademark of Multnomah Books.

Library of Congress Cataloging-in-Publication Data
Herman, Kathy.
    The grand scheme : a novel / Kathy Herman. — 1st ed.
      p. cm. — (Phantom hollow ; bk. 3)
    ISBN 978-1-59052-923-2
  I. Title.
    PS3608.E762G73 2008
    813'.6—dc22

                           2007041513

Printed in the United States of America
2008

10 9 8 7 6 5 4 3 2

To Him who is both the Giver and the Gift.

ACKNOWLEDGMENTS

In the writing of this story, I drew from several resource people, each of whom shared generously from his or her storehouse of knowledge and experience. I did my best to integrate the facts as I understood them. If accuracy was compromised in any way, it was unintentional and strictly of my own doing.

I owe a debt of gratitude to my friend Paul David Houston, former assistant district attorney, Nacogdoches County, Texas, for helping me understand various statutes and criminal charges and for reading selected chapters and helping me with legal terms. Thanks, Paul. I can't tell you how much I appreciate not only your input but also how quickly and thoroughly you responded to my plethora of questions.

I want to extend a heartfelt thank-you to my friend Will Ray, professional investigator, state of Oregon, for valuable input concerning evidence collected during crime scene investigations. Will, thanks for your usual willingness to answer my questions thoroughly and in a timely manner. I hope someday to meet you and Laverne face to face.

I'd also like to offer a special word of thanks to my longtime friend Deanna Tyler for addressing my questions about environmental issues that affect residents on the western slope of Colorado.

To my mother, Nora Phillips, not only for saving all my e-mailed chapters on CD, but much more important, for sharing my excitement as only a mother can. I know you're proud of me. But do you know how very proud I am of you?

A special word of thanks to Pat Phillips, my sister and zealous prayer warrior, for being sensitive to pray for me, especially as I sought to find a satisfying ending to this story, and to my online prayer team for your amazing support. There's no way to measure your importance to this writing ministry. How God is using each of you!

Thanks also to Kim Prothro; Deidre Pool; Susie Killough; Judi Wieghat; Mark and Donna Skorheim; Pearl Anderson; LaVerne McCuistion; my friends at LifeWay Christian Store in Tyler, Texas; my friends at LifeWay in Nashville, Tennessee; and the ladies in my Bible study class at Bethel Bible Church for your many prayers during the writing of this book. It means so much.

To those who read my books and those who sell them, thanks for encouraging me with e-mails and cards and personal testimonies about how God has used my words to challenge and inspire you. He uses you to bless me more often than you know.

To my novelist friends in ChiLibris, thanks for sharing so generously from your collective storehouse of knowledge and experience. What a compassionate, charitable, prayerful group you are! It's an honor to be counted among you.

To my agent, Beth Jusino, thanks for working tirelessly on my behalf; to the team at Multnomah Books, thanks for all you do to get my books on the shelves.

To my editor, Diane Noble, thanks for your gentle way of suggesting ways to strengthen and tighten the story. Your constructive comments go down almost as easily as your compliments. You're a joy to work with!

To my husband, Paul, whose steady words of encouragement are like wind in my sails, thanks for steering me in the right direction, especially when the enemy tries to convince me I'm way off course. What an immeasurable gift you are!

And to my Father in heaven, without whose blessing none of this would matter, I pray that You will take the words I fashioned into story and make them real and relevant in the heart of every reader.

PROLOGUE

*For where you have envy and
selfish ambition, there you find
disorder and every evil practice.*

JAMES 3:16

The drone of deep voices in Jewel's Café turned to silence. Grayson Knolls lifted his gaze to the front door as Rue Kessler came inside and stomped the March snow off his boots.

Grayson fiddled with the bill of his cap and pasted on a bland expression. *Too bad you didn't get run over by a truck on the way over here.* He found the thought amusing.

"There's my future son-in-law." Elam Griffith pushed back his chair and stood, a broad smile appearing just below his mustache.

Rue did a double take and seemed surprised to see the EG Construction crew sitting around several tables that had been pushed together.

Grayson figured it was an act.

Elam shook Rue's hand and pulled him into a half bear hug. "I lured you here under false pretenses. I just got through telling the crew that you've agreed to be our project manager. It's official. Congratulations."

For what? Being handed a job he didn't earn? I'm the one who deserves it.

The crew applauded, and then Joel Myers got up and shook Rue's hand. "I'm looking forward to working with you."

"Thanks, same here," Rue said.

One by one the others got up and offered their congratulations.

Grayson waited until last, then with his fabricated expression still intact, he stood and offered Rue a hearty handshake. "Congratulations. Guess there *are* fringe benefits to marrying the boss's daughter."

Rue laughed. "I never thought of it that way. You know she's my son's mother, and we're finally gonna be a family, right?"

"Yeah, I heard."

Elam patted Rue on the back. "I'm thrilled for Ivy. But I'm excited about having someone in the family as passionate about this business as I am."

Grayson took his seat at the table, wrapped his hands around his mug, and imagined how good it would feel to slap the stupid grin off Kessler's face.

"So when's the wedding?" Joel asked. "I assume my dad's going to perform the ceremony?"

"Yeah, Saturday morning, June 7. I told Pastor Myers that if I had my way, we'd elope. But Ivy has her heart set on having the wedding at Woodlands Community Church."

"So is your kid going to be in it?" Grayson asked.

Rue nodded. "Ring bearer. We're only having a best man and matron of honor stand up with us. The ceremony's gonna be simple."

"But the reception *isn't*," Elam said. "We're having it out at our place, and Carolyn wants to do it up big. We only have one daughter and plan to marry her off in style. Rue, sit down. Have some coffee and decide what you want for breakfast. You're the man."

Still wearing that annoying toothy grin, Rue pulled out a chair across from Grayson. "Life's pretty terrific right now."

"No kidding," Grayson said. "You've got your entire future nailed down. Not bad for a guy who arrived here seven months ago—fresh out of rehab on a temporary work program."

Grayson knew the instant he said it that he shouldn't have. Heat scalded his cheeks in the awkwardness that followed, and he took a sip of cold coffee, waiting for Rue to put him in his place.

"I can hardly believe it myself." Rue's tone was surprisingly non-defensive. "I just thank the Lord for it."

Elam's eyes narrowed as he homed in on Grayson. "I asked Rue to manage the retirement village project because he has more experience than anyone here. But both of you are important players, and it's going to take you two working together to get the first phase done before September. Are we on the same page?"

Grayson bobbed his head, hoping to move past the clumsiness of the moment. "It doesn't matter to me who I call boss as long as we get the work done right."

Jewel Sadler appeared at the table, her white hair flattened by a hair net, a green pad in her hand. "Are you fellas ready to order?"

"We all decided on the skillet scramble," Elam said. "Rue, what about you?"

"Sounds great."

"All righty." Jewel winked at Rue and mouthed, *Congratulations.* "Rita will bring you fruit muffins and a fresh coffee. We'll get your order out to you as fast as we can."

Grayson picked up the plastic carafe and emptied the last of the coffee into Rue's mug. "So how long have you been in construction?"

"Since the day I got my first set of Tinkertoys. Actually, my grand-dad was a builder, and I worked for him every summer from middle school through college. In the twelve years since, I've worked for several builders on a variety of projects, usually as foreman. I was supervisor on the last one."

"I'm surprised. I mean, considering your drinking problem and all."

"Fortunately, I was a functioning alcoholic—till just before I entered rehab, anyway."

"The point is, he kicked it," Elam said. "Let's move on."

Rue rubbed a coffee ring off the table with his index finger. "If I were Grayson, I'd probably wonder if you would've hired an ex-drunk to manage this project if he wasn't about to become your son-in-law."

"Well, the nice thing about owning the company is I don't have to explain my decisions." Elam glanced across the table at Grayson. "But in case anyone is wondering, I didn't just pin a title on Rue, I checked out his references. His work history's broad and impressive. He's an experienced foreman and supervisor, and he was being groomed for a management role on his last project. Plus he's got a bachelor's degree in construction management and civil engineering."

Elam patted Rue on the back. "He's exactly what we need. This project is too involved for me to handle by myself, and having someone with his experience to juggle the details solves a big headache for me and for all of us. And it positions us to be on a fast track as soon as the weather warms up. Am I making myself clear?"

"Crystal clear," Grayson said. "I'm one hundred percent on board." *But what I plan to do when your back's turned is another story.*

1

RUE KESSLER GRIPPED the wheel of his new Chevy Silverado and felt almost as if he were riding on air. Or was it just his mood? He spotted the entrance to Three Peaks Christian Camp and Conference Center and turned left just shy of it onto the private road that led to his in-laws' log house.

He scanned the panorama of wide-open range and was awed by the brilliant kaleidoscope of wild flowers that had overtaken the valley floor. In the distance, the blue gray peaks of the San Juan Mountains formed a backdrop worthy of a travel magazine. Rue let his mind wander, his heart basking in the pristine beauty.

"What's so funny?"

"Sorry, what?" He turned to Ivy, her face radiant, her intriguing gray eyes animated and exuding joy. He mentally snapped a picture of her expression, determined to keep her that happy for the rest of his life.

"You laughed out loud. I wondered what was so funny."

Rue picked up her hand and pressed it to his lips, a smile tugging at the corners of his mouth. "I must be *really* happy because when we turned back there and started driving straight for those majestic peaks, I had this sudden urge to belt out the song from *The Sound of Music*. 'The hills are alive with the sound of music…'"

Ivy laughed. "Listen, mister. If you start singing like that when we get to Mom and Dad's, you're on your own."

"I wonder what they expect me to say. I've never brought someone's daughter home from her honeymoon before."

"I doubt they expect anything, other than to see us happy." Ivy craned her neck and peered out the front window. "I'm surprised Montana wasn't waiting for us when we made the turn. He sounded so excited on the phone."

Rue saw a glint of red on the split-rail fence about a hundred yards up the road. "I'll bet that's him." He tooted the horn.

Montana jumped off the fence and waved his red cap in the air, then raced to the side of the road, flanked by two rollicking balls of fur.

Rue pulled over, and Ivy flung open the passenger door, slid out, and threw her arms around their son, the two huskies yelping and running in circles.

"I thought you'd never get here," Montana said, sounding out of breath. "You've been gone a really, really, *really* long time."

"It's *so* good to see you." Ivy smothered him with kisses, then drew back and studied him. "Oh, my. I think you've grown in the past ten days."

Montana's mop of thick auburn hair fell in bangs just above his puppy eyes and shone like copper in the afternoon sun. "Grandma says she's gonna put a brick on my head because I'm growing too fast."

Rue got out and hurried around to the other side of the truck. He lifted Montana into his arms and whirled him around. "How's my favorite son?"

"I beat Brandon at arm wrestling *two* times."

"That's awesome."

"I've been drinking lots and lots of milk and strawberry yogurt shakes—the kind you said would make me strong."

"Okay, let's have a look." Rue set him on the ground.

Montana bent his arm and flexed his muscle.

"Good grief. Are those *your* biceps? You're turning into the Hulk." Rue put his son in a headlock and tickled his chin, relishing the sound of his giggling. "I missed you. You know that?"

"I missed you, too. So are you gonna sleep over now?"

"Absolutely. My pajamas are right there in the suitcase. You're stuck with me for the rest of your life."

Montana's face beamed. "Good. I always wanted to live with my dad since I was a little kid."

"That long, eh?" Rue winked at Ivy. "How about we ride up the hill and say hi to Grandma and Grandpa? I'm sure they're anxious to see us. Windy and Sasha can ride, too." He put the dogs in the bed of the truck and gave Montana a boost into the backseat.

"Guess what?" Montana buckled his seat belt. "Uncle Rusty's moving here."

"Oh, sweetie. I doubt that," Ivy said.

"Grandpa said so. The animal doctor died, and Uncle Rusty's gonna be it now."

"Doc Henley died?"

"Uh-huh. He got a heart attack in his sleep."

Rue sensed Ivy tensing up and slid his arm around her slender waist. "Well, your brother moving back to Jacob's Ear could be good news."

"Uncle Rusty doesn't like me," Montana said. "But Mom said it's *his* problem."

"That's right," Ivy said. "It has nothing to do with you. Uncle Rusty is just mad at Mommy for some things that happened a long time ago when I was doing drugs. He's decided not to like me or anyone who's important to me."

"Then he won't like Dad, either."

"Don't be too sure about that," Rue said. "I'm completely irresistible."

Ivy sighed, and he realized this wasn't the time to joke around.

"Don't you worry about Rusty, babe. There's no way I'm gonna let him mistreat you or Montana the way he did before. But he knows that moving back here means he'll be running into us. Maybe he's ready to mend fences."

"Or he just wants to drive a wedge between us and Mom and Dad."

Rue pulled into the circle drive in front of Elam and Carolyn Griffith's log home, his mind flashing back to the huge white pavilion that had stood out front and the lavish luncheon reception that had been held there following the wedding. He turned to Ivy just as she turned to him, her face aglow. She squeezed his hand as if to say she was reminiscing, too.

Montana flung open the door and jumped out of the back and ran up the front steps, the dogs on his heels. "They're here. They're here."

By the time Rue followed Ivy up to the porch, his in-laws and Montana had come outside, and in the next second, it was hard to tell who was hugging whom.

"The two of you are positively radiant," Carolyn said.

Elam winked at Rue. "Jamaica will do that to you."

"That must be it." Rue gave Ivy's hand a gentle squeeze. "We can't thank you enough for such a great wedding trip."

"Actually, for *everything*," Ivy said. "We've hardly stopped talking about the wedding and reception. Did any of the pictures turn out?"

Elam chortled. "Oh, just a couple hundred."

"We don't have the professional proofs back yet," Carolyn said. "But the digitals are really good. There's one in particular with Brandon and Kelsey that's priceless. I dare say your best man and matron of honor were almost as stunning as the two of you. Well, come in and have some blueberry cobbler and tell us all about Jamaica."

"I want ice cream on mine." Montana disappeared through the front door.

"Before we go in," Ivy said, "what's this about Rusty moving back?"

"We were surprised, too." Elam put his arm around Carolyn's shoulder. "He's already talked to Doc Henley's widow and made her an offer on the veterinary practice, and she accepted."

"What about his practice in Albuquerque?"

Elam shrugged. "He doesn't seem too concerned about leaving it."

"Has he sold his house?"

"No, but he doesn't think it'll take long to sell it because of the upscale neighborhood and exceptional view. He's put down a deposit on a two-bedroom house in Jacob's Ear and plans to rent until he and Jacqueline find what they want. She and the girls will stay in Albuquerque until the house sells. He's planning to move in this weekend."

"So much for Father's Day." Ivy's expression had lost the joy that bubbled over earlier. "Don't expect me to be happy about it. We all know Rusty lied about being sick so he wouldn't have to come to our wedding. It's obvious he wants nothing to do with us. And I don't want Montana put through the wringer again."

"Hey…" Rue tucked her hair behind her ear, unsettled by the apprehension in her eyes. "I told you I'm not gonna let him mistreat you two like he did before. Don't close your mind already. He might've had a change of heart."

Ivy turned to her father. "Do you think he did?"

"I haven't had a chance to broach the subject with him yet," Elam said. "But I'm with Rue. We're not going to allow Rusty to treat you the way he did before."

"No, I'll just be stuck with the guilt because the family's divided."

"Baloney. We've been divided on this issue since Rusty was here at Thanksgiving. It's not your fault that he chose to be difficult."

Ivy's sigh blew the bangs off her forehead. "I know, Dad, but I'm finally happy. The last thing I need right now is more of Rusty's venom."

The front door opened and Montana stood in the threshold, a much-too-angelic expression on his face. "Hey, how come you guys are still out there when the blueberry cobbler is in here? Better hurry up before I eat it *all*." He laughed a husky laugh.

"Oh no, you don't." Rue grabbed him and started tickling his ribs, evoking a loud squeal and a giggle.

Carolyn chuckled. "All right, people. Sounds like we'd better get in there and divide up the spoils."

Rue ate the last bite of his cobbler and pushed his bowl aside, eager to go home and get unpacked and start his new life with Ivy and Montana. He sat back in his chair, his hands folded across his middle. "Carolyn, that's gotta be the best blueberry cobbler in the known world."

She smiled. "I'm glad you like it. Would you care for a little more?"

"My taste buds would, but my belt's telling me that two bowlfuls is enough."

Montana jumped up from the table. "Are we going home now?"

"Can you handle fifteen more minutes, sweetie?" Ivy said.

"I'll try." Montana stood between Rue and Ivy, one of his arms around each of their necks. "I just wanna give you my surprise sooooo bad."

"At our house?" Rue said.

Montana bobbed his head, an Opie Taylor grin overtaking his face. "Grandma helped me, but it was my idea."

Rue tousled Montana's hair and pulled him into a half hug, relishing the thought of a future with the two loves of his life. "Then we can hardly wait to see it."

"We're *very* excited to get home," Ivy said. "But Daddy and I need to discuss something with Grandma and Grandpa first."

"Okay. I'll go play with Sasha and Windy so you can talk about *Uncle Rusty.*"

Rue smiled. "You're getting too smart for your own good. We won't be long."

Montana whistled for the dogs and, a few seconds later, went out the front door.

Rue studied Ivy's somber profile, feeling helpless to do anything to alleviate her mounting anxiety. Did being married to her for ten days give him sufficient license to assume a role in this conflict? He turned his attention to Elam and Carolyn. "Any suggestions how Ivy and I should respond to Rusty? Think we should call him and break the ice, then offer to help him move in?"

"I vote to leave him alone until he decides to be civil," Ivy said flatly. "If he's hung up on my past, that's his problem. I'm not going to make it ours. Not now. Not when I'm *finally* happy."

Elam tugged at his mustache and seemed to be deep in thought. "Better let me feel him out before you do anything. His decision to move here came about so suddenly that Carolyn and I haven't had a chance to assimilate it, either."

"Now that I think about it," Carolyn said, "Jacqueline seemed distant when we were there in February. I assumed she felt awkward about our not coming for Christmas because Ivy and Montana weren't invited. Maybe there was more to it than that."

"Like what?" Ivy said.

Carolyn twirled a lock of hair around her finger. "I'm not sure. But the timing is very strange, especially since Rusty's made no effort to reconcile with you. Plus they've got everything going for them in Albuquerque. Rusty's practice is growing. They have a fabulous home. Tia and Josie are enrolled in a first-rate preschool. And they just bought a membership to some prestigious new country club. They're not going to be able to duplicate all that here."

"Isn't it possible," Rue said, "that Rusty regrets not coming to the wedding and misses being a part of this family? Maybe he's moving back to make things right."

Ivy stared at her bowl, her sleek, bobbed hair covering her expression. "It's so like you to think the best. But Rusty's not the brother I grew up with. His heart's turned to stone."

Rue guessed from the dark mood that had replaced Ivy's joy that her brother's opinion of her had a profound effect on how she felt about herself.

2

IVY KESSLER CLIMBED into the passenger seat of the Silverado and waved good-bye to her parents, then sat back and enjoyed the ride to the bottom of the hill. For the first time in a decade, her life was *normal* and sweet and full of promise. She wasn't going to let her concern about her brother's move back to Jacob's Ear spoil it.

As Rue turned left into Three Peaks Christian Camp and Conference Center, he winked at her and began whistling the tune to "The Sound of Music."

She stole a few well-spaced glances at her husband. He was a perfect balance of strength and gentleness. Handsome in a rugged sort of way—and *that* enhanced by his Jamaican tan. Montana had his smile. And his kind heart.

Half a minute later Rue passed the main lodge and turned onto Chalet Circle, then pulled into the third driveway and parked next to Ivy's Jeep Liberty.

"We're home." He honked the horn several times and laughed.

Montana pushed open the back door and jumped out, Windy on his heels.

"Dad, let me go in first and make sure my surprise is still there."

Rue smiled. "I'm sure it's fine, champ. The house is locked."

"But I want to see. Can I have the key?"

"Sure. Here you go."

Montana raced to the front door and unlocked it, then glanced over his shoulder. "Wait here. I'll be right back." He followed Windy inside and closed the door behind him.

Rue came around to where she was standing. "He's pretty fired up about his surprise."

"He gets that way about all the gifts he chooses." Ivy looked up at the chalet and then into Rue's inviting brown eyes, feeling as if a tiny bubble machine had been turned on inside her. "I can hardly believe you're going to be living here with us. I don't think it's hit me yet."

Rue slid his arm around her and ran his thumb over her wedding band. "It's generous of Elam and Carolyn to let us stay at Three Peaks as long as we want. But I'm committed to getting our house finished before next summer."

Montana pushed open the door and held it. "Okay, you can come in now."

"Hang on, Mrs. Kessler." Rue lifted her into his arms, then carried her toward the house, the sound of her giggling evoking squeals of delight from Montana.

Rue stepped across the threshold and set her down, then pulled her into his arms and kissed her. For a few glorious seconds she felt as if she had stepped into the pages of a storybook. "I love you," she whispered.

"And I love you—so much." Rue stroked her cheek, then turned to Montana and rubbed his hands together. "Okay, champ, you're next."

He chased Montana out to the stoop, then carried him back into the house under one arm, his belly laugh filling the living room. He kissed him on top of his head, then proudly announced, "It's a done deal. We're officially a family. So where's that surprise you promised us?"

Montana shot them a toothy grin. "Close your eyes and no peeking." He took his parents each by the hand and slowly led them down the hall and into the bedroom that would now be theirs. "Okay…here's your surprise."

Ivy opened her eyes and saw a beautifully framed and matted colored-pencil drawing on the wall next to the bed. She walked over and stood in front of it and realized it was a drawing of Montana, Rue, and her at the wedding. "Sweetie, what a beautiful picture. Are you the artist?"

Montana's face beamed. "I drew it all by myself. For your wedding present."

"This is excellent," Ivy said. "You captured all the detail, right down to the pink in my dress and the stripes on the ascots. Did you draw it from memory?"

"No. Grandma gave me a picture she took at the wedding so I could remember everything. I drew it over and over until I made it just right. It was Grandma's idea to put the date on it, so even when I'm big you can always remember when I drew it."

"I'm crazy about it," Rue said. "This'll be in our room forever."

"The frame is lovely, too." Ivy ran her fingers along the dark rich wood, inlaid with mother-of-pearl. "Did you pick it out?"

"Kind of. The lady at the frame place helped me and Grandma, and I told her I wanted it to be very special because I've never had a family before."

Rue put his hand on Montana's shoulder. "And because this is a very special day, you get to choose what we're going to have for our first meal together as a family."

"Spasketti and meatballs."

Rue glanced over at Ivy and raised his eyebrows up and down several times. "Okay, babe. How about the men bring in the luggage and get the laundry started while you decide what we need from the store? We'll do the shopping and even clean up the dishes afterward."

Grayson Knolls watched the last of the lumber being unloaded from the flatbed truck and noticed Elam Griffith's burgundy Suburban pulling in behind Joel Myers's SUV.

He signed a delivery slip and waved the flatbed on, then met Elam about halfway between his Suburban and the work site.

"How's it coming?" Elam asked.

"Great. We're ready to start framing." Grayson made a sweeping motion toward the model. "Phantom Hollow Retirement Village is about to take shape."

"Good timing. Rue and Ivy got back this afternoon. I told him to go ahead and take tomorrow off. I wouldn't be a bit surprised if he comes out here in the morning. You'll need to fill him in."

"Sure, but he doesn't need to rush back. There's nothing here I can't handle."

Elam put his hand on Grayson's shoulder and seemed to be looking out at the mountains. "I'm grateful for your willingness to step up this past week, Grays. But this project needs a full-time manager. We're all going to benefit from Rue's experience. I know you understand that."

"Of course I do." *You still don't think I can do the job.* Grayson pushed his hands deep into his pockets, aware of the chill in the air as the afternoon sun slipped down behind the peaks.

"I'll let you get back to work. I expect Rue'll have stars in his eyes for a few days, but once he gets his business head back on, I want him moving this project forward as quickly as possible. Our best chance to draw prospective buyers is during tourist season."

Rue put the last of the dinner dishes in the dishwasher and turned it on. "Okay, champ. That's it. Go get the Chinese checkers."

"I get to be blue." Montana raced over to the stairs and climbed up to the loft, Windy on his heels.

Rue chuckled at the sight, glad that he'd followed through with his idea to convert the ladder to wood steps so Windy could get up to Montana's room.

"Hey, Tarzan, watch yourself on those steps," Ivy said.

Rue studied her for a moment and decided she had become even more alluring and youthful since the wedding. Even the signs of premature aging that resulted from her years of doing drugs seemed to be fading. Or was it just that he loved her so?

He went over to the table where she sat and stood behind her, his hands massaging her shoulders. He admired the stonework on the fireplace that dominated the far wall of the living room, his mind flashing back to December, to the first time Ivy had invited him here to have dinner with her and Montana. What started as a fun afternoon of snowmobiling and a home-cooked meal had evolved into the fulfillment of his heart's desire. A sense of awe overtook him as he considered how God's hand had been evident, even then.

"It feels so natural being here with you two," he said.

"It should. You've been over here enough times."

He bent down, his cheek next to hers. "But now I don't have to go back to my place when it's time to go to bed."

"Montana's beside himself that you're finally going to *sleep over.*"

"And how do you feel about it?"

"I'll let you know in the morning."

Rue smiled and blew in her ear, then pulled out a chair and sat at the table next to her. "I can hardly wait to get our house built."

"I know, but don't get ahead of yourself. You're going to have your hands full managing the retirement project."

Rue picked up her hand and kissed it. "I just want to get our house framed before the snow flies so the three of us can build a fire and make s'mores and hang out over there while I do the finish work."

"It's almost too wonderful to think about."

"Okay." Montana set the game box on the table. "The champ is here. Prepare to lose."

Rue chuckled at how grown up he sounded. "You seem mighty sure of yourself."

"Well, how many times have *you* won?"

"I don't know. A few."

Montana pointed to himself with his thumb. "And how many times have *I* won?"

"Most of the time."

"Right." Montana let out a husky laugh. "That's why they call me the champ, baby."

Ivy folded her arms on the table, obviously amused by Montana's choice of words.

Rue placed the yellow marbles on the metal board and let the normalcy of the moment fall softly on his heart. He glanced at his bride and little boy, who wore the same smile as his own, and wondered how life could get any better than this.

The phone rang, and Montana jumped up. "I'll get it. I've been practicing." He ran over to the wall and picked up the phone, his proud grin nearly swallowing the receiver. "Kessler residence. Montana speaking…" His smile quickly disappeared. "It's Uncle Rusty. He wants to speak to Mom."

"I really don't know what to say." Ivy turned to Rue, panic in her eyes.

"Let's both talk to him. Go pick up the extension." Rue got up and took the phone from Montana. "Hello, Rusty. This is Rue. Sorry you couldn't make it to the wedding. I hope you and the family are feeling better now."

"We're fine," Rusty Griffith said. "I called to speak to Ivy."

"She's picking up the extension." There was a click on the line. "You there, babe?"

"Yes, but don't hang up," Ivy said. "Whatever Rusty has to say, he can say to both of us."

Rusty exhaled into the receiver. "I called to say that just because I'm moving back doesn't mean my feelings have changed since you and I talked at Thanksgiving. I just wanted to make that clear."

"And now you have," Ivy said. "But there's no way we can avoid seeing each other. The three of us are out at Mom and Dad's a lot."

"Don't worry, I'll be polite when I see you. I just want to make sure you understand ahead of time."

"Why don't you explain it to me?" Rue said. "Because I don't get it. Ivy's been clean now for more than four years. She's done a great job with Montana. She's been good to your folks. She's fiscally responsible. And now she's married to me, and we're raising our son. She's completely turned her life around. What more do you think she should do?"

"I don't expect you to understand."

"Well, I'd like to," Rue said. "Because I love her and Montana, and anything that hurts them affects me."

"Listen, Rue. Let's get something straight. This conflict is between Ivy and me. I don't have to answer to you. But just so you'll know where

I'm coming from: I watched Ivy's drug habit tear this family apart. My parents spent more money on her rehab than they did putting me through college, and then she up and disappeared without as much as a thank-you. When she *finally* resurfaced, she showed up at my parents' with a seven-year-old kid none of us even knew about, and—"

"I know all about Ivy's past," Rue said. "She got addicted to drugs in high school and spent the next ten years making choices she isn't proud of. But she's clean now. And she's got her head on straight. Do you have any idea what it took for her to come this far?"

"Her? Do you have any idea what she put *us* through? Frankly, I'm tired of hearing about how tough *she* had it. But I suppose it takes one to know one. I hear you've been in rehab, too."

"We each fought our own addiction," Rue said. "And we both kicked it. Count your blessings that you never had to. Your sister's worked hard to fight her way back. She's a gentle, loving person who deserves another chance."

"Fine. Since you understand her so well, you give her another chance. I'm done. I'm going to hang up now. My dad said you offered to help me unload the U-Haul when I arrive. No need. I've got it covered." *Click.*

Rue hung up the phone and waited for Ivy to come back into the kitchen.

"Was Uncle Rusty mean?" Montana said.

Rue pulled Montana into his lap. "He's got a powerful wad of anger in his gut, that's for sure."

"I don't want him to come to our house."

"I doubt he will," Rue said. "But we need to pray that God changes his heart. It's sad for a brother and sister not to want to see each other."

Ivy came in, flopped in the chair across from them, and blew the bangs off her forehead. "Well, one thing about Rusty, you never have to wonder where you stand with him."

"Give it time." Rue reached over and put his hand on hers. "I don't think he'd be moving back here if he really thought the two of you would be at odds forever."

"I don't want Uncle Rusty to move here. He makes Mom cry…and he acts like I'm not even there. It hurts my feelings."

Rue tilted Montana's chin and saw sadness in his eyes. "I'm not gonna let that happen. How about the three of us just enjoy being a family and not worry about Rusty for now?"

3

THE NEXT MORNING Rue woke up to the wonderful aroma of freshly brewed coffee and forgot where he was until he opened his eyes and saw Montana's drawing hanging on the wall. He turned over, draped his arm over Ivy, and nestled next to her, thinking of all the times he had imagined waking up beside her in this room.

"Our new coffeemaker works," Ivy said sleepily.

"I noticed." Rue stroked her arm and relished the softness. Elam told him to take the day off. Did he really need to go out to the site? "I think I'll just stay here with you. Forget about work."

Ivy turned over and faced him, her head on his pillow. "But you won't be able to forget about work unless you go check things out. I don't want you to be distracted when we hike up to Tanner Falls this afternoon." She traced his eyebrows with her finger. "I'm really excited we're doing something fun with just the three of us. You won't have much free time once you go back to work. We both know what construction is like in the summer."

"We'll still have Sundays after church to do things as a family. And after the cold weather sets in, I'll have a lot more free time. We can get back to stargazing and snowmobiling and cozy evenings in front of the fire. I'll make good on my promise to teach Montana how to play hockey. And do the finish work on our new house."

Ivy captured a yawn with her hand. "I wonder what Rusty's going to do about a house?"

"I doubt he'll be happy with anything in Jacob's Ear, but there are some gorgeous homes for sale all over Phantom Hollow and up in the foothills. They're plenty pricey, though."

"I don't think money's a problem. I just don't want him living near us. How sad is that?"

"Certainly reasonable, considering how he treats you."

Ivy sighed. "I did some awful things when I was shooting up. All I could think about was getting another fix. I never intentionally hurt my family."

"Of course you didn't. Rusty doesn't understand addiction and doesn't want to. Let's just be glad he doesn't know the circumstances of how you ended up pregnant with Montana because I'm sure he'd use it to hurt him."

"Mom and Dad would never reveal anything that sensitive to Rusty or to anyone else."

"I know that, babe." He drew closer to Ivy until his lips were inches away from hers and he could feel the warmth of her breath. "And now, if it's okay with you, I'm going to kick your brother out of our bedroom and enjoy a few minutes alone with my bride."

Just after eight, Rue pulled up behind Grayson Knolls's old Dodge pickup and turned off the motor. He got out and ambled over to the model condominium, surprised and pleased to see the framing was underway.

Grayson stood nearby and appeared to be reading something on a clipboard, then came over to him. "Hey, welcome back. So how was Jamaica?"

"Great. But it's good to get back home to these mountains. I see things are progressing nicely."

"Yeah, we're moving along at a pretty good clip."

"Any snags?"

"Not a one. Everything's under control. In fact, I took care of getting the roofing bids for you. Peak Roofers submitted the lowest. I put all that information on your desk."

Rue bit his lip and paused for a moment. Why would he do that? "I'm sure you meant to be helpful, Grayson. But I thought we were clear that Elam left it to me to choose the subcontractors. I'd already started on this. There's more to consider than who gives us the lowest bid."

"Yeah, I know. Peak did a good job for us last time."

Rue hooked his thumbs on his jeans pockets and stared at his boots. "Actually, they didn't. I went out and inspected the work, and we can do better. Elam and I have already discussed this. Peak is out. I wish you'd talked to me before you got involved."

"I thought I was doing you a favor."

"You can see how important it is that we're on the same page so we aren't spinning our wheels." Rue softened his tone. "The retirement village is an extremely ambitious project. We've got a lot to get done before the snow flies. The only way we're gonna stay on schedule is by each of us putting one hundred per cent into the task he's been assigned—"

Angry voices broke Rue's concentration. He turned around and saw the work crew circling two men who were about to go at each other with clenched fists.

"I'd better go find out what's going on," Grayson said.

He jogged over, stood between the two hot-tempered Hispanic men, and spoke to them in fluent Spanish.

Rue listened as Grayson asked what they were mad about and worked out a solution. A few minutes later the men shook hands, went back to work, and Grayson came back over to Rue.

"Just a little misunderstanding. Hernandez and Montoya take everything personal. They're fine now."

"I heard. Where'd you learn to speak Spanish so well?"

"My wife, Tara, teaches it at the high school. If you're done with me, I need to finish working on the scheduling. Sorry I overstepped. It won't happen again."

Late that afternoon, Ivy sat on a smooth boulder with Rue and Montana and watched the spring runoff spill over the top of Tanner Falls and plummet fifty feet into the whitewater of the Phantom River.

"This is amazing." Rue gave her hand a gentle squeeze. "I'm glad you thought of hiking up here."

The scent of pine wafted under Ivy's nose, and for a moment she was a girl again. "This is one of my favorite places. Rusty and I came up here all the time when we were kids. We stood near the falls and let the over spray get us wet."

"Was Uncle Rusty mean to you when you were little?" Montana asked.

"Not really. We had our share of disagreements, but we were the best of friends—maybe because we didn't have any other kids to play with. When we lived in the log house Grandma and Grandpa have now, there was nothing else out there but the stable. Three Peaks hadn't been built yet, and as far as we could see was forestland and wide-open range. In fact, Rusty and I rode our horses all over the land where the camp is now."

"How come Grandma and Grandpa wanted a camp there?"

Ivy brushed the bangs out of Montana's big brown eyes that looked so much like her brother's. "Because after Rusty and I moved away, they got lonesome out there by themselves. They decided to build a place where other people could come and share that gorgeous view."

Windy climbed out of a nearby stream, shook the water off her coat, then jumped up on the rock, her wet tail swiping their faces.

Montana giggled. "You just love the water, don't you, girl?" He put his arms around her and laid his head on her back.

"You and that pup really get along great," Ivy said.

"She was the funnest Christmas present in the whole world." Montana scratched Windy's chin and looked out at the rushing water. "Dad, could we go out on a raft sometime?"

"Sure. But let's ask Brandon where it's safe to be on the whitewater. There's an awful lot of rocks in the river."

Ivy reached into her backpack. "Anybody want another peanut butter cookie?"

"Me." Montana raised his hand. "These taste even better than Grandma's."

Ivy smiled to herself. She had followed her mother's recipe to the letter. Was it just the contentment of the day that had caused him to imagine they tasted better?

Montana wagged his finger at Windy. "You can't have any more." He reached in his jeans pocket and took out a dog treat and gave it to her.

"I'll take a couple of those cookies, babe." Rue held out his hand. "You excited about going back to work tomorrow?"

"I have mixed feelings. It's been a wonderful couple weeks. It's hard to think about getting back in that routine."

"Ever think of quitting?"

Ivy stopped chewing. "I never thought it was an option."

"Elam's paying me good money. There's no reason you have to keep working unless you just want to."

"What would I do at home all day?"

"Bake stuff," Montana said, his mouth chock-full of peanut butter cookie.

"I do that anyway."

"Well, you could keep Windy company so she won't get lonesome."

Ivy laughed. "Lonesome? That pup has the run of the camp, and the guests spoil her rotten." Ivy studied her son's face for a moment and then said, "Maybe you'd like me to be the one to take you to school and pick you up."

Montana shrugged. "Okay. But Grandma likes doing it. I can tell."

"And she also loves having you at her house after school and in the summer. It seems like something you both enjoy."

"Yeah, it's pretty fun."

Ivy gave Rue's arm a gentle squeeze. "What do *you* think?"

"All I care about is that you're happy and wearing that pretty smile at the end of the day."

"I think I'll leave things the way they are for now. At least I don't have any conflicts at work. I honestly don't think I could deal with somebody as insecure as Grayson."

"It's no big deal. He's just trying to impress me with how much he knows. Eventually, he'll accept that we're not in competition, that we both have an important job to do."

Grayson waited until Liz Parker got in her car and drove off, then went up the steps and unlocked the trailer where the on-site offices of EG Construction had been set up. He flipped on the lights and breezed past Liz's desk and down the narrow hallway to Rue Kessler's office. He sat at the desk and opened the folder with the roofing bids.

He knew he was overstepping when he'd jumped into this. But would it have killed Rue to at least commend him for having shown initiative instead of pointing out that he'd failed? How was he supposed to know Peak Roofing hadn't done a good job? Last he'd heard, Elam was happy with their work.

Just because Rue made it through college and had a little more experience than Grayson didn't prove that he was more qualified. He had never actually managed a project before. And though Elam liked to brag on Rue's *impressive* work history, he tended to skip over the fact that it had been overshadowed by a serious drinking problem. As far as Grayson could tell, the only thing Rue had proven to be more skilled at was kissing up to the boss.

He could only guess how much money Rue was making. It would be just like Elam to inflate his son-in-law's salary to make sure his daughter had everything she needed. And Elam could certainly afford it. He probably owned half of Tanner County.

Grayson thought about his own mounting credit-card debt and his wife's complaining that she was burned out and wanted to quit teaching.

Not once in his married life had they even come close to being debt free. And unless he could make a lot more money, it wasn't even possible. Too bad he didn't have a rich father-in-law to give him an easy ride.

Grayson closed the folder and tossed it in the trash. He started to get up, then paused as temptation toyed with his thoughts. He slid open the bottom drawer and removed the folder marked *Phase One*. He tucked it in his waistband and pulled his shirt down over it. He reached into the trash can and retrieved the folder, laid it neatly on the desk, then turned out the lights and left for the day.

4

SHERIFF FLINT CARTER got out of his squad car and paused for a moment to admire the lava-colored streaks painted across Thursday morning's sky. He pushed open the glass door of Jewel's Café and was hit with a gust of warmer air and the familiar aroma of fresh-baked muffins.

"Well, there you are," Rita Benson said. "Jewel was beginning to think you weren't coming today."

Flint sat at the table closest to the moose head. "I'm having breakfast with Elam. He said six thirty, but he's always early, so I decided to split the difference. I'm flattered you would've missed me."

Jewel Sadler came over to the table. "Actually, I'm anxious for you to sample my apricot muffins."

"So that's what smells so good."

"You can have one with your coffee. Be right back." Jewel disappeared through the swinging doors.

Elam Griffith came in the café and took off his cap, then went over to Flint's table and sat across from him. "You're awfully chipper this morning."

"I love this summer weather," Flint said. "It's all I can do not to sneak off with Ian and go trout fishing. So when are Ivy and Rue due back from their honeymoon?"

Elam beamed. "They got home a couple days ago. I've never seen Ivy happier. Does a father's heart good, especially after all that girl's been through."

Rita came to the table with a plastic pitcher and two coffee mugs. "You ready to order or do you need a few minutes?"

"I'll have my usual," Flint said.

"I'll have the skillet scramble and a large orange juice—and you can bring me the bill."

"Okay, it'll just be a few minutes." Rita disappeared through the swinging doors, and Jewel came out, carrying a small plate with two huge muffins.

"Here you go." Jewel set the plate on the table. "You fellas sink your teeth into these, and I'll be back for the verdict."

Flint peeled the paper off one of the muffins, cut it in two, buttered it, and took a big bite. "Mmm…this is great."

"Really tasty." Elam wiped the crumbs off his mustache. "So what's going on with you? I've been so preoccupied with the wedding and the new construction project that I haven't thought of much else."

"The jail's busting at the seams, but violent crime is down. We haven't had a murder in the county since that scumbag Johnson McRae split just before Christmas. In fact, this year is a cakewalk compared to last. I decided to grab a couple weeks later in the summer and take the family to Disney World."

"You'll enjoy it. I remember when Carolyn and I took our kids. Seems like a lifetime ago."

Flint laughed. "It *was*."

"Hard to believe Ivy's thirty and Rusty's thirty-two. By the way, he's moving back here. That's one of the things I wanted to tell you."

"I thought he and Jacqueline were enamored with Albuquerque."

Elam shrugged. "So'd we. But he got the ball rolling with Doc Henley's widow to buy the veterinary practice. He's moving here this weekend."

"Are he and Ivy still at odds?"

"Yeah, but it's all Rusty's doing. It's like he's disowned her—which makes it all the more surprising that he would want to move back here."

"How do you and Carolyn feel about it?"

Elam took a sip of coffee and seemed pensive. "I love my son, Flint. But I don't especially *like* him right now, and I'm not thrilled about his timing, especially with Father's Day this Sunday. But I've got another conflict. Carolyn and I set aside twenty-five acres of prime land for each of our kids a long time ago. We gave Ivy and Rue her twenty-five for a wedding gift. In all fairness, I should give Rusty his, now that he's moving back. He doesn't know anything about it. And the way I feel at the moment, it would be an obligatory gesture, not a gift from the heart. That's not going to change as long as he's hateful to Ivy and Montana."

"Does Carolyn know how you feel?"

"I haven't verbalized it, but she certainly knows that my disappointment with the kids can change me from generous to closefisted in the blink of an eye."

Jewel came over to the table. "All right, what'd you think of my apricot muffins: a go or a no?"

"A definite go," Flint said.

"You're not just saying that to be nice?"

Flint pointed to the crumbs on his plate. "Does that look like I'm just being nice? I'd like to buy a half dozen to take home."

"Ditto," Elam said. "Carolyn will love these."

Jewel pushed back a lock of hair that had escaped her hairnet. "Heavens to Betsy. You boys made my day. Now I've got cranberry, blueberry, apple, banana nut, raisin bran, *and* apricot muffins. Who knows what I might try next?" She glanced over at Rita, who arrived at the table, balancing a big round tray. "Their breakfast is on the house today."

Flint smiled, wondering if he was going to be able to eat what he'd ordered after putting away that huge muffin.

Ivy dropped Montana off at her parents' house, then drove down the long, private drive and turned into the camp. She drove past Three Peaks Lodge and around to the back of Building A, then parked the car and hiked beyond the tall pines to her favorite scenic overlook. She stood on the wood platform, her arms resting on the rail, and drank in the magnificent, unspoiled beauty of Phantom Hollow and the bulwark of rugged peaks that surrounded it. As far as she could see, a colorful potpourri of wildflowers covered the valley and the foothills beyond.

Lord, what a spectacular beginning to a whole new season of my life.

She held out her hand, admired the row of diamonds on her wedding band, and relived the moment Rue had slid it on her finger to seal his pledge of faithfulness. It still seemed like a dream. She had never expected to know the man who had fathered her child, much less fall in love with him. It was pure grace that she and Rue found each other—and that Montana now had both parents in his life.

Ivy closed her eyes and could almost feel the warm Jamaican surf washing over her feet—and her past. The haunting worthlessness that had driven her deeper and deeper into her drug habit was gone. If Rusty was unwilling to accept that God had freed her from drug addiction and blessed her in spite of her mistakes, it was his problem. She had already engaged in far too much self-loathing to allow him or anyone else to put her back under condemnation.

Ivy glanced at her watch and hurried back to the car, eager to put on her new nametag and resume her duties as registration coordinator. How she looked forward to sharing with her husband the smallest details of her day and to lavishing him with love in the privacy of the night. But more than anything else, she wanted the way they raised Montana to bring glory to God.

If Rusty still doubted that she had turned her life around, nothing she did would convince him otherwise.

Rue opened the door to the trailer and walked down the hall to his on-site office and flipped the light switch. He sat at his desk, his gaze lingering on the framed photo of Ivy and Montana, and thought of yesterday's hike up to Tanner Falls. His workday had barely begun, and already he missed being a threesome.

He opened the file folder on his desk and saw all the roofing bids Grayson had solicited. Maybe he'd been too blunt with the guy. But there was no way Grayson had misunderstood Elam's directive that Rue was to handle subcontracting bids. And it's not as though Grayson had ever gotten bids before. This was clearly a ploy to win points with the boss.

Rue read through the folder and noticed that Grayson hadn't solicited a bid from Everhardt Roofing. Everhardt would no doubt come in higher than Peak, but their reputation was second to none, and they were reputed to be competitive.

There was a knock at the door, and he turned. Joel Myers was standing in the threshold, wearing a boyish grin.

"Hey, welcome back, brother." Joel came in the office, and the two exchanged a bear hug. "Montana announced in Sunday-school class that you and Ivy were coming home this week. He's so proud to have a family."

"Jamaica was great," Rue said, "but we missed him so much that we could hardly wait to get back to him."

"Well, the people at church kept him entertained. I even took him fishing a couple times. And out for ice cream."

"Thanks. He thinks the world of you."

"It's mutual," Joel said. "Okay, I'd better get back to work and earn what you're paying me. I've got a ways to go before I can pay my tuition next fall. Talk to you later."

Joel left his office, and seconds later Elam slipped in.

"Good morning."

"Good morning, yourself," Elam said. "So how's my daughter treating you?"

Rue grinned without intending to. "Better than I deserve."

"Takes after her mother. So did Grayson get you up to speed?"

"Pretty much. I'm going to work on the roofing bids first thing. I'd really like to nail a contract with Everhardt ASAP."

"Good. I've had it with Peak. It's been one problem after another."

"Everhardt will be higher. But you'll get the most bang for your buck, and I don't think they'll give you any headaches."

A smile appeared under Elam's mustache. "I could've saved on my Excedrin bill if I'd just hired you sooner."

Rue laughed. "You didn't know me any sooner."

Elam turned his head toward the outer office and waved. "Liz just walked in. I need her to find something for me before I leave. I'll be back this afternoon, and you can show me where we are with Phase One. Good to have you back."

"Thanks. It's great to be back. I know I keep saying this, but Ivy and I can't thank you enough for the land." Rue lifted his eyebrows. "We can hardly wait to get the house finished."

"You're welcome. There *is* a method to our madness. Carolyn and I hope to keep you in Phantom Hollow. We don't want to lose our daughter again."

"No chance of that happening. I'm a little nervous about Rusty moving back, though. Ivy's already dreading the conflict."

"You let me worry about that son of mine. He's got a chip on his shoulder the size of Jacob's Peak. He needs to get back in church and remember what forgiveness is all about."

"Then Rusty's a believer?"

Elam's eyebrows came together. "He accepted Christ at summer camp when he was a teenager. And he went to church with us till he went off to college, but I haven't seen any fruit. Far as I know, he and Jacqueline don't go to church, and Tia and Josie have never set foot in Sunday school."

"Maybe he'll start up again when he comes back."

Elam nodded. "I sure hope so. The kind of bitterness he's got doesn't go away without help."

Ivy set a platter of roast beef, carrots, and potatoes on the table and then sat next to Rue.

"Mmm…does this ever smell good," he said.

"I'd like to tell you I slaved all day, but I just put everything in the Crockpot this morning before I went to work."

Rue said the blessing and then picked up the platter and put a sampling of everything on Montana's plate.

"I like this better than the kind we had at Jewel's when you and Mom were on your huggymoon."

"You mean our *honey*moon."

A smile tugged at the corners of Montana's mouth as he shoved in a big bite of potato. "Me and Ian like to say *huggy*moon. Get it?"

Rue smiled with his eyes. "Yeah, I get it." He filled his plate and handed the platter to Ivy.

"So what did you do all day at Grandma's?" Ivy said to Montana.

She listened as her son bubbled over with excitement about his grandmother's letting him ride one of the tamer horses around the property as long as he stayed inside the split-rail fence. Rue seemed to hang on to every word but didn't have much to say about his own day, other than he had locked in the contract with Everhardt Roofing.

"I had a very busy day," Ivy said. "Of course, it was great seeing Kelsey and reminiscing about the wedding. But we've got a conference ending day after tomorrow and three different age groups of kids coming in for summer camp. The absolute highlight of my day was calling the mother of one of the boys to tell her about a cancellation and introducing myself as Ivy *Kessler*."

"I got the name Kessler before you did." Montana cocked his head and flashed a toothy grin. "Now we all three match."

"We certainly do." Her mind replayed the expression of sheer bliss on Montana's face when she and Rue told him, just days before the wedding, that his last name had been legally changed.

"May I please be excused?" Montana slid out of the chair. "I wanna call Ian and tell him Grandma let me ride Sassy all by myself."

"All right, sweetie. Would you take your dishes to the sink? You can use the phone in our room."

Montana cleared his place and hurried down the hall to the master bedroom.

Ivy turned to Rue and gently stroked his arm. "You seem miles away. Is something wrong?"

"I'm fine, babe. I just misplaced an important file and had to wing it during my meeting with your dad. I would've liked to make a better impression. It's not as though I haven't got my ducks in a row. I just don't know where they are."

"Did you take the file out of your office?"

Rue shrugged. "I could swear I left it in my desk drawer. But I thumbed through every file, and it's not there. I had a lot on my mind the week before the wedding. Maybe I picked it up without even thinking and left it somewhere."

"Did you ask Liz?"

"Yeah, she hasn't seen it."

"You don't have the information entered on the computer?"

"No. I planned to do it when I got back." Rue sighed. "I've got weeks of notes in that file. I need to find it. The last thing I want to do is delay the project—the very thing your dad hired me to avoid."

5

IVY SAT AT A WINDOW table at Jewel's Café and reveled in the bustling sounds and delicious aromas that took her back to when she was a waitress there.

Jewel Sadler came through the swinging doors, rushed over to Ivy, and threw her arms around her. "Rita said you were here. It's so good to see you. How was Jamaica?"

"Fabulous. But it was wonderful coming home and finally being able to move in together as a family."

"So where's that sweet husband of yours?"

"Out at the site. No construction manager worth his salt takes a whole Saturday off in the summer."

"Sometimes my dad lets me wear his hard hat." Montana patted his head.

Jewel reached down and hugged him with the affection of a grandmother. "So how's my favorite young man?"

"Good." Montana seemed relaxed in her arms, his round dark eyes peeping over her shoulder. "In our new house, my dad's gonna build a doggy door so Windy can go out and come back in by herself."

"Good thinking." Jewel kissed Montana's cheek and stood upright. "When will you be in the new place?"

"Hopefully before this time next year," Ivy said. "Rue wants to have it framed by the time it starts snowing again, and then start on the finish work through the cold months."

Jewel glanced around the café. "I want to hear all about it when it's not so busy in here. Has Rita taken your order?"

"Yes, and we're in no hurry. Montana and I are just having a relaxing breakfast before we go do some special shopping."

"Tomorrow's my very first Father's Day in my whole life," Montana said. "I wanna find something awesome for my dad."

"I'll bet you will." The door to the café opened, and Jewel seemed distracted for a moment. "Well, for heaven's sake. I didn't know Rusty was in town for Father's Day."

Ivy felt the muscles in her neck tighten and didn't turn around. "He isn't. He's moving back. He just bought Doc Henley's practice."

"I don't want Uncle Rusty to see me." Montana picked up the dessert menu and held it in front of his face.

"It's so pitiful that we're actually hiding from my brother."

"Rita said something to him," Jewel whispered. "He left."

Ivy pulled back the curtain and saw her brother get into a Lincoln Navigator with a small trailer in tow and drive away. "He was probably trying to find Mom and Dad. He made it clear he doesn't want anything to do with me."

"Uncle Rusty isn't nice." Montana put the menu back on the table. "I don't want him to move here."

"Why do I let Rusty intimidate me?" Ivy said. "He can make me feel so unworthy—like I don't have the right to be happy."

Jewel lowered herself into the chair next to Ivy. "Listen to me, doll. You can hold your head high. The way you've pulled yourself up is a testimony to God's mercy. Don't let anybody steal your joy."

Ivy stared at her hands, her mind racing through the chapters of the past year. "You're right. It was the Lord who restored Rue and me and brought us together. Of course we were unworthy. But isn't that the whole point of mercy?"

"It is." Jewel patted her hand, then slowly rose to her feet. "I'd better keep this body moving before I stiffen up like a block of cement."

"Do you still hurt because that guy in the mask beat you up?" Montana said.

"Sometimes. But I'm not going to sell the café and stay home afraid, because then the bad guy would win." Jewel locked gazes with Ivy. "I don't like it when the bad guy wins. Sometimes we just have to stand our ground."

Rue stood with Elam outside the model condo, pleased at how quickly the framing was coming along.

"If the weather cooperates, Phase One could be completed ahead of schedule," Rue said. "Maybe even by the middle of September."

Elam stroked his mustache, which didn't quite hide his smile. "Making you manager was one of my smarter moves. It's taken a huge load off me so I can concentrate on other things."

"That's why you're paying me the big bucks." *And why I need to find that file.*

Rue heard a car door slam and turned to where the crew had parked their vehicles. A man with hair the color of Montana's got out of a white Lincoln Navigator.

"Well, for crying out loud," Elam said. "It's Rusty." He waved his hand in the air. Rusty acknowledged him with a nod and headed across the open field in their direction. Elam waited until Rusty was a few yards away and then walked up to shake his hand.

So that's the big bad wolf? Doesn't seem very ferocious in a white Polo shirt and navy pants.

Rue, pretending to be reading the notes he'd attached to his clipboard, eavesdropped on the conversation.

"I don't see a U-Haul," Elam said.

"A couple high-school buddies helped me unload it in less than thirty minutes, but I still have boxes everywhere. I have a meeting at one thirty, but I wanted to drop by and say hi to you first. I already went by the house and talked to Mom."

"Any problems on the road?"

"Just Tanner Pass," Rusty said. "Some tattooed freak in a VW bus had traffic slowed to a crawl because he could barely get up the mountain. I don't know why they allow junkers like that on the road. Anyway, I made it."

"Your timing couldn't be better. Come meet Rue."

"I didn't know he was out here. Can't I do it another time? I need to get going."

"It'll only take a minute. He's right over there."

Rue stared at the clipboard a few seconds longer and then lifted his head as the two approached him.

"Hello, Rue…Rusty Griffith." Rusty's no-grip handshake belied his pleasant expression.

"Good to finally meet you." Rue looked squarely at his brother-in-law, who seemed trapped in a long pause. *You're not even going to ask about your sister, are you?*

"Let us take a minute and show you around the site," Elam finally said, noticeably louder than he needed to.

"Sorry, Dad. I've got just enough time to go back to my place and clean up before my meeting with Mrs. Henley."

Rue smiled to himself. The guy was clean-shaven and without spot or wrinkle. Every hair in place. How cleaned up could he get?

"Then what do you say we all gather out at the house for Sunday dinner tomorrow after church?" Elam said. "We can celebrate all the dads."

Rusty put his hands in his pockets and seemed focused on a squawking scrub jay perched in a nearby pine tree. "I really can't commit to anything this weekend. I have a long list of things that can't wait."

"I'm sure eating's one of them," Elam said. "Why not share a meal with us? You don't have to stay long."

"I appreciate the invite, but I haven't even had time to study the legal papers yet, and I'm supposed to go over them with my attorney first thing Monday morning. I'll bring your gift by sometime tomorrow, but I need to play the rest of it by ear."

"It's up to you." Elam shot him a knowing glance. "The invitation stands."

Rusty turned to Rue, a disingenuous smile tugging at the corners of his mouth. "No doubt we'll meet again."

Ivy and Montana are just fine. Thanks for asking. "If you decide you need help with anything," Rue said, "you have our number."

"I do. Thanks."

Elam escorted Rusty back to his SUV, and they seemed to be arguing. A few minutes later, Elam came back.

"Sorry. That son of mine can be a real boor," he said. "It burns me that he avoided any mention of his sister's name and didn't have the common courtesy to congratulate you."

"He got caught off guard, Elam. It was awkward for both of us."

"Well, I'm not making excuses for him. There aren't any."

Grayson opened the door to the trailer and greeted Liz with a wink and a smile, then went down the hall and knocked softly on Rue's open door.

"Hey, Grayson. What's up?" Rue said.

"I was just about to break for lunch and thought I'd check in. You happy with the framing?"

"Yeah, it's coming along great. I was just about to come tell you that Elam's extremely pleased we're ahead of schedule."

"Good. Did you decide on a roofer?"

"I gave the contract to Everhardt." Rue's tone seemed taunting. "You seem surprised."

"They have a reputation for being sky high."

"Actually, they underbid several midrange roofers that don't have as good a track record. Elam doesn't wanna trust his reputation to anyone but the best on this project, especially after all the headaches Peak gave him."

"Why didn't someone tell *me* Peak was a problem?"

Rue folded his hands on his desk. "That's just not the way I do things. When I have a problem, I take it directly to the source and try to get it resolved. Word travels fast in this business, and I don't wanna be responsible for hurting a company's reputation. I let the work speak for itself."

Grayson bit his lip. *As if I'm going to run around telling everyone.*

"Listen, I know it's really different working with a manager," Rue said, "but the only thing that's really changed is that I'm doing most of the work Elam was doing. I'm sure he didn't dump his frustrations on you, either. You've got enough headaches of your own without being distracted by the ones you have no control over."

Grayson cracked his knuckles. "It just seems that I'd be more valuable around here if I was kept informed on everything."

"You're valuable because you're a good foreman."

"But with all due respect, I could do this job in my sleep. I'm ready for more of a challenge. And I need to make more money."

"That's something you need to talk to Elam about."

"I'm already at the top of the pay scale for a foreman," Grayson said. "I remember him saying that on the last project you worked, someone groomed you to move up. Could you do that for me?"

Rue picked up a pencil and bounced the eraser on his desk. "I'm still feeling my way around this job. I really should have more experience before I take someone under my wing."

Liar, Grayson thought. *You're just afraid I'll find out you aren't more qualified than I am.*

Rue sat back in his chair, his arms folded across his chest. "I can tell by your expression that's not what you wanted to hear. If you're trying to find a fast track to working your way up, there isn't one."

Not unless you have a rich father-in-law who hands it to you on a silver platter. "Surely you can understand my dilemma? I've got four growing kids whose appetites are increasing, and my paycheck isn't. I can't make more money unless I take a step up. And I can't step up unless someone pulls me along. It's a Catch-22."

Rue seemed to be lost in thought for a moment and then said, "All right. Once I get comfortable with my job, we can talk about how we might work you toward that goal. Keep in mind, it's not something you learn in a few months. It takes a couple years."

A couple years? "Thanks," Grayson said, trying to sound sincere. "I'm going to lunch."

"I'm about to head out. Have a nice day off tomorrow."

Grayson turned and went down the hall and out the front door of the trailer. He tramped across the open field to his dumpy Dodge pickup and climbed into the front seat. He opened his lunch pack and took a bite of a stale peanut-butter-and-jelly sandwich.

Rue Kessler was an arrogant jerk. Now that he got what he wanted, why should he be in a hurry to help Grayson advance? The guy was clueless about the pressures of maxed-out credit cards, a second mortgage, or a disgruntled wife whining that she wanted to quit teaching so she could be there when her own kids got home from school. Two years to move up might as well be two hundred.

In his side mirror he caught a glimpse of Rue climbing into his shiny black Silverado crew cab. The thing was loaded: Z71 off-road package. Chrome wheels. Bose speakers. OnStar. All the bells and whistles.

Probably costs as much as I make in a year.

As Rue drove away in a cloud of dust, Grayson imagined the Silverado exploding into a giant ball of fire and vanishing in a puff of black smoke. He savored the rush for a moment and then took another bite of his sandwich.

6

RUE SAT WITH IVY and Montana on a gently sloping hill that would one day be their front yard and enjoyed a picnic lunch of cold chicken, coleslaw, and baked beans.

He reached over and stroked Ivy's cheek. "This tastes great, babe. I was starved."

"Me, too." Montana giggled when Windy snapped at his drumstick and missed. "You can't have chicken bones." He reached in his pocket and gave her a doggy treat.

Ivy looked out at the mountains, the June breeze tousling her hair. "Just think…next summer we'll be sitting here on our porch swing enjoying this spectacular view of Phantom Hollow."

"And Ian and me can sleep out in a tent," Montana added.

The scent of pine wafted under Rue's nose, and he clasped Ivy's hand in his. "It's awesome that we own twenty-five acres of planet Earth that no one can mess up."

"Speaking of that, Montana and I were approached by two gals from a group called SAGE—something something God's Earth, I can't remember exactly—putting flyers on cars in Jacob's Ear. They're upset because so much forestland is being cleared to make room for more ski lodges, restaurants, condos, and such. I wasn't about to tell them my dad and husband are involved in building the new retirement village."

"They're fighting a losing battle," Rue said. "In the next few years, White Top and Mt. Byron will draw more skiers than Telluride. Adding all the new facilities has put both those towns on the map. Plus the architectural design of the new structures blends perfectly with the historic buildings. How is that a negative?"

"Maybe SAGE is afraid the developing won't stop until most of the trees are gone and every tract of land has a building on it. And the watershed's always been an issue."

Rue shrugged. "Could be, but it's not their call. Most of the land in Tanner County is privately owned. And property is so valuable that most landowners can't afford *not* to sell it to developers."

"Well, Mom and Dad decided a long time ago never to sell their homestead property, and I don't know how many hundreds of acres that is. They've never sold any piece of land without knowing exactly how it was going to be developed. I'm proud of how they've worked to preserve the character and resources of the area."

"You're preaching to the choir," Rue said. "And between the national forests and all the replanting programs, we're sure not gonna run out of trees."

Montana jumped up and held his arms out wide. "We have a million zillion trees here, and we don't have to cut down any of them—except when we want a Christmas tree, right?"

"That's right, champ." Rue winked at Ivy.

"Sorry, I didn't mean to get off on this," she said. "You mentioned earlier you had something to tell me about your morning."

Rue noticed Montana was finished with his lunch. "Why don't you and Windy go exploring?"

Montana cocked his head, his eyes turned to slits. "Do you really think real Indians lived here?"

"Maybe. Native Americans from the Ute tribe used to live in this part of the state."

"Come on, girl. Maybe we'll find something really cool."

Windy yelped in playful anticipation as Montana gathered his paper dishes and put them in the trash bag.

"Stay close enough to hear us calling you," Ivy said.

"I will."

Rue waited until Montana was out of earshot and then said, "Rusty showed up at the site. Your dad insisted he come meet me, though it was obvious he didn't want to."

"How was he?"

"Phony." Rue relayed the details of the awkward encounter, including Elam's disgust that Rusty didn't even congratulate Rue or mention Ivy's name. "But he wasn't nearly as intimidating as I thought he would be."

"Just wait till he lights into you. Rusty is cold and mean. I don't know him anymore. He probably treated you halfway nice because Dad was there."

"Probably so. But if we stand any chance of getting along with him, we're gonna have to blow off his attitude. Maybe if we don't react, he'll soften."

Ivy rolled her eyes. "Don't count on it. I'm *glad* he's not going to Mom and Dad's after church."

"On a lighter note, I had an interesting conversation with Grayson. He asked me to start grooming him for a better position. I told him I would, as soon as I feel comfortable with my new job responsibilities. I'm not sure he really *gets it* that I'm in training myself."

"He has to admire you."

Rue picked up a twig and etched a cross in the dirt. "I don't know about admire. I'd like to think I've earned his respect, though. I've certainly earned the right to manage this project."

"So is Grayson going to be like an apprentice?"

"That's a good way to put it. He'll learn more by osmosis than formal training. But it's not something that happens in a short period of time."

"I'll bet he was glad you agreed to be intentional about it."

"Yeah, I think he was."

Grayson walked in the front door of his house and heard dishes clanking. He went out to the kitchen and saw his wife emptying the dishwasher.

He grabbed a beer out of the fridge, popped the top, and took a big gulp.

"How was your day?" Tara said.

"Same old. How about you?"

"Busy. Two soccer games, swimming lessons, T-ball. It's so nice being off with the kids for the summer. I'm already dreading teaching again in the fall."

Don't start with the whining. "Where are the kids?"

Tara pulled her long, dark hair behind her head and put it in a ponytail. "The boys are out back. Lindsey's at a sleepover. You look beat."

"I am." Grayson sat at the table and guzzled his beer until he emptied the can. "I'm sorry I have to put in so many hours this time of year. I'm not much help to you, and I hate missing the boys' games."

"Was Rue any nicer to you today?"

"In a smug sort of way. I got him to say that when he's comfortable with his new job, he'll work with me so I can move up. I'll believe it when I see it."

"Would he lie about something like that?"

"I wouldn't put it past him to drag his feet, since he's enjoying being Elam's golden boy right now. He says it'll take a couple *years* for me to learn everything. I hate for you to have to hang on that long."

"It's not like I have a choice."

Grayson crushed the can. "I promised you could stay home when we had kids. Maybe it's time I got a second job so you can quit."

Tara went over and cupped his face in her hands, her disarming blue eyes causing him to regret his resentful tone. "Then I'd *never* see you. I'm as disappointed as you are that Elam didn't give you the job. But we'll manage."

"And while we're trying to *manage,* you should see the new Silverado Rue's driving. I'm sure the sticker on it was over forty grand."

"I'd be content to own a minivan with less than a hundred thousand miles that won't nickel and dime us to death."

Grayson pulled her on his lap. "Come on, Tara. Don't you ever dream about a beautiful new house? A classy four-door sedan with leather seats? Taking a trip to Hawaii? Buying your clothes at The Boutique instead of Wal-Mart?"

"What I *dream* about is paying off the credit cards and the ortho-dontist and the second mortgage and—"

"Some dream. Sounds more like a nightmare." Grayson boosted her to her feet and patted her behind. She was still shapely after four pregnancies, even if they couldn't afford a membership to the gym. "So what's for dinner?"

"Chili cheese dogs, Tater Tots, and salad."

"Have I got time to take a shower?"

"Sure. It'll be twenty minutes before it's ready."

Sheriff Flint Carter parallel parked on the west side of the Tanner County Courthouse, behind Marshal Kyle Redmond's squad car and just feet from the bronze statue of Jacob Tanner that stood at the corner of the grounds. He scanned the row of placard-carriers walking back and forth in front of the historic stone building and saw the mayor standing at the top of the courthouse steps, scowl faced, his thumbs hooked on his red suspenders.

Flint got out of his car and spotted Kyle waving on the other side of a maze of protesters. He walked along the perimeter of the crowd and read some of the placards they were carrying: "Protect His Creation," "Save All God's Earth," "We Answer to the Maker of Heaven and Earth," "God Is Watching."

Kyle cut through the swarm of marchers and bystanders and rushed over to him. "Thanks for coming, Flint."

"I was about to throw some burgers on the grill when you called. What's so important that I needed to come down here and see for myself?"

Kyle nodded toward the protesters. "Those folks carrying signs belong to an environmental group called SAGE. Stands for Save All God's

Earth. They claim to be Christian, and as you can see, they're just exercising their First Amendment rights to draw attention to their cause."

"And I need to know this on a Saturday evening because…?"

"Because the mayor insists they're harassing tourists," Kyle said. "And he wants something done about it. I tried to tell him there's nothing I—"

"It's about time you got here." Mayor Lester Smart came over and stood facing Flint, his expression chiding. "These tree-huggers and their *comrades* are walking our streets, handing out flyers and reciting some well-rehearsed spiel about how Tanner County is being destroyed by demon developers who are raping the forests, upsetting the water tables, and driving out wildlife."

"These complaints are nothing new," Flint said.

"Well, my phone ringing off the hook *is*. The retailers are up in arms that this group is running off tourists. Maggie Easton called from the real estate office, madder than a hatter because a potential buyer withdrew his offer—said he was looking for a quiet retreat, not a war zone. The final straw was an SOS call from Harvey Spade at the chamber of commerce. He wants these troublemakers out of here."

"They're not breaking the law, Lester."

"Can't you tell them to move on?"

Flint shook his head. "I have no legal ground."

"I already told him that," Kyle said.

"Well, can't you make up something?"

"You know better than that." Flint glanced over at the demonstrators, each wearing a green T-shirt with some sort of logo on the front. "We'd have the ACLU parked on our doorstep before midnight. We both know these protesters aren't the only ones who'd like to see a halt to the construction boom. There're plenty of people in Jacob's Ear and surrounding communities who echo their complaints. They have a right to their say."

Lester threw up his hands, a lock of his stringy white hair falling down on his forehead. "Your friend Elam came to my door. Showed me the protest flyer left on his car window. Don't they need a permit or something to do that?"

"It's no different than leaving a pizza coupon under the wiper. I can't force them to leave just because they're expressing opinions you and others disagree with."

"You sound just like Kyle." Lester exhaled loudly, his arms folded across his chest and resting on his rotund belly. "Can't you intimidate these people into leaving? Send them over to White Top or Mt. Byron or someplace else where there's actually construction going on. For crying out loud, the historic buildings protection ordinance doesn't even allow new construction in the city limits."

"This isn't about Jacob's Ear," Flint said. "They're protesting here because it's the county seat. See how peaceful they are? There's nothing I can do. If we don't overreact, they'll probably leave on their own."

Lester took a handkerchief out his pocket and dabbed his forehead. "If that's the best you can do, good luck with reelection. I'm sure the voters will interpret your failure to act as an indication you're more sympathetic to the cause of the activists than to the health of our economy."

Flint rolled his eyes at Kyle, then patted Lester on the back. "I'm going to ignore that remark and assume you'll be sorry later you said it. I'm going home and grill hamburgers. I suggest you do the same. Tell Violet hello for me."

Rue sat at the oblong pine table in Elam and Carolyn's kitchen table, enjoying a bowl of homemade strawberry ice cream.

"We had a great picnic today at the new house," Rue said. "It's starting to take shape. It'll be a couple weeks before I can get the framing crew out there to put some meat on its bones."

"The view is *so* amazing." Ivy put her hand on his, and he relished the softness—and the excitement that sparkled in those big gray eyes of hers.

Elam wiped ice cream off his mustache. "Your mother and I had that land picked out for you ages ago. We just weren't sure you'd ever move back to the area. I doubt there's a prettier view in all of Phantom Hollow."

"Me and Windy like playing there," Montana said. "She found this humongous bone down by the creek. It might be a dinosaur bone—from a long, long, long, *long* time ago."

"You don't say?" Elam ever so slowly moved his spoon toward Montana's bowl, then stuck it in the boy's ice cream and stole a bite.

"Grandpa." Montana giggled and reached over and snatched a spoonful of Elam's ice cream.

"So did you find the dinosaur's footprints yet?" Elam said.

"Nooo." Montana grinned and hovered protectively over his bowl as if he were expecting his grandpa to snatch another spoonful of his ice cream. "But maybe dinosaurs were right where our new house is. Ute Indians, too. I mean Native Americans."

"I'd like to change the subject before I forget to ask," Ivy said. "Did either of you hear about the environmental group that's protesting in town?"

Elam took a bite of a butter cookie. "We talked to a couple members. They were putting a flyer on the windshield as we were leaving Jewel's."

"Did they get ugly?"

"Not at all. Just expressed their feelings about all the tree cutting and construction going on. I know better than to get lured into a conversation that isn't going anywhere. I *am* involved in preserving the integrity of the area, but they won't see it that way."

"Did they know who you were?"

"I doubt it, since neither mentioned the retirement village. I did stop by Lester's house and gave him the flyer. Said his phone had been ringing off the hook. Apparently, members of this group have been passing out flyers all over town. Ruffled a few feathers."

"Doesn't it bother you?" Rue said.

Elam shook his head. "We need groups to raise public awareness. But I'm sure not going to debate them about whether I have the right to develop the land I own. I believe the earth is here to serve us, not the other way around. The issue for me is how to use natural resources in a way that doesn't upset the balance."

"You've probably replanted more trees than they have," Carolyn said.

"I think they're more interested in counting the ones I cut down."

Montana wiped his mouth with a napkin. "Thank you for the ice cream, Grandma. May I please be excused so I can watch a DVD?"

"Yes, you may, sweetie." Carolyn watched Montana leave the kitchen and then said to Rue, "Elam told me Rusty was out at the site today. I'm sorry he was rude to you."

"I wasn't expecting a warm reception," Rue said. "Maybe now that that's out of the way, things will be less strained."

The expression in Carolyn's eyes told him she didn't believe it any more than he did.

7

AT NOON THE NEXT DAY, Ivy sat quietly as Rue pulled the Silverado out of the parking lot of Woodlands Community Church and headed toward town. What had ever made her think this was a good idea?

"You okay?" Rue said.

"I must need my head examined." Ivy stared at the plaid gift bag on her lap. "Rusty will probably trash this before we're out of the city limits."

"Or have it with his coffee." Rue reached over and gave her arm a squeeze. "Don't go soft on me now. I like your idea of leaving a loaf of homemade banana bread on his doorstep with a welcome note. Regardless of what he decides to do with it, he knows it's a peace offering."

"Maybe Uncle Rusty will gobble it up and just be nice," Montana said.

Ivy pulled down the visor and studied her son's sympathetic expression in the mirror. "I hope so, sweetie. He's probably lonesome having to spend Father's Day without Tia and Josie."

Rue slowed the truck in front of Spruce Park, where the traffic had almost come to a standstill.

"What's going on?" Ivy said.

"I'm guessing the protesters are still here. Can you read what's on the signs?"

Ivy scanned the placards. "Let's see…one says, 'The Earth Is the Lord's, and Everything in It.' Another says, 'Our Help Comes from the

Lord, the Maker of Heaven and Earth.' 'Earth' is underlined. I can't make out the others."

"Well, at least they acknowledge *God* made it." Rue pulled around the van in front of him and continued down Main Street.

Ivy felt the muscles in her neck tighten when he reached Silverton Road and turned left.

"Relax, babe. If Rusty opens the front door, just hand him the gift bag. He's not gonna bite. What he does with it isn't nearly as important as what it says about you."

Ivy smiled wryly. "Yeah. That I'm intimidated by my own brother."

"Which is all the more reason why this is an important step." Rue pulled up in front of a small white house with dark green shutters. "This is 108, but I don't see Rusty's car." He turned to her and stroked her hair. "Just leave the bag on the stoop. We'll be out of here in less than a minute."

"You want me to do it?" Montana said. "I'm not scared if Dad's here."

"Thanks, sweetie. I can do it." *I think.*

Ivy slid out of the truck, opened the latch on the wrought-iron gate, and went up on the front stoop. She set the bag in front of the door, then hurried back to the truck and got in, her heart racing faster than the teenager zooming by on a ten-speed.

Rue took her hand, a tentative smile twitching the corners of his mouth. "That wasn't so bad, was it?"

"I'm glad you find this amusing. Let's just go, okay?"

Rue pulled away from the curb and continued down the street, then frowned at something in his side mirror. "You're not going to believe this. Rusty just pulled up."

"What?" Ivy glanced over her shoulder and saw her brother's Navigator parked in front of the house. "Good heavens, we missed him by seconds."

"Should I turn around and go back?"

"No!" Ivy laughed in spite of herself. "Let's head out to Mom and Dad's. I'm starved."

Flint exited Jewel's Café behind his wife and son and spotted Lester and Violet Smart ambling up the sidewalk.

"Good morning, Violet. Mr. Mayor." Flint flashed his friendliest smile, pretending not to notice Lester's sulky expression. "I saw you at church but couldn't get your attention. I trust you're enjoying this fine Father's Day?"

Violet put her hand over her heart. "All our children and grand-children will be here this afternoon. First time since Christmas."

Lester exhaled loudly. "Guess you saw that mess at the park."

"Caused mostly by curious onlookers," Flint said. "The SAGE marchers were peaceable."

Lester grabbed his polka-dot tie, which was being whipped about by the breeze. "Just because they're well versed in Holy Writ doesn't mean their cause is righteous. Or that they have the right to bombard our visitors with it."

"But since there's nothing I can do to prevent them from exercising their First Amendment rights, I'm going to spend Father's Day trout fish-ing with my son."

"Aren't you going to be here to maintain order?" Lester hooked his thumbs on his red suspenders. "What if things deteriorate throughout the day?"

"Bobby Knolls is on duty. If I'm needed, he knows how to reach me."

"You're going to regret not doing something about this." Lester's tone sounded threatening. "I've been talking to retailers. I wouldn't put it past them to run this group out of town."

"Be sure to remind them they could be the ones who end up in the county jail."

Lester pursed his lips. "It's just plain wrong that these tree-huggers can scare off our best source of revenue and that we have no power to stop them."

"How many tourists would you guess they ran off?"

"Hard to say."

Flint folded his arms across his chest and rubbed his chin. "As far as I can tell, the Phantom Hollow Lodge is at capacity. So is the Tanner Hotel, the Miner's Inn, and all the B and Bs. And judging from the traffic on Main Street, I'm confident those guests—and even the protesters—are eating in restaurants and spending money around town."

Lester threw up his hands. "Come on, my dear. Let's go have lunch. It's obvious the sheriff isn't interested in doing what's best for our citizens."

Violet glanced up at Flint, her faded blue eyes wide and apologetic. In the next instant, Lester took her by the arm and ushered her into the café.

Flint went over to his car, slid in behind the wheel, and groaned.

"What was that all about?" Betty Carter asked.

"The retailers are all over Lester to get rid of the protesters. His nose is out of joint because I won't tell them to leave."

"Have they broken any laws?"

"Not as far as I know. But Lester implied that if I don't force them to leave, the retailers will. Anyway you cut it, that's a recipe for trouble."

Grayson laid the Sunday paper on the coffee table, vaguely aware that Tara had turned on the ten o'clock news. He glanced up at the TV and saw that Mayor Smart was being interviewed by field reporter Jessica Monrovia. He picked up the remote and turned up the volume.

"Mr. Mayor, there are rumors aloft that business owners in your town are threatening to take action against the environmental group SAGE, since the town marshal and the sheriff's department have done nothing to deter their activities. Would you comment on that?"

"Absolutely. To say I'm disappointed doesn't begin to cover it. Law-enforcement officials refuse to do anything because this group isn't technically breaking the law—never mind that its presence is hurting the local economy. These activists are allowed to pass out flyers and harass tourists by

spouting the group's mantra concerning the state of the environment. It's bad for the local economy. Bad for tourism. And bad for Colorado."

Grayson turned to Tara. "Have you run into any of these people?"

"Not yet. But they're sure creating a stir. Listen…Sheriff Carter's about to comment."

"I want to assure Tanner County residents that the sheriff's department is committed to enforcing the law. I realize emotions run hot on this issue. But SAGE members have expressed their opinions in a peaceful way. We may not like it when freedom means someone has the right to speak out with opposing views, but that's what free speech is all about."

"That's all the sheriff would say. Marshal Kyle Redmond was unavailable for comment after an incident at Spruce Park this afternoon when SAGE demonstrators were confronted by loggers who took offense at the group's claim that the harvesting of aspen forests is unnecessary and is upsetting the water tables. Sheriff's deputies said that when the demonstrators attempted to express their point of view, the loggers became loud and disruptive to keep them from being heard."

"Good for the loggers," Grayson said. "What does SAGE think trees are supposed to be used for, anyway? What a bunch of losers."

"I'm afraid this situation isn't going to be resolved anytime soon. We'll keep a close eye on the situation and report any breaking news. This is Jessica Monrovia reporting from Jacob's Ear. Watson, back to you."

Grayson rested his head on the back of the couch. "I wonder if anyone's even heard of this group."

"They have now."

Rue handed Ivy the remote and got up to answer the phone.

"Hello."

"Rue, it's Elam. Sorry to call so late, but I figured you were still up."

"Yeah, we were just talking about what a great day it was. We really enjoyed spending the afternoon with you."

"Same here. Thanks for the CDs. I've been wanting those. And how about that drill Montana got you?"

Rue smiled at the memory of his son's beaming face. "Thanks for tipping him off. He wanted his first Father's Day present to wow me. Of course it did. But *he* was the real gift."

"That's the truth. Listen, are you watching the news?"

"We just turned it on. Things seem to be heating up around that environmental group."

"I just got an anonymous call from some punk who says he's a member, and that if I don't put a halt to the retirement project, there will be consequences."

Rue locked gazes with Ivy. "Oh, man. That's all we need."

"Could be bogus. SAGE is known for being nonviolent. At any rate, we're going to forge ahead, but I wanted you to be cautious. Keep your eyes and ears open, especially when you get out to the site."

"I will. Did you talk to the sheriff?"

"Not yet," Elam said. "I'm about to. I wanted to catch you first."

"Thanks for the heads-up. By the way, did Rusty ever come by?"

"Actually he did. Only stayed a few minutes. Not worth talking about. See you in the morning."

"I appreciate the call. Good night."

Rue hung up the phone and flopped on the couch next to Ivy. "Rusty finally stopped by for a few minutes. Your dad didn't get into detail, but I got the feeling he wasn't impressed. But that's not why he called." Rue relayed what Elam had said about the threatening phone call.

"What's SAGE's problem?" Ivy said. "It's not like the mountains and the forests belong to *them*. They're for everyone to enjoy. They can't stop people from moving here. As long as whatever Dad builds fits the character of the area, doesn't mess up the view, and is environmentally friendly, why would anybody threaten him? Especially when he's got thousands of acres of pristine land he's not even going to touch."

"Whoever called him probably doesn't know that."

Ivy lifted her eyebrows. "I doubt if it would make any difference. Some of these people are against picking a blade of grass."

"Don't you wonder why they would wait till the project is up and running to be upset, though? I mean, we broke ground in March. Why'd they wait so long to express their disapproval?"

Flint started to turn out the lights in the living room when the phone rang. He went out to the kitchen and picked up the receiver.

"Hello."

"It's Elam. Hope I caught you before you went to bed. Some young punk called me a while ago. Said he was a member of SAGE. And that if I go forward with the retirement project, there'll be consequences."

Flint sighed. "Wonderful."

"I'm not even convinced it was legit, but I thought you'd want to know about it. I just hope it's not the beginning of trouble."

"Me, too. I wish this group would move on. Lester's all over me to run them out of town on a rail, but my hands are tied."

"I gathered that from the news," Elam said. "Any idea where SAGE originated?"

"All I know is the group is made up of members from several non-denominational churches in Tanner County. I'm sure they're here to raise public awareness for the sins of the logging industry. And apparently the building industry, too."

"I wonder what argument they think we haven't already heard? Most people here want to protect the integrity of the environment. Some of us are just more practical in our approach."

Flint felt his cell phone vibrate, took it off his belt clip, and read the display screen. "I've got to take another call, Elam. I'll talk to you tomorrow."

"Tell Betty I'm sorry for calling this late."

Flint put his cell phone to his ear. "Yeah, Bobby. What's up?"

"The trouble's startin'. One of the female SAGE demonstrators was found unconscious and bleedin' in the ladies' rest room at the park. Took a nasty blow to the head. She's at the ER. That's where I am now."

"Is she going to make it?"

"Don't know," Bobby said. "The doc hasn't come out to talk to me yet."

Flint exhaled into the receiver. "I'll be there in fifteen minutes."

8

FLINT PUSHED THROUGH the emergency room door at Tanner County Medical Center. Lieutenant Bobby Knolls stood to the side of the registration desk with a half-dozen young people clad in green T-shirts imprinted with SAGE's logo. In a row of chairs toward the back of the room, Pastor Rick Myers was comforting two women who were crying.

Bobby acknowledged Flint with a slight nod and came over to him.

"Who's the victim?" Flint said.

Bobby spit his bubblegum into the trash can. "The president of SAGE, Madison Baughman. Age thirty-five. Lives in White Top. Married. Husband's a dentist. Two school-age kids. The doc said she sustained a deep gash on her head and needed stitches, but that she'll be fine. Said she was lucky."

Flint lifted his eyebrows. "I guess lucky is relative. Who found her?"

"Another female SAGE member, Patty something. Called 911 at 9:24, then called the other members' cell numbers and told them what happened and to meet her here. I don't know how your pastor found out."

"When can we talk to the victim?"

"Right now. I was waitin' for you. The doc said to go on back. Mrs. Baughman is expectin' us."

Bobby stuffed a fresh piece of gum into his mouth, then led the way through the open door of the waiting room and down a corridor of examination rooms framed only by curtains. He stopped in front of the third cubicle on the left. "This is it."

"Mrs. Baughman, it's Sheriff Carter and Lieutenant Knolls of the Tanner County Sheriff's Department. May we come in?"

A few seconds later the curtain opened, and Flint stood face-to-face with Terri Myers, Pastor Rick's wife. He patted her shoulder, then went over to the bed where Madison Baughman lay, her upper body elevated, her head wrapped in gauze and resting on a pillow.

"Mrs. Baughman, the lieutenant and I need to ask you a few questions."

"I'll be in the waiting room," Terri said. "We're all praying for you, honey. Your husband should be here anytime."

Madison seemed to stare at nothing and then lifted her eyes and said, "I never saw the man who attacked me."

"Can you tell us what happened?" Flint said.

Madison pushed her tongue along the inside of her lips as if her mouth were dry. "The others had just left, and I was about to drive back to White Top. I went over to use the ladies' rest room at the park. Someone grabbed me from behind and held me in a choke hold. He smelled like beer and had a deep voice. Young. I'm pretty sure he was white."

"What'd he say?"

"That he knows how to shut up female activists who care more about protecting trees than protecting jobs." Madison's eyes brimmed with tears. "He said if I didn't back off, he'd come find me and show me what females were *really* made for…" Madison choked on the words and wiped the tears off her cheeks, almost as if she were angry for getting emotional. "I heard laughing. I think there were at least two other guys. Whoever grabbed me let go, then I felt this horrific thud in my head. The next thing I remember was hearing Patty's voice."

"Any idea what time this happened?" Bobby said.

"I'm not sure. It had just gotten dark outside."

"When the guy told you to back off, what did you take that to mean?"

Madison shrugged. "Step down, I guess. Stop voicing my concerns."

"Would you know the perp's voice if you heard it again?"

"Absolutely. I'll never forget it."

Bobby blew a pink bubble and sucked the gum back into his mouth. "SAGE's presence here created a stink. You must've come up against a lot of angry people."

"Not really. A handful of loggers heckled us at the park, but they never stopped talking long enough for us to address their concerns. SAGE is committed to not being argumentative, so we just let them rant. There were a few others—men *and* women—who told us to go home. But I never sensed we were in danger."

"Well, I suggest you take this seriously," Bobby said.

"Trust me, Lieutenant. I know when I've been threatened. I can hardly wait to get in the shower and wash his filthy handprints off me. But I'm not going to be intimidated into abandoning the cause. I just won't go out alone anymore. None of us will."

Flint nodded. "That's probably smart. At least until we catch this man. Can you remember anything else about him or the men you heard laughing?"

"Just that they sounded young."

"Do you recall any young men at the park eying you in a way that made you uncomfortable?" Flint said.

Madison sighed, her eyes droopy. "There were so many people there, Sheriff. Old. Young. Both genders. Entire families. No one stands out except for the hecklers. And they were forty—give or take. Whoever threatened me sounded much younger."

"What about after the crowd left?" Bobby said. "Did you happen to notice anybody hangin' around?"

Madison shook her head.

"What about vehicles in the parking lot?"

"Sorry. I just didn't pay attention."

9

RUE PARKED HIS TRUCK and walked across the open field toward the temporary offices of EG Construction Company, relieved he hadn't seen anyone or anything suspicious around the construction site. He went up the steps and into the trailer.

Liz Parker was on the telephone. Rue gently rapped on her desk, mouthed "good morning," then headed down the hall and into his office. He sat at his desk and thumbed through his inbox.

Seconds later Elam came in and shut the door. "Did you hear the news this morning?"

"No, what'd I miss?"

"The president of SAGE was attacked last night at Spruce Park."

Rue listened as Elam told him the details he had heard on the radio and confirmed with Flint.

"Man, what a bottom feeder," Rue said. "What kind of guy threatens a woman with something like that?"

"One with a twisted mind. Or who wants SAGE to *think* he's twisted enough to follow through with the threat. The goal is to scare them into silence." Elam tugged at his mustache. "Flint doesn't think it'll work."

"The poor lady who was threatened must be scared to death."

"You'd think. But activists tend to be passionate about their cause. I'd be surprised if it shut her up. She'll probably capitalize on the attention to get her message out there."

"Did you ask the sheriff if anyone else got a phone call like the one you got?"

"No one's reported it yet. But if SAGE *is* responsible, I'm guessing other builders were called."

"Didn't the caller tell you he was from SAGE?"

Elam shrugged. "Sounded awfully young. And not especially bright. You'd think an organization that wanted to convince me to scrap a project would pick their most articulate person to do the talking. Not some young punk who spouts off a nebulous threat like *there'll be consequences.*"

"So you don't think it was SAGE?"

"Doesn't make any difference. I'm not halting this project. I've done everything I know to ensure the retirement village will be environmentally friendly, right down to the solar panels. I refuse to feel guilty because I cut down a few trees to open up the view of those gorgeous mountains." Elam glanced at his watch. "I'd like to meet with you at ten. I need to hear your assessment of where we are on Phase One. Maybe you could chart it out for me?"

With what? All my notes are in the missing file. "Uh, sure. I'll pull something together."

Ivy stood behind the registration desk at Three Peaks Lodge and felt a draft when the entrance door opened. She glanced up and saw Rusty walking toward her, carrying the gift bag she'd left on his stoop.

He set the bag on the counter. "I told you I haven't changed my feelings since we talked at Thanksgiving. I'm not giving you the chance to burn me again. I don't want any personal interaction with you, Rue, or Montana. If we run into each other at Mom and Dad's, so be it. But I don't want anything more. You and I need to settle this right now."

Don't be rude. Don't react. "I remembered you like banana bread. I thought you might enjoy it with your coffee, especially since you were all by yourself on Father's Day."

"Don't change the subject, Ivy."

She focused on her wedding band. "I'm sorry you feel the way you do. Rue is a wonderful man. And Montana is such a sweet child. Tia and Josie would love him."

"I don't want him around my girls," Rusty said flatly. "With all he's been exposed to, it's just a matter of time before he starts acting out."

Ivy blinked the stinging from her eyes. "You said that last time you were here, and you're wrong."

"I'm sure you believe that, but I have a responsibility to protect my daughters from your dysfunction."

Ivy bit her lip. "You know what? I'm not going to let you bring me down. I've worked hard to break old patterns and straighten out my life. I have a responsible job. I'm married to the man I love—"

"Who got you pregnant and skipped out for eight years."

Think what you want. I can't trust you with the truth. "I love him, Rusty. And we've got the sweetest little boy, who reminds me of you as a kid."

Rusty folded his arms across his chest. "Let's hope you don't break his heart, too."

I might as well be talking to a brick wall. "Look, it's your choice not to have anything to do with us. Our door is always open to you."

"Spare me the martyr act, Ivy. Let's agree to avoid each other as much as possible. Just because we're related doesn't mean we have anything in common. We live in two different worlds."

"Not anymore, we don't."

"You know what I mean."

"Yes, you're ashamed of us. I get it. But over time, you're going to see that I've changed. And that Rue's a wonderful husband and father. And Montana's a sensitive, loving boy—probably *because* of what he's been through."

"You make it sound like you're the ideal family. You've been married, what—a little over two weeks? Give it time. Your past is going to catch up with you."

Ivy saw the coldness in her brother's eyes and let out a sigh of frustration. "Rusty, it already did. I stopped doing drugs four years ago. When I came back here, I recommitted my life to Christ. I came forward with the truth about Joe's death and paid for covering it up. Now Rue and I are raising our son in a Christian home. If God can forgive me, why can't you?"

"Because you can't *use* and *abuse* people, then wave a magic wand and make everything all right." Rusty glanced at his watch. "I need to go meet with my attorney. I want to be sure you and I are on the same page about this. There's no reason for Mom and Dad to get pulled into it."

"How can they not when they love us both?"

"The only way they're going to find out about this conversation is if *you* tell them."

"I don't keep secrets, Rusty. Secrets nearly ruined my life."

He smiled derisively. "No, the behaviors that caused the secrets are what ruined your life."

Ivy swallowed the wad of emotion in her throat. *Lord, he's so bitter. How can I ever reach him?* "Rusty, why did you move back? You had to know your attitude would cause division in the family."

"I have as much right to live here as you do."

"You didn't answer my question."

Rusty's eyes turned to slits. "*You're* the one who's divided this family. Not me. I didn't have any conflict with Mom and Dad until you came home and started sucking them dry."

"They helped me get back on feet. But I wasn't passive through the process."

"What would you call it? *They* were the ones doing all the giving. They let you live under their roof. Gave you three squares a day. Bought you a new car. Turned their home into hospice to accommodate your friend Lu. They even bought her headstone, for crying out loud. Then they took care of your kid the entire six months you were in jail. Other than hanging on to the job *they* gave you, I fail to see where you've been actively doing anything."

"You twisted everything." Ivy's eyes filled, and she couldn't stop the tears from spilling down her cheeks. "I'm not going to defend myself to you. I made mistakes I'll always regret. And it's been a struggle getting my life back. Yes, Mom and Dad have helped me, but it took a lot of hard work getting to where I am."

"And where exactly is that? You're a recovering crackhead with a criminal record. You married a recovering alcoholic who finally, eight years after the fact, decided to help you raise your illegitimate son. Don't expect me to pin a medal on you."

Ivy took a slow deep breath, her husband's words echoing in her head. *Rusty obviously doesn't understand addiction and doesn't want to.* "I love you, Rusty. Believe whatever you want about me. Like I said, our door is always open to you. You'd better go. You'll be late for your meeting."

"Fine. Just stay away from me."

As Rusty pushed open the exit door, a gust of air sent a stack of brochures sailing across the floor.

Ivy hurried over and started to pick them up and noticed Kelsey Jones getting a drink at the water cooler. How long had she been there?

Flint sat at the table in his office with Bobby Knolls and Investigator Buck Lowry, going over statements from the night before, Morgan Baughman's and those of the SAGE members who had gone to the ER.

"Bottom line: nobody saw anything." Flint took off his reading glasses. "The perp's remark that Baughman was more interested in saving trees than jobs tells me this is personal."

"Yeah, to almost everybody," Buck said. "Who *wouldn't* be affected if SAGE succeeded in pressuring logging companies and developers into going somewhere else?"

Bobby blew a pink bubble. "Maybe we should start by askin' who else got a phone call from SAGE besides Elam Griffith."

"The call to Elam came during the ten o'clock news," Flint said, "barely an hour after Baughman was attacked in the park. It's possible that someone from SAGE made other calls before that."

Bobby leaned forward, his elbows on the table. "Elam said the caller sounded young. Why don't we track down the youngest male members of SAGE and see if that leads anywhere? I also wanna know if this group did any *official* callin' around, though I'm guessin' we're not gonna find any record of it."

Flint got up and stood by the window, his mind racing with the implications. "Just keep in mind, no complaints have been filed against SAGE for using the phone to threaten anyone. They've been squeaky clean."

Bobby snickered. "Ever met a tree-hugger that couldn't justify breakin' the law to achieve a higher good?"

"Until we have something solid against them, I'm willing to believe they're doing things lawfully."

"With all due respect, Sheriff. A tree-hugger's a tree-hugger's a tree-hugger. They've all got a one-track mind."

"I didn't see them break any laws, Bobby."

"Let's dig deeper. SAGE made somebody mad enough to assault a lady and threaten her."

Flint's eyebrows came together. "It's not our job to demonize SAGE. Just find Baughman's attacker and lock him up before he does something worse."

Ivy lifted the hinged counter at the registration desk and went through to the other side, avoiding eye contact with Kelsey. "I guess you heard Rusty and me arguing."

Kelsey nodded. "I was at the water cooler when he came in. When I realized what was happening, I just stayed there, hoping I wouldn't embarrass you."

"So you heard the whole thing?"

"It was all I could do to keep my mouth shut. Rusty really has no clue what you've been through."

"How do I make him see that I've changed?"

"Well, he's hardly been around you," Kelsey said. "Once he sees the consistency in your life, I'll bet he'll change his tune."

Ivy wiped away a runaway tear. "I hope you're right. I don't know him anymore."

"He probably feels the same way about you." Kelsey came over and took Ivy's hand. "It could be the best thing for both of you that he's moved back. Rusty said he doesn't want any interaction, but there's no way he can avoid it altogether. When he sees how great you and Rue and Montana are together, he's bound to soften."

"If I live through it."

Kelsey smiled. "You will. Just think of everything the Lord's brought you through this past year. He is so faithful."

"I know. I need to trust Him with this, too. But it's so frustrating that I have to deal with it now, when I'm finally happy and things are going well."

"On the other hand, you have Rue to help you keep your perspective. I found it interesting that Rusty never told you why he moved back. Maybe deep down he really wants to set things right between you two."

Ivy shrugged. "I didn't sense the tiniest crack in the wall he's built around himself."

"Do you know if his wife feels the same way?"

"When I met Jacqueline at Thanksgiving, she acted aloof whenever Rusty was around. When he wasn't there, she was a lot more relaxed and friendly."

"There you go. Maybe she'll be the catalyst that will bring you two together again."

"You're a lot more optimistic than I am, but Jacqueline won't even be here until their house sells." Ivy heaved a sigh. "This is terrible to say, but I think Rusty would love to drive a wedge between my parents and me."

"Because he resents them helping you?"

"You heard him. He thinks all I do is take."

"You know better, and so do they."

Ivy brushed a lock of hair out of her eyes. "I can't explain it, Kelsey, but there's something almost evil about Rusty. I'm starting to think it's better if I just stay away from him."

Rue sat at the table in Elam's office, silently bemoaning the missing Phase One file, and presented the timetable chart he'd put together from memory.

"This is a good start," Elam said, "but I was expecting to see something a lot more detailed. I already know most of this."

Rue felt the blood rush to his face and decided he might as well get the inevitable out of the way. "The truth is, I don't have all the information you want. I misplaced the file that had all my notes."

"How'd that happen?"

"All I can figure is that the day before the wedding I was distracted and must've left it somewhere. I've searched high and low and can't find it."

"Can't you pull most of the information from the computer?"

Rue shook his head. "I was on such a fast track before the wedding, I decided to wait till I got back to enter everything into the computer." Rue sighed. "It didn't seem like a big deal. I've never lost a file before. But I don't know where else to search. Liz hasn't seen it, either."

Elam tugged at his mustache, a row of ridges forming on his forehead. "You can't manage this project without sticking to a timetable. How can a file just disappear?"

"I probably stuck it somewhere without thinking. But don't worry. I'll put in as many hours as it takes to reconstruct what I know. I'm not going to let us lose momentum."

"Did you check every file in the drawer to see if it's misfiled?"

"At least a hundred times."

"Did you check at home?"

Rue nodded. "Truthfully, I don't recall ever taking it out of my office. I promise I'll get this worked out. I just couldn't do it in time for this meeting."

The intercom beeped, and then Liz's voice rang out. "Rue, is Elam with you?"

"Yes."

"Line two is for him."

"Thanks."

Elam picked up the receiver. "Hello… Yes, it is… Wait, I—" Elam exhaled and slammed down the receiver. "Another threat."

"Same guy?"

"Sounded like the same young voice. Said he's from SAGE. And if I don't stop construction on the retirement village, there will be consequences."

"What kind of consequences do you think he's talking about?"

"Don't know. But I think it's time I hired a security guard."

10

GRAYSON LEANED ON THE FRONT of his truck and crushed his cigarette with his foot, keeping his eyes on Rue's son playing in the field with an Eskimo dog of some kind.

The boy threw a Frisbee over the dog's head, and it landed next to Grayson's tire. Grayson reached down and picked it up, aware of footsteps pounding the ground.

"Hi." The kid came to a stop at Grayson's feet, sounding out of breath. "I'm Montana. This is Windy."

"What kind of dog is she?"

"Part husky. We don't know what else."

Grayson handed the Frisbee to Montana and scratched Windy's chin. "Beautiful dog. I'm Grayson, by the way."

"I heard my parents say that name before. I think my dad knows you. His name's Rue Kessler. He works here."

"Yeah, we know each other. So what brings *you* out here?"

"My grandma usually watches me in the daytime. But she had to go to the dentist, and it's boring. So my dad said I could come play here. But I'm not allowed to go where the workers are."

"So you've heard your parents mention my name, huh?"

Montana nodded. "I don't know very many people who work here. Just my dad and Grandpa Elam and Liz. And Joel Myers—he's my Sunday-school teacher."

"Well, now you know me, too." Grayson pushed a pine cone with his boot. "So...what did your mom and dad have to say about me?"

A smile tugged at the corners of Montana's mouth. "I don't know."

"Come on, a smart kid like you? I'll bet if you think really hard, you'll remember *something*."

Montana put his finger to his chin and looked up, his eyes moving one direction and then the other. "Well…my dad said you're a real *piece* of work—because *lots* of people work here. Get it?"

"Yeah, I get it. Anything else?"

Montana shrugged. "Not really."

Windy yelped and ran in circles.

"She wants me to play with her," Montana said.

"So you and Windy are pals, eh?"

Montana beamed. "She's the funnest dog in the whole world. We do everything together, don't we, girl?"

"How come I haven't seen you out here before?"

"I come with my dad when nobody else is working. Me and Windy play out here till he's done in his office." Montana pointed to the trailer. "Do you work in there, too?"

"No, I don't need an office." *Thanks to your dad stealing my job.* "But Liz keeps some of my files in her drawer."

"Do you get to wear a hard hat?"

"Yeah." Grayson smiled and glanced at his watch. "I need to get back to work. My lunch hour is over. It was nice meeting you, Montana. You have a real nice dog."

"Thanks, Mr. Grayson. Come on, Windy."

Grayson stood for a moment and watched Montana throw the Frisbee and Windy jump up in the air and catch it with ease. Nice kid. Nice dog. Everything Rue Kessler owned was nice. It was sickening.

A real piece of work. Grayson figured that was probably the least of the unkind remarks Rue had made about him.

He walked across the field to the model condo, resentment chipping away at his Mr. Nice Guy facade, and wondered if the highlight of his afternoon would be breaking up squabbles between Sandoval and Hernandez.

Flint walked into Jewel's Café and spotted Elam sitting at the table by the moose head. He pulled out a chair and sat across from him.

"I never turn down a free lunch," Flint said. "But I assume you've got something bigger on your mind."

"I got another threatening phone call," Elam said. "Sounded like the same young punk. He said again that if I don't halt the retirement project, there would be consequences."

Jewel Sadler came to the table with menus. "Well, heavens to Betsy, Flint. It's not often I get to see you for breakfast *and* lunch. Today's special is chicken spaghetti and a garden salad."

"That's what I want." Flint handed his menu back to Jewel. "Ranch dressing on the side. Black coffee."

Elam nodded. "Same here. I'll save room for dessert."

Jewel flashed an elfin smile. "I thought you might. Be right out with the hot rolls."

Flint leaned forward on his elbows, aware of the pronounced lines across Elam's forehead. "Did the caller give you any indication of what the consequences would be?"

"No. Same vague threat. The guy hardly sounded old enough to shave."

"My deputies are putting SAGE members under a microscope as we speak. If we can get a list of people they called, we might be able to zero in on who had motive to attack Madison Baughman."

"I'm not sure any list you could compile would be inclusive enough. With the hot buttons SAGE is pushing—logging, land development, waste dumping in the old mines—people are so divided and so many jobs threatened that I wouldn't even know where to begin to weed out that lady's attacker."

Flint sighed. "I have to believe a guy who could do that is bound to brag about it."

"Do you think he's a sex offender?"

"Probably not. A sex offender would've seized the opportunity when he had it. But this perp is certainly a loose cannon. It's possible he just wanted to scare her, but we can't afford to assume he won't come back and do what he threatened. He's proven he's capable of violence. I advised Baughman to back off till we get him, but she's not going to."

"Sure hope she doesn't end up regretting that decision."

"That's two of us." Flint fiddled with his fork. "I think it's smart you hired a security guard. But until we know who's out there, I think you should be really careful. Carolyn, too. Probably a good idea to tell your work crew to keep their eyes open for anything suspicious."

"Hey, you're the one who said this group has no history of violence."

Flint nodded. "But their president was never attacked before, either. Someone could be itching to get even."

Rue left the trailer and trudged over to the model condo. He spotted Grayson talking with one of the workers and waited until the conversation was finished, then went over to him.

"Have you got a minute?" Rue said.

"Sure. By the way, I met Montana just before I came back from lunch. He was throwing the Frisbee to his dog. Nice kid."

"Thanks. We think so. Did you hear about the lady from SAGE who got attacked?"

Grayson nodded. "My brother Bobby called me. Pretty sick deal."

"Well, Elam wanted me to tell you that he's gotten two phone calls from SAGE, one last night and another this morning, telling him to stop construction on the retirement village or there'll be consequences."

Grayson's eyebrows came together. "Surely SAGE doesn't think he or someone working for him attacked their leader?"

"I doubt it. Elam got the first call after the attack, and the caller didn't mention it then or this morning."

"Seems a little too coincidental, don't you think?"

Rue shrugged. "I don't know what to think. I don't have all the facts. The security guard'll be arriving before we knock off for the day. I wanted you to know."

Grayson took his handkerchief and wiped the sweat off his neck. "Of all the builders to pick on, why go after Elam? He's done more to protect this area than SAGE has."

"We don't know that EG Construction is the only company they're targeting. But the second phone call was enough to convince Elam he needed to take the threat seriously."

"I wonder what kinds of consequences the caller was referring to."

"Hard to say. But we all need to watch our backs. Keep our eyes open for anything suspicious. I need you to talk to the work crew." Rue put his hands in his pockets and drew a line in the sawdust with his boot. "Grayson, did you happen to see a file around anywhere? *Phase One* was written on the tab."

"No. Should I have?"

"I just misplaced it. That's all."

"Was it important?"

Rue nodded. "Very. If you run across it, I'd appreciate your bringing it to me."

"I will."

Rue lifted his eyes in time to catch a smirk on Grayson's face. "Did I say something funny?"

"No. No. I was just thinking about Montana. I enjoyed talking to him. Kids say the cutest things."

Flint jogged down the courthouse steps and went over to his squad car, his mouth watering for the Yankee pot roast Betty had waiting for him.

He winced when he spotted Bobby Knolls walking in his direction. Was it too much to ask for a relaxing evening?

"I'm glad I caught you before you left," Bobby said, sounding winded. "We just got back. We've been all over the county, chasin' down SAGE members."

"Find anything interesting?"

"Members have to be at least eighteen. Since the caller sounded young, we questioned all male members under the age of thirty. There were twenty-two of them. We pushed plenty hard but got nothin'. They all denied makin' the phone call to Elam—or to anyone else. Most seemed like they'd cry if they stepped on an ant."

"Did they say why they thought Madison Baughman was attacked?" Flint said.

"They all echoed the same thing: there're plenty of people who'd like to shut them up."

"How many of these guys were at Spruce Park?"

"Just three. All were at the ER last night and gave statements. Apparently, the group changes out who's gonna be where when so the same members aren't out every weekend. It was mostly an older crowd that protested here. The average was thirty-nine."

Flint leaned against his car, his arms folded. "I assume you're going to dissect the list of SAGE members and talk to the sons old enough to have made the call to Elam?"

"Buck's gettin' it lined up. We're not gonna leave any stone unturned."

Flint looked out at the mountains and noticed just a few trails of white still on the peaks. He wondered if this case was going to eat up his entire summer. "How much do we really know about the Baughmans? It's possible that the attacker had it in for one of them and wanted us to believe the attack was somehow related to Madison's environmental stand. Could've been completely unrelated."

"Want us to go back and talk to the Baughmans?"

"Not yet. Check out the SAGE members' sons first and eyeball each one that's old enough to have made those calls. If that doesn't raise a red flag, let's go back to the Baughmans and dig deeper."

—

That evening at dinner, Rue listened to Montana chatter away about his day before telling Ivy about his meeting with Elam and how embarrassing it was to admit he had misplaced the important file containing all his notes. He told her he was going to have to put in long hours until he could reconstruct everything that had been lost.

Ivy didn't say anything. She seemed miles away and was pushing a pea around her plate with her fork.

"You okay, babe?" he said.

She jumped at the sound of his voice. "I'm fine. I'm just processing something I heard today. We can talk about it later."

"That means you don't want me to hear," Montana said.

Ivy tilted her son's chin and smiled. "That's the best part of being a kid. You don't have to solve grown-up problems." She touched his nose with her finger. "Why don't you go do your chores and let me talk to Daddy, and then later we can drive into town and get ice cream."

"Yay." Montana jumped to his feet. "I want chocolate with peanut butter sprinkles—*three* dips." He cocked his head and smiled. "Okay, two."

Ivy waited until Montana put his dishes in the sink and went out the front door, and then said, "Rusty came by the registration desk this morning and returned the banana bread. He was just as hateful as he was at Thanksgiving."

Rue listened as Ivy told him everything that had happened from the time Rusty laid the gift bag on the counter until he turned on his heel and left.

"What hurts me more than anything," she said, "is the way he bad-mouths Montana—like that sweet child is some kind of dysfunctional time bomb that's doomed to cause trouble. Rusty said he had the responsibility to protect his girls from *our* dysfunction. He doesn't even know us. How can he say something so mean?"

"Doesn't seem like Rusty has any trouble being mean."

Ivy wiped the tears off her cheeks. "I'm not going to try being nice anymore. I just want to stay away from him."

"I know, but your family is going to be divided until this gets worked out."

"How am I supposed to work it out if Rusty won't bend?"

Rue put his hand on hers. "Don't decide it's hopeless after just one try. You haven't had a breakthrough with Rusty yet, that's all."

"It makes me furious that he thinks you got me pregnant and then skipped out."

"Would you rather he knew I was a john you don't even remember sleeping with? Rusty's clueless about addiction—or the desperation that drives people to do things they're ashamed of."

"Well, I'm sure not ashamed of Montana."

"Definitely not." Rue kissed her cheek. "He's the best thing that's ever happened to either of us. So what if Rusty thinks I skipped out? He can't fault me for wanting to make things right."

"I'm not about to tell him how God brought us together and let him pooh-pooh the whole thing."

Rue nodded. "Let's just commit to praying God will soften Rusty's heart. Listen, before Montana comes back, I need to tell you that your dad got another threatening call, this time at work. Same as last night. He's hired a security guard to watch the building site."

"Was it the same caller?"

"Elam thinks so. The guy sounded young. The sheriff's deputies are talking to every member of SAGE to try to weed him out. Frankly, I'm a little nervous. The group can't be happy about their leader being attacked. Let's just hope they're not planning to retaliate."

11

RUE WAVED AT THE SECURITY GUARD posted at the gate, then parked his Silverado behind Grayson's Dodge pickup. He glanced up at the pastel blue sky and last smattering of stars still visible above the rugged peaks and wondered how many months it had been since he had taken Ivy and Montana on a stargazing adventure.

He locked his truck and made a beeline for the office, the sound of hammering echoing in the stillness of dawn.

He went up the steps and into the trailer, the smell of freshly brewed coffee wafting under his nose.

"Good morning." Liz stood at the coffeepot, decidedly attractive in her snug-fitting jeans and white blouse. If he had seen her only from the neck down, he would never have believed she was sixty-two.

Rue pointed to his watch. "You're here early."

"Early's relative this time of year. Between you and Elam barking orders, I need to grow two more arms to keep up." She winked. "Then again, the overtime's nice. You want coffee?"

"Sure, but I can get it."

Liz arched a penciled eyebrow. "You see that trail of brown spots on the linoleum? Never had that till you fellas decided it was politically correct to get your own coffee. Save me the grief and let me bring it to you before I scrub a hole in the floor, trying to clean up after you."

Rue laughed without meaning to. "You run a tight ship, Cap'n Lizzie."

"And don't you forget it. By the way, did you see Stan outside?"

"Who?"

Liz filled a large mug with coffee and motioned for Rue to head down the hall. "Stanley Pearson—the security guard."

"You're already on a first-name basis?" Rue went into his office and flipped the light switch.

Liz set the mug on the desk, then put her hands on her hips. "I happen to think it's a good idea to be on a first-name basis with someone I may have to scream for. With all this SAGE nonsense, anybody wanting to get to Elam would have to take me out first."

"That's an awful thought. Totally crazy. But awful."

Liz tapped him on the chest with her forefinger. "Well, we're dealing with crazies. A girl can't be too safe."

"If it makes you feel better, our man Stan was standing at the gate. I waved to him on the way in."

The phone rang and Liz picked it up. "Good morning, EG Construction. No, I'm sorry he's not. I don't expect Mr. Griffith until mid-morning. Would you like to speak with the project manager…? May I tell him who's calling…? Thank you. One minute, please." Liz put the caller on hold and hung up the receiver, her face ashen. "It's *him*. He says his name is John Smith, but I recognize his voice. It's the guy who called yesterday and threatened Elam. I know it."

Rue took a slow, deep breath. "Okay, let's stay calm." He moved his head next to Liz's and picked up the receiver so she could listen in. "This is Rue Kessler. How can I help you?"

"We warned you *twice* to stop the construction or there'd be consequences. You should've listened, dude."

The phone went dead.

"Hello, Mr. Smith…? Are you there…? Talk to me…" Rue slammed down the receiver and stood mute for moment, then heard himself say, "Liz, grab that pad and write down exactly what he said before we forget."

Liz scribbled the words on the pad. "I'll go call the sheriff."

"Okay, that's good. That's good." Rue fumbled around for his cap and realized it was on his head. "I'll go tell Stan about the call. Then I'll be back."

"No." Liz grabbed his shirt. "Call his pager. I'm not staying here alone. You have no idea where that guy was calling from. He might be on the property."

Ivy set a plate of pancakes and sliced bananas on the Spider-Man place mat.

"Sweetie, your breakfast is ready."

Montana turned off the TV and raced to the table. "Yum."

The phone rang, and he jumped up and grabbed it. "Kessler residence. Montana speaking…Hi, Dad…Okay, sure." Montana handed the phone to Ivy. "He wants to talk to you."

Ivy smiled and put the receiver to her ear. "Miss me *already?*"

"We got another threat, babe. I took the call myself fifteen minutes ago. The sheriff's on his way and thinks we need to take this seriously. Try not to worry Montana, but I don't want you leaving him at your mother's today. In fact, Elam doesn't want Carolyn to stay at the house, either."

"Should I take Montana to work with me?"

"No, Carolyn's on her way to our house and is going to watch Montana there. They'll be safe at the camp. It's just not smart for them to be in that big house with no one else around. Not with this threat hanging over Elam."

Ivy glanced over at Montana and forced a smile. "Okay, I'm sure that'll be fun for a change."

"I take it Montana's within earshot?"

"Uh-huh."

"I don't think we can shelter him from this completely. All of us need to be tuned in to our surroundings. I'd feel better if he didn't go outside unless Windy's with him."

"And I should say this is because…?"

"Tell him that someone wants to stop Grandpa Elam from building the retirement village, and until the sheriff figures out who it is, we think it's a good idea for Grandma not to be at their house without another grownup."

"That might raise more questions."

"Explain it however you think he'll understand it, but try not to worry him. We don't know what *consequences* the caller was talking about. But now that he knows my name, too, I just think you need to stay alert. If anything feels off or if anyone seems suspicious, call camp security."

"What about you?"

"This place is crawling with deputies. Nobody's going to do anything out here."

Flint leaned on his squad car and took his ringing cell phone off his belt clip. He read the display screen, not surprised that Bobby Knolls was calling. He pushed the Talk button.

"Hi, Bobby. Grayson's fine, in case you were wondering."

"Yeah, I was. Thanks. So tell me about the threatening phone call."

"A guy who identified himself as John Smith called EG Construction about seven this morning. Elam's office manager, Liz Parker, gave the call to Rue Kessler and listened in on the conversation."

Flint relayed to Bobby what Liz and Rue had told him, including the caller's exact words.

"This guy always cuts to the chase," Bobby said.

"Keep that in mind when you're talking to the sons of SAGE members today. Maybe one of them will stand out. But in case you don't know, both Smiths on the membership roster are women, and neither has a spouse or a son named John. We're checking Elam's phone records to determine what phone number was used to place the calls to his house and his office. Maybe our troublemaker didn't know we could do that."

"Do you think somethin's about to go down?" Bobby said.

"We have to respond as if it is. The caller didn't specify the threat to mean bodily harm, but I suggested Carolyn Griffith not stay home alone until we find whoever's doing this."

"I'm thinkin' everyone workin' for Elam should watch his back. If the caller wants to make an example of EG Construction, it might not matter to him which employee he targets."

Flint glanced over at the work crew talking to detectives. "So far, the calls have all been made to Elam."

"I thought you said Kessler took the call."

"But the guy asked for Elam. Since he wasn't there, Liz put him through to Rue."

Bobby exhaled into the phone. "I have a bad feelin' about this. If this bogus Mr. Smith can't get to Elam, how do we know how far down the chain he'll go to make his point?"

Ivy stood at the registration desk in Three Peaks Lodge, aware of the front door opening and closing. She heard footsteps and lifted her eyes, expecting to see another arrival for the men's conference.

"Rusty. What're *you* doing here?"

"My attorney heard on the news that Dad's been getting threatening phone calls. I can't get an answer at the house. Do you know where Mom and Dad are?"

"Dad's probably out at the construction site. Mom's at our house." Ivy told Rusty the details of her conversation with Rue right after he had taken the threatening call.

Rusty's eyes turned to slits. "Well, no one bothered telling *me*."

"They didn't know how seriously to take the threats until the third one came in this morning. It's just been a few hours. Maybe they thought you were busy with your attorney and didn't see any point in bothering you until they know more."

"They could've left a message on my cell phone. You have any idea how embarrassing it was hearing from a third party that Dad's getting threatening phone calls—and being totally clueless?"

"I'm sure they didn't intentionally withhold it from you, Rusty. I doubt if they knew it was on the news. I would've been glad to call you, but you don't want to hear from me."

"I shouldn't have to hear things like that from *you*. I'm the one who's always been there for them. I'm the one who dried their tears when you broke their hearts."

Ivy let out a breath and blew the bangs off her forehead. "That was a long time ago, Rusty. I'm the one who's working hard to stay close to them *now*. If you feel left out, maybe you need to do something about it."

"Oh, so now you're the expert on Mom and Dad?"

"I lost ten years with them. Ten years. And we've grown closer in the past twelve months than I ever thought possible. I'm not going to let you make me feel guilty because they've forgiven me. No one is trying to shut you out. You're doing that all by yourself."

Rusty glared at her. "No, I'm not. I knew when you came back to Jacob's Ear they would invest everything in you and all your *needs*. You're a loser, Ivy. You may have Mom and Dad fooled, but you don't fool me. You'll keep taking until you drain them. And one of these days you're going to break their hearts again. You and that kid of yours."

Ivy blinked back her tears and willed away the emotion that left her mute.

"I've got my eye on you and that parasite you married. Don't think for one minute that I'm going to sit back and let the two of you suck them dry." Rusty turned on his heel and stormed out of the lodge.

Ivy stood stunned for a moment and then groped her way to the adjacent file room and closed the door. She leaned against the cold metal cabinet, her face in her hands, and wept.

12

IVY LAY ACROSS HER BED, aware of the dishwasher running in the kitchen and Montana and Windy roughhousing up in the loft. The sound of their playing was the only thing about her entire day that felt normal, and she decided to let Montana think she didn't hear him using his bed as a trampoline.

How could all this be happening—and just one week after coming home from her honeymoon? Threats from activists. Verbal attacks from her brother. Rue working impossible hours in an effort to reconstruct the information in his lost file.

At least her parents felt comfortable going home after her dad decided to hire an additional security guard to watch their house and property. He also alerted the security personnel at the camp to keep a close eye on the chalet.

But the vague threat hanging over EG Construction was the least of her worries. After today's confrontation with Rusty, she was mad enough to take on every member of SAGE with her bare hands.

How dare her brother accuse her of shutting *him* out when he had rebuffed every effort she'd made to draw him in—not just once, but over and over? And how dare he insinuate that she and Rue were out to get as much as they could from her parents?

You're a loser, Ivy. You may have Mom and Dad fooled. But you don't fool me. You'll keep taking until you drain them.

How much did Rusty think they'd given her? When she first moved back, they bought her some clothes so she could work at Jewel's. And a car so they wouldn't have to run her back and forth to work. And when she accepted the job at Three Peaks, they offered her free lodging as a perk—the same as they'd done for several other staff members.

The land they gave her and Rue for a wedding gift was a complete surprise. She had never expected or even considered such a generous gift. But her parents were worth millions, and accepting twenty-five acres from the thousands they owned could hardly be considered "draining."

Ivy sighed. There was something dark about Rusty. His eyes seemed vacant. He never smiled. Never said anything positive about anybody— other than himself. His behavior was prideful but reeked of self-loathing.

Lord, please don't let my hurt feelings make me as bitter as he is.

A loud thud rocked the ceiling, followed by giggling and yelping.

Ivy smiled in spite of herself and decided she'd better go up to the loft and see what kind of mischief Montana and Windy were getting into.

Rue turned the key, surprised not to hear barking, and pushed open the front door. Windy ran in circles and then sat whimpering, her tail swishing from side to side, looking as if it was all she could do to keep from jumping up on him.

He reached down and scratched her chin. "You knew it was me, didn't you?"

Ivy, dressed in her pink nightgown, shuffled toward him from the hallway. "Not till after she barked loud enough to wake the dead."

"At least she was being protective, babe. Sorry she woke you."

"Actually, I wasn't asleep." Ivy slid into his arms. "You must be exhausted. Were you able to make any headway?"

"Oh, sure. I knew if I could get quiet and focus, I could remember most of the timetable I'd set up for Phase One. It'll take a few days to make some calls and double-check the details I'm a little fuzzy on. But we're not gonna lose momentum because I lost the file. So why are you still awake? Are you worried about the threats?" Rue heard Ivy sniffle and drew back and studied her face. "What's wrong?"

"Everything."

"Why don't we sit down and talk about it?"

Ivy nodded and went over to the couch.

Rue sat next to her, his arm around her. "What's got you so upset?"

"Rusty. He came by registration this afternoon after he heard Dad was being threatened. He was mad Mom and Dad hadn't called him and weren't answering their phone. He wanted to know if I knew where they were. Of course, he didn't waste the opportunity to make everything my fault."

Rue listened as Ivy went through the conversation she'd had with Rusty, detail by detail.

She wiped the tears off her cheeks. "I'm sick of him calling me a loser. And how dare he call you a parasite. Does he honestly think you married me because Mom and Dad have money?"

"Consider the source." Rue tilted her chin. "And you're anything but a loser. Your brother's jealous that your parents have rallied around you in spite of the pain you caused."

"Just because they welcomed me home doesn't mean they love him any less."

"No, but for ten years, they showered all their attention on Rusty, the dutiful son. He probably resents that attention being turned on you when, in his mind, you've done nothing to deserve it."

Ivy sighed. "Can't our parents just love me because I'm their daughter?"

"Absolutely." Rue brushed away the strands of hair that had stuck to her wet face. "We just need to blow off most of what he says right now and pray that he changes over time. Hopefully, you won't have to see him again for a while."

"Good."

"Other than Rusty, how'd you do today?"

"I talked to Montana about the calls, and we're being cautious. But I'm not convinced SAGE is going to come after us. Or even after Dad, for that matter. I'm more inclined to think if they're going to break the law, they'd do something to stop the building project—like destroy equipment and supplies or existing structures."

"Your dad thinks so, too."

"Of course, that makes me glad you have a security guard at work. But I just don't see this group going after people. They've never done it before. And they're committed to protecting life."

"Actually, the sheriff thinks it could be a member acting on his own."

"Great. All we need is a wild card." Ivy saw something out of the corner of her eye and realized Montana was standing at the railing in the loft. "What's the matter, sweetie?"

"Windy was barking and woke me up. Dad, will you tuck me in?"

"Sure." Rue kissed her cheek. "Why don't you warm up my side of the bed? Maybe now we'll all get some sleep."

Flint sat in his easy chair and downed the last of the Sleepytime tea. Betty said it would relax him, but all it did was keep his bladder busy. He reread the notes he had scribbled on a ruled pad before he came home. All they knew about the caller so far was that he sounded young. Had a deep voice. And got right to the point. There was no John Smith listed on the SAGE membership roster. No husbands or sons by that name, either.

It was likely they were dealing with one man, even though there was no way to trace the calls, since a prepaid cell phone was used in each case. Liz and Elam seemed sure that all three calls came from the same individual. But since they each heard the caller only two of three times, and for just seconds, it was speculative at best.

Flint set his reading glasses on the table. He had hoped that the interviews with SAGE members would reveal that someone in the organization had kept a record of calls made to companies the group took issue with. At least that would've narrowed down the list of who may have had motive to attack Madison Baughman.

Hair and skin-cell DNA were collected from Baughman's T-shirt and probably belonged to the attacker, but they were still waiting for the results. Whatever object the attacker used to strike her head had not been found.

"Are you ever coming to bed?"

Flint glanced up at the doorway where Betty stood, dressed in her pink satin pajamas. "I'm so wired, I'd just keep you awake."

"Sorry the tea didn't work."

"Yeah, me, too. I've been over and over what we know so far. I'd like to get some rest."

"You think this guy's going to go after Elam?"

"He never threatened bodily harm. But whatever he meant by *consequences,* I feel pretty certain he'll follow through with it. Elam thinks he'll try to sabotage the building project somehow."

"He'd have to get past the security guard, wouldn't he?"

Flint nodded. "But the guard can't be everywhere at once. I've got deputies posted on the road about hundred yards from the gate, and it'd be impossible for anyone to drive up to the work site without being seen. If he decided to go on foot, he'd have to cut through the barbed-wire fence and hike over some pretty rugged terrain in the dark. The security guard would spot a flashlight."

"I just can't imagine SAGE doing this. One of the men who volunteers with me at the Miner's Museum has a granddaughter who's a member. He says they're good people and are schooled never to get pushy or hateful with their views on the environment."

"I don't think we're dealing with the organization, hon. I think this is probably some radical who's unhappy with the progress the group is making and decided to try intimidation tactics. But Buck and Bobby couldn't get anyone in SAGE to name an affiliate who might be zealous enough to act on his own. So we're right back where we started."

Flint faded in and out of wakefulness, aware that the Mylanta he took
before he went to bed had not put out the fire in his gut. A chilly breeze
blew the curtains, and he turned on his side and pulled the blanket up
to his ears, wishing he could stay asleep.

Madison Baughman's face popped into his mind, and he replayed
what she had told him and Bobby at the ER. If she was right that at least
two other men were present when she was accosted, maybe someone
other than the man who threatened her had struck her over the head.

Flint felt himself drifting off and gave in to it, hoping he might get
a couple hours' sleep…

A loud ringing noise startled him. He groped the nightstand and
hit the Snooze button on the alarm clock and realized it was his cell
phone ringing. He found it and put it to his ear.

"Sheriff Carter."

"It's Bobby. I'm on my way to the Griffiths'. The missus just called
911 and reported that someone turned the horses loose and set the stable on fire."

"Where was the security guard, for crying out loud?"

"Don't know yet. Pumper trucks from White Top and Mt. Byron
are on the way. I knew you'd wanna know."

Flint let out a sigh of exasperation. "Yeah, Bobby. Thanks. I'll meet
you out there."

13

FLINT BARRELED DOWN Three Peaks Road, siren blaring, and just before he got to the camp entrance, he turned onto the private road that led up to Elam and Carolyn's place. He pressed the accelerator and raced toward the stable, the moon barely visible through a blanket of smoke.

He drove around behind the Griffiths' log house and out about fifty yards to where flames shot up from the blazing stable and licked the predawn sky.

He pulled up behind Bobby Knolls' squad car, relieved to see that two pumpers were already there. Firefighters held high-pressure hoses and directed torrents of water into the inferno. He saw the Griffiths and the Kesslers trying to corral horses into a pen.

Flint popped two Tums, then opened the door, a handkerchief held to his mouth, and stood leaning on his squad car for a few moments before realizing the smoke was drifting in the other direction.

Bobby hurried over to him. "Appears to be a total loss, Sheriff. But Elam's pretty sure all his horses were let out before the fire was set."

"It's definitely arson, then?"

"We'll have to wait for the official word from the fire marshal. But we all know who did it."

Flint heard shouts and looked up just as the roof collapsed in on itself and sent sparks flying everywhere. Firemen scrambled to put out small brush fires that sprang up and were able to quickly contain them.

A white Navigator pulled up behind Flint's car, and he recognized Rusty Griffith when he got out and jogged over to his parents.

"So where's the security guard?"

Bobby popped a pink bubble. "His truck's gone. Wouldn't it frost you if he was in on it?"

Ivy gasped in disbelief as the stable that had held so many wonderful childhood memories seemed to melt before her eyes.

Rue slid his arm around her, his lips to her ear. "Rusty just arrived."

"So what?" She glanced over at him hugging her mother.

"We should go say something," Rue said.

"If my brother has something to say to me, he can come over here."

"Babe, this isn't the time to dig in your heels. Your folks need us."

She assessed Rue's sooty expression and saw only kindness. "You're right."

"Just stay close to me," he said. "Rusty wouldn't dare smart off with me and your dad there."

Rue took her hand, and they went over and stood next to her mom and dad.

"Sorry we couldn't save it," Rue said.

"Thanks for helping us try." Carolyn sighed. "At least we didn't lose the horses."

Elam put one hand on Ivy's shoulder and the other on Rue's. "Why don't you two take your mom inside and get cleaned up? Maybe you can help her answer questions for Flint and the fire marshal while Rusty and I go round up the rest of the horses."

Ivy eyed her brother's Polo shirt and wrinkle-free khakis, amused that they were going to smell like a sweaty horse by the time he got back.

"I've got plenty of rope in the shed," Elam said, "just in case we need a lasso. But Sasha's good at rounding up the horses. It shouldn't take long now that the sun's almost up." He turned to where the other horses were penned and seemed to be studying them. "We're missing four, including Sassy, Montana's favorite."

Ivy could almost see Rusty bristle at the mention of her son's name and was glad when Sheriff Carter came over and stood next to her dad.

"I'm going to nail whoever did this, Elam."

"I know you will. Right now, I'd just like to wring the security guard's neck for leaving us out here like sitting ducks."

An hour later, all the missing horses had been retrieved, and Ivy sat at the kitchen table having breakfast with her parents, Rue, and Rusty and trying to ignore the disgusting smoky odor that lingered in their clothes and hair.

"I'd have that security guard's head on a stick if I were you." Rusty slid a piece of sausage off the platter and onto his plate, then passed it on to Carolyn.

Elam glanced at his watch. "The business office at Southwest Security opens in fifty-five minutes. Believe me, I plan to be on their doorstep and give somebody an earful. They assured me this Tom Nicholson was a trusted, longtime employee."

"What're you gonna do with the horses?" Rue said.

"I'll make arrangements to board them at Horseshoe Ranch till we can get a new stable built. I'll get with the insurance company later this morning."

"Montana's going to be relieved Sassy's all right." Ivy stole a glance at her brother and relished being able to say her son's name out loud without Rusty making a cutting remark. "He loves that horse. Actually, she reminds me a lot of Rusty's first horse, Zorro. Remember him?"

"I never forget anything." Rusty flashed an angelic grin and stuffed it with another bite of sausage.

You hypocrite, she thought. *If Mom and Dad only knew how vicious you've been.*

The doorbell rang, and then Ivy heard footsteps moving in their direction. Seconds later, Flint Carter came into the kitchen.

"We just found the security guard tied to a tree at the edge of the south woods. He seems disoriented and isn't making much sense right now. His truck's missing. Maybe he can give us a description of whoever did this."

Shortly before nine, Ivy took her place at the registration desk at Three Peaks Lodge, showered and smelling like herbal shampoo. She was still waiting to hear if the security guard had told the sheriff anything helpful.

A few minutes later Kelsey breezed in the front door of the lodge, her purse strapped to her shoulder, her long hair wet and tied back in a ponytail. "I think I got ready in record time."

"Thanks again for coming over to stay with Montana. I really didn't want to expose him to the chaos." *Or his ruthless uncle.*

"I was glad to help." Kelsey came over and stood at the counter. "Brandon said that your dad told camp security to patrol your street 24/7."

"Just a precaution. The threats were all directed at my dad. He's the one I'm worried about."

"Truthfully, Brandon and Jake are concerned. Elam owns Three Peaks, too. What if SAGE decides to strike here? We're probably the most vulnerable place of all. And especially with so many kids here for summer camp."

"I just don't see SAGE endangering anything *living,* especially children."

"I hope you're right. I guess all we can do is use good sense and trust the Lord." Kelsey played with her fingernails. "Listen, I have a confession to make. I overheard you and Rusty arguing again yesterday before lunch. I was coming out here to refill my water bottle when I heard Rusty's voice, so I stood behind the door and eavesdropped."

"How much did you hear?"

"I came in about the time he called you a loser and accused you of draining your parents and said you're going to break their hearts again. That about killed me. But I nearly lost it when he referred to Montana as that 'kid of yours' and Rue as a 'parasite.' He went right for the jugular."

"It hurts to admit he talks to me this way."

Kelsey's eyes brimmed with tears. "It hurts me *for* you. Rusty is downright abusive—and so wrong. Have you told your parents?"

"No, just Rue. But if it keeps up, I'm going to have to see if my dad can intervene. I can't live with this kind of tension. You know what's so maddening? He acted like a perfect gentleman when my parents were there. This morning at breakfast he got in a dig at me. But because he smiled and was oh-so-pleasant, I'm the only one who realized it. If it had been just the two of us, he would have cut me to shreds."

Kelsey nodded. "I believe you. Well, I'd better get busy. Jake was understanding about me coming in late so I could help you, but I'm sure he's got a mound of work waiting for me."

"I hope you don't have to stay late because of this."

The corners of Kelsey's mouth twitched. "Heaven forbid."

"Why are you smiling?"

"I keep forgetting this is your first summer working here. When camp's in full swing, I could work around the clock and never get caught up. Brandon and I see each other from noon Saturday until noon Sunday. And it's going to be that way until school starts. Believe me, working late is no big deal."

Flint went up on the porch at Elam and Carolyn's house and saw them sitting together on the glider.

"The fire marshal confirms it was arson," he told them. "We'll know more later, but based on what he saw, his best guess is that the exterior walls of the stable and the hay inside were soaked with gasoline, and then a torch or a Molotov cocktail was tossed in through the open door. The fire started in the front."

Elam shook his head from side to side. "Honestly never occurred to me anybody would strike there. I was worried about the house."

"Unfortunately, Nicholson didn't see it coming. He was standing in your driveway next to his truck, listening to the 3:00 a.m. news on the radio, and remembers someone grabbed him from behind and held a cloth over his face until he blacked out.

"Here's what we think happened: the perps parked their vehicle on Three Peaks Road, approached the house on foot, used chloroform to put Nicholson out, then put him in his truck and took him to the woods. They tied him up, drove his truck to the stable and set the fire, then used his truck to get back to their own vehicle. We've got an APB out on Nicholson's truck, but they probably ditched it somewhere nearby."

"*They?*" Elam said. "So there was more than one person?"

"We took three different shoe impressions around the area where Nicholson was tied up. And found a cigarette butt. Also tire tracks consistent with the tread pattern found on the other Ford trucks Southwest Security uses. We followed those tracks from the woods to your stable and around the side of your house to the driveway. Didn't either of you hear a motor running in the night?"

Carolyn shook her head. "I took a sleeping pill. I wasn't aware of anything till I got up to use the bathroom and heard the horses pitching a fit."

"Sasha kept barking at the security guard," Elam said. "I put her downstairs in the bathroom around eleven thirty so I could get some sleep. I crashed after that."

"Why wouldn't you? You thought things were covered. By the way, Nicholson's gun is missing, too."

Elam tugged at his mustache. "This is very disturbing, Flint. But I'm not going to stop work on the retirement village. For one thing, it'd put a lot of breadwinners out of work, including my son-in-law. For another, I won't be intimidated into caving in to the demands of a group that's too ignorant to realize I'm on *their* side."

"What more do they think he should do?" Carolyn said. "The project is about as environmentally friendly as it gets."

Elam nodded. "I even purchase my lumber from companies that don't log in the aspen forests and are engaged in replanting programs that exceed the requirements. Think I should go to Madison Baughman and explain all that? Or to the media?"

"It couldn't hurt," Flint said. "But truthfully, it doesn't ring true to me that someone serious about preserving the environment would torch your stable—with demon gasoline, no less—knowing the smoke would pollute the air and trees would be cut to rebuild it. Or use chloroform to knock out Nicholson. And throwaway cell phones to threaten you. Just doesn't fit the profile."

"Good point," Carolyn said.

Flint moved his eyes from Carolyn to Elam. "I think we should start at least considering that this may be someone other than SAGE. Can you give me a list of former employees or competitors or anyone who might be angry enough to want to hurt you?"

"I don't have any enemies that I know of. I let two workers go last year after they repeatedly came in late. One of them had a drinking problem."

"Okay, why don't you fax that information over to me," Flint said. "I'm going to head into town. I wouldn't count on this being over. Might want to consider some stronger security measures. I'm going to have a cruiser patrolling this end of Three Peaks Road. That should help deter any thought of those jerks coming back for an encore."

14

GRAYSON KNOLLS TOOK the last puff of his cigarette and crushed it with his boot just as Rue got in his truck and left for lunch.

He went up the trailer steps and into the temporary business offices of EG Construction, the Phase One file tucked in his waistband and hidden under his plaid shirt. He decided he had punished Rue long enough. It was time to put the folder back in the file drawer before he got caught with it.

"Hey, Liz," he said. "How're you holding up?"

She stopped typing and turned her attention on him. "I'm nervous as a kitten. And with good reason."

"Yeah, I can't believe Elam's stable was burned down."

"Well, I sure can. That caller warned us there'd be consequences. It's not like it should've been a big surprise to anyone. This place is probably next."

"I don't know. It'd be a trick getting in here with barbed wire around the property and deputies staked out on the road."

"Tell that to Stan."

"Stan who?"

Liz peered over the top of her half glasses. "Our security guard, Stan. After what happened to the guard at Elam's place, I'm sure he's not wild about this gig. Is there something I can do for you?"

"No, thanks. I just need to borrow Rue's desk while he's at lunch. I want to fill out the crew's work schedule for next week." Grayson headed down the hall. "It'll only take a few minutes."

He flipped the light switch in Rue's office and sat at the desk. He slid open the file drawer and started to unbutton his shirt when his eye was drawn to some notes written on a ruled pad that lay face up on top of the files.

Talk to Elam about GK's aptitude test. Multitasking not his strength. Not suited for project management.

Grayson's mind raced in reverse. Rue's notation had to be in reference to that test Elam had asked him to take months ago. Many of the questions seemed ambiguous, which had made his multiple-choice selections merely guesswork. He told Elam that at the time. Elam said not to worry about it, that he didn't take these tests seriously.

Grayson had forgotten all about it, but now he wondered why Elam had never talked to him about the results. Had the test been a factor in his being passed over for the management job? And how did Rue get his hands on such personal information?

Grayson shut the drawer, his hope of advancement shattered. He sat for a moment, feeling crushed and furious and vengeful.

He got up and turned off the lights and went out the front door without even speaking to Liz.

Later that afternoon Rue sat at his desk and continued reconstructing the information he had put in his Phase One file.

Elam came in and shut the door. "How's it coming?"

"Great. I think I'm about done. I have a few more details to double-check, and then I'll draw it out on a timeline. Man, I dodged a bullet on this one. From now on, I'll keep my notes in the computer and back it up." Rue lifted his eyes. "So did you talk to the insurance company?"

Elam gave a nod. "Yeah, everything's covered. I just thank the Lord they didn't burn down the house instead of the stable. Carolyn and I could've been trapped upstairs, and you and I might not be having this conversation."

"I don't even want to *think* about that. Did the sheriff find out any-thing else since this morning?"

"I haven't heard. I faxed over the names and addresses of the two guys I had to fire last year. But I don't even know that they're still in the area." Elam pulled up a chair and sat next to Rue's desk. "Ivy and Rusty seemed okay with each other this morning, don't you think?"

"It was an act. Nothing's been resolved."

"Neither of them is talking to us about it. You want to fill me in?"

Rue told Elam about the phone call Ivy got from Rusty before he moved back and the two run-ins she'd had with him at the lodge. He stated verbatim the cruel and demeaning remarks Rusty had made.

Elam shook his head from side to side, his eyebrows a dark bushy line. "I'm so sorry. I thought for sure he had softened a little."

"I don't care what he says about me, but when he puts Ivy down, I can hardly stand it. I told her we should blow off most of what Rusty says right now and pray that he changes over time. But I don't know how long I can practice what I preach. I'd like to go knock some sense into him."

"Let me take care of it."

"All right. But truthfully, I don't know that your running interfer-ence will change anything."

Elam tugged at his mustache. "It won't change Rusty's heart, but it might force a change in his behavior. I guarantee you he doesn't want to get on *my* bad side." Elam glanced at his watch. "Let's shift gears and talk about Grayson. You said you had something to ask me."

"I do." Rue opened his desk drawer and pulled out the ruled pad where he'd made some notations, and also Grayson's file. I was cleaning up the personnel files like you asked me to and noticed that Grayson had taken a job aptitude test back in December."

"Yeah, a friend of mine in the business gave it to everyone on his management team and thought it was an eyeopener. I don't put much stock in tests, but I was curious enough to take it myself and asked Grayson to. He thought some of the questions could be taken more than one way and was uncertain how to answer. Frankly, the results didn't ring true to me, especially the part about multitasking not being his strength. He was already doing a good job of it."

"Did you discuss it with Grayson?"

Elam waved his hand. "No. I blew it off."

"Just as well. I don't think this is a true picture of Grayson's strengths and weaknesses."

"Doesn't matter. He's doing a good job as foreman. I'm content with that."

"But Grayson isn't. He came to me on Saturday and asked if I would start grooming him for a better position. I explained it takes a couple years, and that I need to get comfortable with my new responsibilities first. But I'm convinced it's the logical next step. If EG Construction keeps growing and taking on bigger projects, you're going to need more than one manager."

"You think he's up to it?"

"I do. I trust my instincts. And for the record, I don't do as well on multiple-choice tests, either. I often find the questions ambiguous. If it's okay with you, I'd like to work with him. It'll be an ongoing process. And if he doesn't have what it takes to deal with project management, it'll show up. I don't see that we have anything to lose."

Elam nodded. "Okay. Just be fair with yourself. Take some time to settle in before you get involved with Grayson."

"Thanks. I will."

Elam stood. "I need to get home. I'm sure Carolyn won't feel safe there by herself. Don't stay too late. I imagine Ivy's feeling a little vulnerable, too."

"Yeah, I'll be out of here in thirty minutes."

Flint waited for Buck and Bobby to come into his office, then closed the door and joined them at the table.

"Okay," Flint said. "Fill me in. Buck, you first."

"My team found Nicholson's truck abandoned in the tall grass about fifty yards on the other side of Three Peaks Road, across from the Griffiths' property." Buck leaned forward on his elbows. "We went over the truck inside and out. Dusted for prints. Nothing identifiable except Nicholson's. We discovered six five-gallon gasoline cans in the bed of the truck—all empty. No distinguishable prints there, either."

"Good work," Flint said. "Anything else?"

"The red dirt found in the tire tread is consistent with the soil near the south woods of the Griffiths' property. We found a set of tire marks in the grass next to where Nicholson's truck was recovered. The width suggests the perps' vehicle was a truck or SUV."

"Did you find Nicholson's gun?"

Buck shook his head. "The gun wasn't in the vehicle. We're waiting to hear back on the trace and DNA evidence we collected from the interior of the vehicle. That's it so far."

Flint scribbled a note on his pad. "Thanks. Bobby…?"

"We concentrated on the area where Nicholson was found and the vicinity of the stable." Bobby folded his arms across his chest. "We cast three different shoe impressions, each found at both locations. A size ten, an eleven, and an eleven and a half. We're waiting to hear back on brand identification."

"What about the towel you found near the tree where Nicholson was tied?"

"It was soaked with a do-it-yourself type of chloroform made with bleach, acetone, and ice—probably somethin' the perps learned how to do on the Internet. Strong enough to keep Nicholson out for a while and make him disoriented when he finally came to. The rope used to tie his hands could be found anywhere and wasn't helpful."

"Were you able to question Nicholson?"

Bobby blew a pink bubble and sucked it into his mouth. "Yeah, we had him go over his story several times. Seems consistent with the evidence we've recovered so far."

"All right," Flint said. "Let's put this together. Three perps hid their vehicle across Three Peaks Road and walked up to the Griffiths' house, probably each toting two five-gallon cans of gasoline. Those things weigh what—forty pounds apiece?"

Bobby nodded. "So we can assume the perps are young, or at least physically fit."

"Right." Flint continued. "During the 3:00 a.m. news on KTNR radio, one of them grabbed Nicholson from behind and held the chloroform-soaked towel over his face. The perps then drove his truck to the woods, tied him up, drove to the stable, set the horses free, torched the stable, then drove it back to their own vehicle and fled. You want to add anything?"

Bobby and Buck each shook his head.

"All right, then. We need to process all the evidence and see if we can put together a—"

"Excuse me, Sheriff…" Flint's administrative assistant's voice resounded over the intercom, "Deputy Slade is on line one for you. He thought you'd want me to interrupt your meeting."

"Thanks, Sandy." Flint went to his desk, picked up the receiver, and pushed the blinking light. "What is it, Slade?"

"I'm out at Phantom Hollow Veterinary Clinic. Madison Baughman's collie was poisoned. She and a neighbor rushed the dog over here, and the new vet just happened to be in the building, getting things set up. Unfortunately, he couldn't save the animal."

"Does he know what the dog died from?"

"Ingested poison—probably strychnine. But it was no accident. Mrs. Baughman got a call from a young male who never identified himself. His exact words were, 'Go watch your dog die. That's what you get for setting this morning's fire.' She hung up and rushed out to the back-yard and found the dog convulsing. It wasn't a pretty sight. I saw it."

"Did she think the caller was the man who assaulted her?"

"She was sure it *wasn't* him. This man's voice was young, but not deep."

Flint sighed. "Great. Still *another* perp thrown into the mix. I'm assuming the new vet you referred to is Rusty Griffith?"

"I only talked to him for a few seconds, but that sounds right. Let me read the sign taped on the door. Says the clinic will reopen on Monday, June 30, at 8:00 a.m., and the new vet is Russell Elam Griffith, DVM. Is that Elam's son?"

"Yeah, it is. All right, Slade. You've got your work cut out for you. Don't miss a step. Looks like we're in the middle of a turf war between SAGE and somebody who wants to shut them up."

Grayson turned his truck off the highway and onto the graded road that led to his favorite fishing spot. He pulled down his rearview mirror and, through the cloud of red dust kicking up behind the truck, could see that no one had followed him. He drove about two miles and stopped in front of the old cottonwood tree marked with a white X.

He sat for a moment, his pulse racing and his temples throbbing, then grabbed the can of gasoline from the box on the floor and went over to the stone grill that had been there longer than he had been alive.

He unbuttoned his shirt and took out Rue's Phase One file, slammed it on the rusty grill, and soaked it with gasoline. Then soaked it some more. Finally, he turned the can upside down and emptied it.

Liar. Rue never had any intention of grooming him for a better position. It was all talk.

He stepped back and put a safe distance between him and the grill. He held a cigarette between his lips and lit it, entertained by the thought that he was about to sacrifice Rue's hard work on the altar of revenge.

He stared at the file for a moment and savored the feeling of power. He took a puff of his cigarette, then tossed it on the grill and held his arms in front of his face as the file exploded into flames with a loud whoosh.

Grayson stayed and watched the fire devour the file and regurgitate the ashes. Let Rue think he'd had the last laugh. Two could play this game.

15

AFTER DINNER, RUE HELPED Ivy load the dishwasher and noticed Montana sitting intently in front of the TV, watching a special news report about the fire that destroyed his grandparents' stable and the poison that killed Madison Baughman's dog.

"Hey, how about a game of Chinese checkers?" Rue said. "It's time you got beat."

Montana grinned and pointed to himself with his thumb. "No, *I'm* the champ."

"Then you'd better turn off the TV and come defend your title."

"Okay." Montana started to get up, then seemed distracted again when he saw his uncle Rusty talking to a reporter outside the Phantom Hollow Veterinary Clinic.

Rue snuck over and grabbed Montana from behind, evoking a playful shriek. He tickled the boy's ribs until he was belly laughing so hard there was no sound. Rue finally stopped, and the two of them sat on the floor and tried to catch their breath.

Windy ran in circles and barked, trying to get into the action.

Rue glanced up at Ivy. "You should try this, babe. It's a great stress breaker."

"I'll take your word for it."

Montana lay on his back, his arms out wide, and Windy swiped his face with her tongue. He put his arms around the dog's neck and pulled her down next to him, her tail swishing back and forth. "You wanna play, too. Don't you, girl?"

"Well, if you're going to play Chinese checkers, you'd better get started," Ivy said. "You're not going to be happy until you turn it into a tournament, and I want you in bed by nine."

Montana got up on his feet and went over to the table and sat. "Why did somebody poison that lady's collie?"

"There're a lot of sick people in this world," Rue said. "Whoever poisoned the dog did it to make the owner feel sad."

"Because she loves her pet like I love Windy?"

Rue nodded.

"Why couldn't Uncle Rusty make the dog well?"

"Somebody fed the dog strychnine. That's the worst kind of rat poisoning. There's really nothing anybody could do."

Montana reached down and scratched Windy's chin. "Is Uncle Rusty the only vet around here?"

"Pretty much," Ivy said. "People bring their pets to the Phantom Hollow Clinic from all over Tanner County. That's why Rusty bought it when Doc Henley died. It's been there since we were kids."

Montana's eyes grew wide. "Whoa. That's a really long time—longer than my whole life." He put his elbows on the table, his chin resting on his palms, and seemed deep in thought. "What if Windy gets sick or needs her shots? Will we have to take her to Uncle Rusty?"

"Uh…" Rue pasted on an I-hadn't-thought-of-that expression and turned to Ivy, "I'm sure there must be another vet somewhere."

"Of course there is," Ivy said. "I'm sure there are several—just not as close to Jacob's Ear."

Montana lifted his eyes, his chin still resting on his palms. "What if those mean men come back and burn Grandma and Grandpa's house down?"

"That absolutely can't happen," Rue said. "Sheriff Carter has deputies watching the road that leads up to the house. Nobody can get past the deputies."

Montana's eyebrows came together. "What if they fall asleep?"

"You know what?" Ivy said. "All this scary talk is silly. You are completely safe here with us. And Grandma and Grandpa are safe at their house. Why don't you put the marbles on the board, and I'll get some trail mix for us to snack on?"

Grayson gripped the remote and surfed through every TV channel and realized he was back where he started.

"What's wrong with you tonight?" Tara said. "You can't focus on anything for two seconds."

"Sorry, honey. I'm just tired."

He wasn't about to tell her that he'd stolen an important file from Rue's desk and then torched it in a fit of rage—and that he'd do it again in a heartbeat. Or that if he'd had a stick of dynamite he would've blown Rue's truck to smithereens without giving it a second thought. He had a right to be mad. And he wasn't going to let Tara make him feel guilty about it.

"Why don't you turn on the ten o'clock news?" she said. "I want to hear the latest on what happened today."

Grayson turned it to KTNR, though he couldn't have cared less about what happened to anyone else today.

"Good evening. This is Jillian Parker…"

"And I'm Watson Smyth. Welcome to the ten o'clock news. An early morning fire on the homestead property of real estate developers Elam and Carolyn Griffith destroyed the couple's horse stable and may have provoked a second attack against environmental activist Madison Baughman, the president of SAGE…"

Grayson got up and walked out to the kitchen and poured himself a bowl of raisin bran and drowned it in milk. He wasn't going to feel sorry for Elam. Not today. So what if the stable burned? The insurance company would just build him a new one. It's not like it was going to shake the mighty Griffith *dynasty*.

He felt his face turn hot. Why was he reveling in Elam's misfortune? It was Rue he resented.

He picked up his bowl and went over and stood in the doorway and continued watching the news. Reporter Jessica Monrovia was interviewing Sheriff Carter.

"Sheriff, the fire marshal confirmed that the blaze at the Griffiths' was set by an arsonist. And we know that Mr. Griffith received threatening phone calls from a man who claimed to be a SAGE member. We also know the man who called Mrs. Baughman this afternoon said, and I quote, 'Go watch your dog die. That's what you get for setting this morning's fire.' End quote. Has SAGE claimed responsibility for the fire? And did anyone claim responsibility for poisoning Baughman's dog?"

"I'm not going to comment on the nature of those phone calls during the ongoing investigation. But I will say that no one has contacted the sheriff's department and claimed responsibility for anything."

"Isn't it reasonable to suspect the fire was set by SAGE in retaliation for the assault on Mrs. Baughman?"

"I can't comment on that during an ongoing investigation. But keep in mind the Griffiths had nothing to do with that assault."

"But Mr. Griffith is one of the chief land developers in Tanner County and has drawn sharp criticism from SAGE. It's certainly possible that SAGE might have targeted Griffith to make an example of him and let it be known they won't be intimidated."

"Speculation is dangerous, Jessica. I deal with facts. It's a fact that Mrs. Baughman was assaulted. It's a fact that the fire at the Griffiths' was arson. It's a fact that Mrs. Baughman's dog ingested strychnine. I'm not going to comment beyond that. Now, if you'll excuse me, I need to get back to the case."

The sheriff turned and disappeared through the front door of the courthouse, and Jessica faced the cameras.

"There's a lot Sheriff Carter couldn't say. But a number of residents we talked with are convinced that there's an organized effort underway to silence SAGE's criticism of logging and land development in Tanner County.

And after Baughman's dog was poisoned earlier today, people are worried that the proverbial ball is now in SAGE's court. This is Jessica Monrovia for KTNR News. Watson, back to you…"

Grayson went over and put his bowl in the dishwasher. He could understand people being mad enough to fight back. He'd never resented anyone as much as he resented Rue Kessler.

"Are you okay?" Tara stood in the doorway.

"Yeah. I told you I'm just tired."

Tara sighed and folded her arms across her chest. "Are you sure that's all it is?"

"Good grief, woman. Can't a man be tired without his wife making a federal case out of it?" He brushed past her. "I'm going to bed."

Flint captured a yawn with his hand and closed the case file. He glanced across the table at Bobby. "My mind's fried. Let's call it a day."

"Our investigation of SAGE sure didn't give us squat."

"*Yet.* I want your team to tear SAGE apart until we find out who set that fire at Elam's. For now, we have to go with the premise that at least three people in the organization have decided to break rank. I want Buck's team to investigate the logging companies, real estate agencies, and retailers and find out who's mad enough to keep going after Baughman before we end up with a dead person and not just a dead dog."

Bobby sat back in his chair, his weight resting on the balls of his feet. "I know the mayor said the business community was worried that SAGE was runnin' off tourists. But I can't think of any business owner gutsy enough to puncture a tire—much less assault a woman, threaten her, and poison her dog. We've got a bunch of loudmouths. But I don't think any of them would really act on it."

"No one ever thinks they will until they do."

"Good point."

"I'm also having Buck dig into the Baughman's personal life to find out if someone might be holding a grudge completely unrelated to her environmental stance. Maybe we'll get some leads and make some arrests soon. I hate it when we come across like we don't know up from down."

Bobby chortled. "We don't."

"Maybe we do and we just don't know it. We've certainly got all kinds of facts. We just need to fit them together. Go home, Bobby. Get some sleep."

"See you in the mornin'."

Flint sat for a minute, aware of the lieutenant's footsteps squeaking down the hallway. He opened Madison Baughman's case file again. She stated emphatically that the man who had attacked her at the park had a different voice than the man who told her to go watch her dog die. There were at least two perps involved in harassing Baughman. Was it possible that there really was an organized effort to silence SAGE? And how much retaliation would the opposition put up with before the perp who assaulted Baughman followed through with his threat to do worse?

Any man capable of poisoning a dog with strychnine, knowing what a violent death it would cause, might be capable of sexual assault and even murder.

Grayson lay in the dark, thinking about Rue's having deceived him and getting angrier by the minute. He waited until he was sure that Tara was asleep, then tiptoed into the bathroom and got dressed. He tiptoed out to the garage, gathered what he would need in a plastic bag, then got in his truck and headed toward the camp.

It was bad enough that Rue made him feel inferior. But Rue's talking to Elam behind his back—and over a stupid test that didn't prove anything—was over the top. If the creep didn't plan to help him advance, he should've just said so.

Grayson felt his gut tighten. Did Rue have any idea what it was like to bust his tail month after month just to make the minimum payment on maxed-out credit cards? Or tell his stressed-out wife she had to keep working because they had no hope of ever getting out of debt? All Rue had to worry about was kissing up to the boss and keeping that fat salary coming in.

He went through his list of grievances against Rue over and over until he had almost reached the end of Three Peaks Road. He slowed the truck and turned on Road G2 and parked his truck behind a stand of trees. He sat for a minute, his hammering heart the only sound, and wrestled with what he was about to do. Was it worth the risk? Sure it was. And if he got away with it, SAGE would be blamed. What he needed to do was get in and out quickly without being seen.

He grabbed the bag off the front seat, grateful for the light of the full moon, and moved surreptitiously toward the camp, staying close to the trees at the edge of the woods. He spotted a deputy sheriff's squad car parked about fifty yards away on the private drive leading up to Elam's place. He stayed hidden among the trees until he was just a few yards from the entrance to Three Peaks. He took a deep breath, darted across the road and through the open gate of the camp, and jogged toward Chalet Circle, which he remembered was the first street past the main lodge. He glanced over his shoulder, relieved that no one was behind him.

Just before he came to Chalet Circle, he cut through the backyard of the first chalet and within seconds spotted Rue's Silverado in the third driveway. He went down to the empty lot across from Rue's place and hid behind a tree. He reached in the sack and took out the rubber gloves.

Grayson surveyed his surroundings and didn't see anyone. He crossed the street and hunkered down between the Silverado and a Jeep Liberty and listened intently. Not a sound.

He reached in the sack and removed the pocket saw his boys had gotten him for Christmas. It was supposed to cut through almost anything, even metal. He paused a few moments and let the gravity of what he was about to do sink in. He pulled the blade out of the handle and into place, then held it against the front quarter panel of the Silverado and walked down the side and back again, leaving deep gouges in the shiny black paint. He repeated the process several times and finally just started slashing, reveling in the destruction and imagining Rue's disgust and disappointment when he discovered it.

Grayson finally backed up and leaned against the Jeep and sized up the mutilation. What a rush. He reached in the sack one last time and pulled out a can of white spray paint and wrote the letters *S-A-G-E* on the side of the truck. He put the spray paint and the pocket saw back in the plastic bag just as he spotted a car moving slowly down the street in his direction.

He ducked down between Kessler's vehicles and made his way around to the front of the Silverado. Had he been seen? A beam of light moved across the front of the chalet and then across the driveway and between the cars. He didn't move or breathe.

After what seemed an eternity, the vehicle continued on down the street. Grayson poked his head around the side of the Silverado and read the words *Camp Security* between the taillights.

He waited until the car was out of sight and then took off running in the opposite direction toward the front entrance. When he got to the gate, he hid in the shadows for a minute and caught his breath. He peeked around the stone wall and noticed the deputy sheriff's squad car was still parked in the same place. Could he dart across the moonlit road a second time without being seen? Or was he tempting fate?

He decided it was too risky. He put his back flat against the stone wall and worked his way down to the end until he reached the wooded area on the other side of Three Peaks Road. He stayed close to the trees at the edge of the woods until he came to marker G2, then ran across Three Peaks Road and over to where he'd hidden his truck. He climbed in the front seat and locked the doors as if that would somehow keep him from being caught.

He sat in the stillness for a moment, then started his truck. He didn't turn on his headlights until he was on Three Peaks Road headed back to Jacob's Ear. He pushed on the accelerator and glanced in his rearview mirror. No one was following him. He did it. He pulled it off!

Grayson leaned his head back and laughed and then laughed harder. So what if Rue thought he wasn't smart enough for project management? He was smart enough to get the last laugh and pin it on SAGE.

16

On Thursday morning just before daybreak, Rue climbed in the Silverado and headed for the work site. He and Ivy had tossed and turned all night and wondered if Elam and Carolyn had been able to sleep. He tried to imagine what kind of person could be so vehemently opposed to Elam's construction project that he'd abandon the purist mentality and use gasoline and chloroform in the act of getting even.

He pushed a Selah CD into the Bose player. *Lord, help me represent You well today. And help me stay focused. I'm really tired.*

Rue lost himself in Selah's words of praise until he arrived at the work site. He waved at the deputies who were parked on the road, then drove through the open gate and pulled up on the left side of Grayson, who was just getting out of his truck.

"Good grief, man," Grayson exclaimed. "What happened to your truck?"

Rue got out and hurried around to the passenger side to see what Grayson was reacting to. He stared in disbelief at the deep gouges and slash marks and the spray-painted letters and felt sick inside.

Grayson shook his head. "SAGE sure did a number on you."

"I can't believe this," Rue said. "I honestly never thought they'd come after me. They must've done this last night. I didn't notice it when I left for work."

He felt hot all over. Who'd had the gall to come to his home and violate his property this way? Curse words he had long ago stopped saying now polluted the same mind that had praised God all the way to work. He breathed in slowly and let it out. Then did it again. *Sorry, Lord. Help me get a grip. It's just a truck.*

"At least no one got hurt," he heard himself say. "It can be fixed."

"But wouldn't you like to get your hands on whoever did this?" Grayson said. "I mean, they ruined it. It'll never be right."

"A good paint-and-body shop can fix it so you can't even tell it was vandalized."

"Aren't you even mad?"

"Of course I'm mad, but I can't change what happened. I need to report it so the sheriff can figure out who's responsible."

"That's it?" Grayson said. "If I paid over forty grand for a truck and somebody trashed it, I'd want to tear him limb from limb."

"I'm sure not happy about it, but no one hurt me or my family. No one poisoned my dog. No one burned my stable. It could've been a lot worse."

Grayson stood watching the work crew install the windows in the model condo. Rue's reaction had been disappointing and hardly seemed worth the risk. Couldn't he have at least lost his cool? Shown a little outrage? Shouted a few cuss words?

His thoughts turned to the potential consequences. What if someone saw him? What if he left evidence that could be traced back to him? What if he got arrested? What explanation could he offer Tara and the kids—that his jealousy got the best of him? That his actions went against everything he had taught his kids, and yet he wasn't sorry—not one bit?

He mentally retraced his steps. He was almost positive no one saw him. Besides, no one would ever suspect Bobby's brother of doing something like this. Plus Tara would swear he was home asleep. As far as anyone knew, SAGE had struck again.

—

Later that morning, Rue sat in his office at EG construction and finished answering questions for Sheriff Flint Carter.

"I'm sure the reason I didn't hear anything is because the attic fan was on," Rue said. "Even Windy didn't bark. I'm so disgusted that I was awake most of the night and had no clue what was going on right outside."

"My deputies searched your driveway and yard. And dusted your truck for prints. Ivy's Jeep, too. Unfortunately, they didn't find anything useful."

"So much for camp security."

Flint arched his eyebrows. "Actually, they patrolled your street about every fifteen minutes and never saw anything suspicious."

"What about the people staying in the other chalets?"

"None of them saw anything other than the camp security car. Which leads me to think the vandal was on foot."

"He would've had easy access, since the front gate is never locked. It's not like they've had problems before." Rue sighed. "When I took that call for Elam and the guy said, 'You should've listened, dude,' maybe the *you* included me. You think giving him my first and last name set me up?"

"Not really. Anyone who wanted to find out who worked closely with Elam could get that information with no sweat."

"That's not very comforting."

"What's not comforting is that someone in SAGE seems to be itching for a fight." Flint stood and stretched his back. "I'm going to go talk to Madison Baughman and see if she can help us put a stop to this before it turns violent."

Ivy hung up the phone after talking to Rue about his conversation with Sheriff Carter. She let out a low moan. Why did life have to be so complicated?

She lifted the hinged counter and walked through to the other side. She set the "Attendant Will Be Back in Five Minutes" sign on the registration desk and then pushed open the front door of the lodge and went outside.

The scent of pine wafted under her nose, and a warm breeze brushed her cheek. In a nearby tree, a scrub jay squawked at a crow—or maybe it was other way around. She sighed. Even birds couldn't get along.

She went out to the parking lot and leaned on her Jeep and wondered if the vandal had done the same thing. Sheriff Carter's deputies had gone over it, but she hadn't heard whether they found anything helpful.

She would have preferred Montana not be out of her sight right now but knew her mother would use good judgment. There was no reason to panic. The sheriff would figure this out soon.

She heard a familiar cough and lifted her head. "Rusty. What are you doing here?"

"I got chewed out by Dad. That's what I'm doing here. Did you go crying to him because you and I had a fight?"

"I haven't discussed anything we've talked about with Dad *or* Mom."

"Well, that pinhead husband of yours must have. I told you there's no reason for either parent to get involved in this. It's between you and me."

"Nothing's between you and me, Rusty. I'm not perpetuating this animosity. And I'm not keeping secrets. I'm just not going to hurt our parents by admitting how abusive you are."

"Good. Leave them out of it." Rusty's eyes seemed to search hers. "I ran into Pastor Myers at the bank. He asked me if I'd been out to see the new house Rue is building you. What new house? I thought you were living at the camp."

"We are." Ivy's heart sank. She didn't want to tell Rusty anything about the new house or the land their parents gave her and Rue for a wedding gift.

"Then what was he talking about?"

"I'm not going to discuss my personal life with you, Rusty. You made it clear you want nothing to do with me or my family."

Rusty's eyes became slits, and he shook his head from side to side. "I knew it. You conned Mom and Dad into giving you property, didn't you?"

"I need to get back to work." Ivy turned and headed for the lodge.

Rusty grabbed her arm and spun her around. "I'm going to find out whether *you* tell me or not."

"I'm not discussing my personal life. Let go of me."

Rusty tightened his grip. "Like I said before, you'll keep draining them as long as they let you. You're the same loser. Nothing's changed."

"You don't have a clue what my relationship with them is like. You don't *want* things to be resolved because then you wouldn't have anyone to pick on."

Rusty started to say something and then didn't.

Ivy yanked her arm free, her eyes brimming with tears. "What happened to you, Rusty? You used to be such a sweetheart. Now you're the rudest, cruelest, meanest man I know."

"Hey, is there a problem?"

Ivy recognized Brandon Jones's voice and felt her cheeks burning. She turned and saw him approaching. "My brother and I were just having a discussion."

"Yeah, I heard. *Everyone* did."

"Rusty, this is Brandon Jones, the camp director."

Brandon didn't offer Rusty his hand. "I need Ivy to get back to registration."

"We're done," Rusty said. "I was just leaving."

"Our guests come here to relax." Brandon folded his arms across his chest. "If you've got a beef with your sister, I suggest you deal with it when she's not on the clock and someplace where the guests don't have to hear it."

"I'm sure you're aware that my dad owns this camp," Rusty said.

Brandon took a step toward Rusty. "And I'm sure you're aware your dad would agree with me."

"Touché." Rusty flashed a phony smile, then went over and got in his Navigator.

"You okay, Ivy?" Brandon said.

She blinked to clear her eyes. "I'm fine. Thanks for coming to my rescue."

"No problem. I was on my way to the office to pick up something and just happened to hear you two fighting. Kelsey told me how mean Rusty can be. I never realized how bad it was. Does Rue know?"

"Sure. But we agreed to blow off most of what Rusty says right now and just keep praying for the Lord to change his heart."

"I'm all for the Lord changing Rusty's heart, but I don't think it's healthy for you *or* Rusty to just let him walk on you. Anyhow, that's my two cents' worth." Brandon glanced at his watch. "I've got to hustle. You know what summer camp is like."

"I'm learning. See you at church Sunday?"

"Absolutely."

Rue sat under the leafy branches of a cottonwood tree on the bank of Phantom Creek, soothed by the sound of rushing water and cooled by the rainbow mist. The damp, earthy smell reminded him of his boyhood days in Missouri when he would go hunting for worms after a good rain.

In the distance the San Juans stood like a formidable fortress around Phantom Hollow, only a few spider veins of white still visible on the jagged peaks.

Rue loved it here. Close to nature. Alone with God.

Lord, please protect Ivy and Montana and me. Protect Elam and Carolyn, and Grayson and Tara and their kids, and anyone else SAGE might be targeting.

He entered into the quiet and allowed the peace to relax him. His eyelids grew heavy, and he blinked several times to clear the sandy sensation. What he wouldn't give to just lie down and take a nap…but he needed to get back to the office.

He looked forward to the day when he could sit out on his own front porch and feel this same sense of tranquillity but wondered if his plan to have the house finished by next summer was too ambitious.

Rue heard a car motor and turned around in time to see Elam wave as he pulled his Suburban next to the Silverado.

Elam got out and examined the damage on Rue's truck and shook his head, then came over and sat beside him on the ground. "Quite a day, huh?"

"It's just a truck."

"I know. That's how I felt when my stable burned and my horses were spared. So how're you doing?"

"All right. I just came out here to eat my lunch and get quiet. So what do we do now? I'm concerned about Grayson, since he could be next."

Elam nodded. "I had a talk with him. He's going to be extra careful. Said his brother Bobby's going to make sure deputies are patrolling his street."

"Do you think SAGE will stop with just property damage?"

"They've never lashed out until now, so we don't really know what they're capable of. But I can't afford to scrap this project because they have a problem with it."

"But is it worth someone getting hurt?" Rue said.

"Of course not, but stopping the project will put every man on my crew out of work. That's a hurt of a different kind. And I don't see that backing off because of SAGE's bullying will resolve anything. They'll just target someone else."

Rue sighed. "I thought these people were supposed to be Christians."

"That's what they claim."

"How can they justify their actions?"

Elam shrugged and shook his head. "Beats me. I don't see anything biblical to support their tactics."

"Maybe we should go talk to the Baughman lady—not as construction guys, but as fellow believers."

Elam's eyebrows formed a bushy line. "Flint might frown on us doing that while he's still investigating."

"Don't you think the woman should know that we had nothing to do with her being attacked? Or her dog being poisoned?"

"Flint told her that. And she claims she knew nothing about the fire at my place or the vandalism on your truck."

"Maybe she's telling the truth. I mean, how dumb is it for an organization like SAGE to do this stuff openly and risk being shut down?"

"Flint still thinks it could be a rogue member who's acting on his own."

"But that still doesn't explain who's out to get Mrs. Baughman."

"No, it doesn't." Elam tugged at his mustache. "Let me change the subject. I had a heart-to-heart with Rusty last night."

"About what's going on?"

"And about harassing his sister."

"What'd he have to say for himself?"

Elam sighed. "Not much. He thinks Ivy's supersensitive and blows everything out of proportion. I put in a good word for the three of you and suggested he try getting to know you. But I could tell he shut me off."

"When are Jacqueline and the girls coming?"

"Not till the house sells. They've gotten a few nibbles, but no solid offer."

"Can't the real estate agent deal with that?" Rue said. "Seems like it would be better for the family to be together. And it might improve Rusty's disposition."

"I asked him about that. He said Jacqueline didn't think it was a good idea to pull the girls out of swimming, dance, and gymnastics."

"Those things are more important than being with their dad?" Rue picked up a twig and made lines in the dirt. "Any chance they could be having marital problems?"

"Nah. Jacqueline adores him. The girls, too."

Rue laughed to himself. How could anyone adore Rusty Griffith?

17

GRAYSON SAT OUT ON THE PATIO, his mind replaying Rue's calm reaction to the damage done to his truck. Even when Rue was interviewed on the news, he had shown remarkable control and kept saying over and over that it was just a truck.

Grayson took a gulp of beer. So the truck wasn't as important to Rue as he'd thought. How would he react if he lost something that *couldn't* be replaced?

The sliding glass door opened, and Tara came and stood next to his chaise lounge. "Are you coming to bed?"

"Not just yet."

"You do realize that's the end of the beer till payday?"

"I know. I'm a little tense tonight, okay?"

"The deputies are parked out front. Bobby promised they'd be there until morning."

"Yeah, I know. You go on to bed. I need to wind down first."

Tara put her hand on his shoulder. "Bobby's not going to let anyone near this place."

"SAGE never really threatened *me* anyway. It's just a precaution. I'll be in soon. Make sure the alarm is set for five."

"Good night." Tara went back in the house and slid the door closed.

Grayson set his beer on the table and zipped his sweatshirt, then stuffed his hands in the pouch and looked up at the full moon. It had been surprisingly easy to get in and out of the camp without being seen. And even though the damage he'd done to Rue's truck hadn't produced the reaction he'd hoped for, there was something thrilling about having a secret no one else knew about. He hadn't felt this alive in a long time.

He and Tara sure didn't have much to say to each other anymore. Not that the marriage had completely fizzled out, but her resentment at not being able to quit her job wasn't exactly an aphrodisiac. And it didn't help that every cent of their income was spent before they ever signed their paychecks. They had long ago stopped going to movies and eating out and buying birthday and Christmas gifts for each other. They spent that money on the kids.

Tara finally quit smoking to save money. He cut back to a pack every other day and reduced his beer consumption to one can a night. Tonight he'd had four…and wished he'd had another four.

He downed the last of the beer, then crushed the can with his hand and threw it against the fence. He could forget building a new house with a two-car garage, a double oven for Tara, and built-in desks in the kids' rooms. It wasn't going to happen now—not ever. He wondered what kind of fabulous house Rue was building for his wife and son.

Grayson sucked in a breath and blew it out. Why was he so obsessed with Rue? Why couldn't he just let go of the anger he felt at having been passed over for project manager and get on with his life? Then again, what life?

Rue had the life he wanted—*and* enough self-confidence to run the company when Elam finally decided to hand it over to him.

Sure he was jealous of Rue. But he hated him, too—the way he hated his father for making him feel like a flunky because he got a construction job instead of becoming a partner in the family's insurance agency. His dad never even congratulated him when Elam made him foreman. Rue's uppity attitude left him feeling just as deflated.

Part of him was scared that the intensity of his feelings had driven him to do something as risky and spiteful as vandalizing Rue's truck. And part of him wished he could do something worse.

Rue pulled back the curtain and peered outside into the moonlit night and didn't see anything moving, then crawled into bed and nestled next to Ivy, too exhausted to fall asleep. He thought about closing the window and locking it but decided he wasn't going to live in fear. At least it was cool enough in the house that he didn't have to turn on the attic fan. Windy would hear every noise and alert him if the vandals came back. Not that he would be asleep.

He said a quick prayer for Grayson and his family and hoped whoever these rogue SAGE members were, they weren't planning to strike there next.

His thoughts wandered to Ivy's unpleasant encounter with Rusty earlier that day—and Brandon's timely intervention. What more did Rusty expect his sister to do to make things right with the family? She had swallowed more pride in a year than he had in a lifetime and had done everything possible to build back a loving, trusting relationship with her parents. All Rusty was doing was rubbing her nose in past failures.

Rue felt his fist tighten. He was tempted to confront Rusty and goad him into throwing the first punch so he'd have an excuse to deck him. But if he allowed Rusty's hateful behavior to evoke the same behavior in him, then how was he any better? Surely, there was a way for Ivy to learn to stand up to her brother without the other men in her life running interference.

He heard a rustling noise outside. Or was he imagining it? Windy didn't bark. There it was again. Rue jumped up and held back the curtain and craned his neck to see the driveway, but he could only see the right quarter panel of Ivy's car.

He moved stealthily to the living room closet and grabbed Montana's Louisville Slugger, then unlocked the front door, his heart racing. *Lord, protect me.*

Windy charged down the stairs from the loft, her tail swishing the way it did whenever she anticipated going for a ride.

He pushed open the door and let her out just as something metal-lic crashed onto the driveway. He flipped on the porch light, holding tightly to the bat, just in time to see an orange ball of fur dart across the driveway and into the dark, Windy in pursuit. He spotted the trash-can lid on the driveway near what appeared to be chicken bones from last night's supper.

"Should I call 911?" Ivy whispered from behind him.

"No, babe. It was just Jake and Suzanne's cat raiding our trash can. Montana must not have gotten the lid on tightly." He went outside and tossed the bones back in the trash can and put the lid on, then went back in the house. "Sorry I woke you up. False alarm."

Rue whistled for Windy and let her back in the house, then set the bolt lock on the door, sure of only one thing: he was going to be tired in the morning.

Flint lay on his side watching Betty sleep. In the moonlight flooding the room, she looked almost as young as when he married her. He stroked her hair and hoped he wouldn't have to postpone their long-awaited trip to Disney World with Ian. It was still a month away. Maybe the attacks would stop by then and his department would have solved the case.

He thought back on his interview with Madison Baughman earlier in the day. It was obvious she was shaken—and not just about the sin-ister threat hanging over her and her dog being poisoned. She seemed genuinely upset that any member of SAGE would break rank and com-mit arson and vandalism against Elam Griffith and his right-hand man. But was she playing dumb about knowing which members might be capable of it?

Flint rolled onto his back, his hands clasped behind his head. The entire SAGE membership was to gather on Saturday for a day of prayer. Madison promised that she would let him know if she noticed anyone acting suspiciously. But would she really be willing to give up one of her own?

He still struggled with the plausibility that anyone serious about the environment would actually cook up a batch of chloroform or set a gasoline fire that poisoned the pure mountain air with billows of black smoke. But it didn't seem likely that either of the workers Elam had fired last year could have done it—both lived over a hundred miles away and had solid alibis.

Flint groped the nightstand and grabbed the bottle of Tums and popped two. For now, he had to consider that one to three SAGE members were zealous enough to justify vandalism and arson, but not the killing of Elam's horses. And that the opposition drew no such line.

Strychnine had been outlawed in Colorado, even for controlling the pesky ground squirrels that threatened food crops and hayfields and carried fleas infected with bubonic plague. Anyone callous enough to feed strychnine to Madison Baughman's dog was probably capable of worse.

18

EARLY THE NEXT MORNING, Grayson waved at the deputies parked on the side of the road and drove his truck through the open gate and into the field adjacent to the work site. He parked next to Joel Myers's SUV and sat for a moment, bemoaning the start of another twelve-hour day.

"Hey, Grayson."

He turned toward the voice and realized Joel was standing at his window. "Hey, yourself. I'd like to say TGIF, but we both know that won't be true again till September."

Joel smiled. "Six-day weeks already got you down?"

"Not really. I just didn't sleep well, that's all."

"Anything happen?"

"Nah. I really didn't think it would, but Bobby sent a cruiser to watch the house, anyway. SAGE never showed."

"That's good. Not that I believe the SAGE leadership is behind this."

"Why's that?"

"My folks spent time with Mrs. Baughman and some of the members the night she was attacked. They're totally not into using force or threats."

"Rue and Elam might beg to differ."

"Well, I'm glad you're okay. I prayed you would be."

"Thanks. I'm not used to people praying for me."

Joel patted him on the back and flashed a grin. "You kidding? I pray for you all the time. I wish you'd reconsider coming to church with me. My dad's a great preacher. Really relevant."

"I've never seen much point to religion."

"Me, either. But Christianity is really about enjoying a relationship with God. Anyhow, the invitation's open."

"I know it is. Thanks." Grayson had no intention of ever going to church. His old man never missed a Sunday and was still a total jerk.

He got out of the truck, started walking up to the work site with Joel, and noticed Rue had just pulled up.

Grayson paused and admired his handiwork on the passenger side of the Silverado and was hit again with a sense of euphoria.

"Too bad about Rue's truck," Joel said.

"Yeah. A crying shame." Grayson laughed to himself. As long as everyone thought SAGE was responsible, why not take it to another level and give Rue some real grief?

Rue sat at his desk and savored his first cup of coffee while he cleared out his inbox.

Elam came into his office and closed the door, then sat in a chair, his hands folded between his knees. "Flint just called with bad news. Everhardt Roofing burned to the ground last night. Arson."

"Well, that explains why the roofers haven't shown up. Man, this thing is out of control."

"Red Everhardt got a call at home after the place was completely engulfed. A young male caller using a prepaid cell identified himself as a SAGE member and said the fire was a payback for whoever poisoned Madison Baughman's dog."

"But why target Red? He had nothing to do with that."

"We had nothing to do with attacking her, either. It's almost like SAGE is randomly hitting people in the construction industry."

Rue shook his head from side to side. "Just frosts me that they profess to be believers. This kind of thing completely blows their witness and makes all Christians look bad. Does Flint have any suspects?"

"No. And he's hot. He's pulling out all the stops to catch these guys. He's considering calling the ATF and asking for help."

"I thought the ATF dealt with alcohol, tobacco, and firearms."

"They're also experts at cracking arson cases."

Rue combed his hands through his hair. "This thing's making me crazy. I was awake all night worrying about Grayson and wondering if the vandals might come back to our place." He told Elam about hearing a noise and following Windy outside, clutching Montana's Louisville Slugger. "Talk about edgy."

Elam nodded. "I sat in the living room until I couldn't keep my eyes open any longer. I kept checking to make sure the security guard was out front. It was totally unnecessary. A deputy sheriff's cruiser was parked in our private drive, and no one could get up to the house without being spotted."

"I imagine it's hard to relax after what happened to the last security guard."

"Yeah, it is. I'm not that worried about my property, but I couldn't handle it if something happened to Carolyn."

"Exactly."

"So how're you coming with the schedule for Phase Two?"

Rue smiled. "Good. And I'm entering everything into the computer as I go. I learned my lesson."

Elam stood and patted him on the shoulder. "No harm done. We're still ahead of schedule. I just wonder how long we'll have to wait now to get our roofing completed."

"I'm sure Red will call me sometime today," Rue said. "I just hope he can get a temporary office set up and won't have to shut it down over the summer. I've got a backup plan if that happens."

"I figured you did. I think I'll try to reach Red at his home number. He could probably use a little encouragement. I know how hard this must be."

Flint stood at the window in his office, his arms folded, and focused on the gray clouds that had covered Jacob's Peak. This merry-go-round was getting more dizzying by the minute. The man who called Red Ever-hardt identified himself as a SAGE member and told Red his building was on fire, and that it was a payback for the poisoning of Madison Baughman's dog. He was adamant that SAGE didn't have anything to do with vandalizing the Silverado, that it must be a "poser." Flint, Bobby, and Buck decided not to release that information to the media and asked Red to keep it to himself.

The intercom clicked on, and then Sandy's voice filled the room. "Sheriff, the mayor is here to see you."

"All right, Sandy. Send him back." Flint stayed where he was and listened to the footsteps moving closer to his door.

Finally, Lester Smart breezed through the doorway, his thumbs hooked on his red suspenders. "Do you have any idea how upset people are?"

"Of course I do. *I'm* upset. But I don't have any solid evidence against any member of SAGE. And your hollering at me isn't going to change that."

Lester took a step forward, a lock of his stringy white hair falling down on his forehead. "So round up the whole lot of them and hold them till someone fesses up. My phone is ringing off the hook. Everyone SAGE could possibly target is calling me and demanding action."

"Oh, stop whining. Our phones are ringing off the hook, too. Why don't you try supporting our efforts while we sort this thing out?"

Lester dropped into a chair. "You may not know who attacked that Baughman woman and poisoned her dog, but you sure as shootin' know that SAGE burned down Elam Griffith's stable and Everhardt Roofing. And vandalized that Kessler kid's truck. Can't you hold Mrs. Baughman till she talks?"

"Not when she denies knowing anything about it. We've already interviewed every member in the organization, and no one stands out as being capable of this kind of spiteful retaliation."

Lester snorted. "This is ridiculous. We know someone in SAGE is responsible."

"Not until we can prove it, we don't."

"But each of the callers admitted to being a member of SAGE."

"Saying it doesn't prove it. And if they are SAGE members, they're likely renegades who've secretly broken rank."

Lester smoothed his wispy hair. "Whose side are you on, Flint?"

"The side of justice. I can't arrest someone just so people will feel better. I don't have enough evidence to hold anybody, much less press charges."

Lester shook his head slowly from side to side. "That won't set well with taxpayers, I can tell you that."

Flint came over and leaned on his desk facing the mayor. "People elected me to be county sheriff, not county magician. I have procedures I'm required to follow and hoops I have to jump through. Like it or not, it all takes time. You can badmouth me, or you can support my department's hard work. It's up to you. But I'm not going to apologize for not being able to solve this yet. There's a lot more involved than meets the eye."

Lester folded his hands on his belly. "Like what?"

"You know I can't discuss the details of an ongoing investigation." *Especially to a blabbermouth like you.* "But I assure you, we're doing everything we can to figure out who's attacking whom and why."

"That's not especially comforting now that there's been a second fire."

Flint rolled his eyes. "Who said anything about comforting? I'm trying to get at the truth. And I doubt it's going to be pretty. In fact, I'm seriously considering asking the ATF to assist us in the arson cases. And maybe the FBI to help us profile the perps. I don't want the next dead body to be human."

"I should think not." Lester wiggled back and forth in the chair and finally used the arms to push himself to his feet. "I trust you're going to tell that to the media."

"Of course." Flint walked him to the door. "Lester, we've known each other forever. Trust me to solve this."

"Took you ten years to solve Joe Hadley's murder."

"That was a cheap shot. We had nothing to go on. Even the FBI was baffled. May I remind you that it took us just nine days to solve the class reunion shooting last spring and link it to Joe's murder? I'm not a miracle worker, Lester. But I am thorough and persistent and would appreciate your support instead of your criticism."

Lester stared at his hands, a sheepish expression on his face. "Violet says I get testy when everyone's on my case."

"Well, that makes two of us."

"All right, Flint. I'll support your investigation while you weed out these renegades and get them behind bars. Like you said, we don't want the next body we find to be human."

Flint sat at the table in his office and moved his eyes from Bobby to Buck and back to Bobby. "We're in over our heads."

Bobby blew a pink bubble and sucked it into his mouth. "At least we've identified what brand shoes our perps were wearin' when they set the fire at Elam's."

"Tell me again," Flint said.

Bobby picked up the report and turned the page. "A size ten True Wilderness chukka boot, an eleven-and-a-half Sperry Top-Sider, and a size eleven New Balance, model 1122, high-tech, extended-mileage sport shoe. Definitely a step in the right direction." Bobby lifted his eyebrows up and down. "Sorry, bad joke."

Buck exhaled. "I was surprised the man who called Red Everhardt denied that SAGE was responsible for vandalizing Kessler's truck. I didn't see that coming."

"Makes sense, though," Bobby said. "If each attack since Baughman's assault was in retaliation for the previous one, then one of these tit-for-tats is out of sync. And since the fire's consistent with the first one, I'm guessin' the caller was truthful about SAGE not bein' responsible for Kessler's truck."

Flint nodded. "Agreed. So what are we dealing with?"

"A poser," Bobby said. "Isn't that how the caller referred to him?"

"But why would someone go after Kessler now, Bobby—in the midst of all this other?"

"Don't know yet, but it's the least of our worries at the moment."

"Let's talk about Madison Baughman," Buck said. "I finished a pretty exhaustive check into the Baughmans' background. There's nothing there to make me think the attacks on her were personal rather than political, so let's stick with that premise. She seems sure the caller who told her to go watch her dog die was *not* the man who attacked her. So are these guys working together?"

Flint folded his arms across his chest. "That's my guess. Remember Baughman said she heard at least two other men laugh just before she was hit over the head. Listen, guys. We all agree this case is pulling us in too many directions. I'd like to see what the ATF and FBI can do to help us. The arson fires don't seem complicated, so with a little back-and-forth, the ATF may be able to work with the fire marshal without having to supply manpower. But I'm going to ask Special Agent Nick Sanchez to come help us profile the perps."

Bobby smiled wryly. "Mr. FBI himself? I'll dust off his throne."

"You can cut the sarcasm," Flint said. "Nick was amazing when that lunatic McRae threatened my wife and son."

"Aw, I'm just kiddin'." Bobby swatted the air. "Nick's an okay guy for a fed. If you can get past his arrogance, he's great at what he does."

"And that's exactly why I'd like to get his spin on what's going on here."

19

ON SATURDAY MORNING, Grayson walked out of the model condo, satisfied that the work was running at least a week ahead of schedule and certain that Rue was going to take credit for it.

He heard playful barking and spotted Montana Kessler playing Frisbee with Windy out in the open field. The dog was a beautiful animal with husky markings so distinctive that he probably would never have noticed she was a mix if Montana hadn't told him.

Grayson waved, and Montana waved back, then came running over to him, Windy on his heels.

"Hi, Mr. Grayson."

"Hey, big guy. Anything exciting going on?"

"Well, tomorrow after church, I get to help my dad build our new house. We're gonna eat hotdogs out there. That's my favorite picnic, and I like a really lot of relish on mine."

Grayson smiled and wondered how Rue ended up with such a personable kid. "So what kind of work does your dad let you do at the new place?"

"Hammer in the nails. Sometimes he hits them again to make sure they can't come out, because he's stronger than me. But I'm a really good helper."

"I'm sure you are. By the way, I'm sorry about what happened to your dad's truck."

Montana shrugged. "Me, too. But he said we should be thankful nobody got hurt."

"I wouldn't be that nice about it, if it were mine."

"Well, my mom cried and got really mad. She didn't know I could hear when she told my grandma that whoever ruined my dad's truck and burned my grandparents' stable was a *monster*. But there's really no such thing," Montana quickly added. "She was just saying that."

"I knew that."

"The insurance got my dad a different truck till his gets fixed. But I like the Sliverado better."

Grayson smiled at Montana's mispronunciation. Why did the kid have to be so likable? It just made him feel guilty for the thoughts he was having. "Don't worry. He'll get his truck back good as new."

"Yep."

Windy ran in circles and barked, then sat, her tail swishing back and forth, looking as though she were ready to pounce.

"She wants me to play Frisbee some more. Don't you, girl?"

Grayson clapped his hands, and Windy came over to him and yielded to his rubbing her coat and scratching her chin. "She's a great pal, huh?"

"She's the funnest dog in the whole world."

"Does she like hotdogs as much as you do?"

"She likes everything, but she goes bonkers over hamburger. We have to chain her up when my dad grills them, because she whines and whines."

"Well, I need to get back to work. Hope you have fun helping your dad build the new house."

Montana nodded. "Thanks. I will."

Grayson stood for a moment and watched Montana run back to the field and throw the Frisbee. He wondered how long it had been since he'd had a conversation like that with one of his own boys.

Grayson stood in the doorway of Rue's office and saw him working at the computer. He knocked.

Rue glanced up and continued typing. "Come in, Grayson."

"Liz said you wanted to see me. What's up?"

"Red Everhardt set up a temporary warehouse and is back in business. The roofers will be here first thing Monday. We'll hardly miss a step."

"Good. My work crew's done a bang-up job of staying ahead of the game."

"I appreciate that." Rue stopped typing and turned his head toward the doorway. "You should probably be careful, Grayson. I doubt this thing with SAGE is over."

"Don't worry about me. Bobby's got a cruiser in the neighborhood. By the way, I saw Montana outside playing with Windy. He told me he's going to help you work on the house tomorrow after church."

Rue smiled. "He and Ivy don't know anything about this, but I stopped by there last night before I went home, and the framing is almost done. I can hardly wait to see their faces now that it's starting to look like a real house."

"You guys going to keep Windy inside—or are you building her a pen?"

Rue smiled. "She goes wherever Montana goes. Sleeps right next to him. He doesn't have any siblings or neighbor kids to play with, so Windy's filled a big void. She's part of the family."

"Yeah, I'll bet. My three boys have each other to play with. We've never had a dog." *Some of us can't afford another mouth to feed.*

"Now that we've got Windy, Ivy and I don't worry when he's off exploring. The property is a kid's paradise—wide-open spaces, woods, and even a creek. I don't think he'll ever run out of things to do. You should bring your boys out sometime and turn them loose."

Grayson had already been out there, but he wasn't going to give Rue the satisfaction of admitting how awesome it was—or that he'd been curious enough to go uninvited. "Thanks, I will. Was there anything else you wanted to see me about?"

"No, I just wanted to relay the good news that the roofers were coming Monday."

Grayson stood mute for a moment, silently prodding Rue to say something about the results of his aptitude test. There was no way he could bring it up without Rue knowing he had been in the file drawer. Didn't the guy have the decency to at least tell him to his face that the stupid test had blown his chance of moving up? Was Rue going to just let him live with the illusion?

"Grayson, is something wrong?"

"Huh? Oh, not really. I just remembered something I forgot to do. If you're finished with me, I need to get back."

"There is something I've been meaning to talk to you about, but it can wait till Monday. Hope you have a nice Sunday off."

"You, too." *But I wouldn't count on it.*

Flint sat at the table in his office, Bobby and Buck on either side of him, and finished laying out the details of the case for Special Agent Nick Sanchez of the FBI.

"That's it, Nick." Flint handed him a five-page summary he had put together. "We've got a three-ring circus on our hands."

"You sure know how to pick them," Nick said.

"So are you going to be able to give us a profile of who's doing this?"

Nick smiled. "You're in luck, Sheriff. Three-ring circuses just happen to be my specialty. I'll study the file over the weekend, and we can meet again on Monday. My first impression is that everything seems too obvious."

"How so?"

"I'm having trouble with the idea of three against three. Three guys lash out against Baughman. Three SAGE members break rank and strike back. Especially since the attacks allegedly perpetrated by SAGE are inconsistent with the group's history."

"So what are you saying, Nick?"

"I'm saying I have a lot of work to do before I can profile who it is we're looking for. I don't think it's as cut and dried as it seems. And I agree with you that whoever vandalized Kessler's truck was a poser. And not even a good one."

Bobby blew a pink bubble and sucked it into his mouth. "Isn't it possible that both sides are just strikin' randomly and we aren't gonna find any kind of consistent pattern?"

Nick nodded. "Sure, but both arsons followed an attack on the SAGE leadership. And now we've got the shoe impressions to prove that the same three guys were present at both fires. That smells like a pattern, Lieutenant."

Grayson sat out on the patio, disgusted that he was out of beer and couldn't afford to buy more until payday. He had checked the TV listings and noted there was nothing worthwhile on. Tara was sewing. His three sons were on a campout. His daughter was talking on the phone. And he was sitting alone in the dark—bored and wondering how he had become so unimportant to everyone. He felt almost as insignificant at home as he did at work.

He didn't have any real friends, other than Tara. Fifteen years of being a family man and working long hours hadn't left him time for much else—other than fishing and hunting, which he often did alone. But now that Tara seemed distant, he felt as if he were coming home to a vacuum. He could only imagine how much better life would be if he were drawing the kind of salary Rue was. No one was going to convince him that money couldn't buy happiness, though he'd be happy just getting the pressure off. Anything was better than this.

His father's words rang in his mind. *You blew it when you turned down my offer to join me in the agency. You'll have to work twice as hard for half as much.*

Grayson had zero interest in the insurance business. And as mad as he was that his father never validated his desire to build something rather than sit at a desk all day, the man's words now seemed almost prophetic.

He and Tara started out from day one spending more than they made. If they wanted something, they charged it. For years they played the game of transferring their credit balances to new cards with less interest. But it finally caught up with them. Unless they could get a higher credit limit, he didn't know how much longer they could meet their obligations.

He'd seriously considered going to a credit counseling service for help, but he hadn't been able to swallow his pride. Until now, he'd always held the hope that eventually he would be promoted and could start paying things off. He might as well kiss that thought good-bye.

Grayson put his hands behind his head and looked up at moonlit sky. Was it normal to think about hurting people who made him feel stupid? He'd entertained those kinds of thoughts all his life but hadn't acted on any of them until he vandalized Rue's truck. Had he known how easy it was to pull it off, he might've planned something that at least caused Rue to suffer a little.

The same obsessive thought that had played in his mind all afternoon popped into his head with greater urgency. He still had an open window of time in which he could act and SAGE would get the blame. He had already toyed with a perfect time and place. It was just a matter of getting up his nerve.

20

THE NEXT DAY AFTER CHURCH, Rue drove back toward Three Peaks Christian Camp and Conference Center and turned the loaner truck onto Road G6, Ivy and Montana buckled in the front seat and Windy riding outside in the bed. The delicious aroma coming from the to-go sack Montana was holding permeated the cab.

"I'm so hungry I could eat all these deli dogs by myself." Montana leaned down and took a big whiff. "Mmm."

Ivy tousled his hair. "If you're still hungry after eating two, you can have my second one. But I also bought us potato salad, baked beans, and chips. And brownies for dessert."

"Your brownies are better than these kind. But deli dogs are *dy-no-mite.*"

"Oh no," Rue said. "What if they blow your mind?"

Montana glanced up at him, wearing a silly grin, then elbowed him in the ribs. "I get it, Dad. Could me and Ian camp out at our new house sometime?"

"You mean before it's finished?"

"Uh-huh. In my pup tent I got for my birthday."

"You boys can't stay out here by yourselves. Where would Mom and I sleep?"

Montana shrugged. "The house could be your tent, and you could put a blow-up mattress in there."

"Or we could just set you up at Three Peaks—right outside the chalet."

"But that's not special. If we get to camp out at the new house, we might see coyotes. Or a bobcat or something. Maybe even a *bear*."

"Yeah, right," Rue said. "And what would you do if you saw any of those things?"

"Yell like crazy for you to come save us." Montana let out a husky laugh. "Please?"

"We'll see. I think we're gonna have to sell your mother on the idea. She's not much of a camper."

Rue winked at Ivy and then slowed the truck and turned onto the graded road that led up to the house. "Anyone notice that something's changed since we were out here last?"

"The wildflowers have really thinned out." Ivy looked out the side window. "And there's hardly any snow left on the peaks."

"You're right, but I was referring to something else."

"*I* know," Montana said, "the road's not muddy, and the truck's not getting all yucky."

"True. But there's something *much* more exciting than that."

Ivy turned to him, the corners of her mouth twitching. "You going to give us a hint?"

"What did we come out here to see?"

She turned and peered out the front window just as he drove past the last of the trees and the house was visible in the clearing. She sucked in a breath and put her hands to her cheeks. "The framers weren't supposed to come for a couple weeks."

"They had to postpone work on another project. I didn't say anything because I wanted to surprise you."

"Wow. Wait till Ian sees *this*." Montana craned his neck to see out.

Rue drove the truck rocking and bouncing over the uneven terrain, then parked it where the driveway was going to be.

"I wanna see *my* room." Montana climbed over Ivy and jumped out. "Come on, girl."

Windy shot over the side of the bed and raced ahead of him.

Ivy couldn't seem to take her eyes off the house. "It's really happening. It's starting to look like the drawing on the plans."

Rue laughed. "That's the way it works. Come on, babe. Let's go dream a little. This is where it starts to get fun."

Grayson finished reading the sports page of the *Denver Post* and laid it aside, wondering how long before Tara would insist they cancel their subscription and use the money for something else. He drank the last of his coffee and sat back in his chair, hungry, but not in the mood for a peanut butter sandwich.

Tara was out on the patio reading a novel. His daughter was talking on the phone—again. And his sons weren't due home from their campout until after dinner. He had the entire day to do his own thing. He told Tara he was going fishing. But that was only to lock in an alibi in case he got up the nerve to turn his fantasy into action. He regretted lying to her, but she would never understand or sanction what he wanted to do.

Not that he completely understood it, either. He had never been consumed with jealousy before, and he felt powerless to turn it off. It was as though the rush he felt after vandalizing Rue's truck had created a lust for more that wouldn't be satisfied until Rue was hurting as much as he was.

His mind replayed each of Rue's offenses and then seemed to zoom in on the wedding reception. It was hard to believe that anyone bought the phony humility that Rue had exuded when Elam toasted his accomplishments and touted him in front of the guests. To hear Elam talk, Rue was a direct answer to prayer.

Grayson grunted in disgust. If there was a God, he was sure He couldn't stand Rue, either. It was so unfair that a slosh head fresh out of rehab had everything working in his favor.

Grayson rubbed his throbbing temples and went in the bathroom to take something for the pain. It was exhausting to have the slide show of Rue's offenses playing over and over in his mind, but he didn't know how to stop it. And the longer the loop played, the more driven he was to act on his anger.

He popped two Excedrin and swallowed a few gulps of water. Maybe he should tell Tara what was going on in his head. Let her hold him accountable. Once she knew what he was thinking of doing, he would be too ashamed to go through with it.

Rue sat with Ivy and Montana on the living room floor of the new house, their backs against the far wall, and gazed at the magnificent peaks through the enormous cutout that would soon become a wall of windows.

"Before you know it," Rue said, "we'll be sitting right here in front of a roaring fire, watching the snow come down, snug as a bug in a rug."

Montana flashed him a mustard-framed grin. "What does *that* mean?"

"It means we're gonna feel right at home—just like Windy over there sleeping in the sun."

Ivy put her hand on Montana's knee. "It's really special that Grandma and Grandpa picked out this land for me when I was your age."

"And they never ever *ever* would sell it?"

"That's right, sweetie. They saved it for me, even when I was doing drugs and they had no idea where I was or if I would ever come home."

Rue picked up Ivy's hand and kissed it.

"I honestly would've been content to live at the camp." Ivy sighed dreamily. "I never expected anything like this."

"Grandma and Grandpa must love you a lot," Montana said.

"They sure do—all three of us. Did you get enough to eat?"

Montana put his hands on his middle and nodded. "I *love* deli dogs. Thank you for the picnic. Can me and Windy go play?"

"I thought you were going to help your dad."

"How about if I whistle for you in a little while?" Rue said.

"Okay." Montana got on all fours, then turned around and faced them, sitting on his heels. "I wish we could come out here every single day."

"Won't be long, champ." Rue brushed the hair out of his eyes. "Have fun out there. Don't get close to the stream."

"I won't."

Windy bounded toward them, her tail swishing back and forth, her coat full of sawdust.

Rue cupped the dog's face in his hands and made eye contact with her. "Take care of my boy, you pretty thing."

Windy whimpered, her body trembling with excitement.

"Okay, go play."

Windy darted out the door, and Montana followed. Seconds later the two raced down the gently sloping hill and finally disappeared.

"I think Montana was as surprised as you were to see the house starting to take shape."

"He really was."

Rue slid his arm around her. "We're so blessed, babe. Sometimes I'm overwhelmed when I stop and realize that you're really my wife, Montana's our son, and we get to live on this gorgeous land and build our own place. God is so good."

"I still haven't gotten over Him putting the broken pieces of our lives back together and entrusting us with that precious little boy."

"Me, either."

Ivy put her head on his shoulder, the herbal scent of her hair wafting under his nose. "So what are you going to have Montana help you with?"

"Oh, I thought I'd let him drive some nails around the doorways. There's really nothing that *needs* to be done, but he doesn't know that. I want him to feel part ownership. Once I start the finish work, there'll be plenty of things he can help me with. You, too, if you want."

"I'd love it."

Rue entered into the stillness and closeness with Ivy. He drank in the splendor of the rugged, majestic peaks and relaxed to the swishing sound of wind in the pines. Somewhere in the distance, he heard Windy's playful barking.

Minutes passed and finally Ivy said, "I wonder if Mom and Dad picked out land for Rusty, too. I can't imagine they wouldn't have done the same for both of us."

"Why don't you just ask them?"

"What if they're planning to give him the land next to ours? I don't want us living that close to him and his sour disposition."

"Babe, there're acres between this house and our property line in any direction. Who cares what they give Rusty or where it is? This is a great place to live. Montana can roam all over this property without us having to watch him like a hawk the way you did when you lived in Denver."

Grayson loaded his fishing gear into the bed of his truck and secured it to his metal storage box. He went in the house to tell Tara he was leaving.

"I'm going to fish till my arms drop, so if I'm not back by dinner, go ahead without me." The lie pricked his conscience.

Tara turned the page on her book and kept reading. "Hope the fish are biting."

"You want me to bring any home?"

"We've got plenty in the freezer."

"All right. See you when I see you."

He went out to the truck and climbed in the front seat, sobered that he had come this far and still hadn't talked himself out of it. He might not get another chance to pull off something like this and let SAGE get the blame. He was sure of that, but could he live with the guilt? This would be a lot worse than messing with Rue's truck.

Grayson put the key in the ignition. He was tired of arguing with himself. He'd made his decision. He just wanted get it over with.

He backed out of the driveway and drove to end of the block, then turned toward the highway. He decided to stop at the Gas-N-Go and top the tank on the truck and make sure he told someone besides Tara he was going fishing.

Rue patted Montana on the back as he finished hammering the last nail.

"Good job."

"Wow, I must've pounded a zillion nails." Montana laid the hammer on the toolbox and held up his right hand, his fingers spread. "I even have blisters."

Rue gently ran his thumb across the red marks. "Those are calluses, champ. Means you did a man-size job. We're done for today."

"It's still early," Ivy said. "You want to play awhile before we leave?"

"Can I hike down to where the dirt road starts and back?"

Ivy smiled. "That's a long walk."

"I can do it. Please?"

"All right. You and Windy stick together. Come right back. Don't go anywhere else."

"We won't."

"Thanks for helping me," Rue said. "Someday when the house is finished, we're going to feel great that we all pitched in to make it happen."

"I like helping. Come on, Windy."

Rue returned the hammers to his toolbox. "While those two are walking off all that energy, let's go outside and enjoy the fresh air. We can sit under that big old cottonwood tree and try to picture this place a year from now." He took Ivy by the hands and pulled her to her feet. "What's wrong?"

"Oh, nothing. It's just hard letting him be so independent."

"He's a responsible kid, babe. We'd better get used to it if we're going to live out here. You and Rusty had a lot of freedom to roam the property when you were kids."

"I know, but he's only eight. And Rusty and I had each other."

Rue stroked her cheek with the back of his hand. "He's got Windy. He'll be fine." He pointed to his watch and smiled knowingly. "But if he's not back in one hour, we'll get in the truck and go get him."

21

GRAYSON GLANCED IN HIS REARVIEW mirror and didn't see any vehicles behind him on Three Peaks Road. He slowed his truck and turned onto an unmarked road and drove about the length of a football field, then veered into the tall grass and stopped near a pond. He got out and released the tailgate, then climbed up in the bed of the truck and took his hunting rifle out of the metal storage cabinet.

There was no doubt in his mind that had he told Tara his obsessive thoughts, he would not be on his way to Rue's new house with a loaded rifle in his hands. But he would've lost what little respect she still had for him. He wasn't about to let Rue take that from him, too.

Grayson jumped down from the back of the truck, his rifle strapped to his shoulder, and trudged through the high grass toward the Kesslers' property. He'd been there before, and there were plenty of places he could hide and observe the wide-open area around the house.

Shooting Windy shouldn't be any more difficult than shooting any other unsuspecting animal he'd hunted. If he could get her in his sights, he could take her out relatively painlessly. He hated that Montana would probably see the whole thing, but it was all part of making sure that the kid's arrogant father suffered this time.

If he could get a clear shot, it would be over quickly. Rue would lose something he cared about. SAGE would be blamed. And Grayson would go fishing for a few hours and return home around the same time he did every Sunday, no one the wiser. It was a perfect scheme.

He came to the split-rail fence and climbed over it, struck by a possibility he hadn't considered: what if the Kesslers didn't go out to the new house after church? Or what if they were already gone? Or didn't bring Windy? What if he'd come to this torturous decision only to be denied the satisfaction of finally taking the control away from Rue?

Grayson's pulse raced. He stopped and leaned against a tree, torn between the fear of succeeding and the fear of missing the opportunity. He breathed in deeply and let it out slowly. And then did it again. If he didn't get his chance today, it was over. There was no way he could get up his nerve a second time.

He lingered a few moments, then continued tramping through the high grass until he found the trail he had discovered before. He followed it into the woods and across a small stream, then hiked uphill through a densely wooded area and stopped at the edge of a clearing.

He peeked out from behind a pine tree and spotted the two-story house about fifty yards away and Rue's loaner truck parked out front. The place was starting to shape up. He'd never been invited to go over the blueprints, but he guessed it to be four thousand square feet, give or take. Rue's fat salary must be even fatter than he thought.

Anger flooded every fiber of his being. He and Tara and their four kids were crammed into fifteen hundred square feet—with only a bath and a half. And he couldn't even afford to paint it. This was so excessive.

Was that a dog barking? He listened intently and turned toward the sound, then spotted Windy and Montana coming up an unpaved road. They were about a hundred yards from the house and half that far from where he stood. What a picture of innocence.

Grayson observed the two, the pounding of his heart echoing in his ears. Could he really do this? What kind of miserable human being would actually shoot a dog—especially one loved by such a sweet kid? Was getting back at Rue worth the price?

Sure it was. It had to be. He'd already made his decision and wasn't going to get another chance. This was not the time to start second-guessing himself.

He took the rifle case off his shoulder, laid it on the ground, then removed the rifle and braced himself against the tree. He put his eye to the telescopic sight and positioned the rifle until he had a good fix on Windy. This was no different than shooting a deer or an elk or even a rabbit. All he needed was one clean shot.

He put his finger on the trigger and held Windy in the cross hairs of the scope, aware that he was shaking. Who was he kidding? This was nothing like hunting a wild animal. Shooting that kid's dog would be cruel and despicable. Montana would never get over it. There had to be a better way to get back at Rue.

A loud rustling noise startled him, and the rifle went off. The moment seemed to freeze in time.

He glanced over his shoulder just as a mule deer disappeared into the woods, then whipped back and saw Montana's body sprawled on the road, Windy licking his face.

Grayson stood dazed, and then he fell to his knees, his body trembling, his jaw clenched. He dug his fingers into his face. This couldn't be happening. He had changed his mind. He wasn't even going to shoot the dog. Everything in him said *run,* but how could he just leave the kid there to bleed to death?

He heard a car coming and realized it was the loaner truck barreling down the road to where Montana lay. A wave of nausea swept over him, and he retched until he had emptied his stomach.

He groped the ground for his rifle and put it back in the case, then stumbled to his feet—and fled.

22

RUE GRIPPED THE STEERING WHEEL and sped toward the place in the road where he'd seen Montana fall, the memory of the lone shot ringing out sending chills through him all over again. This couldn't be happening. Surely he was caught in a nightmare and would wake up soon.

"There he is!" Ivy shouted. "Stop!"

Rue hit the brakes, and before the truck had come to a complete stop, Ivy flung open the door and jumped out.

Seconds later, he knelt beside her where Montana lay. He gasped when he saw his son's blood-soaked shirt and gaping wound.

Ivy stifled a sob. "Oh no."

Rue raked his hands through his hair, his gaze fixed on the little boy he loved more than life itself, and tried to think. "We need to stop the bleeding. I'll be right back." He darted over to the truck, rummaged through the cab till he found a clean T-shirt, then went back to Montana and dropped down next to him. *Lord, please don't let him die.*

Montana moaned, and his eyes fluttered briefly, then closed.

Rue covered his son's wound with the T-shirt and applied direct pressure, but the second he let up, the shirt was soaked with red.

"It's not working," Ivy said.

"We've got to get him to the emergency room as fast as we can."

Ivy nodded robotically, the color drained from her face.

"Let's go, babe. Get in the truck, and I'll put him on your lap."

Rue followed Ivy to the truck and gently placed his son's limp body on her lap, aware that his own hands and arms were covered with blood. "Hold the shirt directly over the wound—like this—and keep pressing as tightly as you can. Try not to let up."

"Hang on, champ." He stroked Montana's hair. "We're going to get help. You're going to be all ri—" Rue choked on the words.

He let Windy up in the bed of the truck, then slid in on the driver's side, terrified that they were already too late.

Sheriff Flint Carter sat out on his front porch enjoying a glass of lemonade and reading Sunday's *Denver Post* when he saw Bobby Knolls' squad car pull up.

Bobby got out of the car and jogged across the lawn and up on the porch. "A 911 call just came in from Rue Kessler. His boy was shot by an unknown assailant. They're en route to Tanner County Medical Center."

Flint's heart sank. "Good grief, Bobby. Where'd it happen?"

"Out at their new place. The Kesslers heard a shot and saw their son on the ground. That's all I know. I was a few blocks away when the call came in and thought I'd swing by on my way to TCMC and make sure you knew before Ian heard about it."

"Does Nick Sanchez know?"

"I'm sure he does, Sheriff. He's been workin' in your office all day. You comin' to the hospital?"

"Yeah. I'm five minutes behind you. I need to figure out how to handle it here first."

"Okay. See you over there."

Flint's mind flashed back to last December and how helpless he felt when Ian and Betty were held hostage. Elam stood with him through every gut-wrenching moment until the crisis was over. The sound of Bobby's tires squealing brought him back to the moment.

He walked in the house and found Betty sitting at the kitchen table, copying a recipe. He pulled out a chair and sat across from her. "Where's Ian?"

"Outside playing. Why? What's wrong?"

Flint took her hands in his. "Montana's been shot."

Betty stared at him blankly for several seconds and then shuddered. "Is he…?"

"I don't know. The 911 call literally just came in. All I know is it happened out at the new house, and the assailant is unknown at this time. Bobby swung by to tell me, and I need to get over to the medical center. I don't see any point in alarming Ian at this stage. Why don't you steer him away from the TV? I'll call you the minute I know something more."

Betty's eyes brimmed with tears. "It was just a matter of time before these poachers hurt someone."

"Let's hope it's that cut and dried."

"What do you mean?"

The silence that followed screamed with possibilities.

"There's no point in speculating, hon. I need to go."

Betty grabbed his sleeve, her eyes probing. "Are you thinking SAGE would actually shoot Elam's grandson to intimidate him into scrapping the retirement project?"

"What *I'm* thinking is irrelevant. Let's wait for the facts."

Rue felt a blast of cold air as Ivy pushed open the emergency room door at Tanner County Medical Center. He hurried inside, carrying Montana's limp body, and went up to the attendant's desk, aware of something warm trickling down his arms.

"Please help us. Our son's been shot."

Time seemed to stand still, then two men in green scrubs burst through the swinging doors pushing a gurney. They took Montana from his arms and gently laid his blood-soaked body on a clean, white sheet.

Rue explained to them what had happened, then bent down and whispered in Montana's ear. "I'm still here, champ. Don't be afraid."

"You'll need to wait out here until the doctor gets your son stabilized," one of the men said.

No way. What if Montana had lost too much blood? What if he was dying? "I'm not leaving him," Rue said.

"Sir, I know this is hard, but your boy's in very capable hands. We'll come get you in a few minutes."

"Why don't you and your wife come with me?" he heard a woman say. "We can get the paperwork out of the way while you're waiting."

Rue followed the woman into a cubicle and sat in a vinyl chair, the ER noise muffled except for the sound of Ivy's sniffling.

He let Ivy give the woman Montana's full name and all his personal information, including a recap of his childhood illnesses, and the necessary insurance information. Then he and Ivy pieced together the details of what happened, and the woman entered the information into the computer, seemingly in slow motion.

"You know we have to report this to the authorities?" she said, never taking her eyes off the computer screen.

"I already called 911," Rue said. "Sheriff's deputies are meeting us here. Are you about finished with us?" He hated that he sounded abrupt, but he just wanted to be with Montana.

"I believe so. Why don't you and your wife take a seat in the waiting room? Someone will come get you shortly and take you to your son."

Rue stood and exited the cubicle after Ivy, feeling almost as if he were a prop in someone else's nightmare.

Grayson sat on the bank of Phantom Creek, scared and shaken and keenly aware that his life was ruined. He couldn't shake the image of Montana's small body sprawled on the road. How devastated would he be if he'd found one of his own kids shot and left for dead? He could only imagine Rue's horror but found no satisfaction in having inflicted it. How ironic that his plan had backfired all the way around.

If only he had listened to his inner voice and leveled with Tara about his obsessive thoughts. She would've shamed him into abandoning his foolish plan, and this tragedy would never have happened. There's no way he could tell her about it now—not ever.

His cell phone vibrated and he jumped, his heart racing. He took it out of his pocket and saw his home number on the lighted screen.

Stay calm. Sound natural. He breathed in deeply and let it out slowly, then hit the Talk button. "Hi, honey."

"How's the fishing?" Tara said.

"Really good. How's the novel?"

"Wonderful." Tara sighed. "I finished it a few minutes ago. I can't wait to get to the library and check out the sequel. Glad the fish are biting."

"Me, too, but I changed my mind. I'll be home in time for dinner. I've missed the boys this weekend and want to hear about their campout."

"It would be nice if we could all eat together. They should be home between five and six. I'll have dinner on the table at six thirty."

"Anything else going on?"

"Not a thing. It's been a relaxing day."

"Yeah, same here." *Other than I shot a kid and ruined my life.* "I'll see you soon."

"Okay. I love you."

"Love you, too."

Grayson closed his cell phone and put it back in his pocket. Obviously, she hadn't heard about the shooting. Of all times for his truck radio to be on the fritz. How could he find out how much the authorities knew without creating suspicion?

Flint stood in the corridor outside the waiting room at Tanner County Medical Center, talking with Bobby and Nick.

"I don't know what's going on," Nick said, "but I'm not buying that SAGE has struck three times in a row without further provocation from the opposition. It's conceivable that SAGE members acting alone could've set the arson fire at the Griffiths' stable and then at Everhardt Roofing, each in retaliation for the attacks on Baughman and her dog. But the vandalism on Kessler's truck and this attempt on his son's life don't seem to be paybacks for anything. I think there's something else at play here."

"Makes sense," Flint said. "After the fire at Everhardt's, I would've expected another attack against Baughman or someone in her organization."

Bobby seemed pensive, his jaws working out on the piece of gum he was chewing. "SAGE hasn't claimed responsibility for this."

"That's exactly right, Lieutenant." Nick rubbed the stubble on his chin. "And in my experience, it takes someone with ice in his veins to shoot a kid in cold blood. We get that with gangs and kidnappers and serial killers. And occasionally, the mob. But not environmental groups."

"Could've been an accident," Bobby said. "We've been havin' problems with people trespassin' and huntin' on private property."

"That's a possibility." Nick glanced at his watch. "Why don't we head out to the Kesslers' property and see if our investigators have found anything useful?"

Flint glanced into the waiting room and saw Elam pacing, and Carolyn sitting in a corner with Rue and Ivy. "I'd like to wait it out until Montana's out of surgery. Why don't you follow Bobby out to the Kesslers' property? I'll call your cell if the doctor gives us the green light to talk to Montana. But I don't think it'll be anytime soon."

Grayson decided his best crack at finding out the full extent of what he'd done was to call Bobby and see if he volunteered anything. He took out his cell phone and pressed the auto-dial.

"This is Knolls."

"Hey, big brother. I'm sitting out here at my fishing hole, hauling in quite a catch. Why don't you come out and join me?"

"I'd love to, Grays, but I'm on duty. We've got a serious situation goin' on."

"Sorry to hear that. What's up?"

"I hate to tell you, but your boss's son was shot."

"Rusty Griffith was *shot*?"

"No, Kessler's boy. Montana."

"Oh, man. That's terrible. I just talked to Tara, and she never mentioned it. Was he playing with a gun or something?"

"You know I can't discuss the details, but it happened out on the property where the Kesslers are buildin' their new house."

"I can't believe this," Grayson said. "Is Montana going to be okay?"

"Don't know yet. He's in surgery. I'm in my car on the way out to the scene with Special Agent Sanchez ridin' my tail. Don't you know he's havin' a stroke that he has to follow *my* lead for once?"

"The FBI's involved?" Grayson's pulse quickened.

"Flint asked Sanchez to help us sort through the cases. It's gettin' real complicated."

"And I'm getting real nervous. What if SAGE decides to come after one of my kids next?"

"No one said SAGE did this."

"You didn't bring in the FBI for nothing, Bobby. And they already went after Elam and his son-in-law. Why not his grandson? Doesn't take a rocket scientist to add it up."

"But this is over the top. Just between you, me, and the wall, we aren't convinced SAGE is behind this one."

"You think it was somebody else?"

"I've already said too much. One thing about Sanchez: he can be as irritatin' as a rock in your shoe, but he knows his stuff. If anyone can figure out *who's* doin' *what,* he can."

Grayson didn't like the sound of that. "Everything I've heard on the news or read in the newspaper indicates SAGE is striking back for the attacks on that Baughman lady. They've even claimed responsibility for it. Are you saying that's not true?"

"Let's just say I'm expandin' my thinking."

"That sounds like a yes."

"You didn't hear it from me. Listen, I'm about to turn on a dirt road and need both hands on the wheel. I'll talk to you soon."

"All right, Bobby. Good luck with the investigation."

Grayson disconnected the call and put his cell phone back in his pocket. It had never occurred to him the authorities would question SAGE's involvement.

He thought back on his hasty departure after the shooting. He couldn't think of anything incriminating he might've left behind, other than the shell casing—and the bullet they would pull out of Montana. And since lots of hunters use the same caliber, the only way authorities could trace it to him was to get a ballistics match. Which he knew couldn't happen unless they got a search warrant for his rifle. And why would they?

Grayson rubbed the back of his neck. The most important thing he could do now was to stay under the radar.

Rue sat in the waiting room at Tanner County Medical Center, clutching Ivy's hand and staring at the mural of the San Juan Mountains on the wall.

Why couldn't he have been the one who was shot? It was his job to protect Montana. If only he hadn't let him walk down that road.

"Stop it," Ivy said. "I know what you're thinking. This is *not* your fault."

"I should've listened to you."

Ivy wiped a tear off her cheek. "I was worried Montana would get tired walking that far or curious enough to get sidetracked. Neither of us could've foreseen this."

Rue glanced over at his in-laws, who looked as solemn as he felt. If only he could turn back the clock.

He was suddenly aware of the blood all over the front his shirt, and images he would just as soon forget popped into his mind. "I'll never forgive myself if he loses that arm." *Or his life.*

"You can't play God, Rue. It's not like we can protect Montana from every danger. We just have to trust that God will take this evil act and use it for His good purpose."

Purpose. That's not what he wanted to hear. He wanted his son to be healthy and whole and unscathed. Too late for that.

Elam stood as Brandon and Kelsey Jones came into the waiting room. In the next second it was hard to tell who was hugging whom.

Rue was aware of Kelsey talking to Ivy and of Brandon taking the seat next to him.

"I'm so sorry," Brandon said. "Is there anything I can do? Call someone? Go get you something to eat?"

Rue shook his head. "Just pray."

"We did that all the way over here. Jake called the staff and asked them to pray, too. And he stepped in for me so Kelsey and I could be with you guys. By the way, what'd you do with Windy?"

"Flint took her to his house so Ian could watch her. He thought Ian might cope better if he felt like he was helping."

"Good idea." Brandon glanced around the room. "Is Rusty here?"

"No. Elam left word on his cell phone, but he hasn't called back. Just as well. I'm so tense I'd probably flatten him the first time he made a wisecrack."

"I guess Ivy told you about my run-in with him?"

Rue nodded, swallowing the emotion that tightened his throat. "The last thing we need at the moment is being with someone who doesn't give a rip about our son."

Brandon put his hand on Rue's shoulder. "Any word on how the surgery's going?"

"Just that it's underway. They won't know the extent of the damage until they get in there and remove the bullet."

23

RUE LEANED AGAINST the warm brick wall outside the hospital, his hands in his pockets, and caught a glimpse of the same majestic peaks that had formed the backdrop for the deli dog picnic he and Ivy had enjoyed with Montana at the new house. It had been such a great afternoon. Now he wondered if he would ever again be able to see these mountains without hearing that shot ring out and seeing his son collapse on the dirt road.

He shuddered. What kind of sick monster would shoot a child? If SAGE had done this to intimidate Elam, it worked. The man was devastated. He was talking about shutting down the retirement village project and getting out of construction altogether. Flint had suggested he not jump to the conclusion that the shooting was intentional or even connected to the other crimes—that they should reserve judgment until the authorities had finished their investigation.

Rue's mind was too foggy to process the implications. He was just so grateful his son was alive. Had the bullet veered to the right and struck his chest, they would be planning a funeral instead of waiting for him to come out of surgery.

He pictured Montana out rollicking with Windy and throwing the Frisbee. Would he regain full function of his right arm? Be able to swing a hockey stick? Throw a baseball? Shoot baskets? Even write legibly? He was confident that Montana could learn to function with just one arm as thousands of others had done—and probably without ever losing his infectious smile and agreeable disposition.

But how would any of them deal with the fear, especially with so many unanswered questions? Had the shooter intended to kill Montana? Were he and Ivy targets, too? Was there anywhere they could go and feel safe?

Maybe Elam was smart to get out of the construction business. He certainly had the means to do whatever he wanted—including living off his investments.

Rue decided not to worry about what closing down EG Construction would mean for him and Grayson and the work crew. Or whether he and Ivy might have to postpone their plans for the new house. The only thing that mattered at the moment was taking care of their son.

Rue glanced up and saw Brandon standing there.

"How're you doing?" Brandon asked.

"I'm pretty numb. I probably should go back inside and be with Ivy."

"She's okay at the moment. Pastor Myers just arrived." Brandon hesitated for a moment and then said, "Rusty called. I'm not sure what was said, but I think Elam hung up on him."

"Too bad he's not out of cell range—permanently. Is he on his way over here?"

"I don't know. Your mom and Ivy were talking to Kelsey and didn't see Elam answer the phone, and he never mentioned it to them. He's got that look he gets when he's about to blow. I just wanted to give you a heads-up."

Rue sighed. "This is probably one of those times when I should ask myself, 'what would Jesus do?' But it would feel *so* good to grab Rusty by the collar and shove him up against the wall. Show him how it feels to be bullied."

"I can relate to that emotion, but we both know it would only complicate things."

"I don't know, friend. A couple of good punches might actually clear things up." Rue flashed a phony smile. "I'm half kidding…but I've had about all of my new brother-in-law I can stomach."

"You and everyone else."

"I never realized how protective I'd feel when I had a family. The way Rusty treats Ivy and the hateful things he says about her and Montana are hard to hear and even tougher to ignore. Sure doesn't make me feel like turning the other cheek."

Brandon nodded. "I have to hand it to you, you've shown amazing restraint."

"Thanks. It's certainly the opposite of what I'm feeling."

Rue heard someone call his name and Brandon's and spotted Kelsey motioning them to come inside.

"Montana must be out of surgery." Rue's pulse quickened, and his feet felt as if they were nailed to the sidewalk. *Lord, please let him be okay.*

Brandon put his hand on Rue's shoulder. "Lord, I ask that You give Rue and Ivy each a calm spirit and clear head as they listen to what the doctor has to say. Thank You for sparing Montana's life. We leave him in Your hands and pray for Your perfect will and the doctor's clear direction in this situation. We thank You now, in Jesus's name."

Rue felt a pat on the back and realized his legs were moving toward the door.

Grayson helped his sons put their sleeping bags in the attic, then washed his hands a third time in the laundry room sink as if that would somehow remove his guilt. It's not as though he had to worry about gunshot residue. No one would ever suspect him of the shooting.

He dried his hands and then followed the aroma of something delicious all the way to the kitchen, where he found Tara taking her meat loaf out of the oven.

"Did you get everything put away?" she said.

"*And* their dirty clothes put in the washer. Need help out here?"

"No, thanks. I'm about to put it on the table."

He stepped into her unusually cheery mood and felt some of the tension leave him.

"It'll be nice seeing all of us around the dinner table," Tara said. "That's been happening less and less with your summer work schedule and the kids' activities."

"I've been preoccupied with our finances, too, and I've got to stop it. The kids'll be grown before we know it, and I don't want to wake up one day and regret I wasn't more involved."

Tara set her oven mitts on the countertop and put her arms around his neck. "I'm so glad to hear you say that. They really do need you."

"I know. The situation with Rue's son sort of puts things in perspective."

"That's for sure. I wonder if Bobby knows how Montana's doing?"

"Think I should call him after dinner?"

"Well, I wouldn't think of calling the Kesslers or the Griffiths. Can you even imagine what they must be going through?"

Unfortunately, I can. "Has to be a nightmare."

Tara laid her head on his shoulder. "I'm so relieved Bobby doesn't think SAGE was behind it. At least we don't have to worry that our kids might be targets."

Flint disconnected the call and put his cell phone in his pocket. He popped two Tums, then went over to Rue and squeezed his shoulder.

"You and Ivy hang in there. Montana's in good hands. I'll go check on Elam."

"Thanks," Rue said. "We really appreciate your being here."

Flint went out to the hospital courtyard, where Elam was sitting by himself on a wrought-iron bench.

"Okay if I join you?"

Elam gave a slight nod.

"Sorry Montana's surgery turned out to be more complicated than anticipated. But I'm impressed the surgeon had the smarts to call in a pediatric orthopedic specialist to assist. Montana's got the best doctors working on him."

"Only matters if they can save his arm."

"Well, I've got a good feeling they can."

Elam sighed. "You really should be out there tracking down the shooter instead of waiting here with me. I'll be fine."

"I've got plenty of people working the case. In fact, I just got off the phone with Bobby. They found a shell casing at the edge of the clearing about fifty yards from where Montana was shot—a .223 Remington."

Elam lifted his eyebrows. "So the creep used a varmint rifle to shatter our lives. Did you get his fingerprints off the casing?"

"No. But once we have the bullet, ballistics can match it to the rifle used. It's an important piece of information."

"*If* you find weapon."

"We will," Flint said. "But it's important for another reason. How many environmentalists do you think own a varmint rifle?"

"What are you saying?"

Flint sat on the bench next to Elam, his hands folded between his knees. "I think we have to consider the possibility that SAGE wasn't behind the shooting."

"Come on. SAGE openly opposes the retirement village project. They vandalized Rue's truck, claimed responsibility for burning my stable and Everhardt's place."

"Madison Baughman doesn't believe any of her people are capable of this stuff."

"What'd you expect her to say?"

Flint cracked his knuckles. "I can't get into specifics and would appreciate it if you'd keep this to yourself, but Nick Sanchez thinks we've got another thread sewn in."

"What kind of thread?"

"An additional perp."

Elam put his hand on the back of his neck and moved his head to one side and then the other. "I'm too overwhelmed to take in anything else right now."

"I know. It's complicated. But before you shut down the retirement project, I wish you'd give us a chance to work this angle."

Grayson sat across from Tara at the kitchen table and dialed Bobby's cell number.

"Knolls."

"Bobby, it's Grayson. Tara and I are really concerned about Montana Kessler and wondered if you've heard anything."

"Actually, Flint called from the hospital a few minutes ago. The kid's still in surgery. His right arm was blown to bits, and they called in a pediatric orthopedic doctor. It's not good."

"Meaning life threatening?"

"Could be. He lost a lot of blood goin' in. And we both know things can go wrong in long surgeries. I really feel for his parents, you know?"

"Yeah, I do." Grayson glanced over at Tara and gave her a thumbs-down. "So how's the investigation coming? You still out at the Kesslers' property?"

"Yep. We're goin' over every inch of this place."

"Any leads?"

"Nothin' I can talk about."

"Come on, Bobby. Throw me a bone. It's my boss's kid, for cryin' out loud."

"You and Tara can't say anything, all right?"

"I know that."

"We found a handkerchief. So we may have the perp's DNA. Even if it's not on file, once we start sortin' through suspects, we can nail the sucker."

"How do you know it's his?"

"We don't, but it's too fresh to have been out there long. And just feet away from where we found the shell casing."

Grayson's pulse quickened. "What did that tell you?"

"That the perp used a varmint rifle. When we recover the weapon, ballistics can match the bullet to the rifle."

"Man, where do you start searching for someone like that? Half the guys in Tanner County own a varmint rifle."

"Oh, we have ways of narrowin' things down. Just takes time."

24

Rue sat in the waiting room of Tanner County Medical Center, Ivy's hand in his, and listened to Dr. Gregory Andover's explanation of Montana's condition, feeling as though the words were garbled in his brain.

"Do you have any questions?" Dr. Andover said.

"Probably," Rue said. "But truthfully, my mind's on overload, and most of what you said didn't compute."

Ivy squeezed his hand as if to show she agreed with him.

"Sorry, I have a bad habit of sounding too technical." Dr. Andover pulled up a chair and sat facing them, weariness in his eyes. "Here's what you need to know: your son is going to be all right.

"The bullet shattered the bone in his upper arm, but we feel confident that we repaired the damage. He's got some hardware in there that will need to come out down the road. There's also been considerable tearing of the muscles and tendons as well as some nerve damage. But with time and the proper rehab, he should regain full function. He's weak from the blood loss, and I've ordered two additional pints of blood. Twenty-four hours from now, he'll probably be asking for pizza." Dr. Anchor smiled. "You must have a direct line to the Man upstairs. I expected to find a much worse situation."

Thank you, Lord. Rue blinked to clear his eyes and pulled Ivy close. "We can't thank you enough for all you've done."

"When can we see him?" Ivy said.

"He'll be in recovery for a while yet. As soon as we have him settled in a room, you can go on back. Feel free to stay with him through the night if you'd like."

"When can we take him home?" Rue said.

"Two days. Maybe three. I'd like to see some movement in his fingers first. I want to make sure he understands how important it is to keep the Velcro cast on 24/7. And I think he probably needs a little time to let it all sink in."

"We all do." Rue helped Ivy to her feet, and they each shook Dr. Andover's hand. "Thanks again for all you've done."

"You're welcome," the doctor said. "I'm pleased at the outcome."

Rue watched the doctor walk away, suddenly aware that Carolyn and Elam were standing next to him. Flint, too.

"Praise the Lord." Elam's voice sounded shaky. "Why don't I take us out to get something to eat? Anybody hungry?"

Everyone shook his head.

"Me, either." Elam turned to Flint. "Thanks for sitting this out with us. You should get home and tell Ian and Betty the good news."

"I'm on my way," Flint said. "For a while there, I wasn't sure things were going to be this promising. I can't tell you how relieved I am. And how determined I am to catch the guy responsible. And mark my word, we *will* get him."

Elam's phone rang.

"I'll let you get that," Flint said. "I'll check in later and see how Montana's doing. I'd really like to ask him a few questions tonight, but only if he's up to it."

"Thanks for your support, Flint. We'll talk to you later." Elam took his cell phone off his belt and put it to his ear. "Hello… What do *you* want…? I meant what I said, Rusty…" Elam lowered his voice. "Take all the time you need to deal with it. Just don't inflict it on us. I don't need you here with that attitude… Yes, Montana made it. They saved his arm, and he's going to be fine… I don't want to hear your lame excuses, Son.

Things have changed. You can either get over the past or wallow in it by yourself." Elam disconnected the call.

Carolyn's eyes brimmed with tears. "I don't even know Rusty anymore."

"At least he called back." Rue was careful not to let his tone reveal his cynicism.

"Only because he knows Dad's mad at him," Ivy said. "He doesn't care about Montana."

Grayson helped his seven-year-old fix the stuck zipper on his jeans. "There you go. Good as new."

"Cool. Thanks." Samuel gave him a high-five. "Would you play Uno with me again some time?"

"Sure I will." Grayson pulled the boy into his arms and hid the emotion that was just under the surface. What if the authorities knew more than Bobby had told him? What if they figured out he was the shooter and all this was snatched away? The life he had so bitterly resented suddenly seemed precious. He blinked to clear his eyes and patted his son on the behind. "Go get your shower."

He walked into the living room, where Tara sat on the couch, darning a pair of socks.

"Come sit with me," she said.

Grayson gladly complied, having no desire to be alone with his guilt.

"It was so nice having dinner together as a family," Tara said. "Why don't we set aside one night a week and make it family night? We can play games or do something else fun together after dinner. The kids would love it."

"Okay by me. Probably should've done it before now."

Tara stopped darning and seemed to study him. "You seem sad."

"Well, I'm certainly not sad about being home. I just can't get the Kesslers off my mind. When I was helping Samuel just now, it hit me that he's only a year younger than Montana. That's pretty sobering."

"I'll say." Tara started darning the sock again. "They wouldn't want me on the jury. As far as I'm concerned, they can lock the shooter up and throw away the key."

"Assuming it was deliberate…but it might've been an accident."

Tara's eyebrows came together. "So what? There's no excuse for leaving a wounded child."

"Of course not. I just have trouble imagining that anybody could actually shoot a kid on purpose."

Tara shook her head. "Even if it *was* an accident, anybody who could leave a helpless little kid lying in his own blood deserves to be punished with the same kind of indifference."

Rue stood at the window in Montana's hospital room, his arms folded, and watched Elam and Carolyn cross the parking lot and get into the Suburban.

He glanced over at Ivy, who was sitting in a chair and appeared to have dozed off, and was glad for a few moments to be alone with his thoughts. He was sure it hadn't hit him yet that Montana was going to be all right. He had grappled with the possibility of losing him until it seemed inevitable. When Dr. Andover came out and told them he was going to be fine, it was too much to take in.

He turned his attention to Montana's ashen face and wondered how much blood the child had actually lost and how close he had come to dying. Rue wondered if he would have ever accepted losing him—or if his newfound faith would've failed.

It was hard to remember what it was like before he knew he had a son. Even though it had been only seven months, he couldn't imagine his future without Montana.

He looked out at the San Juan Mountains silhouetted against a dusky sky, all too aware that he had ignored the biblical admonition not to let the sun go down on his anger. He wasn't sure who had made him angrier, the cruel monster who had shot his son or his heartless brother-in-law who couldn't care less.

"Dad...where's Windy?"

The sound of a tiny voice brought him back to the moment. He hurried over to Montana's bedside and gently stroked his hair. "She's with Ian. He's taking very good care of her until you're better."

Montana stared at him blankly and didn't respond.

"You're in the hospital. You got hurt."

"Windy...licked...my...face."

"Do you remember what happened before that?"

Montana batted his eyes sleepily and then closed them.

Rue bent down and whispered in his ear, "I love you, champ. You're gonna be all right. Mom and I are right here."

The sound of his son's deep breathing was comforting. Rue didn't care how long he slept—just as long as he woke up.

Flint sat in the porch swing and rested his eyes, his mind racing through the events of the day. He was disappointed he hadn't heard from the Kesslers, but even if Montana was awake, it was too late to go back to the hospital tonight. He would head over there first thing in the morning. Maybe the boy saw something—anything—that would help investigators.

The night air was cool and refreshing, and the rushing water of Phantom Creek soothing. How he wished he could capture the peace of the moment and draw on it in the midst of tomorrow's hectic schedule.

He fully expected a media circus after today's shooting and wondered how SAGE would respond to the accusation that someone from their organization was responsible. But it just didn't add up. Nick Sanchez was right. There had to be another thread in these crimes.

Flint's cell phone vibrated, and he picked it up. "Sheriff Carter."

"Nick here. I hope you weren't planning on sleeping tonight."

"What now?"

"The 911 dispatcher just got a call from Madison Baughman. There's a brush fire raging in the field behind her house. A male caller told her to look outside, that it was a payback for the fire at Everhardt Roofing."

"This is getting ridiculous."

"Agreed, but did you notice the caller didn't say it was a payback for the shooting? I doubt if he even knows about it yet. This pretty much confirms we've got a third party playing for fun."

"Yeah, Nick. I think we're on to something."

"We did get a break, though. Baughman recorded the caller's voice this time. I'm on my way out there now."

"I'm right behind you." Flint rose to his feet. "See you in fifteen."

25

RUE WALKED OUT of Montana's hospital room and almost ran head-long into another man. They locked gazes.

"Why are *you* here?"

Rusty Griffith puffed out his chest. "I want to set something straight."

"No one's confused about where you stand."

"I resent everyone acting like *I'm* the black sheep of the family just because I'm unwilling to pick up where I left off with Ivy."

Rue glanced into the room and saw Ivy was still asleep in the chair. "I don't want to talk here. Follow me to the vending machines. That's where I was headed."

Rue moved briskly down the shiny hallway, Rusty on his heels. "If you resent being the black sheep, why don't you do something about it?"

"Because I refuse to pretend everything's hunky-dory," Rusty said. "I may be hard-nosed, but I'm not two-faced. Believe whatever you want, but Ivy's bad news. She ruined this family."

Rue stopped and turned around, his fists clenched. "Open your eyes, bud. You're the *only* one who thinks it's ruined."

"I've known my sister a lot longer than you have. She destroys everything she touches."

"I know at least five of us who disagree with you. No one's denying Ivy made poor choices in the past. But all that's behind her. She's a beautiful person with a heart even bigger than that chip on your shoulder. You're the only person who can't see it."

Rusty smiled derisively. "Or the only one who's smart enough not to set himself up to get dumped on again. I'm done with Ivy. I already told you that."

"Then why are you here?"

"To put a stop to you and Ivy poisoning my parents' minds against me."

"Give me a break. You're doing a great job of convincing them you're a real jerk without our help." Rue went over to the vending machine and put in the correct change, then pushed the button for his selection.

"How dare you judge me?"

Rue put the package of Ritz Bits in his shirt pocket, spun around, and glared at his brother-in-law. "But it's okay for you to judge Ivy?"

"Her past deeds judged her, not me."

"That's why it's called the *past,* Rusty. Have you noticed you're the only one living in it?"

"Actually, I'm the only one living in reality."

Rue let out a sigh of exasperation and shook his head. "What do you want from me? I need to get back."

"I want you and Ivy to stop turning my parents against me. I know you talked to Dad about my conversations with Ivy because he chewed me out over it."

"I told him what happened because I knew he'd be rational and talk me out of coming after you. I've had it with your abusive attitude toward Ivy and Montana."

Rusty snickered. "What are you going to do, beat me up?"

Rue grabbed the front of Rusty's Polo shirt and shoved him against the vending machine. "Listen, pal, I'm only gonna say this once: keep your stinking hands off Ivy and stay away from us. I'm not letting you hurt her anymore. I'm not kidding." He gave Rusty a slight shove and let go.

A nurse walked by and gave them a double take, and Rue manufactured a smile. "Hi. How're you doing?"

Rusty straightened his shirt, his face suddenly crimson. "Why am I not surprised you would try to settle this with your fists? It's the only way you good ol' boys know how to deal with conflict."

"Well, *Doc*. I hadn't noticed you were handling it any better. Guess your veterinarian degree didn't educate you on how to treat *people* humanely."

"I have compassion when it's warranted. I held my parents together the entire decade Ivy was sleazing it, and it nearly killed me. I refuse to open my heart to her again. Period."

For the first time, Rue sensed more pain than anger in Rusty's words. *Lord, I'm not handling this well. Help me.* Finally, he said, "I can't know how hard it was for you. And you can't know how hard it was for Ivy battling her addiction. Both sides suffered. No question. But it's over. Why don't you let it go?"

Rusty threw up his hands. "Ivy ruined everything, and you want me just to let it go?"

"The only thing that's *ruined* is your perspective. You've got Jacqueline and the girls, a great career, and a family here who wants a relationship with you. You're blessed, man. Can't you see that?"

Rusty grimaced. "Save the preaching. I didn't expect you to understand. Bottom line: I'll stay away from Ivy as long as I don't find out you're badmouthing me to my parents. Can we agree on that?"

"Sounds good to me."

Rue offered Rusty his hand, but he refused it and made an about-face, then marched down the hall toward the exit.

"By the way"—Rue's voice echoed in the corridor—"Montana's still alive. Thanks for asking." *You miserable excuse for a human being.*

Rusty pushed open the exit door and slipped into the darkness outside.

Flint saw a parade of flashing lights on the street outside Madison Baughman's house and pulled up behind Nick Sanchez's car. He also spotted the KTNR News van and a camera crew.

He popped two Tums, then got out of his squad car, the air thick with smoke, and cut across the lawn to the front door. He squeezed past an FBI agent he didn't recognize and entered the living room, where he saw Nick Sanchez sitting with Madison Baughman and her husband.

Flint went over to them and shook hands. "Sorry to meet again under such grim circumstances."

"It's never going to end, is it?" Madison dabbed her eyes.

"We've got three law-enforcement agencies focused on it," Flint said, "but we haven't had much to go on. I understand you recorded the caller's voice this time."

Madison glanced over at Nick. "Yes. I was just telling Special Agent Sanchez that I had the presence of mind to hit the record button on my answering machine. I'm positive it *wasn't* my attacker's voice. It was the young man who called me after my dog was poisoned. He told me to look outside and see the payback for the fire set at Everhardt Roofing. I smelled smoke and raced over to my kitchen window and saw the field burning."

"Firefighters have it under control," Nick added.

"Thank the Lord." Ken Baughman put his sweater around Madison's shoulders. "It's one thing to go after my wife, but we've got two young children. Can't you do something to stop these people?"

"Having the caller's voice is a big step in the right direction," Flint said. "We've also got the attacker's DNA off your wife's T-shirt, though it's not on file at NCIC."

"What's that?"

"The FBI operates a National Crime Information Center in Washington, DC. Nick, why don't you explain it?"

"NCIC is a computerized information system that stores records on wanted persons and stolen property," Nick said. "Law-enforcement agencies in every state are linked through local terminals and can get information at any time. Unfortunately, we can't match your wife's attacker's DNA to anyone on file."

Ken rolled his eyes. "So what good is it?"

"Vital, if he ends up on our suspect list. We can nail him with it.

Right now, his DNA is all we have, except for your wife's statement that he had a deep, young voice. As for the telephone caller, I'm guessing he used a prepaid cell tonight—same as after your dog was poisoned. But now we've got his voice."

"None of this will do you any good without suspects."

"But they're important pieces to the puzzle, Mr. Baughman. That's how we come up with suspects." Nick rubbed the stubble on his chin. "It's no secret that SAGE has a lot of opposition. We've questioned the higher-ups at several logging companies and a few of the more vocal retailers and builders in the region. No one stands out. Without a description, fingerprints, or identifiable DNA, trying to narrow it down is like searching for a needle in a haystack. That's why the sheriff's deputies have been so focused on getting your wife to help them determine which SAGE members might be capable of setting the other two fires. If we can catch them and pick their brains, the trail might lead us to her attacker."

Madison sighed deeply. "How many times do I have to tell you that it's unconscionable that any of my people would've set those fires?"

"Well, someone who claimed to be a member of SAGE *did*," Nick said. "We took identical shoe impressions at both scenes. We will be revisiting your membership again with this new evidence."

Madison shook her head. "We had an all-day retreat and prayer meeting on Saturday, and every member of this organization was present. I personally spoke with each one and am absolutely convinced none of them is capable of destroying someone's property—not by arson or vandalism or anything else. We pride ourselves in not using force but rather the power of persuasion."

"With all due respect," Nick said, "if someone in your organization decided to break rank and take *persuasion* to a higher level, I don't think you'd get a heads-up."

"Unless you present me with proof, I'll never believe anyone in SAGE set those fires."

Nick sat forward, his hands folded between his knees. "Does your organization have enemies capable of committing these crimes and letting SAGE take the hit?"

"Not that I know of. We're on good terms with other environmental groups. I can't imagine any of them—not even the more radical ones—would throw their convictions in the toilet and risk losing everything to stop one building project, especially when there are dozens of others underway."

Nick's eyes narrowed. "Well, somebody is. And they claim to be you."

"Nothing about this makes sense," Ken said. "The man who hit Madison over the head essentially threatened to sexually assault her if she didn't back off. She hasn't changed her agenda one bit, other than she doesn't go out without several guys with her. Don't you find it odd that he hasn't called and at least restated his threat? Instead, a different man called to say her dog had been poisoned and a grass fire was burning behind her home—as payback for those two arson fires. Not a word about Madison not backing off. The whole thing's driving me nuts."

Us, too, Flint thought.

"Something noteworthy," Nick said, "is that the attacks against Mrs. Baughman have been unsophisticated, cruel, somewhat impulsive, and extremely personal—consistent with what we might expect from angry rednecks scared they're going to lose their jobs. But the retaliatory arson fires required considerable organization and planning, and we—"

"I know what you're driving at," Madison snapped. "But you're wrong. Would you please just listen to the caller's voice? Maybe it'll lead somewhere."

Rue sat in Montana's hospital room, his arms folded on the bedrail, and watched the rise and fall of his son's chest. He seemed so pale and fragile and small hooked up to all those machines. For a split second he saw Montana arranged in a casket and blinked away the image, his heart pounding.

Lord, thank You for not letting him die. I don't think I could handle losing him.

Rue thought back on those horrific minutes after the shot rang out. He could still hear Ivy's sobbing and feel the dread that overtook him as he carried their wounded son to the truck, afraid they couldn't get him to the hospital before he bled to death. He had almost no recollection of the drive to the hospital or even the 911 call he made.

And he hadn't even begun to deal with his anger at the shooter, much less his pathetic brother-in-law. Both were despicable and undeserving of any mercy. He'd never understood hate before now and was surprised at how easy it was to justify it.

"Dad…what is this place?"

Rue came back to the moment and realized Montana's eyes were open. He reached over and stroked his hair. "You're in the hospital, champ. You got hurt, but you're gonna be okay."

In a heartbeat, Ivy was at their son's side. "Oh, sweetie. It's so good to hear your voice."

Montana's eyes looked glazed and his expression confused. "My arm hurts really a lot."

"Do you remember what happened?" Rue said.

"I got shot."

Ivy's eyes brimmed with tears. They had both hoped he wouldn't remember.

Rue slid his arm around her. "That's exactly right. Ian's dad is working hard to figure out who did it. Do you remember seeing anybody?"

"No. I just heard a loud bang, and it knocked me down." Montana's voice was soft and labored. "It hurt so bad, but I remembered not to move—not even a little."

"What did you remember that from?" Rue said.

"When those big kids at that school got shot, and they didn't want the man with the gun to shoot them again. So they pretended they were dead. That's what I did."

"You were playing dead?" Ivy said.

Montana nodded, a tear rolling down his cheek. "I was really, really scared."

Rue swallowed the wad of emotion that seemed stuck in his throat. "And you were really smart."

"Why did I get shot?"

Ivy wiped the tear off his cheek with her thumb. "We don't know yet. It could've been an accident. Ian's dad will figure it out. Right now, we just need to get you better and take care of that arm."

Montana seemed to notice the sling for the first time. "Can the doctor make my arm stop hurting?"

"I'll bet he can." Rue pushed the Call button.

"May I help you?" said a female voice.

"This is Mr. Kessler. My son is awake now. Did the doctor order something for pain?"

"Yes sir. I'll be right there."

"Where's Windy?" Montana said.

"Ian's taking good care of her until you're better, so Mommy and I can be here with you."

"Can't I go home?"

"Not for a couple days, champ. We have to make sure your arm is okay first. You had an operation to remove the bullet. And the doctor had to do some repair work on the inside."

"Can I see the bullet?" he said sleepily.

"Maybe later on. Sheriff Carter's deputies have it. It might help them find the bad guy."

Montana got quiet, his eyelids heavy. Finally, he said, "We better pray for the bad guy. I don't think he has Jesus in his heart."

Rue was caught off guard by Montana's concern for the person who had shot him and was relieved when the nurse breezed into the room.

"Well, you really are awake," she said. "Look at those big brown eyes. I brought something to make you a lot more comfortable. This won't hurt at all. I'm going to inject some medication into the tube in your arm, and it's going to take away that awful achy feeling. Might make you a little dizzy, is all. You ready?"

Montana nodded.

Rue stood aside and let the nurse do what she had come to do. He knew there would be no instant fix for the emotional pain his family would feel once the numbness wore off. The reality was, someone tried to kill Montana—and he was still out there.

26

THE NEXT MORNING, Flint pushed open the door to Jewel's Café, his eyelids heavy, his mind plagued with doubts that he and Nick would ever be able to uncover who was behind the attacks that seemed to be spiraling out of control. He went over to the table next to the moose head and flopped in a chair.

Jewel Sadler came rushing through the swinging doors, wiping her hands with a towel. "There you are. I've been waiting for you to get here."

"You just turned on the Open sign."

"I just found out about the shooting this morning when I turned on the radio. I've been beside myself with worry. How's Montana?"

"He had us all worried for a while there, but he's going to be fine. He lost a lot of blood."

"Poor little guy. How's his arm?"

"Thankfully, the doctor was able to repair it. Said with the proper rehab, he should regain full function. I'll tell you this: I'm making it my life's mission to find the loser who shot him."

"How are Ivy and Rue handling it?"

"They're pretty shaken. Who wouldn't be?"

Jewel sat in the chair opposite him, her arms folded on the table, her eyes glistening. "What's going on, Flint? People here used to respect each other. It just grieves me."

"Me, too. When you start pitting environmental concerns against economic growth, you're bound to have some serious clashes. But shooting a child is off the chart."

"Can't you close down this SAGE group?"

Flint shook his head. "Not without proof they broke the law. Their president swears she knows nothing about any of the crimes."

"But I heard on the news that SAGE claimed responsibility."

Rita Benson came over and poured Flint a cup of coffee.

He nodded a thank-you and took a sip, his thoughts focused on not saying more than he should. "Jewel, there's a lot of information floating around out there that I can't confirm or deny during an open investigation. Just don't forget this isn't one-sided. Someone instigated the whole thing by attacking SAGE's president."

"Well, they started a chain reaction that no one could've imagined. And the Kesslers and the Griffiths are paying for it."

"Seems that way."

Jewel's eyes narrowed. "But you don't think so?"

Flint took a sip of coffee and avoided eye contact.

Jewel pushed back her chair. "Goodness. Listen to me. You came in here to enjoy your breakfast in peace, and here I am interrogating you."

"One of these days, we can have a real conversation about it. For now, I'd better stick with breakfast. I'll have my usual. And maybe one of your fruit muffins. Racking my brain makes me hungry."

"Coming right up."

Bobby Knolls came in the door and over to the table, then sat across from Flint. "You sure had a busy night."

"Yeah, I had finally started to unwind when my cell phone rang and Nick told me Baughman had called 911."

"I listened to the voice you recorded off her answering machine." Bobby blew a pink bubble. "The guy sounds young, but we already knew that."

Rita came over and placed a mug of coffee on the table in front of Bobby. "Would you like a menu, Lieutenant?"

"Nah, I can't eat this early. Coffee's fine. Thanks." Bobby wrapped his hands around the mug. "So why'd you ask me to meet you here?"

"The lab finally confirmed that the shoe impressions found at Everhardt Roofing were identical to what we found at the Griffiths' stable. I want you and Buck to get a warrant and revisit each male member of SAGE, husbands and boyfriends of female members, and sons old enough to drive. Let's find out if anyone's shoes match the size and brand names."

"I thought you were hedgin' on the idea that SAGE set the fires."

"I can hedge all I want, but I certainly can't eliminate them. See if you can link the shoe impressions to anyone associated with the organization. While you're doing that, Nick and I are going to talk to Montana Kessler and see if he saw anything."

Rue stood on the sidewalk outside the hospital, his hands in his pockets, and admired the shades of golden orange that dawn had painted across Monday morning's sky.

A sparrow hawk sat atop the light pole at the edge of the parking lot and faced the open range, seemingly to wait for some unsuspecting prey to show itself within striking distance.

On the other side of Phantom Hollow, the jagged peaks of the San Juan Mountains took on a reddish hue in the glow of sunrise. The air was dry and crisp and fresh. Hardly a cloud in the sky. Everything pointed to it being a perfect summer day.

Rue blinked to clear the sandy sensation from his tired eyes. How could the day be anything but perfect when his son was alive and going to make a full recovery?

So why was he still too fighting mad to sleep? He'd spent the night wide-awake at Montana's beside, unable to silence vengeful thoughts of what he'd like to say and do to the lowlife who shot his son. And to Rusty for not caring whether his nephew lived or died. He imagined how satisfying it would be to deliver one blow after another until he beat the smug self-righteousness out of Rusty.

He spotted a red-tailed hawk soaring overhead and wished he could yield himself to God's Spirit with such ease. It was wrong to harbor these thoughts, and he knew it. Maybe he was mad at himself for not protecting Montana. If only he'd listened to Ivy and not let him go walking by himself, none of this would've happened.

He was suddenly aware of footsteps and then Ivy's voice.

"The nurse came in to give Montana a sponge bath," she said.

"Did he eat his breakfast?"

Ivy shook her head. "He was feeling sick to his stomach."

"Probably the heavy drugs. I'm not expecting him to feel good for a while."

"I don't know, Dr. Andover said he'd be asking for pizza by tonight." Ivy linked her arm in his and nudged him to walk. "I'm just so grateful he's going to be all right. I don't think I've ever begged the Lord for anything before."

"Don't you wonder why He let it happen?"

"Sure, but that's a dead end. Bad things happen to good people all the time. I'd go nuts if I tried to figure out why. God certainly didn't pull the trigger."

"But He could've stopped it. Why didn't He?"

"He could've prevented you from abusing alcohol and me from doing drugs, too. But He let us make our own choices."

"What choice did Montana have?"

Ivy stopped and turned to Rue, her eyebrows forming a straight line. "Are you angry with God? Pastor Myers said that might happen."

"I don't know. I'm angry. I'm not sure where to direct it, other than I'd love to make a punching bag out of Rusty. I can't believe he never even asked if Montana was going to be okay."

"Dad already told him he was."

"Yeah, but it takes someone really cold to go to the hospital and harass a parent who's just gone through a life-threatening ordeal with his child."

Ivy lifted her eyebrows and started strolling again. "I tried to tell you Rusty's heart turned to stone. I guess we'd better get used to it."

Grayson walked in the trailer at the work site and saw Liz sitting at her desk, typing at the computer.

"Hey, Liz. Have Elam or Rue come in yet?"

Liz peered over the top of her half glasses. "You're kidding, right? Haven't you heard the news?"

"Yeah, it's terrible what happened to Montana. That's why I came over here. I wanted to tell them how sorry I am and see how he's doing."

"Well, don't expect to see Rue today. Elam's planning to put in a couple hours this afternoon. But last I heard, Montana pulled through and should get back the use of his arm. Elam said he might have a lot of physical therapy ahead of him." Liz shook her head, her lips pursed. "I'd love to get my hands on the good-for-nothing that shot that sweet child."

"Did Elam say whether the sheriff had any suspects?"

"I got the impression he does, but Elam couldn't get into detail." Liz snickered. "When they get the guy, we ought to save the taxpayers money and have a good old-fashioned lynching. Why should we listen to whatever sob story the creep coughs up? He doesn't deserve to live in society another day."

Grayson wanted to shout that it was an accident, that he wasn't a monster. "You're sure Montana's going to be all right?"

"Far as I know. He'll be in the hospital a couple days."

"Can he have visitors?"

Liz stared blankly for a moment and then said, "Never thought to ask. You want me to check with Elam?"

"No, that's okay. Don't bother him with it. I'll call the hospital and find out."

"It's right nice of you to think about going over there. I'll bet Rue and his wife could use the moral support."

Grayson considered the irony of slipping into the role of comforting the people whose child he shot. Could he even face Rue? He decided he had to—and the sooner he did it, the better. The most important thing now was to avoid suspicion.

Flint stood at the window in his office staring at the mountains. He was hungry but didn't have the energy to go out and pick up something for lunch.

"Hey, Sheriff." Nick glided into his office. "I just heard from one of my agents who's helping Bobby and Buck with their *foot* work. They haven't found a match for the shoe impressions yet, but they're only about halfway through the list of *possibles*. We might get lucky… Why are you so glum?"

Flint sighed deeply. "What kind of world do we live in that an eight-year-old knew to fake being dead so he wouldn't get shot again? It never occurred to me that Ian and Montana worried about such things and had even talked through what they would do if it happened to them."

"School shootings have forced kids to become streetwise, Sheriff. Frankly, it was brilliant of the Kessler kid to fake being dead. Might've saved his life. Too bad he didn't see the shooter, though."

"Well, we're going to get him. Any luck coming up with profiles?"

Nick nodded and waved the paper in his hand. "Right here. Is this a good time?"

"You bet. Let's sit over here at the table."

Nick sat across from him and slid the piece of paper across the table. "Read it out loud."

Flint put on his reading glasses and picked up the paper. "Okay, regarding Madison Baughman's attacker. This perp is male. Twenty to thirty years of age. High-school education. Probably a middle child who felt he had to fight to be heard and is reliving that same sense of helplessness in his job. He's likely blue collar. Possibly out of work. He considers himself a leader of the underdog, and that's where he finds his voice. He refuses to be silenced and draws attention to himself by orchestrating chaos. He is capable of inflicting bodily harm, but only impulsively, and he feels great remorse afterward. For that reason, it's unlikely he would threaten someone with bodily harm and then follow through later. Instead, he will resort to fear tactics. He's all about using fear to control. It's not so much about following through with threats as making the victim think he will. The likelihood that he would plan a rape is almost nonexistent."

Flint folded his glasses. "Impressive. What about the perp who made the phone calls?"

"I think he's a follower. Does whatever he's told. The guy we want to focus on is the one calling the shots. And that's the best I can do, based on what we know."

"Okay, thanks. What about our arsonists? Did you work up a profile on them?"

A row of lines formed on Nick's forehead. "Not yet. There's just so much that doesn't add up. I don't want to waste any more energy on it till we hear from Bobby and Buck and see if they can match the shoe impressions we took to anyone associated with SAGE."

27

RUE SAT AT A CORNER TABLE in the hospital cafeteria having lunch with Ivy, Elam, and Carolyn.

"I was so glad to see Montana finally eat something," Ivy said. "He had a bowl of chicken noodle soup and some crackers. And then polished off the vanilla pudding and asked for another."

Carolyn smiled. "Good. I'll bring him a piece of that frozen lemon dessert he loves."

Rue noticed his father-in-law seemed distant and had only eaten a few bites of his sandwich. "Elam, why don't you let Liz hold down the fort and go home and get some rest this afternoon?"

"I'm all right," Elam said. "It's just been a lot to take in. I should've heeded the threats and shut down the retirement village project until Flint got this thing figured out. I let my stubbornness take over, which put my grandson at risk."

"You couldn't have foreseen that," Rue said. "And for what it's worth, I wouldn't have shut it down, either. You start caving in to their threats, and the environmentalists will run us all out of business. Besides, Flint doesn't sound convinced that SAGE did the shooting."

"Yeah, that's what he said. Could've been an accident, I suppose. We've sure had a rash of poaching going on lately." Elam stared at his plate and seemed lost in thought.

"Is something else wrong?" Rue said.

Elam tugged at his mustache for a few moments and then lifted his eyes. "I called Rusty this morning and told him I hoped he had a good first day at the clinic. It was my way of trying to put yesterday's tension behind us and start over. The conversation was downright awkward, and he finally told me he came over here last night—and why. I lost it. We pretty much had a knock-down-drag-out."

"I'm sure I didn't help matters any," Rue said. "I suppose Rusty told you I grabbed him and told him to keep his stinking hands off Ivy?"

"Yeah, but he knew he had it coming. I just don't understand the irrational anger he's got for Ivy and Montana. I can't get him to talk to me about what he's feeling. Every time I try, he closes down. There's so much I'd like to do for that boy, but the wedge he's driving between himself and the rest of us brings out the stingy in me real quick."

Ivy folded her hands on the table. "I assume you and Mom set aside land for Rusty, too."

"Sure we did," Elam said. "Twenty-five acres right next to yours. We've never said anything to him about it because acreage in Phantom Hollow wasn't going to do him any good when he married Jacqueline and moved to Albuquerque. Land values were soaring and his veterinary practice was going so well that we decided when the time seemed right, we'd give him the dollar equivalent outright. But the way Rusty's behaving at the moment, I've half a mind to cut him out of the will altogether."

"You wouldn't do that," Ivy said.

Elam's face flooded with red. "No. But until he gets his head on straight and decides to be a caring part of this family, he's not getting a share of the homestead property."

Ivy wiped a tear off her cheek. "I'm sorry it's come to this. I wish I knew what I could do to fix things."

Carolyn put her hand on Ivy's. "You've done your part, honey. For some reason, Rusty can't seem to move past the things you did wrong and see the things you're doing right. Not to defend his behavior, but he was devastated that after we paid for your rehab, you disappeared without telling us where you were. We could hardly mention your name to him after that. And it hasn't gotten any better since you moved back here."

"So how do we get him to step into the present?" Rue said. "He thinks he's the only one of us living in reality. He told me that."

Elam shook his head. "Actually, he's the only one of us who *isn't*. Maybe I'm being hard-nosed, but I don't have any sympathy for him. He wasn't any more wounded than Carolyn and I. He's a grown man. He needs to step up and forgive his sister. That's all in the world that's wrong with him. I'm sure not going to coddle him."

Grayson thanked the nurse and walked down the long shiny corridor to Room 118, carrying a bag under his arm. He saw the name Montana Kessler in the wall slot next to the door and knocked softly and then peeked inside. Montana lay in bed, an IV tube in one arm that was hooked up to a bottle of something clear. No one else was in the room.

"It's me, Grayson. Mind if I come in?"

Montana flashed a toothy grin. "You're my very first company, except for my family."

"I heard you had a rough time of it."

"Yeah, I got shot. But I'm not gonna die. My dad said so."

Grayson handed Montana the bag. "I brought you a present." *Thirty more bucks I owe MasterCard.*

Montana opened the sack and pulled out a stuffed Siberian husky. "It looks just like Windy." He hugged it tightly with his good arm. "Thanks, Mr. Grayson. They won't let real dogs in the hospital."

"I thought you might be missing her."

"I am. Really a lot. But my friend Ian is taking care of her. His dad's the sheriff. He's gonna find the guy who shot me."

"I know he is. Did you know my brother Bobby Knolls works with the sheriff?"

Montana cocked his head, the corners of his mouth twitching. "Me and Ian call him Lieutenant Bubblegum. Get it?"

Grayson smiled in spite of himself. "Yeah, I get it. So how're you feeling?"

"I almost threw up this morning and didn't want my breakfast. But I'm much better now. Did you see my sling? I have a blue Velcro thingy on my arm. I can't take it off for six weeks—not even for one second."

"Pretty fancy. I hear you're going to be good as new."

"The doctor said my arm might not work right for a while. So I have to go to this place called rehab. I don't know where it is, but my mom can take me. I don't have to stay there."

"Does it hurt much?"

Montana focused his attention on the stuffed dog and fiddled with its nose. "Sometimes…but they give me stuff so it'll stop. When I got shot it hurt really, *really* bad. I wanted to cry, but I didn't dare move." He lowered his voice to a whisper. "I pretended I was dead so the bad guy wouldn't shoot me again.'

Grayson's mind flashed back to the sight of Montana's tiny body sprawled on the ground. "I'm sorry you had to go through that."

"Me, too. Don't tell my parents, but I'm kind of scared he might come back." Montana glanced up at him. "I don't want to get shot again."

Grayson's heart sank. "Oh, I don't think you have to worry about that."

"But what if they don't catch him?"

"You kidding? How can he get away with Sheriff Carter and Lieutenant Bubblegum on the case?" The truth of Grayson's words hit him the moment he said them.

"You know what's the hardest thing?"

"Tell me."

"I can't throw the Frisbee very good with my left arm. I guess Windy and me will have to play something else till I'm all better."

"Hey, Grayson."

He turned around just as Rue and Ivy entered the room.

Rue offered him a firm handshake. "How nice of you to come."

"Well, I'm pretty fond of Montana. I couldn't believe what happened. Tara and I have been on the phone with Bobby, trying to keep up with his condition. We're so glad he's going to be all right."

"Thanks. We are, too."

"See what I got from Mr. Grayson?" Montana held up the stuffed dog. "Doesn't it look like Windy?"

Ivy laughed. "Definitely. What a thoughtful gift, Grayson. He's really been missing that pooch."

"Yeah, I figured. I should get back to the site and check on the roofers. They were hitting it hard when I took off for lunch. Rue, is there anything you need me to do? "

"Just keep the crew on schedule. I hope to be back at work in a couple days."

"All right." Grayson pointed his finger at Montana. "You take care, buddy."

"I will. Thanks for my Windy dog."

"You're very welcome. Glad I was able to find one."

Grayson walked down the long corridor toward the entrance, his rubber soles squeaking on the shiny floor, and decided that if he gave up his one beer a night for a couple months, it would cover the cost of the stuffed dog he put on his credit card.

Flint reread the profile Nick had worked up for Madison Baughman's attacker and closed the file. He picked up the phone and dialed home.

"Hello."

"Hi, Betty. It's me. Have you heard from Ivy or Rue since this morning?"

"Actually, Montana called Ian just a little while ago."

"Really?"

"Yes, they had a delightful conversation. Montana's feeling much better. He said someone who works with his dad brought him a stuffed dog that looks like Windy. And that his parents were ordering him a pizza for dinner."

Flint smiled. "That's great. Speaking of dinner, what are we having?"

"I thought we could grill chicken and vegetables and eat out on the patio. It's too hot in the house to turn on the oven. There are only a few days a year I wish we had air-conditioning. This is one of them."

"Can you believe tomorrow is July first? We'll be off to Disney World before you know it."

"I know," Betty said. "Do you even want me to make plans for the Fourth of July? It's this Friday, and I know you're not going to take a long weekend right now."

"But I should be able to schedule myself off on the Fourth. Maybe Montana will be out of the hospital, and the Kesslers and the Griffiths would like to come over for a cookout."

"That's an idea."

Flint heard a knock on the open door and lifted his eyes just as Nick Sanchez breezed into his office. "I've got to go, hon. Why don't you try to line something up. I should be home by seven."

Flint hung up the phone. "You're much too alert for a guy who was up all night. I must be getting old. I'm wasted."

"I'm sure I'll crash tonight," Nick said. "I came to tell you our teams finished revisiting all male SAGE members, spouses, significant others, and teenage sons. Everyone was surprisingly cooperative. They got a match on the size eleven-and-a-half Sperry Top-Sider: a fifty-eight-year-old accountant by the name of Ron Jerrard. He's the husband of SAGE member Susan Jerrard. The guy isn't the least bit interested in anything SAGE does and has never attended a meeting or a rally. His wife says he was home asleep with her when both fires occurred. He willingly surrendered his hardly-ever-worn Top-Siders for trace analysis. My agents think Jerrard is clueless. Bobby and Buck agree with them. We'll have trace process the shoes, but I don't expect to find anything. There were no matches on the True Wilderness chukka boot or the New Balance sport shoe."

"So whose feet were at those fires?"

"Good question, Sheriff. We've got our work cut out for us."

"You any closer to coming up with a profile for these guys?"

"Not really. But now I need to give this some serious thought." Nick half smiled. "Which means I may not get any sleep tonight, either."

28

ON TUESDAY MORNING, Flint strolled with Nick Sanchez along one side of the charred field behind Madison Baughman's home and stopped when they reached an unmarked road, which ran parallel between the burned property and a new building site.

"The perp doused the back edge of the field with gasoline," Nick said, "and ignited it here at this corner. The dry weeds sparked quickly, and the wind pushed the flames toward Baughman's house. Could've pulled the whole thing off in just a couple minutes and split."

"Who owns this land?"

"Some builder named Nigel Reynolds. The property on either side of this road is being developed into a golf course and gated community called Deer Tracks. The project entrance is a half mile east of here. Only someone living, delivering, or working in this area would know this road was here."

"Or someone stalking Mrs. Baughman."

Nick smiled. "Bingo. We found traces of gasoline along the curb on this side. Also a wad of chewing gum with readable DNA that doesn't match anything on file. And a small white button. We're still questioning everyone who's working the Deer Tracks project, but no red flags."

"It was dark when the fire was set," Flint said. "Maybe the perp left his headlights on so he could see what he was doing. It's possible someone saw him."

"I thought of that. We questioned all the residents whose houses back up to this open field. No one saw anything."

Flint surveyed the black field where the flames had scorched a section of the Baughmans' privacy fence. "So where does this perp fall into the profile?"

"Definitely a follower. My guess is he did what he was told by the ringleader, whom, you'll recall from the profile, considers himself a leader of the underdog."

"Okay," Flint said. "The ringleader is all about using fear to control. I get that. But if he's not as interested in following through with threats as making the victim think he is, why not just threaten to burn her house down and let her sweat it? Why tell his lackey to set the fire and then call and warn her?"

"It's just a guess, but I'm thinking he felt outdone by the arsonists and needed his work to be visible—his way of refusing to be silenced."

"This stuff makes my head hurt."

Nick smiled and patted him on the back. "That's why *I'm* here. Come on, let's go grab some lunch. Then I want to drive out to the Kesslers' new place and do another walk-through while it's still a crime scene."

Rue and Ivy stood in Montana's hospital room, finishing up a conversation with Dr. Andover.

"I see no reason why you can't take Montana home tomorrow," the doctor said. "I'll leave the discharge papers and a set of instructions with the nurses. And a couple prescriptions you'll need to get filled. The main thing to remember is to keep the Velcro cast on him 24/7, and keep it from getting wet. When he wants to take a shower, just slip a small plastic bag over the cast and secure it with rubber bands. You'll need to make an appointment to have his stitches removed the first part of next week. And we'll get him started on rehab in about six weeks, after the soft tissues have healed. Do you have any questions?"

Rue turned to Ivy and then to the doctor. "No, I think you answered everything."

Dr. Andover moved over next to the bed. "I bet you're ready to go home."

Montana shrugged. "To my old house, but not my new one."

"Don't worry, champ. Sheriff Carter's gonna lock up the guy who shot you long before we're ready to move out there."

Dr. Andover patted Montana's good arm. "I'll stop by and see you in the morning before you leave. You've been a wonderful patient. I wish all my young patients were as cooperative and brave as you."

Dr. Andover motioned for Rue and Ivy to come out into the hallway.

"Your son seems to be handling this trauma better than I would have expected," the doctor said. "But don't be alarmed if you notice some anxiety once you leave the hospital and he doesn't feel quite so safe."

"What should we watch for?" Ivy said.

"He might be easily startled. Have frequent nightmares, restlessness, or difficulty concentrating. You might even notice him acting out the trauma when he's playing. Don't be alarmed, but be prepared. Much of the time, these symptoms go away after a month or so. But if the symptoms persist, he may need counseling for posttraumatic stress disorder."

"I've heard of that," Rue said. "What is it?"

"PTSD is a psychological illness in which a person repeatedly relives or dreams about a terrible experience."

Ivy blew the bangs off her forehead. "I sure hope he doesn't have long-term effects from this. But truthfully, he seems to be handling it better than I am."

Dr. Andover put his hand on her shoulder. "That's quite possible. It had to be horrific for you and your husband, especially when you thought he was going to bleed to death before you could get him here. Don't be surprised if you experience nightmares and flashbacks or feelings of anger, fear, helplessness, or guilt. You might even feel numb and isolated from others. That's all part of it. I suggest you stay sensitive to Montana and let him express his feelings, and that the two of you do the same between yourselves. But if it goes on beyond a month or so, by all means seek professional help."

"We will." Rue shook hands with the doctor. "See you in the morning. We're eager to get back to real life and try to put this behind us."

Rue went back in the room and saw that Montana's eyelids were heavy. He pulled the covers up and tucked them by his side. "I can tell the pain med the nurse shot into your IV kicked in. Why don't you take a nap?"

Montana yawned and batted his eyes slowly, then reached for the stuffed dog and clutched it tightly. "Tomorrow I get to see Windy."

"Absolutely." Rue kissed his forehead. "While you're napping, Mommy and I will be outside in the fresh air. We'll see you when you wake up."

Rue sat on a wrought-iron bench in the hospital courtyard, his arm around Ivy's shoulder, his head tilted back. He nestled in the silence and let the afternoon sun bathe his face.

He hadn't told anyone about his fear of going home. What guarantee was there that the shooter wouldn't come to the camp and finish the job? If only he knew what it was the guy wanted.

Lord, be our refuge and our strength. Protect us from this unknown enemy. I don't know where else to turn.

Rue swallowed hard and blinked the stinging from his eyes. Had he ever felt more helpless? Dr. Andover said he and Ivy should talk to each other about their feelings. But this seemed like the wrong time to show weakness. Wasn't it more important that he be strong for her? If she realized how scared he was, wouldn't that make her even more frightened and vulnerable?

He wondered if they should take Elam and Carolyn up on their offer to stay out at their house. At least there was safety in numbers. And with the security guard in place and Sasha and Windy barking at every leaf that blew, maybe they would all feel safer until Flint and Special Agent Sanchez could arrest whoever was terrorizing them.

"Mr. and Mrs. Kessler?"

Rue opened his eyes and saw a young couple that looked vaguely familiar. "Yes."

"I'm Madison Baughman," the woman said. "And this is my husband, Ken. Could we talk?"

"Uh, I…I guess so."

Ivy linked her arm in his. "Why are you here?"

"First of all," Madison said, "let me say how very sorry we are about what happened to your son. We're parents, too, and can only imagine what you've been through. We want you to know we're praying for you. The other reason we came is to tell you face to face that neither I nor anyone in SAGE had anything to do with shooting your son, vandalizing Mr. Kessler's truck, or setting either arson fire."

"Shouldn't you be telling this to the sheriff?" Rue said.

"We have—ad nauseam. I think SAGE is being framed. I don't know who called and claimed responsibility for those crimes, but I'm confident it wasn't someone from my organization. I wanted you to hear it directly from me. I doubt the authorities are going to divulge anything I tell them during an open investigation."

Rue paused and tried to process the implications. Would she risk having this potentially volatile confrontation if she were lying?

"Why should we believe you?" Rue said.

"SAGE has a history of peaceful protesting. We've never been violent. I know that you're members of Rick Myers's church. I'm appealing to you as a brother and sister in Christ to believe me when I tell you that I'm at a loss to know what's going on."

"Even if *you* are," Ivy said, "how can you be sure someone in your organization isn't doing this?"

Madison's eyes brimmed with tears. "I can't. But I know these people. They're strong Christians. They're my friends. We've laughed and cried and prayed together. I just don't believe they're capable of doing these awful things."

"Have you told that to the sheriff and FBI?" Rue said.

"A thousand times. But they keep asking the same questions, and I keep telling them I have no idea who it is that wants to hurt me, or who it is that's striking back. Maybe you don't believe me, either, but I felt impressed by the Lord to come here and tell you."

Rue couldn't have found his voice if he'd had something to say. How did she expect him to respond to that?

Ken Baughman finally spoke. "I'm sorry this is so awkward. It wasn't our intention to intrude on your privacy. All we ask is that you take this before the Lord and pray for justice to be done. We'll do the same thing. Surely we can agree that the guilty parties on both sides need to be caught before someone ends up dead?"

Rue nodded. "Definitely."

"We're sorry for all that's happened to you, too" Ivy said. "We have no idea who's behind any of it."

"I believe you." Madison wiped her eyes. "Thanks for listening. We'll be praying your son gets better and better each day. And that justice is served."

The Baughmans turned and walked hand-in-hand across the hospital courtyard in the direction of the parking lot.

Rue sat stunned for a few moments and then said, "Did that really just happen?"

"Uh-huh."

"Call me naive, but I think she's telling the truth."

"So do I."

Grayson scratched the last item off the list on his clipboard and glanced at his watch. He took his cell phone off the clip and hit the auto-dial for home.

"Hello."

"Hi, Tara. It's me."

"How's it going at the site? Did Everhardt's guys make it?"

"Yeah, they're slapping that roofing down in record time. How's your day going?"

"Busy. I drove the boys to the YMCA in Mt. Byron for their swimming lessons. Then I took Lindsey to the orthodontist and ran some errands and got groceries on the way home. Have you heard any more about Montana?"

"Actually, I have. I went over to the hospital to see him during my lunch break. He was a little washed out, but he's in good spirits. Has to have some rehab, but he's going to be all right."

"What a relief. Did you see Rue and Ivy?"

"Sure did."

"I hope you told them how sorry I am about what happened."

"Of course I did. Listen, I bought Montana a gift from us—a stuffed dog. Looks just like Windy."

"That was sweet of you. I assume you charged it?"

"Yeah, I did. I just didn't see how I could go see him empty-handed. I wanted to show how sorry we are."

Tara sighed. "Of course you did. I'll figure out where to cut something else to pay for it."

"I've already thought of that. I'll just cut out my beer for a couple months."

"Well, Grayson Knolls. You never cease to amaze me. You'd be willing to do that?"

"What can I say? I like Montana. Listen, I need to go. There's a lot more to do with Rue and Elam both out. I doubt if I'll get out of here much before eight."

"I'll save your dinner."

"Thanks. Love you."

"I love you, too."

Grayson put his phone back on his belt clip and headed for the model condo.

All afternoon he'd had the strangest desire to go back out to the Kesslers' place. Maybe going there and reliving what happened would comfort him and remind him he wasn't the monster the media portrayed him to be. But what if he was spotted by investigators and questioned? What if he couldn't make them believe he was there out of curiosity?

All it would take for him to get charged with shooting Montana was a ballistics match on the bullet and a DNA match on the handkerchief. If there was one thing he had learned from Bobby, it was that evidence didn't lie.

He thought about selling the rifle, but that might raise a red flag. And his two older boys were especially fond of that old Winchester Featherweight. It seemed smarter just to keep things in his life as normal as possible.

A loud bang echoed above the sound of hammering. Grayson ducked behind a bulky pile of wood scraps and covered his head. A few seconds later he heard loud bursts of laughter.

"Hey, Grayson. You can come out. It was just Hank's old clunker backfiring."

Grayson emerged, his pulse racing, heat flooding his face. He forced himself to smile at the roofers and join in their laughter. But the incident jolted him back to reality. Getting caught wasn't the only thing he had to worry about. Someone really *was* out to shut down the retirement village project—and he couldn't afford to assume he wouldn't be targeted.

29

RUE PARKED HIS TRUCK in front of his in-laws' log house and waved to Elam and Carolyn, who were sitting together on the porch swing. He bounded up the steps and leaned against the railing, his arms folded across his chest.

The pair stared at him as if they were expecting bad news.

"Everything's fine," Rue said. "I went home to shower and change clothes and wanted to stop by and tell you Montana's being released in the morning. And Ivy and I have talked about it, and we'd like to take you up on your offer to stay out here till the dust settles."

"I'm so relieved," Carolyn said, her hand on her heart. "I won't worry as much if we're together."

Elam nodded. "Ditto. Smart decision."

"I'm not sure what time we'll actually get away. But once we get Montana settled here, we'll go home and get some clothes and a few odds and ends. Let's hope this thing doesn't drag out."

Elam tugged at his mustache. "It might. Flint didn't sound to me as if he thinks they're close to making an arrest."

"Well, the other thing I came to tell you is that Madison Baughman and her husband came to see Ivy and me at the hospital this afternoon. We were shocked. Though, actually, they're very nice people." Rue gave them the details of the conversation.

"I'll have to ask Pastor Myers for his spin on this," Elam said. "I don't trust anybody associated with SAGE right now."

"Well, if it was an act, they should win an Oscar. They said all the right things with all the right emotion. Ivy and I believe them."

Carolyn folded her hands in her lap. "If SAGE isn't retaliating for the attacks on Madison Baughman, then who is?"

"Exactly," Elam said. "That's why I'm not eliminating SAGE until the authorities do. Baughman could be clueless about what's going on with some of her members right under nose."

"She seems as sure about her members as we are about the people we go to church with. Can you imagine anyone at Woodlands Community doing something like this?"

"If there's one thing I've learned over the years," Elam said, "it's that given the right circumstances, everyone is capable of anything. I don't mean to sound negative, but I'm not convinced SAGE is squeaky clean, even if the Baughmans are."

Rue nodded. "I can't blame you. It's pretty confusing. At any rate, we really appreciate being able to hole up here with you. The doctor talked to us about posttraumatic stress disorder and some things we need to watch for." Rue explained what Dr. Andover had cautioned them about. "Montana seems okay. I think he'll feel safer here than at the camp right now. Ivy, too. She's pretty fragile."

"And what about you?" Carolyn said.

"Oh, I'll be okay." *I have to be.* "I think it's just a matter of getting some time between us and the shooting."

Flint set his cell phone and the paper with Rue's cell number in his lap, then leaned back in his easy chair, his eyes closed, his ire just under the surface.

"You okay?" Betty asked.

"No, I'm not okay. The Baughmans did something we asked them not to do." Flint told her about their surprise visit with the Kesslers. "Nick and I and our people don't even discuss our doubts about SAGE's involvement with the outside. The last thing we need is the public getting wind of this. If we've got a third thread in this case, we want the perps to go on thinking we suspect SAGE. If they know we're on to them, we may never catch them."

"So who was on the phone?"

"Elam. Rue just left there. Apparently, the Baughmans convinced him and Ivy that SAGE isn't involved. I need to make sure the Kesslers keep it to themselves." He picked up his cell phone and entered the number Elam gave him. "This case is going to give me a stroke."

"Hello."

"Rue, it's Flint. I just talked to Elam, and he told me that you and Ivy talked to the Baughmans this afternoon."

"Yeah, we did. They came to the hospital to tell us they weren't involved in Montana's shooting or any of the other crimes. They were believable. They're even praying for us. I was going to call you in the morning and tell you about it."

"Listen, it's imperative that you and Ivy keep this to yourselves. I can't get into details, but it's important that the media keeps reporting that we suspect SAGE is involved."

"But what if they aren't?"

Flint traced the stitching on the arm of the chair. "We don't know that for a fact. And even *if* it turns out to be true, which we're a long way from proving, whoever is doing this needs to think we're after someone inside the SAGE organization. If they think we've eliminated SAGE as a suspect, they may throw us a curve and we'll never catch them. These are dangerous people we don't want to get away. I want to lock up whoever torched your father-in-law's stable and Everhardt Roofing. And trashed your truck. And shot your son. Are we on the same page?"

"Sure. I'll talk to Ivy. We won't say anything."

"Thanks. How's Montana?"

"Good. He's being released in the morning. We've decided to stay with Elam and Carolyn until things settle down. We're all a little skittish about going home."

"Understandably. Hang in there. We're going to solve this. See you on the Fourth."

"We're all looking forward to it."

Flint had no sooner disconnected the call than his phone vibrated again. He read the LED screen and saw that it was Investigator Buck Lowry.

"Yeah, Buck. What's up?"

"I just got a call from my friend Jack who tends bar at the Blue Moon Tavern in Mt. Byron. He said three guys he's never seen before are in there shooting off their mouths about Madison Baughman. Calling her every name in the book and saying how extremists like her put breadwinners out of work and wreck families. He's stopped serving them because they've had enough to drink, so he figures they won't stay long. I called the Mt. Byron marshal's office and left a message on his answering machine. I'm ten minutes away and have backup coming."

"Great work, Buck. This might be the break we've been waiting for."

Rue strolled on the sidewalk at the hospital, wishing the night sky was dark enough for him to identify the constellations. He hadn't been stargazing since last spring. And given the shorter summer nights, his longtime hobby had taken a backseat to romancing his bride. But even their passion had waned in the chaos that had consumed them since they got home from their honeymoon.

He thought back on the lull of the surf in Jamaica and the timeless, carefree hours he and Ivy had spent in each other's arms. He wondered if life would ever be peaceful again—or safe. It was almost beyond comprehension that their world had been shaken to the core and they hadn't even been married a month.

At least Montana was alive. And was going to recover and live a normal life. Rue had been so afraid they were going to lose him that even the flood of relief seemed to have hit like a tidal wave and knocked the wind out of him.

How he longed for some alone time with Ivy. Living at Elam and Carolyn's for a while was probably the best choice, but he doubted that sleeping under his in-laws' roof would do much to foster intimacy between Ivy and him. And he was sure the unresolved issues with Rusty would permeate every wall in his parents' home, including the guest bedroom.

He thought it ironic that he had matched Rusty's resentment with a good deal of his own. Where would the cycle end? Or would it? He wondered if his role in this family was going to include an endless battle with his brother-in-law over Ivy's past.

Too bad Rusty couldn't understand the miracle of mercy. It was such a God thing that he and Ivy had met again nearly nine years after the sordid sexual encounter that resulted in her unwanted pregnancy. A drug addict and a john brought together by the God of the universe to raise a son born in shame. A union made holy by mercy and grace.

Rue blinked to clear his eyes. It was still so humbling it was all he could do not to drop to his knees right there on the sidewalk.

And how he adored Ivy. She wasn't just the mother of his child. She was the love of his life. The other half of his soul. The woman he hoped to toast on their fiftieth wedding anniversary. Was it selfish of him to want time and privacy to make love to her without everyone else's problems dousing their ardor?

He sighed. They wouldn't be at Elam and Carolyn's forever. It was important that Montana felt safe. And that Ivy did. Without that, no time they spent together would be relaxed and normal. And he was *so* ready for relaxed and normal.

Flint paced on the front porch, the evening air chilly and still. It had been twenty-five minutes since Buck called. Surely he knew something by now. Flint was tempted to call his cell but thought better of it. Buck would call the minute he had something to report.

How he wanted this over with. If they could arrest the three young men who had attacked and threatened Madison Baughman, the retaliatory attacks should stop. Then again, would he be happy with locking up only half the problem? He wanted to nail the guys who burned Elam's stable and Everhardt Roofing. But his gut told him that the third thread was going to be much harder to figure out."

His cell phone vibrated, and he picked it up. "Yeah, Buck."

"I missed them, Sheriff. My friend Jack tried to keep them here by giving them a free pitcher of beer in spite of their being three sheets to the wind. But a couple tough guys told them to shut up or they were calling the cops. So they split. I probably missed them by five minutes."

Flint gripped the porch rail and spouted off the one swear word he still allowed himself to use on occasion. "Did anybody see what they were driving?"

"Yeah, Jack did. But he couldn't read the license number. It was a white late model Ford F150. That narrows it down to about a million trucks just like it in the state."

"Could he describe the men?"

"Yeah, and Jack remembers details. I'm sure Nick Sanchez will want him to work with the sketch artist. He saved their beer mugs, too. Maybe we'll get prints. In a nutshell, these guys were in their early twenties. Dressed in faded jeans and T-shirts. Overdue for haircuts and shaves. And the mouthiest of the three had a heart tattoo on his left bicep. As soon as I arrived, I detained all the patrons in the bar. My backup's arrived, and we've begun questioning everyone. Maybe someone will remember something important."

"Good work, Buck. I'll call Nick and fill him in. Call me back if you get anything earthshaking. Otherwise, I'll see you in the morning."

"All right, Sheriff."

Flint set his cell phone on the round table next to the wicker chair, aware that Betty had come outside.

"I heard you on the phone. What happened at the Blue Moon?"

Flint told her everything Buck had told him. "Can you believe we missed those guys by just minutes?"

"But how great that you have a description. I hear bartenders are really observant."

"Let's hope. It was quick thinking on Jack's part to call Buck when he did. We may a get a break out of this yet."

Grayson lay in the chaise lounge on the patio, wide-eyed, and wondered how he was going to roll out of bed at five in the morning if he didn't get some sleep.

He had lingered a long time in his son Samuel's room after the boy fell asleep, trying to come to grips with the pain he'd caused Montana. He couldn't imagine going through something like that with one of his kids. The fear he'd seen in Montana's eyes haunted him. The child's honest admission that he was scared the man would come back and shoot him again tore at Grayson's heart. It was never his intention to hurt anyone besides Rue.

He had to stop this. There was no point in lamenting over something he couldn't undo. What was done was done. It might not have been a total waste if he'd gotten even a tad of satisfaction out of making Rue suffer. But even that backfired.

30

ON WEDNESDAY MORNING, Rue and Ivy were waiting in Montana's hospital room for the nurse to bring the discharge papers when Joel Myers squeezed through the doorway carrying a bouquet of brightly colored balloons.

"Hey, Joel!" A smile stole across Montana's face. "Whoa! How cool."

"They're from your Sunday-school class. Each kid used a Magic Marker and wrote a greeting on one of the balloons." Joel winked at Rue and Ivy. "We got together last night to make this bouquet, and then we prayed for you. The kids wanted to come over here with me, but we knew your doctor wouldn't think that was a good idea."

"Wow, that's a lot of balloons!"

"Well, you've got a lot of well-wishers." Joel took the bundle of balloon strings and tied them to the bedpost. "You and your folks will have to read them together later."

"Did you see my sling?" Montana said.

"Sure did. I hear you have to keep that Velcro cast on for a few weeks."

"Yeah, but I can use my other arm till this one gets well."

Joel tousled Montana's hair. "You might even feel well enough to come to Sunday school this week."

Montana's eyebrows came together, and his expression turned somber. "Do I have to tell what happened?"

"Absolutely not. Everyone already knows. We just like it when you're there. Besides, you're the champ at memorizing Bible verses. You don't want to lose your title, do you?"

Montana shook his head.

"By the way, Rue," Joel said, "things are going well out at the site. The roofers are blowin' and goin'. Grayson's keeping us on target. Don't worry about a thing."

"That's great to hear. I appreciate everybody working to keep the momentum going. I'll probably be out there in the morning."

"All right, Montana, my man." Joel gave him a playful punch on his good shoulder. "I need to go to work."

"Thanks for the humongous balloons. I hope they can fit in the truck."

"Don't worry," Rue said. "I brought your mom's Jeep, so we have room for all the flowers and plants there in the window *and* all these balloons."

"And my Windy dog!"

"Yep. That, too."

Flint sat at the table in his office and captured a yawn with his hand. He wondered how Buck could be so alert when he'd been up half the night.

Bobby opened a pack of bubblegum and offered them a piece. "I wonder what's keepin' Nick?"

"I'm here!" Nick hustled through the doorway and over to the table and sat next to Flint.

"Sorry to keep you waiting," he said. "First of all, great job, Buck. We've got our sketch artist working with your friend Jack, and we're about to get our first glimpse of these clowns. We also got DNA off the three beer mugs—none on file at NCIC. We got prints, but several people handled the mugs, so we're still sorting through that. They paid cash, so we don't have a credit-card receipt. But we're moving in the right direction."

"It's about time we got a break," Bobby said.

"There's more." Nick thumbed through the papers in his hands. "Buck got statements from everyone who was at the Blue Moon when these guys were ranting. Most had never seen them before. But one fella, Patrick Winn, thinks the guy with the heart tattoo works for Sullivan Logging. We're checking that out right now."

Buck folded his hands on the table. "We should have Jack listen to the recording of the voice on Mrs. Baughman's answering machine, too. Maybe he'll recognize it. I feel like we're on to something."

Nick nodded. "As relates to the crimes against Baughman, anyway. The retaliatory crimes are another story. I'm not ready to rule out SAGE altogether, but it's seeming less and less likely that anyone from that group set the fire at the Griffiths or at Everhardt Roofing. And I'd bet the farm that SAGE wasn't involved in either of the crimes against the Kesslers.

"So…Bobby, I want you to talk to the Kesslers and start digging into their backgrounds for someone who might want to hurt them. Ivy was deep into the drug world. Maybe there's someone from her past that has it in for her and is piggybacking on the attacks as an opportunity to hurt her family and avoid suspicion."

"I'm on it," Bobby said.

"Buck, I want you to team up with my agents and track these three men from the Blue Moon."

Grayson went into the trailer at the work site and poured himself a cup of coffee.

"So how's it going, Liz?"

"It's a little lonesome with my guys out," she said. "But Elam's coming in this afternoon. And Rue will be back in the morning. If that's all I have to whine about, lucky me."

"Isn't that the truth?" Grayson blew on his coffee. "I saw Montana yesterday during my lunch break. He wasn't doing too bad, all things considered."

"He's going home this morning."

"I didn't know that."

"Rue and his family are going to stay out at Elam's for a while," Liz said. "They thought being together might help them all deal with the fear. I'll sure be glad when they lock up the slimeballs that are doing this stuff. By the way, Rue said to tell you thanks for keeping things running. Joel stopped by the hospital this morning and put in a good word for you."

Grayson took a sip of coffee. "I'm glad to help."

Liz stopped typing and peered over the top of her half glasses. "I hope someone's watching your back. Elam and Rue have both been attacked. If someone's out to shut down this project, you could be next."

"I hope not. When the trouble started, my brother Bobby had a deputy cruiser parked in front of our house. The authorities are stretched too thin to do that now. But I haven't been threatened. I doubt SAGE is going to go after a construction foreman as long as they can get to the brass."

"Well, I'd be freaked if it were me."

Grayson glanced out the window. "I can't afford to freak. I've got too much to do. I'm going to head over and see how the roofers are doing. Page me if you need me."

As the morning wore on, Grayson became even more obsessed with the idea of going back to the scene of the shooting.

He took his cell phone off his belt clip and hit the auto-dial.

"This is Knolls."

"Hey, it's Grayson. What are you up to?"

"Oh, just doin' some grunt work for Special Agent Sanchez. He's crawled up on his throne and is really enjoyin' dolin' out orders."

"Any breaks in the shooting?"

"Nothin' new. We finished our investigation of the scene. Now it's a matter of comin' up with suspects."

"Still don't think SAGE was involved?"

There was a long pause, and then Bobby said, "Listen, Grays. I don't mean to shut you out, but I really can't talk about this stuff. There're too many angles right now, and I already said more than I should've."

"I'm just fond of Montana and anxious for you to get the guy who hurt him, that's all."

"That's the plan. I gotta get back to work."

"All right, Bobby. Talk to you later."

Grayson disconnected the call and glanced at his watch, then keyed in the auto-dial for the office.

"EG Construction, this is Liz."

"It's Grayson. I'm going to lunch. I have an errand to run, so I'll be gone for an hour. Any idea what time Elam's coming in?"

"He said around three."

"I should be back by one thirty."

"Okey-dokey. I'm not going anywhere."

Grayson put his phone on the belt clip and walked over to his truck and climbed in the front seat. He backed out and drove down to the gate, then waved at the security guard and headed for Three Peaks Road.

Rue sat on the front steps at his in-laws' house and scanned the open range and the postcard view of the mountains. At the bottom of the hill, about two hundred yards from where he sat, he could see the log buildings of Three Peaks nestled in the trees.

He had always regarded the chalet as a temporary home, but he wondered if his excitement to build on the new property would ever come back now that the ground had been soaked with Montana's blood. Could his family ever be happy there in the shadow of such a horrible memory?

He was immensely grateful that Montana wasn't going to suffer long-term effects from the gunshot wound. So why did he feel as if a two-ton weight were still sitting on his chest? Why was he moping? Why couldn't he muster any energy?

Elam came out and sat next to him on the step. "How're you doing?"

"I'm numb, I guess. I can't seem to get excited about anything at the moment. Maybe I'm finally allowing myself to crash."

"I just talked to Flint. He said they're really stepping up the pace on the investigations. They want these guys as much as we do."

"Good." Rue cracked his knuckles. "Elam, does all this stuff scare you?"

"You bet it does. Montana's getting shot knocked the wind out of me. If throwing in the towel on the retirement project would stop the violence, I'd do it in a heartbeat, regardless of the financial loss. But Flint's discouraging me from doing that."

"I don't think he believes SAGE did any of this. I don't know why he won't just come right out and say it."

"He's not going to say anything until he has proof. And I'm not convinced he thinks SAGE's hands are clean." Elam turned to him. "Why'd you ask if I was afraid?"

"Because I am. Deep in my gut. It's the *not* knowing who did it and if he's going to strike again that gets to me. I can't really say anything to Ivy because I don't want to make her more afraid than she already is. If I get weak, who's she gonna lean on?"

"I know you want to be strong. Just don't try to take the Lord's place. Right now, He's the One we all need to be leaning on."

"You ever wonder why He lets stuff like this happen?"

Elam tugged at his mustache. "Sure. But it seems like every time I come through something difficult, I'm a little stronger."

"Has the situation with Rusty made you stronger?"

Elam smiled gingerly. "Not yet. I honestly don't know how to get through to Rusty. Maybe you and I should get together and pray about that and everything else."

"You serious? Because I'd really like to."

"How about we take a few minutes in the mornings before we start work?"

"That'd be great. I've never done much praying with other men. But being afraid is something I would find difficult to pray with Ivy about."

Elam put his hand on Rue's shoulder. "Don't feel bad. Carolyn and I share almost everything, but I don't talk to her about that kind of thing, either. I guess we guys find it easier to let down with each other."

There was a long comfortable silence, then Rue said, "What if we can't get past this and the memory overshadows our excitement about the new house?"

"Give it time, Son."

Son. No one had called him that since his father died. He sat quietly for a moment and let it soak in. Finally, he said, "You really think time will erase the memory?"

Elam stroked his mustache. "No, only God can do that. But time will give you space to get excited again. Right now, you're angry and scared and beat-up. You've got to work through that first. Maybe we can do it together."

Rue heard a car motor and saw what appeared to be a squad car coming up the long drive. "Is that the sheriff?"

Elam squinted and seemed to study the vehicle for a few seconds. "That's not Flint's car. It's Bobby's."

Rue sat with Ivy, Elam, and Carolyn at the kitchen table, eager to hear Bobby Knolls explain the reason for his visit.

"We're makin' headway on the attacks against Mrs. Baughman," Bobby said. "Also on the arson fire here and at Everhardt's. But we can't find anything to link them to the vandalism or the shootin'. Special Agent Sanchez wants us to pursue a different angle, and that's where I come in. I need both of you to stretch your thinkin' and try to imagine someone, past or present, who might have a bone to pick with you."

Ivy made a tent with her fingers. "I hung out with some unsavory characters in my drug days. But as far as I know, I don't owe anybody money. I don't really have any enemies."

"What about you, Rue? You were boozin' it pretty heavy for a while. Did you step on somebody's toes?"

"Not that I know of. I wasn't a belligerent drunk."

Bobby shifted his gaze to Ivy. "You witnessed Joe Hadley's murder and sat on it for ten years. Who might wanna get back at you for that?"

"I can't imagine."

"Well, try. The Baughmans would have you believe that SAGE didn't have anything to do with the fires or the attacks on your family. So let's find another explanation."

Ivy shrugged. "I don't know. I made peace with Joe's parents. Everyone else involved is dead."

"Well, we can't blow off the possibility that someone from your past is tryin' to get back at you through your family."

"Hold on, Lieutenant," Rue said. "This thing started when someone attacked Madison Baughman and threatened her. And then someone burned Elam's stable as a payback. I don't see that Ivy fits into this scenario at all."

Bobby blew a pink bubble and sucked it back into his mouth. "If you want us to get whoever shot your son, we need to explore every angle—even the ones that make you uncomfortable."

"All right," Rue said. "But I don't know what we can tell you."

Bobby scribbled something on a ruled pad. "Let's talk about work. Elam handed each of you good jobs in spite of your recent bouts with addiction and rehab. Must've created some resentment."

"Stop right there," Elam said. "Let me set the record straight. First of all, Rue is well qualified to manage the retirement village project. He's got the experience and the education to back it up. I didn't *hand* him anything. Second, the staff at Three Peaks was one hundred percent behind me hiring Ivy to run registration. And she's done great. Everyone out there loves her."

Bobby turned his attention to Ivy. "Is that how *you* see it?"

"Everyone's been very accepting…and they're all nice people. None of them is capable of something like this."

"Rue, what about you?" Bobby said. "Any friction at work?"

"Nothing out of the ordinary. Everyone seems to respect what I've brought to the table. I just don't see anyone there wanting to hurt me or my family."

"What about subcontractors or someone you deal with? Ticked anybody off?"

"I don't think so. I'm just beginning to know these people. I've put my best foot forward."

"Ever put your foot in your mouth?"

Rue's eyebrows came together. "Probably. But nothing specific comes to mind."

Elam exhaled loudly. "Bobby, if anybody in this family has rubbed someone the wrong way, it's me. You know I don't mince words and have no trouble speaking my mind. But so help me, I can't think of anybody I've offended that would shoot my grandson."

31

GRAYSON GLANCED IN HIS REARVIEW mirror and didn't see any vehicles behind him on Three Peaks Road. He slowed his truck and turned onto the same unmarked road he had taken last time, then veered off into the tall grass and parked near the pond.

He sat in the truck a few minutes, watching a great blue heron stalking a fish, and considered the futility of going back to the scene of the shooting. What was done was done. But saying that over and over didn't ease his conscience. He had to do this. He had to retrace his steps and come to peace with it being an accident. He had to relive it so he could let it go.

Grayson hung his binoculars around his neck and got out of the truck. He trudged through the high grass, then climbed over the split-rail fence. What if the feds had determined this is where the shooter had entered the property? What if they had hidden surveillance cameras in hopes that he'd come back? He stopped and surveyed his surroundings. Why was he being so paranoid? The odds that they had been able to pin that down were next to nothing. He continued tramping through the high grass until he found the trail he had discovered before. He followed it into the woods and across a small stream, then hiked uphill through a densely wooded area and stopped at the edge of the clearing.

He put his palms against the same tree he had used to steady himself and looked down at the road. The horror of the moment came rushing back: Windy spotted in the cross hairs...the deer startling him...the rifle going off…Montana's body sprawled and bleeding on the road. His heart felt as if it were falling down an empty elevator shaft.

God, in case You really do exist, I'm sorry. I never meant for this to happen.

Did sorry even matter? He focused on the road, reliving the accident over and over in his mind until it didn't seem quite so overwhelming.

He heard a noise and realized it was a car motor. He stayed behind the tree and put the binoculars to his eyes as a white SUV appeared on the road and pulled up in front of the house. The male driver got out and stood with his arms folded, seemingly studying the house. The man appeared to be younger than he. Probably a subcontractor Rue had hired.

Grayson noticed the time and decided he should be heading back to work. He started to leave when the man opened the rear door of the SUV and took out what appeared to be two large plastic containers of gasoline.

Grayson felt as if his feet were staked to the ground. Was this the guy who had torched Elam's stable and Everhardt's office building? What should he do? What *could* he do? Confronting him was out. The guy could be armed. And if he called 911 on his cell, the call could be traced to him, and he would be forced to offer an explanation of why he was there.

The man set one of the gas cans next to the door and stepped inside, carrying the other. Grayson could hear his own heartbeat pounding in his ears. How weird was this? He had the power to finger the guy who had set the fires, and yet he didn't dare. Then again, why would he want to stop him? Wouldn't having Rue's house go up in smoke achieve what he had wanted all along?

Rue shifted in his chair, too exhausted to think clearly, and wished Bobby Knolls would wrap it up.

"Lieutenant, are we about done?" Rue said. "We've been over the same questions at least twice. We're not hiding anything from you.

We just don't know who might want to hurt our family. If we did, we would tell you. No one wants this creep locked up any more than we do."

"Yeah, I know." Bobby made some notes on the pad. "Sorry if it feels like I'm pushin' too hard, but we can't afford to lose momentum. It's critical we get as much information as possible if we're gonna think beyond SAGE to who else might wanna hurt you."

"But haven't we covered everything?"

"We're gettin' close. Did you have professional enemies when you were a construction foreman in Denver?"

"Not that I know of," Rue said. "I got along with everybody. That's probably why I advanced to foreman as quickly as I did."

"Any chance someone could've been jealous of you for that?"

"I suppose there's a possibility that someone with a twisted mind could've resented it. But it's a stretch. It's not like I was drafted into the majors, for crying out loud."

"All right." Bobby directed his attention to Ivy. "Is there any chance Montana's biological father might want to hurt him?"

There was a clumsy moment of silence, then Ivy exhaled loudly as if to show her annoyance. "*Rue* is Montana's biological father, Lieutenant."

Bobby's face turned redder than the pen he was writing with. "Sorry, I thought Rue adopted him."

"We had his name changed, that's all," Ivy said.

Rue put his arm around her. "Is there anything else? We're both pretty exhausted."

"That oughta do it for now. Sorry for the intrusion. But we really wanna nail this guy, and we're pullin' out all the stops."

Rue stood as if to signal Bobby to do the same. "We're all for that. If we think of anything later on, we'll give you a call."

Grayson barreled down Three Peaks Road and headed back to the work site, fifteen minutes behind schedule. He didn't expect Liz to ask questions. Not that she would know the exact time he returned anyway.

He couldn't believe he had just witnessed an arsonist soak Rue
Kessler's house inside and out, and then turn it into a bonfire. He pulled
down his rearview mirror and saw dark smoke billowing into the bluebird sky. He didn't want to be seen in this area. Not now. Not today.

Grayson was flooded with the same rush he felt when he had vandalized Rue's truck. Satisfaction at last! And he didn't even have to strike
the match. The idea of Rue losing his dream house didn't faze him in
the least. He could always rebuild. *Now* he would understand how it felt
to lose something important.

He heard a siren and spotted flashing lights in his rearview mirror.
Was the officer coming after him? Should he pull over? Speed up? Pull
off and make a run for it? Had someone been watching him after all? If
so, they would know he hadn't gone within fifty yards of Rue's house. He
took in a slow deep breath and let it out. No need to panic. He hadn't
done anything wrong. Just stay calm. Be cool.

He noticed the car seemed to be slipping back and then saw it turn
toward the Kesslers' property. Someone must have seen the smoke and
reported it.

Grayson stepped on the accelerator and pushed his old truck as fast
as it would go. He figured whoever was in that squad car was about to
pass the arsonist driving in the other direction. All he wanted was to get
out of there.

Rue leaned forward in the passenger seat of Elam's Suburban as it rocked
and bounced over the uneven terrain and finally came to a stop in front
of the flaming house.

He heard a siren and assumed the pumper truck was coming. Didn't
matter. The house was engulfed. Nothing could save it now.

He got out of the car, coughing in the smoky air, and stared in disbelief at what was left of the dream house he'd planned for Ivy. He was
glad he talked her into staying at her parents' house while he and her
father came to investigate. She didn't need to see this.

Lord, why are You allowing these awful things to happen to us?

Bobby Knolls came over to him. "When I was leavin' your in-laws' place I saw the smoke and had a bad feelin', so I headed over here to investigate. I'm really sorry you got hit again."

"You think it's arson?"

"We'll have to wait for the fire marshal to call it," Bobby said. "But the way things've been goin' lately, it wouldn't surprise me."

"Did you pass anyone on the road, Lieutenant?"

"Nah. But the perp could've gone the other way and wound around to Road G9 and gotten on Three Peaks Road."

"How'd you know that?" Rue said.

"It's my job to know everything. We combed every inch of this property after the shootin'. There're fresh tire tracks and footprints around the house. Maybe that'll give us somethin'."

The siren was louder now. Through the trees, Rue got a glimpse of the pumper truck turning on to the dirt road. He felt a hand on his shoulder.

"You okay?" Elam said.

"I seriously doubt it."

"Flint and Nick are going to get these guys, Rue. We've just got to believe that."

"Well, no one from SAGE called to warn us. Maybe the lieutenant is right about someone from the past wanting to hurt us. Nothing else makes sense."

Rue heard a loud cracking noise and realized the roof was collapsing in on itself. He shielded his face as sparks flew everywhere and his dream was reduced to a pile of burning rubble.

Grayson arrived back at the work site and realized he had forgotten to eat his lunch. He inspected the work on Building Three and then Buildings Four and Five, amazed that the roofers were finished and had moved on.

His pager beeped. He smiled when he saw the number. Of course it was Liz. She was about to tell him about the fire.

He took out his cell phone and pressed the auto-dial for the office. *Just sound surprised and outraged.*

"EG Construction. This is Liz."

"It's Grayson."

"Elam just called," she said. "You're not going to believe this, but Rue's new house burned to the ground. The sheriff thinks it was arson."

"What?" Grayson shouted. "Man, this is getting ridiculous! In broad daylight?"

"Yep. Rue's place is out in the sticks. But still…" Liz sighed into the receiver. "I think the whole world's gone mad. Tell that brother of yours he needs to get busy and figure out who's doing this. You could be next."

"Maybe Bobby will put a cruiser back on our street."

"Sure seems warranted. Anyhow, Elam won't be in this afternoon and wanted me to make sure you would be."

"Yeah, I'm here. I'll stay till the guys knock off. It's the least I can do."

"Watch your back, you hear?"

"I will. Page me if you find out any details about the fire."

Grayson disconnected the call and saw Joel Myers coming his way.

"Did you hear about Rue's house?" Joel said.

"Yeah, just. Liz told me. How'd *you* know?"

"My dad called. He and Mom were on their way out to Elam's. Rue and Ivy are staying there for a while, and my folks thought the whole family could use spiritual support. It's been some week." Joel put his hands in his pockets. "I don't mind telling you I'm concerned about you and Tara and the kids. I'm praying you'll be safe."

"Thanks. Bobby's not going to let anything happen to us."

Joel gave a nod. "Good. I'll get back to work. Just wanted to check with you."

"Thanks, Joel." Grayson's cell phone rang. He took it off his belt clip and put it to his ear. "This is Grayson."

"It's Bobby. Have you heard about the fire at the Kesslers' place?"

"Yeah, Liz just told me. What's the deal?"

"The fire marshal says it's arson and is workin' with the ATF specialist to determine if the arsonist used the same MO as the fires at the Griffiths' and Everhardt's. I hate to say it, but we're stretched too thin right now for me to send a cruiser again. Don't let your guard down, okay? If anything seems suspicious, call me—anytime, day or night."

"I will. Talk to you later."

Grayson disconnected the call, struck by the irony and an ominous foreboding that he really might be next.

32

RUE SAT IN THE GLIDER on Elam and Carolyn's front porch, too numb to deal with any of the feelings that were competing for his attention. Why would anyone want to hurt him or Ivy badly enough to shoot Montana? And burn down their new house? Or even vandalize his truck? *Was* it someone from his past—or Ivy's?

His mind had raced back through the past several years until his head hurt. He couldn't remember ever stepping on anyone's toes enough to warrant this kind of retaliation. Ivy was admittedly too stoned to remember huge chunks of the years she was hooked on drugs. Maybe this was somehow linked to a drug debt or a disgruntled dealer.

He couldn't ignore the possibility that the caller who had warned Elam to shut down the retirement village project decided to go after Elam's family when burning the stable didn't persuade him.

Rue rubbed the back of his neck. How would the authorities ever figure out what was going on? About the only thing he felt relatively sure of was that SAGE wasn't behind it. But even that was up in the air.

He heard the door open, and a second later Windy darted out and his son crawled up in the glider and nestled next to him.

"Don't be sad," Montana said. "I can help you build the house again. I'm a good helper. I'll work really, really hard."

Rue swallowed hard and blinked the stinging from his eyes. "Thanks, champ. I know you will."

"Everything's gonna be all right, Dad. I asked Jesus to help the sheriff find the mean guys."

"Thanks." Rue turned and kissed the top of Montana's head, wishing he were as trusting.

"Joel told us that Jesus listens to children. So I'll keep asking, okay?"

"Absolutely. Mommy and I will ask Him, too. And Grandma and Grandpa. Everything's going to work out." *I hope.* "How's your arm feeling?"

"It hurts really a lot."

Rue looked down just as Montana looked up, his face flushed. Rue felt his forehead. "You're warm. Did Mommy give you Tylenol for the fever?"

"Uh-huh. Before I came out here. Will you take me to see where the fire was?"

"Sometime. But not today. I think we all need to get some rest. Plus it might be upsetting for you to go back where you got shot. Maybe it's good to wait a while."

"Can Ian come visit me?"

"Sure. Have you talked to him yet?"

Montana nodded. "His mom said it's okay, but he can't stay long till I'm better."

"Maybe tomorrow, okay? I think we need to spend the rest of the day being quiet."

There was a long pause. Finally, Montana said, "Do you wanna be quiet because you're scared?"

"Why would you ask me that?" Rue kept his eyes on the mountains.

"Well, *I'm* scared. But I'm trying to be really brave so Mom won't be afraid. It makes me sad when she cries."

Rue put his arm around Montana. "Me, too. I know things are a little scary right now, but you let me worry about it, okay? It's my job to try and protect you and Mommy while Jesus helps the sheriff find whoever's doing these awful things."

"I prayed for the mean guys, too. They must not know Jesus, or they wouldn't want to hurt us."

Rue hid his vengeful feelings from the light of his son's forgiving spirit. The last thing he felt like doing at the moment was praying for the losers who were trying to destroy them.

Flint stood outside the smoldering ruins of Rue and Ivy's house. What kind of perp was brazen enough to strike the Kesslers twice in only a matter of days? And for what purpose? This crime just didn't have the feel of someone wanting to persuade Elam to shut down the retirement project. He saw Nick Sanchez coming over to him.

"It appears we've got another gasoline fire," Nick said. "Started on the far living room wall. The fire marshal believes the arsonist made a Molotov cocktail out of a beer bottle and tossed it through one of the openings where the front windows were going to be."

Flint popped a couple Tums and chewed them. "It's a crying shame. About the only good news is that the financial loss won't be catastrophic at this stage. It shouldn't take too long to build back what they had."

"The ATF specialist can't say for sure that this was done by the arsonists that set the fires at the Griffiths' and at Everhardt's. But no one called to warn the Kesslers or claim responsibility."

"Maybe they tried and couldn't get an answer at their house, since the Kesslers are staying at Elam's."

"Good thinking," Nick said. "We'll check it out. But we didn't find any of the same shoe impressions out here. Mostly work boots. And a size nine-and-a-half athletic shoe or oxford. We'll see if we can identify the brands. But it could take time matching the shoes to the wearer, since this place has been crawling with different work crews over the past few weeks. We gathered all kinds of evidence: aluminum cans, bottles, wrappers, gum, cigarettes, wads of chewing tobacco. But tracing whatever

DNA we find to specific individuals, especially if it's not on file at NCIC, is almost impossible."

Flint made a sweeping motion with his hand. "What about all these tire tracks?"

"Most are overlapping and didn't leave distinct tread impressions. We're checking out the few that did. But again, matching the tread to the tire, the tire to the vehicle, and the vehicle to one of many workmen could be time consuming. Most of the tracks suggest the size tire we'd expect to find on trucks or SUVs."

"Did you find tire tracks on the road?"

Nick folded his arms across his chest. "Nothing recent. The impressions we found were made when the road was muddy from the rains a couple weeks ago. That graded road is packed down now and didn't tell us anything. We assume the perp exited the back way, since Lieutenant Knolls didn't pass him on the way up here. It's possible he was on foot, but I doubt it."

Flint shook his head. "Why do I feel really dumb?"

"Well, don't. This is complex. We're going to get these guys…but we've sure got a puzzle to solve."

"I assume you've given up trying to come up with a profile on the arsonists?"

Nick sighed. "I'm afraid so. I think we're dealing with different scenarios, perps, and motives. And I have strong doubts that SAGE was involved at all."

"So where does that leave us?"

Nick eyed the smoldering remnants. "Stumped at the moment. I'm thinking the perps who attacked Mrs. Baughman, poisoned her dog, and torched the field behind her house make up the first thread in the case. The arsonists who burned Elam's stable and Everhardt's office building are the second thread. And whoever vandalized Rue's truck and shot Montana and torched the house is the third thread. But if we eliminate SAGE as the retaliatory second thread, I'm really baffled."

Rue sat at his in-laws' kitchen table, grateful for a delicious dinner and a safe place to stay, but wishing life were back to normal and he was home with Ivy and Montana.

"This salmon is great," he said to Carolyn. "I don't know what you put in the glaze, but it's really tasty."

"I'll give Ivy the recipe. It's easy."

The phone rang. "Want me to get it?" Rue said.

Elam nodded.

"Griffith residence, this is Rue Kessler speaking."

"Why am I not surprised you're over there?"

"Hello, Rusty. Did you want to speak with one of your parents?"

"I'm returning my dad's call."

"Hang on." Rue handed the phone to Elam.

"Rusty, I'm putting you on speakerphone. This concerns the whole family." Elam signaled for Rue to push the Speaker button. "Did you watch the evening news?"

"No, I just got home. Why?"

"Ivy and Rue's new house was burned to the ground today. Arson."

"What in the world's going on?" Rusty said. "First you. Now them. Am I going to have to look over my shoulder, too? Why doesn't the sheriff just shut down that environmental organization?"

"It's complicated. Even the feds aren't sure SAGE is setting the fires."

"Well, they'd better figure it out before someone really gets hurt."

"They're trying," Elam said. "Thankfully, Rue and Ivy have insurance, and rebuilding won't be a problem. I just wanted you to hear it from us."

"Thanks for that. I don't like hearing our family business from other sources."

"You made that clear, Son. That's why I called. Did you hear any more from Jacqueline about the nibble you had on your house?"

"It didn't amount to anything. The couple made an offer on another house. Guess it just wasn't meant to be."

Elam glanced over at Carolyn. "I wish you'd let your mother and me fly Jacqueline and the girls here for a visit."

"I appreciate the offer, Dad, but this isn't a good time. The girls are involved in too many activities. And I'm spending every waking moment at the clinic."

"Then how about a long weekend?"

"Maybe later. Listen, my call waiting is beeping. It's probably Jacqueline. I'll talk to you later. Tell Rue and Ivy I'm sorry about the fire."

"They're sitting right here, Rusty. Why don't you tell them?"

"I thought I just did. I need to take this call. Catch you later." *Click.*

Elam handed the phone back to Rue. "At least he said he was sorry about the fire."

"Yes, and he was just oozing with concern about our son's condition," Ivy said, "like someone hasn't *already* been hurt!"

Elam tilted her chin. "Baby steps, honey. It's a start. I sure wish he'd let me fly the girls here for a short visit. I don't think it's good for the family to be apart."

"In some ways," Carolyn said, "it may be easier on them if he has concentrated time to devote to the clinic. It has to be a challenge taking on someone else's practice. He would probably be distracted anyway."

Elam nodded. "I suppose. He just seems more agreeable when the girls are around."

"Not at Thanksgiving, he wasn't," Ivy said.

Rue kicked her under the table. "So what's the plan for the Fourth of July? Is it still on at the Carters'?"

"If Montana's up to it," Carolyn said. "We'll have a cookout around five. Later, we can drive over to Tanner Lake for the fireworks display."

"I'm going!" Montana said.

Rue took Ivy's hand in his and squeezed it. "It'll be a much-needed mental break for all of us."

Ivy's eyes brimmed with tears. "You're right. It's been a horrible week. I just don't want to think about it anymore."

Later that evening, Flint and Nick had a follow-up meeting with Buck Lowry and Bobby Knolls.

"All right, gentlemen," Buck said. "Here's the artist's sketch of our rednecks from the Blue Moon Tavern." He gave everyone present three sheets of paper, each sheet displaying a different facial drawing. "Scruffy characters, all of them. The blond guy is the one with the heart tattoo. We showed his picture to the HR person at Sullivan Logging and found out his name is Sonny Halstead. Age twenty-two. Worked for Sullivan until April of this year when he was laid off along with nine other loggers. We matched the prints from one of the beer mugs to his driver's license. He's also the registered owner of a white 2006 Ford F150. He's moved and left no forwarding address, so we don't know where he is just yet. But we'll turn over every rock till we find him. We're checking out the other nine loggers who were laid off."

"Excellent," Nick said. "Lieutenant, how'd you make out?"

Bobby leaned forward. "I talked to the Kesslers and turned their pasts inside out. Rattled their chains. Neither of them could think of anybody who'd wanna get back at them—or at least that they'd admit would. They seemed cooperative and scared. If they're holdin' back, they won't for long."

"And you're the one who discovered the Kesslers' house burning?" Nick said.

"Yeah, after I left the Griffiths' place and got on Three Peaks Road, I spotted a billow of black smoke comin' from what appeared to be the Kesslers' property. I stepped on it and raced over there. And through the trees, I could see the house burnin', so I called it in, and then called the Kesslers. Didn't pass anyone on the road leadin' up to the house. When I arrived, the place was engulfed."

Nick folded his hands on the table. "The fire marshal and ATF specialist confirmed that the arsonist's MO is the same. But we didn't find any of the same shoe impressions. And no one called to warn the Kesslers or claim responsibility."

Flint listened as Nick explained to Buck and Bobby how he viewed the three threads of the cases.

"I admit I'm stumped at the moment." Nick studied the papers with the artist's sketches. "I think our best shot now is to find Sonny Halstead and to identify these other two clowns. If it turns out this trio is responsible for the attacks on Mrs. Baughman, maybe they can shed some light on who's doing the retaliating. Buck, I want you to stay on it. That'll keep us moving on thread one."

Buck nodded. "You got it."

"I'm going to have my agents dig deeper into the arson fires at the Griffiths' and Everhardt's," Nick said. "If SAGE isn't responsible, then we need to figure out who is. That'll keep us moving on thread two.

"The third thread bothers me more than the others because these incidents seem highly personal and vindictive. Lieutenant, you're the best at getting the truth out of people. Stay on the Kesslers and keep them talking. Find out if there's anyone—past or present—that wants to hurt them. There may be someone they haven't thought of yet."

Bobby gave a slight nod. "If there is, I'll get it out of them."

"Also, I want you to dig deeper into the vandalism incident. Go back to Three Peaks and search for anything we might've missed that would offer a clue as to who might've defaced Rue's truck. I'll have my agents continue to investigate the shooting and fire on the Kesslers' property. That'll keep us moving on the third thread. Any questions?"

Flint stroked the stubble on his chin. "If SAGE is eliminated as a suspect, do we even have a *motive* for the arson fires that make up the second thread?"

"No." Nick blew out a breath. "And we sure need to find one."

33

GRAYSON SAT ON THE COUCH with Tara and turned on the ten o'clock news, figuring the lead story would be the arson fire at the Kesslers' house.

"Good evening. This is Jillian Parker…"

"And I'm Watson Smyth. Welcome to the ten o'clock news. Tanner County residents are outraged, and authorities are scratching their heads after an arson fire today destroyed the home of Rue and Ivy Kessler, just three days after their eight-year-old son Montana was shot by an unknown assailant on the same property where today's fire was started."

Grayson picked up the remote and turned up the sound.

"A lieutenant in the sheriff's department just happened to be in the area and saw smoke and reported the fire. But the house, which was under construction, was engulfed before the pumper trucks from White Top and Jacob's Ear arrived on the scene.

"Sources inside the sheriff's department told us that Madison Baughman, the president of SAGE, is not believed to be linked to any of the crimes. Roving reporter Jessica Monrovia has been knocking on the doors of some law-enforcement officials to get answers. Jessica, what can you tell us?"

"Oh, come on," Grayson said. "Everyone knows SAGE did it."

"Watson, I attempted to get a statement from Marshal Redmond, Sheriff Carter, and Special Agent Sanchez of the FBI, but all declined to comment, citing the ongoing investigation. However, Mayor Lester Smart of Jacob's Ear was certainly not at a loss for words, as you'll see in this clip from my interview with him…"

"This ought to be good," Grayson said.

"How do I feel?" The mayor hooked his thumbs on his red suspenders. *"Sick and tired of the rhetoric. It's unconscionable to me that authorities haven't shut SAGE down until this circus of an investigation is completed. Are we supposed to just* blow off *the anonymous caller who claimed SAGE was responsible fore the first two fires? The situation is out of control. A little boy was shot, for Pete's sake. Is someone going to have to die before authorities deal with the obvious?"*

"My sentiments exactly." Grayson gave the mayor two thumbs up. "I knew there was a reason I voted for him."

"Watson, as you could tell, the mayor was visibly shaken and upset. He had a lot more to say that I didn't include. But I thought it was only fair that we give SAGE a chance to respond, so I spoke with the president, Madison Baughman, who offered a very different perspective. Here's what she had to say..."

Grayson turned to Tara and rolled his eyes. "Like she's going to admit knowing anything."

"Jessica, I can only tell you and your viewers what I believe from the bottom of my heart: that no one in my organization is capable of doing the things we're accused of. We are peaceful, God-fearing people who have a passion for saving all God's earth. That's who we are. That's what we do. But we do it prayerfully, lawfully, and without coercion or violence. My husband and I personally met with the Kesslers after their son was shot and expressed our deep concern for their pain and assured them that SAGE had nothing to do with the shooting or the fires or even the vandalism. They agreed to join with us in praying for the guilty parties to be caught. I can't speak for the authorities. But until they decide to speak for themselves, I fully intend to deny publicly and emphatically that SAGE was involved in any of these crimes."

Grayson folded his arms across his chest. "So now they're going to hide behind their *religion?*"

"Watson, there are so many pieces to this puzzle that don't fit, it's no wonder the authorities aren't talking. But one thing is sure: families are hurt-

ing and suffering loss. And no one seems to know how to stop this madness. This is Jessica Monrovia, back to you…"

"Thanks, Jessica. We will keep on top of this story and report any breaking news as it happens. In other news tonight, the principal of Tanner County High School—"

Grayson patted Tara's knee, then went to the kitchen and poured himself a glass of water. He felt surprisingly little compassion for Rue's loss. So what if he lost his big fancy house? He could always rebuild. He still had his twenty-five acres, his adoring wife, and his fat salary.

The image of Montana lying on the road, sprawled and bleeding, popped into his head, and he blinked it away. He was not going to let his remorse over the shooting accident spoil his satisfaction that Rue had finally been dealt a blow he deserved.

"Grayson, you okay?" He felt Tara's hand massaging his back.

"Yeah, honey. I'm just a little rattled about the Kesslers losing their house. They've really been through it."

"I know. It's awful."

Grayson pulled her into his arms. "You scared?"

"Of course I am. I feel like a target, especially now that there's no deputy cruiser parked out front."

Grayson considered the cracker box of a house they owned. Not that he wanted someone to burn it down. But he wondered if he'd come out ahead financially if they did.

The phone rang. Grayson glanced at the clock. "That can't be good."

Flint took a can of Orange Crush out of the fridge and went outside on the porch, where it was cool. He sat on the glider and popped the top on the can and took a big gulp of soda. The cold liquid seemed to put out the fire in his gut. Why was he letting this case get to him? He almost never fell into a deep sleep anymore, and he was eating Tums like candy. Now he found it hard to focus on anything else. He just wanted the whole thing to go away—only it wasn't.

His cell phone vibrated. He blew out a breath. What now? He put the phone to his ear. "Sheriff Carter."

"Flint, it's Pastor Myers. I'm sorry to bother you so late, but I'm not sure what to do. Joel hasn't come home from work and hasn't called. He never does that. I checked with the foreman, Grayson Knolls. He said Joel left the construction site around eight. He wouldn't not come home without telling his mother or me."

"Have you checked with friends?"

"I have. No one's seen him."

"Does he have a girlfriend?"

"No one steady. Something's wrong, Flint. This kid always calls when he's going to be late. But he's never been *this* late. After what's been happening to Elam and Rue, I'm really nervous."

"When did you talk to Grayson?"

"Just a couple minutes ago. Do I need to file a missing person's report or something?"

Flint took a gulp of Orange Crush. "It's a bit premature for that. Do you know if Joel comes home the same way every night?"

"I think he usually takes Miner's Highway. But once in a while he likes to listen to teaching tapes and takes the long way through Tanner Canyon. Terri is beside herself. I'm about to go searching for him."

"Why don't you let me pick you up, and we'll ride out to the canyon together? In the meantime, I'll send a deputy to check out Miner's Highway. What's Joel driving?"

"That black 2004 Nissan Pathfinder Terri used to drive."

"Don't worry, Pastor. We'll find him."

Rue sat out on the steep hill next to his in-laws' house and gazed up at the night sky. He spotted Vega high overhead, its brilliant blue white color like a diamond within the constellation Lyra. Too bad Montana and Ivy had gone to bed. He would like to have pointed it out to them—and showed them the Summer Triangle. He could hardly believe how long it had been since the three of them sat under the stars and just marveled.

His focus on the heavens didn't last thirty seconds before his thoughts turned again to his circumstances. He was more nervous about what might be coming than what had already happened. What if these losers went after Ivy? Uninvited images popped into his mind. He shuddered.

Lord, I prayed for protection, and You let this happen anyway. I know You're there. I believe You care what happens to us. But it's hard to let You be my refuge and strength when You keep letting me down.

He glanced up and saw Elam's silhouette moving up the hill toward him.

"Mind if I join you?"

"Not at all."

Elam flopped down beside him. "Much cooler out here."

"People say that the mountain air will cure anything that ails you."

"I'm really sorry about the house, Rue."

"We can rebuild."

"Of course you can. But it has to hurt."

"Oh well."

Elam patted his knee. "You've been hit with a double whammy. You don't have to be stoic."

"Don't I?"

"Not with me."

Rue's eyes filled, and he swallowed the emotion that was just under the surface. "It's not just the house. It's the uncertainty. How long can we live in fear? Even with a security guard, I'm scared to let them out of my sight. And I need to get back to work."

"Maybe you and I can take shifts. I'll stay here in the mornings, and you can stay here in the afternoons."

Rue wiped his eyes with the bottom of his T-shirt. "Thanks, but that'll mean we lose momentum on the retirement village project."

Elam shrugged. "Big deal."

"I thought timing was everything."

"Actually, family's everything. Timing is relative to the *priority*. At the moment, the project has ceased to be one."

Rue rested in comfortable silence. Finally, he said, "You really kept your cool with Rusty on the phone."

"Thanks for noticing. His attitude can turn me into an ogre if I'm not careful. Burns me that he didn't even ask about Montana. It's almost like he pretends the kid doesn't exist. Of course, who am I to talk? I did the same thing when Ivy first came home."

"You suppose he feels threatened that Montana is getting close to you and Carolyn when his girls don't get that kind of time?"

"I don't know. Maybe. But that's about to change if he'll let it."

"What's Jacqueline like?"

"Dark hair and deep blue eyes—same as their daughters. Pretty. She did some modeling in college. Soft spoken and thoughtful. We've spent limited amounts of time with her, but she's always been really nice to Carolyn and me. And I think she understands Rusty in ways we don't."

"You think Jacqueline will accept *us*?"

Elam tugged at his mustache. "Hard to say. I've never seen her defy Rusty. When they were here for Thanksgiving, Ivy could hardly be in the same room with Rusty, but she and Jacqueline were polite to each other. I think they maintained an emotional distance to keep from irritating Rusty. Be glad you weren't here. Rusty was downright cruel. He and I came to blows over it, especially the way he treated Montana."

"Well, I've seen him act plenty cruel already. I wish I knew how to break through all that bitterness. I don't have a brother. I think I'd enjoy having a brother-in-law if he'd ever take off the boxing gloves."

"Well, you've got enough to worry about without the two of you going a few rounds. Now that the clinic's open, he's too busy to think about anyone but himself."

Flint pulled up in front of the familiar yellow Victorian house and saw Rick Myers leaning on the wrought-iron fence. He opened the passenger door and climbed in.

"Thanks for getting here so quickly," Rick said. "It's all I could do to convince Terri to stay home in case Joel calls."

Flint pulled away from the curb and drove to the Stop sign, then turned right on Main Street and headed toward Tanner Canyon. "There has to be a logical explanation for him not calling. Maybe he's ministering to someone, and it just didn't work for him to stop and call."

"I thought of that. That would be the best possible scenario. I won't allow myself to consider the worst."

"Isn't Joel going to college in the fall?"

Rick nodded. "Wutherford College in Vermont. He wants to major in world history and then teach it. I was hoping he'd consider the ministry, but he hasn't felt the call."

"Joel's a great guy. Ian loves being in his Sunday-school class."

"He loves those kids. He always connected with the kids he worked with at Three Peaks when he was a summer counselor. Still writes to a couple of them."

Flint drove out of the city limits and turned onto Old Sandstone Highway. "Funny how this road never seemed narrow when I was a teenager. Maybe the cars have just gotten bigger." He felt his cell phone vibrate and took it off his clip. "Sheriff Carter."

"It's Deputy Slade, sir. I drove Miner's Highway from Myers's work site to Jacob's Ear and didn't spot a black Pathfinder. I'm going to make another pass just to be sure."

"All right, Slade. Stay in touch."

"Roger that."

"My deputy didn't spot him. He's going to make another pass." Flint turned on his bright lights and continued driving slowly on the narrow road that took him deeper into the canyon.

"I don't see any sign of him," Rick said. "Or anyone else, for that matter."

Flint popped two Tums. "It's not even five miles to the bottom, and there aren't many pull-offs. If he's in the canyon, I don't think we can miss him."

The road cut through a swatch of scrub oaks and boulders and became noticeably steeper. Flint spotted a sign: "Scenic Overlook 100 Feet." "Why don't we turn in here?" He pulled his squad car onto the paved turnoff and grabbed his flashlight, then got out and stood next to the guardrail and shone the beam across the tops of the trees below.

"We're still pretty high," Flint said. "I haven't been out here in a long time. But if I remember right, the road gets narrower from this point."

Flint got back in the car, pulled onto the roadway, and continued his descent into the canyon.

"I don't have a good feeling about this," Rick said. "Lord, You know where Joel is. Please help us find him."

Flint drove another fifty yards or so and saw a road sign indicating a curve up ahead.

"There!" Rick pointed to an object in the middle of the road. "I think it's a tire!"

Flint hit the brakes and stopped just before he hit it—and then spotted skid marks and a broken guardrail.

34

RUE WOKE UP AND REALIZED it was morning and he had fallen asleep in the glider on the front porch. He glanced at his watch: *7:30!* He got to his feet and stretched, bemoaning that he should already be out at the site. He pushed open the front door and heard Elam talking on the phone.

"All right, Flint. Thanks for the call."

Elam was sitting at the kitchen table, his face buried in his hands.

"You okay?"

Elam looked up, his eyes wet. "Joel Myers's Pathfinder went off a curve last night in Tanner Canyon. They airlifted him to Swedish Medical in Denver. He's not expected to make it."

Rue sank into a chair and let the reality catch up with the words.

"Joel lost a tire before he went off the road, and Flint suspects it wasn't an accident. But he's waiting for investigators to get out there this morning and try to reconstruct what happened. All that's left of the Pathfinder is scrap metal. They had to use the Jaws of Life to get Joel out."

Rue shook his head, his heart heavy. "And he thinks it could be the same guys who've hit us?"

Elam nodded and seemed to stare at nothing. "I'm shutting down the retirement project. Enough people have been hurt."

"Can't you just put it on hold for a while?"

Elam got up and stood at the sink, his back to Rue. "Maybe I should get out of construction all together. It's not like it's a passion with me. I can find plenty of other things to do. Who needs this?"

"You can't blame yourself."

"Maybe not. But if I'd done what they wanted, Montana wouldn't have been shot. You wouldn't have lost your house. And Joel wouldn't have lost his life."

"Maybe he'll pull through."

Elam let out a loud sigh that made it clear he didn't think so.

Later that morning, Grayson, still reeling from the news about Joel Myers's accident, sat in Rue's office and finished telling the sheriff everything he knew, eager to wrap it up so he could call Tara before it hit the news.

Flint's eyes were bloodshot, his expression somber. "We're almost done, Grayson. I know it's hard to even think right now. You said Joel left work around eight last night. Did he mention he was going to drive through Tanner Canyon?"

"No, but I'm surprised he'd take the scenic route when it was getting dark."

"Pastor Myers said he takes the long way home sometimes so he can listen to teaching tapes. I'd sure like to know if he told anyone he was driving home that way."

"I don't know, Sheriff. Is that important?"

"Could be. Did Joel seem nervous about the attacks on Elam and Rue?"

"Not for himself. But he came to me yesterday after he heard about the fire at Rue's and told me to be careful."

Flint's eyebrows formed a bushy line. "If only he'd taken his own advice. Any idea how he heard about the fire?"

"Yeah, his parents told him right after it happened. Said they were on their way to Elam's to offer spiritual support." Grayson studied the sheriff's face. "You don't think this was an accident?"

Flint didn't answer.

"Why would anybody want to hurt Joel? He's the nicest guy you'd ever want to meet. Everybody likes him. And his parents went to the hospital when Madison Baughman was attacked. Even SAGE doesn't have any reason to want to hurt him."

Grayson thought about the man he'd watched start the fire at Rue's house and wondered if he'd done something to Joel. Did he dare keep the information to himself, knowing his own family might be at risk? He could always buy a disposable cell phone and make an anonymous call to the sheriff's department to describe the guy. No one could trace his call that way. But how could he explain the credit-card purchase to Tara? It was probably safer to use the pay phone at the Quik Stop. But what if the authorities traced the call and someone remembered seeing him there? Or got his prints or DNA off the receiver? Or Bobby recognized his voice?

"Did you want to say something?" Flint said.

"Huh? No, I was just thinking about Joel. You think he's going to make it?"

Flint stood and appeared to be leaving. "It's doubtful. His condition is grave."

Rue knocked on Montana's open door, then walked in and sat on the side of the bed. "How're you feeling, champ?"

"Better. Can Ian come over today?"

"We can talk about that later. Right now there's something I need to talk to you about, man to man."

Montana grinned. "What?"

"Joel Myers had a car accident last night. It's pretty bad."

Montana fiddled with the button on his pajamas. "Did he die?"

"No." Rue tilted Montana's chin and saw fear in his eyes. "But he might die. It's very serious."

"Did somebody run into him?"

"The sheriff isn't sure exactly what happened because Joel was knocked out. But he thinks Joel was driving through Tanner Canyon when his tire came off and caused him to lose control. His car went through the guardrail

and down a very steep hill before it finally came to a stop. He was banged
up very badly and was taken by helicopter to a hospital in Denver."

Montana's face fell. "Ian said they only bring the helicopter when
someone dies."

"Not always. It's the fastest way to get someone to the hospital when
they really need help. And Joel really needs help. And our prayers."

Montana reached over and touched the strings on the balloons next
to his bed. "Where does he hurt?"

"I don't know that he hurts at all because he got knocked out in the
accident and isn't awake yet."

Montana seemed miles away for a minute or so and then said, "Could
you take me to him?"

"He can't have visitors right now. And it's a long way to Denver."

"Then would you take me to the cemetery where we buried Gramma
Lu?"

"Sure. But why?"

Montana sighed. "Well, if Joel's going to heaven, then I need to go
tell Gramma Lu what he looks like so she can find him. Then he won't
be lonesome."

Grayson disconnected his call to Tara and put his cell phone on his belt
clip. He lifted his eyes and saw Bobby's squad car pull up. He waved and
met him halfway across the field.

"Hey, big brother. I figured you were covered up with work after
what all's happened in the past twenty-four hours."

Bobby didn't shake his hand but folded his arms and stood silent.

"What's wrong?"

"I expanded my investigation of the crime scene at Three Peaks and
found a yellow rubber glove at the edge of the woods, not far from the
front entrance. Size extra large."

Grayson didn't flinch. The gloves he'd worn were stashed with the
pocket saw and the spray paint. "Okaaay… Why do I need to know that?"

"You can wipe that angelic look off your face. Your fingerprints are all over it."

Grayson's pulse quickened. Had he dropped one of the gloves? He never thought to check the contents of the sack before he hid it. "Now that you mention it, I noticed I was missing a glove when I was fishing Sunday. Must've blown out of the back of my truck. I have no idea how it ended up at Three Peaks."

"Is that so?" Bobby's gaze burned into his conscience like a laser. "Can you explain why the lab found traces of paint residue on it—an exact match to the spray paint that was used on Rue's truck?"

Oh, boy. His heart pounded so hard that he was sure the front of his T-shirt must be moving. "Beats me. Maybe whoever vandalized Rue's truck stole the glove out of the back of my truck and planted it to frame me. It could've been someone who works here."

"Oh, cut the act, Grays. There's no way a glove with your finger-prints—and *only* your fingerprints—just mysteriously showed up out at Three Peaks. Why don't you start shootin' straight with me?"

Deny it. He can't prove anything. "For crying out loud, Bobby. I don't know what you want me to say. I told you what happened. Do you really think I would vandalize Rue's truck?"

"I don't know. Would you?"

Grayson threw up his hands and let out a string of swear words. "Are you so desperate to finger someone you'd accuse your own brother? How'd you know they were my fingerprints, anyway?"

Bobby stepped closer, his nose a foot in front of Grayson's. "Because your fingerprint was registered with the state when you got your driver's license. When I got a match on that, I compared the other prints on the glove to the prints you left on the mug in my garage when you and I worked on the pickup. *All* the prints on the glove are yours."

"So what? Whoever lifted that glove out of my truck could've made sure he didn't touch it with his hands."

"I wanna hear you say it outright. Did you vandalize Rue's truck or not?"

"Not."

"You'd better be levelin' with me."

Grayson shot his brother the most indignant expression he could muster. "I can't believe you even have to ask. What possible motive would I have for wanting to mess with Rue's truck? Besides, I was home asleep when it happened. Ask Tara."

"You have to admit it looks bad."

"Then start talking to the men on the crew and find out who took that glove. Listen, Bobby. I'm already on overload. Whoever's doing this stuff could hit my family next. I can't handle any more pressure. I didn't do this. You should be using your energy and resources to find the guy who did."

"Whaddya think I'm tryin' to do?"

"Fine." Grayson held out his wrists. "Go ahead and haul me down to the station. You can interrogate me all night, but you're wasting time and taxpayers' money."

Bobby's eyes seemed to search his. "All right. I'll accept your explanation and put it on the report. But if it turns out you're lyin' to me, I'll come at you with everything I've got. You're not above the law. Don't think you can hide behind my badge."

Grayson went through the motions, but he couldn't concentrate on his work. The last word he had on Joel's condition sounded grim. The guy was probably going to die. His murder would have people screaming for an arrest, which meant law enforcement would crank their efforts into high gear.

Why did Bobby have to find that stupid glove? If the authorities could prove that Grayson had vandalized Rue's truck, it was just a matter of time before they nailed him for shooting Montana. Then they'd try to pin him with the arson fires and tampering with Joel's SUV. Who was going to take the word of a monster who had shot a little kid?

It was time to ditch the rifle. Bobby knew he owned a Winchester Lightweight and had been target practicing with the boys as recently as last month. Pretending he'd sold a firearm without producing proof of a legal sale would open a door he didn't want to walk through. If the authorities got a warrant for the rifle, he would lead them to the metal storage box in his truck and act shocked that the rifle was missing—same as the glove. Whether they believed him or not, without examining the rifle, ballistics couldn't prove he shot Montana.

He thought back on the day of the shooting. Bobby would have no reason to doubt he'd gone fishing, since it was a routine part of his Sunday ritual. And the clothes he'd worn had been washed twice since. Gunshot residue wouldn't be an issue.

The handkerchief! Grayson remembered Bobby saying a handkerchief had been found near the shell casing, and that it contained the perp's DNA. What if Bobby slapped him with a warrant to obtain a DNA sample? There was no way he could explain his way out of a match.

His brother's words rang in his mind. *We have ways of narrowin' things down. Just takes time.*

Grayson took in a slow, deep breath and let it out. Then did it again. This was not the time to panic. There had to be a way to throw Bobby off his trail and keep that warrant from ever being issued.

Just about sunset, Grayson headed into the house, where the air felt thirty degrees warmer.

Tara met him at the door and wrapped her arms around his neck. "I didn't know you were going to be this late again."

"I thought I told you. Sorry." He kissed her cheek. "The house feels like an oven."

"There's no breeze tonight. I'll serve you dinner out on the patio. I can't believe what an awful day it's been for you."

You don't know the half of it. "I talked to Rue on the way home. Joel hasn't regained consciousness and has all kinds of internal injuries. He'll be lucky to make it through the night."

Fear lines formed on Tara's forehead. "I wasn't as worried when the attacks were confined to Elam's family. But after what happened to Joel, I feel vulnerable. Don't you?"

"I'm certainly going to be cautious, but I don't think we need to panic."

"I'm not panicked, Grayson. But our smoke alarm is broken, and the thought that someone might try to burn our house down while we sleep is scary."

"Of course it is. But all the attacks have happened in remote areas, not in a residential neighborhood. And no one was in any of those buildings when the fires were set."

Tara's face relaxed. "That's true."

"I doubt anyone's going to try anything here with neighbors close by."

"Maybe you're right." She wiggled out of his arms. "Why don't you go shower, and I'll warm up your dinner."

"Where are the kids?"

"Lindsey's in her room—on the phone, no doubt. The boys went to a birthday party at the skating rink. They'll be home around nine."

Grayson glanced at his watch. He might as well get it over with. "This seems like a good time to tell you about something puzzling that happened today. Why don't we talk in the bedroom so Lindsey won't overhear us?"

He followed Tara into the bedroom and shut the door, then sat next to her on the bed. He relayed the entire conversation he'd had with Bobby about the missing glove, careful to act sufficiently hurt that his own brother would think he was capable of vandalizing Rue's truck.

Tara squeezed his hand. "Poor Bobby's under so much pressure to make an arrest, he's obviously not thinking clearly."

"In all fairness to him, it *should* raise a red flag that the glove was found out at Three Peaks. But anyone could've taken it from my storage box and worn it when he spray-painted Rue's truck."

"Well, it's a moot point. You were here with me all night. Did you tell Bobby that?"

"I'm sure I must have. But don't be surprised if he asks you."

Tara kissed his cheek and then got up. "Deep down, Bobby knows it's absurd. By the way, do you have to work tomorrow?"

"Just till noon. We can take the kids out to the lake tomorrow night and watch the fireworks, if you like."

"Oh, the kids will be so excited. They've been begging me to take them."

Grayson sat in the quiet, his mind fast-forwarding through every detail of what he needed to do to cover his tracks. He had stopped by his fishing hole on the way home and hidden everything he had in his possession that could be potentially incriminating. He had one last thing to do in the morning on his way to work. If he succeeded, Bobby might believe he was innocent and focus his investigation somewhere else. If it backfired, he could be looking through iron bars until he was an old man.

35

RUE WOKE EARLY, the heaviness that had oppressed him since Montana was shot still weighing on him. He remembered that Joel Myers was dying. That it was the Fourth of July. And that Elam was thinking about shutting down construction on the retirement village.

He had to know what a huge economic hit would result, not only for Carolyn and him, but for all the men on the crew. Most lived from paycheck to paycheck and couldn't survive a month without income.

Rue hadn't said anything to Elam, but as insistent as Grayson had been about his need to make more money, he wondered if being out of work even for a short period of time would have serious financial repercussions for his family.

The week was already gone, and his intention to meet with Grayson and discuss a mentoring plan for the next couple years had gotten tabled by one crisis after another. Maybe it was just as well. If Elam went through with the shutdown, they wouldn't be working together anyway. He wondered if Grayson would be able to find a foreman job this late in the busy construction season. Or if he would have to join a work crew and go back to making the same wage as the men he was now supervising.

The heaviness suddenly felt as if it were going to crush him. Why was he thinking all these negative thoughts? There was nothing he could do to help Grayson or any of the other employees. It was Elam's decision—and certainly a gut-wrenching one. Whatever Elam decided to do, he would support it. But he also didn't have as much to lose. He knew his in-laws would make sure he and Ivy and Montana were taken

care of until he could find another job. And that Elam's being well connected would probably make that happen sooner rather than later.

Rue sighed. How depressing it would be to break up the team. He
had enjoyed seeing the project take off and could visualize what an
attractive addition the retirement village would be to the region. Why
anyone would oppose it was beyond him.

He turned on his side and studied Ivy's sleeping face. She looked so
peaceful. He stroked her hair and wanted to take her into his arms and
get lost in her kisses and the warmth of her embrace. But was it selfish
to wake her in order to satisfy his desire when she was so exhausted and
fragile?

He kissed his finger and pressed it to her lips, then got up and went
downstairs to watch the sunrise.

Grayson checked the rearview and side mirrors of his pickup to be sure
no vehicles were behind him, then turned onto the unmarked road that
led to his fishing hole. He didn't want company.

He drove about two miles and pulled over in front of the old cottonwood tree marked with a white X and turned off the motor. He got
out of the truck and scanned the area. When he was sure he was alone,
he hiked down an earthen path to the space between two boulders where
he had stashed the incriminating evidence the night before. He picked
up the plastic lawn bag next to his rifle case, carried it back to the passenger side of his truck, then took out the pocket saw he had used to vandalize Rue's Silverado.

He pulled out the blade and locked it, then held it against the front
quarter panel of his truck and walked all the way down the side and
back, leaving deep gouges and slashes. When he had inflicted sufficient
damage, he shook the can of white spray paint, then wrote the letters
S-A-G-E across the passenger door. He stood back with a discriminat-
ing eye. What else could Bobby conclude but that the same vandal who
trashed Rue's truck had trashed his?

He grabbed the pocket saw and climbed up in the bed of the truck and sawed off the padlock on the metal storage box to make it appear someone had broken into it. He hopped down and tossed the pocket saw and can of spray paint in the bag where he had already dumped all his boxes of Remington .223 shells and the other rubber glove.

He stripped off his jeans and T-shirt and stuffed them in the bag, then put on the change of clothes he brought with him—just in case Bobby didn't buy his story and decided to test his clothes for paint residue.

He grabbed the shovel from the back of the truck, picked up the lawn bag, and took the path back to where he had stashed his rifle. He dug a hole next to the boulders and buried the bag and rifle, then put the dirt back, packed it down, and spread pine needles over the top.

All he had to do now was stop at a service station and wash his hair, face, arms, and hands to be rid of any paint residue.

Rue went out on the front porch at Elam and Carolyn's, the mountains reddish in the glow of sunrise, and was surprised to see Montana sitting on the glider with Windy curled up next to him.

"Hey, champ. What are you doing up so early?"

Montana shrugged.

"Does your arm hurt?"

His son seemed to stare at nothing for several seconds and then said, "I don't want Joel to die."

"Me, either. Your grandmother called the prayer chain, and hundreds of people besides us are praying. But we just have to trust that God knows what's best." Rue expected the phone to ring at any moment with news of Joel's passing.

"You didn't take me to the cemetery so I can talk to Gramma Lu."

Rue nudged Windy off the glider and sat next to Montana. "How about if we go this morning?"

"Joel's gonna like Gramma Lu." Montana put his head on Rue's shoulder and clutched his arm.

"I wish I'd met her. She took such good care of you when Mommy was on drugs."

"Gramma Lu was soooo nice, Dad. I know I get to see her in heaven someday." Montana sighed. "I just wish someday didn't take so long. If Joel goes to heaven, I won't see him until someday, either."

"Well, the good part is that they'll be with Jesus and will be happier than we can imagine. And we won't always feel sad about missing them. It'll get a lot better."

"Did Ian's dad catch the bad guy who made Joel's tire come off?"

"Not yet, champ. But he will. So do you feel up to going over there for a cookout and fireworks at the lake?"

"Okay."

Just okay? "I know you must have all kinds of confusing thoughts running through your mind. You might even hate whoever shot you and burned the house and caused Joel's car to go off the road."

"And burned Grandpa Elam's stable."

"Yeah, that, too."

A tear trickled down Montana's cheek. "Joel says we're supposed to love our enemies and pray for them."

"That's a tough one, champ. I still struggle with it."

"Do you think he's praying for whoever made his car crash?"

"I doubt if Joel knows what happened. He's been knocked out since the accident. He may just wake up in heaven."

"Then *I'll* pray for his enemies."

"You don't need to take on that responsibility." He pulled Montana closer. "You just need to get better."

Rue marveled at his son's forgiving spirit, ashamed of what he'd like to do to whoever was hurting the people he cared about.

Grayson slowed the pickup when he reached the work site gate, waved at the security guard, then pulled into the field and parked in such a way that somebody was bound to spot what he'd done to the passenger side.

He walked over to the trailer, surprised to find the door unlocked, and was hit with the inviting aroma of freshly brewed coffee when he stepped inside.

"Hey, Liz. I didn't expect to see you working today."

Liz Parker peered over the top of her glasses. "You really think I'm going to have a relaxing Fourth of July with all the work piling up around here?"

Grayson sensed her stern demeanor was her way of dealing with worry. "I'm sure it helps to stay busy and not have to think about all the awful things happening. Any word on Joel?"

Liz shook her head, her eyes suddenly brimming with tears. "Don't start me blubbering again or I'll never get anything done."

"Hey, it's okay. We're all upset over what happened to Joel."

"He's one of the finest young men I've ever met." She brushed a tear off her cheek. "I've never heard Elam sound so down. I think it's finally getting to him. He and Rue aren't coming in today, either."

"That's all right. I'll keep things rolling."

Liz took off her glasses and seemed to be staring at nothing. "You think Elam would shut down the project?"

"No way. He's one of the toughest guys I know. Did he say something that made you think that?"

"Not directly…but in the twenty years I've worked for him, I've never seen him this defeated. Usually conflict makes him dig in his heels."

"He's been through a lot lately."

"Yeah, but I think it's seeing what it's doing to the people he cares about that's got him so down." Liz rested her elbows on the desk, her chin on her palms. "If he decides to throw in the towel, I guess I'll retire. I've worked for him too long to put up with anybody else."

Grayson's pulse quickened. He had never once considered that Elam might actually scrap the project and he might lose his job!

The door opened and one of the workers came inside. "Hey, man. Why didn't you tell us SAGE hit you, too?"

Grayson manufactured a puzzled expression. "What are you talking about?"

"Your truck."

"What about it?"

"Oh, man. You'd better come see for yourself."

Flint sat at the table in his office for an early morning update from Nick Sanchez, Bobby Knolls, and Buck Lowry. He hoped it wouldn't last long, since he had promised Betty and Ian he would help get the house ready for their afternoon guests. Not that he was in the mood to celebrate the Fourth.

"Gentlemen," Nick said, "I appreciate you coming in on a holiday, and I'm about to make it worth your while.

"First of all, we found a Go Fast receipt in Joel Myers's room dated the day before the accident. His SUV was serviced and his tires rotated by a mechanic named Cruise Foster. My agents went to Go Fast yesterday morning and talked to Foster's supervisor, who told them he was due in at any moment. About that time, a blue van turned left into the parking lot in front of an oncoming vehicle and almost caused an accident. The driver turned out to be Foster. It took my agents about thirty seconds of talking to him to realize he was drunk. His blood alcohol level was off the chart. Come to find out, he lost his wife a couple weeks ago and has been hitting the bottle pretty hard. The supervisor is his brother-in-law. Says he knew Foster was drinking but swears it wasn't affecting his job.

"Investigators think it's highly probable that the lug nuts on the left front wheel of Myers's SUV were not sufficiently tightened, and the wheel came off due to Foster's negligence. I realize that doesn't lessen the tragedy, but we don't think there was foul play. We turned the case file over to the DA. If Myers dies, Foster will probably be charged with criminally negligent homicide. Either way, he's the DA's problem."

The DA's problem? Flint could only imagine the agony Pastor Myers and Terri were going through as their only son lay dying.

"Now for the really good news. Buck, you first…"

Buck folded his hands on the table. "Our investigation at the Blue Moon Tavern paid off. Sonny Halstead's DNA is a perfect match to the

DNA we found on the cigarette butt at the scene of the Griffiths' fire. He was definitely there. My guess is he was wearing one of the shoe types we cast there and at the Everhardt fire. We've put out an APB on him."

"Hold on," Flint said. "Halstead's our suspect in the attacks against Baughman, not—"

"Wait." Nick held up his palm, a grin spanning his cheeks. "It gets even better. Halstead's DNA *also* matches the DNA on the gum we collected near the burned field behind Baughman's house and the DNA found on her T-shirt. And his fingerprints match the set we found on her dog's collar."

Flint's mind screamed with the implications. "Are you saying Halstead played both sides—that he staged the conflict between Baughman's attackers and SAGE?"

"The evidence certainly suggests it. My hunch is that Halstead and his cronies started the ball rolling with Baughman's attack and then staged each of the retaliatory crimes on both sides. Halstead's been having a good laugh at SAGE's expense—and ours."

"Fits with the profile," Flint said. "He orchestrated the chaos to draw attention to himself. And used fear tactics to control the situation without inflicting bodily harm."

Nick nodded. "This new evidence answers many of our questions about the first two threads, but none about the third. We can't connect Halstead to any of the crimes against the Kesslers, and there's no way he's capable of shooting that boy. I think we've still got a loose cannon out there."

"I think you're right," Flint said.

Nick seemed to be processing for a moment, then turned his attention to Bobby. "Let's hear from you, Lieutenant. I saw on your report that you collected additional evidence out at Three Peaks where Kessler's truck was vandalized. Anything new to report?"

Bobby blew a pink bubble and sucked it into his mouth. "Nothin' conclusive yet."

36

RUE TOOK MONTANA by the hand and strolled past the wrought-iron gate into the cemetery at Woodlands Community Church. They passed by the guardian angel that marked Ivy's infant sister's grave and stopped in front of a white marble cross in the back row.

Montana gripped his hand a little tighter. "Read me what it says."

Rue read the words out loud:

LUCIA GUADALUPE MARIA RAMIREZ
Born January 5, 1937 — Died April 14, 2007
Forever at Peace with Her Lord

"That means she's in heaven," Montana said.

"Would you like me to leave you here by yourself for a while?"

"Okay."

"I'll just go sit in the churchyard until you're done. Take as long as you want."

Montana nodded and let go of his hand.

Rue felt strangely excluded from this private room of his son's heart. No matter how many times they talked about Lu, it was no more than a glimpse of the special relationship that belonged only to them. He was just grateful that God put someone so loving and protective in Montana's life during the time Ivy was addicted to drugs and he was oblivious that he had fathered a child.

He trudged up the hill to the churchyard and sat on the bench. The lawn was green and wet and perfectly manicured, and the beds around the evergreen bushes were covered with white alyssum—a contrast to the natural beauty of the open range that lay beyond the parking lot and stretched as far as the eye could see.

In the distance, the jagged peaks of the San Juans seemed to touch the sky and stood like an age-old citadel around Phantom Hollow. As he prepared to celebrate Independence Day, it seemed ironic that he no longer felt safe in the greatest country on earth—and not because of the terrorist threats, but because of some personal, unnamed enemy that wanted to destroy his family.

He glanced over at the cemetery and spotted his wounded son sitting cross-legged in front of Lu's grave, his arm in a sling, and imagined that he had a great deal more to talk to her about than Joel Myers.

His cell phone rang, and he felt the muscles in his neck tighten. "Hello."

"It's me," Ivy said. "Pastor Myers just called from the hospital."

Rue's heart sank. "And?"

There was a long pause, and he heard Ivy's sniffling. "Joel's sitting up in bed, sipping a cup of broth."

"No way! What did the doctor have to say?"

"Just that Joel must have some powerful people praying for him."

Rue laughed. "The doctor has it backward—more like a bunch of desperate people praying to a powerful God."

"I don't think it's hit me yet that he's actually alive and going to recover."

"This is so amazing, honey. Let me go tell Montana. We'll see you soon. I love you."

"Love you, too."

Rue disconnected the call and spent a few moments thanking God for sparing Joel's life. He blinked to clear his eyes, then focused on the window of Montana's Sunday-school class, thankful that there would be rejoicing on Sunday instead of mourning.

—

Grayson sat half in and half out of his truck and spotted Bobby's squad car coming through the gate. What took him so long? He waited until his brother pulled up next to his truck and then got out, knowing he needed to put on the performance of his life.

"Can you believe this?" Grayson threw his hands in the air. "What am I supposed to do now? I don't even have insurance on this old thing!"

Bobby's eyebrows came together. "When'd it happen?"

"I'm guessing last night, but I didn't see the passenger side when I left for work. One of the guys on the crew spotted it and came and got me. You can't really believe SAGE didn't do this?"

Bobby unzipped a vinyl bag and took out a pair of rubber gloves and put them on, then walked down the passenger side of the truck and inspected the damage. He reached in the bag and grabbed a magnifying glass and held it over several places on the spray-painted letters. "There's an awful lot of road dust. Some of it seems bonded to the paint."

"Does that tell you something?"

"That the paint wasn't dry yet when you drove to work."

Grayson's heart pounded. *Stay calm. He can't prove anything.* "Then it must've happened just before I left this morning."

"Deputy Slade cruised past your house right at six. Never noticed it."

"I don't know what to tell you, Bobby. I didn't see anything. But this has to be the work of whoever vandalized Rue's Silverado."

"Probably so." Bobby gestured toward the bed of the truck. "Did you know the padlock's been cut on your storage box?"

"No way!" Grayson swore under his breath and kicked the tire. "I was so focused on the other, I never even noticed. I suppose they cleaned me out?"

Bobby climbed in the bed and opened the box. "Yep. What was in it?"

"I don't remember exactly. My toolbox. The boys' jackets. A couple ball caps. My hunting rifle. Flashlights. A pair of work boots. I'm not sure what all."

"I need to take pictures, collect trace evidence, dust for prints. I don't need you here for that. No reason to keep you from your work. Tara said you were only workin' half a day."

"You talked to Tara?"

"Yeah."

"About what?"

"A few loose ends."

"What loose ends?"

Bobby pulled a camera out of his bag and started snapping pictures. "I can't just make the glove go away, Grays. It's evidence. I have to eliminate you as a suspect. For starters, I need to establish what kinda relationship you have with Rue."

"So you asked Tara instead of me?"

"Only because I went by the house and inspected your driveway before I drove all the way out here."

"Inspected it?"

"For trace evidence," Bobby said. "You know, spray-paint residue, paint and metal scrapings, cigarette butts. Stuff like that. Didn't find a thing. No way was this truck vandalized there."

"Then it must've happened after I got to work."

"Do you have the keys?"

Grayson reached in his pocket and pulled out his key ring. "Yeah, right here."

"Is this where you parked the truck when you got here?"

"Uh-huh."

"Well, if it hasn't been moved, how do you account for all the road dust? That stuff didn't come off a paved highway. And you didn't get all that between the gate and here."

"How am I supposed to know? You act like I have the answers."

Bobby took a step toward him. "Here's one you have the answer to: how do you feel about Rue Kessler?"

"What does that have to do with anything?"

"Answer the question, Grays."

"I supervise the work crew. He juggles the project details. We do fine."

"I didn't ask how you do. I asked how you feel about him. You like him?"

"What difference does that make?"

Bobby's eyes narrowed. "Come on, there's no way you thought it was fair that Rue got the project manager's position."

"So what? Life isn't fair."

"Forty is knockin' at your door, and the guy robbed you of your big chance at the job you deserved. Has to eat at you."

"I never said that."

"You had to find an outlet for all that anger. Why not destroy the shiny new toy he could afford and you couldn't?"

Grayson felt his face get hot and hoped his anger would come across as indignation. "That's insane, Bobby. Besides, I make decent money."

"But not enough. You're in debt up to your eyeballs."

"How do you know that?"

"Why don't you just admit it and get it off your chest."

"Admit *what*?"

"That you vandalized Rue's truck outta spite."

"Oh, right. And I suppose you think I vandalized mine, too?"

"Did you?"

Grayson stared at Bobby, his thoughts racing. How was he supposed to answer that? Finally, he blurted out, "I resent being put on the defensive. I'm the victim here."

"Are you?" Bobby stepped even closer. "I don't like bein' messed with. Especially by my own brother."

"I'm not doing that."

"Is that so? I went back and dusted the *inside* of the glove I found at Three Peaks. Your prints were the only ones there, too. If someone else wore the glove, there would be prints."

"For crying out loud, Bobby. You think I'm lying to you?"

"Let's just say it doesn't add up."

"Maybe the vandal put my glove on over his glove—to frame me."

Bobby took a wad of gum out of his mouth and threw it. "Keep talkin', Grays. At some point you're gonna run out of answers and hang yourself. Why don't you just level with me now and let me try to help you?"

Grayson wanted the pressure off. He needed Bobby's help. But if he confessed, how long would it be before he was suspected in the shooting? Bobby would know the rifle hadn't really been stolen. And that's the one piece of evidence he couldn't let the authorities get their hands on.

Flint sat at his desk clearing out his inbox. The great news about Joel regaining consciousness seemed to have taken the edge off and helped him get in the mood for the Fourth of July backyard cookout with the Griffiths and the Kesslers.

Bobby knocked on the door, then came inside and closed it. "Can we talk before you leave?"

"Sure. Pull up a chair. What's on your mind?"

Bobby reached in a manila envelope and handed him some photographs. "I took these pictures of Grayson's truck. Tell me what you see."

Flint flipped slowly through the stack. "There's considerable road dust visible on top of the spray-painted letters, which indicates the truck was driven after the letters were written. Pretty basic."

"Right." Bobby handed him two more photos taken with the telephoto. "In these pictures, you'll notice spots where the surface dirt appears to be bonded to the spray paint, a good indication the truck had been driven before the paint was completely dry. The lab confirmed it."

"Go on."

"So I'm thinkin' the vandal had to have struck shortly before Grayson left for work at 6:00 a.m. And yet Deputy Slade drove by Grayson's around that time and didn't notice it, even though he came down the side of the street where the passenger side was clearly visible. How could he miss somethin' like that?"

"We're working everyone too hard," Flint said. "Slade was about to end a double shift. After driving by on the hour from dusk till dawn, he might've just seen what he expected to see."

"But there's not a speck of evidence on Grayson's driveway to suggest the truck was vandalized there. I mean *nothin'*. See those deep gouges? There would be metallic shavings all over the place."

"What does Grayson have to say?"

Bobby threw his gum in the trash can. "Plenty. But it doesn't add up."

"Back up and start at the beginning," Flint said. "I want to hear how this thing evolved."

Flint listened as Bobby told him everything that had happened from the time he first confronted Grayson about the glove until he went out to the site, inspected the damage, and discovered the padlock on the metal storage box had been cut and the contents stolen.

"The theft doesn't add up, either," Bobby said. "What thief is gonna take flashlights, kids' jackets, ball caps, work boots—stuff like that? He's gonna rummage through whatever's there, take the valuables, and toss out everything else. There should've been stuff strewn all over that truck bed."

"So what's your explanation, Bobby?"

"I hate to say it, Sheriff, but I think my brother pulled off somewhere between his house and the work site and vandalized his own truck. My guess is that after I confronted him yesterday about the glove, he realized he was about to go down for vandalizin' Kessler's truck. So he staged the whole thing to make himself appear to be a victim and not a vandal. He probably thought the theft would make it seem more believable."

"Did he have a motive for vandalizing Kessler's Silverado?"

Bobby leaned his head back and let out a sigh. "Grayson was hopin' to be promoted to project manager. It would've meant a lot more money. He denies it, but I think he resents that Kessler got the job."

"Well, we've certainly got enough to bring him in for questioning. But I think we need to take you off the case."

Rue sat at a window table at Jewel's Café with Ivy and Montana and his in-laws, waiting for their breakfast order. The café was abuzz with a seemingly relaxed holiday crowd, many of whom knew the Griffiths and came over to the table to express their outrage and concern for the attacks on both families—especially the shooting.

Jewel Sadler waltzed through the swinging doors and over to the table, carrying a waffle smothered with raspberries and blueberries, and topped with whipped cream, red and blue sprinkles, and a tiny American flag. She set the plate in front of Montana. "As promised: my first-ever Fourth of July waffle. You're the very first person to try it."

"Wow!" Montana's grin was wider than Jacob's Gulch. "I love waffles."

Jewel tilted his chin. "I know you do, sweetie. And I made this extra special just for you because I'm so glad you're going to be all right."

Someone at the next table started to clap and then someone else and someone else until the café resounded with applause and whistles.

Jewel's eyes glistened, and her nose turned red. "See? I'm not the only one who feels that way."

Montana sat wide-eyed and seemed a little overwhelmed but managed a polite, "Thank you."

Rue thought he spotted Rusty sitting alone at a corner table, but the guy had turned around with his back to them and seemed to be reading the newspaper. He decided not to mention it. Why ruin everyone's day?

The waitress came up behind Jewel, carrying a large tray. "Okay… I've got the rest of the orders."

Rue's phone vibrated, and he put it to his ear just as the waitress put his skillet scramble on the table in front of him. "Hello."

"Rue, it's Liz. I thought you should know that Grayson was just escorted out of here by a sheriff's deputy and an FBI agent."

"*Why?*"

"I'm not sure. He came over to the office to get coffee first thing this morning, and one of the workmen came in and told him his truck had been vandalized. Just like yours, actually—passenger side and all. His brother came out and made a report, and that's the last I heard about it till just now."

"Why didn't you tell Elam that Grayson's truck was vandalized?"

"I tried but haven't been able to reach him. I left messages at his home and on his cell phone, but he hasn't called back."

Rue lifted his eyes and locked gazes with Elam. "That's okay. I'll tell him. Do you have a hunch what this is about?"

"None."

"All right, Liz. Thanks. Call back if you hear anything."

Rue disconnected the call and repeated the conversation for everyone at the table.

"You don't think Grayson was involved in any of the crimes, do you?" Ivy said.

Rue shook his head. "I can't imagine."

"Honey, Grayson's worked for me for years," Elam said. "He's always shot straight with me. I'd trust him with my life."

37

AT THREE THAT AFTERNOON, Rue pulled his loaner truck in front of Flint and Betty Carter's house and parked behind Elam's Suburban. He wasn't really in the mood for a backyard cookout and a night of fireworks, but it was worth the effort just to see Montana's excitement.

He got out and let Montana slide out on the driver's side, and a few seconds later, Ian Carter was standing next to him, admiring his Velcro cast and sling.

The boys disappeared through the front door, and he noticed that Flint and Betty and Elam and Carolyn were sitting on the porch. He waved, then linked arms with Ivy and went up the front steps.

"We're so glad you're here," Betty said. "Can I get you some lemonade? Soda? Iced tea?"

"Lemonade would be wonderful," Ivy said.

Rue nodded. "Sounds great. Thanks."

"Make yourselves comfortable." Flint appeared relaxed, dressed in khaki shorts and Hawaiian shirt and sipping a frosty glass of lemonade.

Rue sat next to Ivy on a wicker love seat and admired the green lawn and the baskets of flowers hanging along the porch. "What a nice place. I love these old Victorian homes—especially the big porches."

"We've been here a long time," Flint said. "Sometimes it's hard to keep up with the maintenance on an older home. But we had it remodeled a few years ago and eliminated a few headaches."

Elam tipped his glass and crunched a mouthful of crushed ice. "Flint, why don't you tell them what's going on with Grayson?"

"All right. As you know, Grayson called in this morning to report his truck had been vandalized—much like Rue's, right down to the S-A-G-E spray-painted on the passenger side. We're in the process of asking him questions in an effort to clear up some inconsistencies."

"What kind of inconsistencies?" Rue said.

"We're just trying to piece together exactly what happened." Flint took a sip of lemonade. "On this fine Independence Day afternoon, I think we should put everything on the back burner and celebrate not only our freedoms, but the fact that Montana and Joel escaped near tragic situations. We have a lot to be glad about."

Grayson opened the front door of his house and closed it behind him. He went in the kitchen and laid two six-packs of ice-cold beer on the countertop and removed a can from one of the cartons.

Tara came in the patio door. "Thank heavens, you're home. Why in the world were you answering questions for the sheriff and the FBI?"

"Where are the kids?"

"The boys are in the tree house. Lindsey's at a girlfriend's." Tara shot him an I-thought-you-gave-up-beer-for-two-months expression.

"Let's go in our room and talk." Grayson followed her into the bedroom and closed the door. He leaned against the dresser, popped the top on the can of beer, and took a swig. "How'd you know where I was?"

"When you didn't answer your cell, I called Liz. She said you were at the sheriff's department answering questions about what happened to your truck. I can't believe you didn't call me. It's like I'm the only one who doesn't know anything."

"I'm sorry, honey. It all happened so fast that I wasn't really think-ing clearly. Bobby's been a real jerk."

"Really?" A row of lines formed on Tara's forehead. "He was nice when he was here this morning."

"He didn't seem strange?"

"Not really. He told me he came to gather evidence from the driveway to confirm that's where your truck was vandalized. I was embarrassed you hadn't even told *me,* so I pretended I knew what he was talking about."

"Did he ask you questions about me?"

Tara sat on the end of the bed. "Right before he left, he asked me what kind of relationship you had with Rue. I thought that was random."

"What'd you tell him?"

"That he should ask you, but I thought you and Rue got along okay."

"Did you tell him how disgusted I've been that I didn't get the promotion?"

Tara shook her head. "It's not my place to speak for you, and I told Bobby that. Would you please tell me what actually happened to your truck? Bobby didn't come right out and say because he assumed I knew. And you never bothered to call me back."

"Sorry. Every time I started to, things got crazy." Grayson tilted his head back and guzzled the rest of the beer. He had agonized all the way home about having to lie to Tara. What choice did he have?

"I didn't know anything about it till after I got to work." He put into sequence everything that happened from the time he arrived at the site until one of workers came to the office and told him to come take a look at his truck.

"I about croaked," Grayson said. "The passenger side was messed up just like Rue's—right down to SAGE's signature in spray paint. Naturally, I called Bobby immediately. Took him forever to get out there, and he told me he stopped by here first. I couldn't believe how weird he acted."

"Weird how?"

"Like he thinks I had something to do with it."

"That's ridiculous. Why would he think that?"

"After he confronted me with the glove yesterday, he went back and dusted the inside of it and found only my prints there, too. He said if someone else wore it, there'd be other prints. But the vandal could've put that glove on over another glove to frame me. I didn't mess up Rue's truck. And I sure didn't mess up my own. Does he think I'm nuts? We don't even have insurance to cover this."

"It's not like Bobby to doubt your word."

"Yeah, well. Bobby's under a lot of pressure to make an arrest. He's a desperate man."

"Desperate enough to point a finger at his own brother?"

"Apparently." Grayson crushed the can and tossed it in the trash can. "I just spent two hours being grilled by Buck Lowry and that FBI agent that's working the case. It was humiliating."

Tara got up and went over to him and nestled in his arms. "I'm so sorry, Grayson. I can't imagine what would make Bobby turn on you."

Flint heated up the barbecue grill on the back patio, feeling surprisingly lighthearted and carefree. He wondered why he and Betty didn't entertain company more often.

His cell phone vibrated. Not now. He was enjoying his guests, the beautiful weather, and a short block of time to forget about all the unanswered questions that awaited him at the office. It vibrated again, and he put it to his ear.

"Sheriff Carter."

"It's Nick. Sorry to interrupt your plans, but I wanted to give you some good news. Our APB on Sonny Halstead hit pay dirt. A marshal over in Telluride recognized his truck and picked him up. He didn't even resist. It's almost like he was expecting to be found—maybe even hoping he would be. We picked him up, and he's down here now."

"Did he lawyer up?"

"Not yet. If we feed his ego and tell him how ingenious he was to come up with such a clever scheme, maybe he'll confess to the arson fires and all the attacks against Baughman."

"That'd be nice." Flint ambled over to the hummingbird feeder, his back to the curious listeners on the patio, and brushed a spider off the glass. "So how'd it go with Grayson?"

"Oh, we rattled his chain big time for a couple hours and then let him go. There's no point in coercing a confession and then having some hotshot lawyer get it thrown out later. We need to do this right. Even with the glove, we can't put him at the scene of the vandalism with absolute certainty."

"So he's sticking to his story about the missing glove and someone framing him?"

"Oh yeah," Nick said. "And we can't prove he pulled a copycat with his own truck till we determine where he did it. He tested negative for spray-paint residue. We can't prove he faked the theft, either. But the lieutenant's right, it doesn't add up."

Flint strolled back to the grill. "I'm proud of Bobby for playing by the rules."

"Yeah, couldn't have been easy implicating his brother. I'll call you later and let you know how this plays out with Halstead. So how's the backyard cookout coming?"

Flint smiled nonchalantly at five pairs of eyes staring at him from the umbrella table. "I'm standing in front of a hot grill, decked out in my chef's hat and apron, ready to cook for the masses. You're not going to lay a guilt trip on me, are you?"

Nick laughed. "No way. Enjoy the time with your family and friends. Relax while you can. I think this thing's about to come down."

After a magnificent fireworks display at Tanner Lake, the Griffiths and the Kesslers said good-bye to the Carters and all piled into Elam's Suburban. Montana fell asleep almost immediately, his head on Ivy's shoulder.

"He really overdid it," Rue said.

Ivy nodded. "It was probably too soon after surgery for him to be this active. But it was so good for him to be with Ian. He can sleep all day tomorrow."

"Not me. I've got to go to work."

Elam started the car.

"Dad, wait!" Ivy said. "Is that Grayson and Tara?" She pointed to a couple with four kids getting into an old minivan.

"It sure is," Rue said. "I'll be right back."

Rue got out and made his way through the crowd. "Grayson! Wait up!"

Grayson turned toward Rue, a sheepish expression on his face.

"Weren't the fireworks great?" Rue said.

"Yeah, very nice. My kids had a good time. Did you bring Montana?"

"We did. He loved it. Probably was a little too much too soon. But it was worth it just letting him have some fun."

"So he's feeling better?"

"Much better, thanks. Listen…Liz called and told me what happened to your truck. I've been trying to reach you."

"Sorry I didn't return your calls. Dealing with my truck took a lot of time. And I promised my family I'd spend the afternoon and evening with them."

"Liz mentioned you went down to the sheriff's department to answer questions. Everything okay?"

Grayson glanced over at his kids buckled up in the van. "Yeah. Just a little misunderstanding, that's all."

"Good. I'm coming in tomorrow. See you in the morning."

"Okay."

"Good night, Grayson."

Rue went back to the Suburban and climbed in the backseat. "I'm glad we ran into him."

Elam pulled down the rearview mirror. "What did he have to say about being questioned?"

"That it was just a little misunderstanding."

"Flint didn't act like it was a big deal," Elam said. "Maybe we made too much of it."

Just before midnight, Flint stood at the two-way mirror of the interrogation room, watching Nick Sanchez and Buck Lowry wrap up their questioning of Sonny Halstead.

"Start at the beginning, and tell me one more time," Nick said. "An abbreviated version will do."

Halstead ran his hands through his stringy hair, then rested his elbows on the table, his chin in his palms. "How many times do I have to tell you, dude? Me, Josh, and Simon went to the SAGE rally at Spruce Park and waited for Madison Baughman. I threatened her. Simon hit her over the head with a rock. And then we split. I wasn't gonna attack her. I just wanted her to sweat it. Her big mouth cost me my job."

Nick folded his arms across his chest. "Go on."

"Scaring the high and mighty Madison Baughman was such a rush that I got the idea that me and Josh and Simon should fake a feud between SAGE and the opposition. So we set the fire at Elam Griffiths' and claimed SAGE did it. Then we fed poison to Madison's dog. We set the fire at Everhardt's and claimed SAGE did it. Then we torched Madison's backyard. That's it. After we heard that kid had been shot, we left town. We didn't want someone trying to pin *that* on us."

"Tell me who made the phone calls," Nick said.

"Dude! How many times do I have to tell you? I made the calls to Elam Griffith and Red Everhardt. Josh made the calls to Madison Baughman."

"And which of you vandalized Kessler's truck, and shot his son, and burned his house?"

"That's a trick question, right?" Halstead grinned. "I already told you we didn't do that stuff. Had you stumped, though, didn't we?"

"Definitely." Nick rubbed the stubble on his chin. "Your plan was ingenious. I've worked a lot of cases, and this is the first time I've ever encountered anything like *this*. Truthfully, it wouldn't surprise me if you got a book deal out of it. Maybe even a miniseries."

"You think so?"

"Oh yeah." Nick put a pad and pen on the table in front of Halstead. "Before we can tell the world your story, we need you to write it all down—every clever detail. Investigator Lowry and I are going to leave you here to work on that."

Halstead lifted his eyebrows up and down. "Just make sure the media spells my name right."

Nick followed Buck out of the room and walked around to where Flint was standing and slapped him on the back. "See? No coercion needed." He laughed. "I would've asked for his autograph if that's what it took."

"Did he name his accomplices, Nick?"

"Josh Ruddman and Simon Allister. Both twenty-four. Halstead said they're staying with some girl in Silverton. We hope to have them in custody shortly." Nick turned to the two-way mirror and observed Halstead writing feverishly. "I'm convinced he and his cohorts didn't vandalize Kessler's truck, shoot Kessler's son, or burn Kessler's house."

"Well, I don't think Grayson Knolls did all that."

Nick arched an eyebrow. "He had motive. Opportunity. And I'd bet the farm that he vandalized his own truck. The only reason for a guy doing that is to cover up something. And I intend to find out what."

38

THE NEXT MORNING, Flint sat at his desk, his hands wrapped around a mug of coffee, his eyelids grainy with sleepiness.

Nick strutted through the door, wearing a smug grin that seemed out of place with his bloodshot eyes.

"Our two accomplices finally confessed," he said. "I knew they wouldn't hold out for long, given the evidence and the fact that Halstead ratted them out and took all the credit for masterminding the operation. Talk about a narcissist. I sure missed *that* when I worked up his profile."

"Wait'll he figures out he's not getting a book deal." Flint stifled his smile with the rim of his mug and took a sip of coffee. "I can't believe he fell for that."

"Hey, my method was perfectly legit. I just told him to write down the details of what happened. I didn't tell him it had to go on for pages and sound like a book proposal." Nick laughed. "Talk about a blow by blow. We know exactly what happened in each of the crimes. At the very least, we've got them for engaging in organized criminal activity."

"You're good. Two threads down. One to go. I can hardly wait to tell our disgruntled mayor."

"We've got time to get our ducks in a row before we go after Grayson Knolls. We need to build a case without making him nervous enough to lawyer up." Nick smiled. "I love this job."

"By the way, I danced around our suspicions about Grayson with the Griffiths and the Kesslers yesterday. All they know is that we were questioning him about some inconsistencies concerning the vandalism of his truck."

"That's about to change," Nick said. "We know Grayson is guilty of criminal mischief. Let's see what else he did."

Grayson went up the steps and into the trailer at the work site, his desire for a cup of coffee stronger than his dread of having to be social.

"Good morning, Liz."

Liz peered over the top of her glasses. "Good morning, yourself. Did you get things squared away about your truck?"

Grayson went over to the table and stood with his back to her and filled a paper cup with coffee. "Yeah, I think so."

He heard footsteps and then Rue's voice. "Have you got a minute? I've been meaning to talk to you about something for over a week, but with everything that happened, I haven't had a chance."

"All right."

Grayson picked up his cup and followed Rue to his office and sat in a vinyl chair.

Rue shut the door and then sat in the chair next to Grayson. "Elam and I recently had a conversation about you working toward a management position and me being involved in helping you reach that goal. We agree that it's a good idea, and just as soon as I can get back into the swing of things around here, I want to talk to you about ways we can begin that process."

"You do?"

"You seem surprised. Isn't that what you and I talked about?"

"I remember you saying that once you got comfortable you'd start working toward that goal. But I got the impression it'd be a while." *Like never.*

Rue nodded. "Well, I've had time to think more about it. There's really a lot I can teach you now. Sorry it's taken me so long to get back

to you. But all this stuff with SAGE and then the shooting and our
house burning down…well, needless to say, my mind hasn't been on
my work."

"I'm sure not."

Rue folded his hands between his knees. "Having said that, I need
to level with you about something. Elam's so shaken by what's happened
to my family that he's seriously considered shutting down the project. I
know that's not really what he wants to do. I've got him talked into going
forward—at least for now. I don't want to mislead you in any way. My
hope is that EG Construction will go on with this project and many
more down the road. If we do, then I'll be glad to teach you what I know
so you can eventually work into a better-paying position. But if you need
to explore other job opportunities, given the uncertainty here, I would
certainly understand."

Grayson took a sip of coffee and sized up Rue's demeanor. Why
was he suddenly so willing to be a teacher? Willing to share something
as private as Elam considering a shutdown? Was Rue trying to get him
to quit?

"I appreciate your honesty," Grayson said. "Elam's been good to
me. I'm not going to bail on him."

"Good. Obviously, you need to keep this confidential. There's no
point in worrying the work crew about something that may never
happen."

Grayson grew increasingly agitated as the morning wore on. If Rue
wanted him to quit, why was he being so nice about it? The thought
that he might have misread Rue all along wouldn't leave him alone.
And the implications were more than he could deal with.

His cell phone rang and he put it to his ear. "This is Grayson."

"It's Bobby. Where are you?"

"Out at the site."

"I need to talk to you, face-to-face."

"Tough. I'm working."

Bobby sighed into the receiver. "I know you're mad. But believe it or not, I'm on your side. When do you go to lunch?"

Grayson glanced at his watch. "Any time I want."

"Leave now and meet me at the abandoned Texaco station out on J93. I'll explain when we get there." *Click.*

Grayson disconnected the call. He wasn't meeting Bobby anywhere. He had nothing to say to him. The traitor! He started to go back to work and then had second thoughts. As disgusted as he was with Bobby, he couldn't afford to make an enemy of him.

He hit the auto-dial on his cell.

"EG Construction. This is Liz."

"It's Grayson. I'm going to lunch. I'll be off premises. I've got something I need to do."

"Have a good one."

He put his cell phone on his belt clip and marched across the field to his truck. He winced when he saw the passenger side. The red auto paint he used to cover the damage clashed with the faded red on the rest of the truck. But it was better than driving around with SAGE spray-painted across the side.

He climbed in the front seat and drove to the gate, then waved at the security guard and headed in the direction of the Texaco station.

How much longer could he keep his lies straight? Conceal his guilt? Keep his cool? How long could he look Tara in the eyes and pretend to be a victim? Or dodge Bobby's pointed questions?

Grayson spotted the faded red star on the Texaco station, which was just about the only thing out this far on Highway J93. He slowed his truck and saw Bobby's squad car parked on the side of the boarded-up building. He turned in and pulled alongside his brother, then got out, his arms folded across his chest.

"All right," Grayson said. "I'm here. Want to tell me why?"

Bobby's face was somber, his eyes pained. "I've been taken off the case. I'm here because I care what happens to you."

"Yeah, Bobby. Keep telling yourself that."

"There's no point in beatin' around the bush." Bobby opened the door to the backseat. "I recovered your *stolen* stuff."

Grayson's heart pounded so hard he was sure Bobby could hear it. He scanned the items on the backseat and saw his rifle case, shells, can of spray paint, pocket saw, one yellow rubber glove, a pair of jeans, and a white T-shirt. Even if he'd known what to say, the words would never have escaped his throat.

"Didn't take me long," Bobby said, "to figure out where the red dirt on the spray paint came from. I went out to your fishin' hole and found metal shavings on the ground where you usually park. And I assumed you hid whatever you used to fake the vandalism on your truck—maybe even pitched it in the river. I hiked down the path toward the water and just happened to spot some fresh dirt up on a boulder. I knew it didn't get there by itself, so I started rootin' around. You did a pretty good job of coverin' your tracks, Grays. But not good enough."

Grayson glanced over at Bobby and noticed his eyes brimming with tears. He'd never seen his brother show emotion before, not even when their father died.

"I was puzzled why you staged the theft. Then I remembered you said your rifle was stolen. I tried not to think the worst. But when I found your .223 Remington shells buried with it, it all came together: *You* shot Montana Kessler. How could you do that? How could you shoot a little kid?"

"I…I never said I shot anybody."

"You didn't have to…" Bobby's voice cracked. "Your fingerprints aren't the only thing I got off the mug in my garage. I compared your DNA to the DNA on the handkerchief we found next to the .223 Remington shell at the scene. A match. And we both know ballistics is gonna prove the bullet that hit the Kessler boy came from that rifle. You did it, Grays. The only question is *why*."

Grayson leaned with his hands against Bobby's squad car and hung his head between his arms. "It was an accident. I meant to shoot the kid's dog."

"Well, guess what? You missed."

"I know that, Bobby! This is hard enough without your sarcasm!"

"You think *this* is bad? Wait till Nick Sanchez gets ahold of you!"

Grayson swallowed hard. He couldn't escape the evidence. How was he going to face Tara? The kids? Rue? Elam? *Montana?*

"Why in the world were you gonna shoot the kid's dog?"

"Because I'm stupid, that's why! Isn't that what you want to hear?"

"You're *not* stupid, Grays. That's why I'm so blown away by this. Just level with me. You're in big trouble, and I'm the best friend you've got."

Grayson took a couple of slow, deep breaths and let a wave of nausea pass. When he finally started talking, he felt as though he were someone else saying the words. "I've been jealous of Rue since the day Elam announced he was going to be project manager. That job should've been mine."

He went on to tell Bobby how he had stolen Rue's Phase One file and then destroyed it, and how he had snuck into Three Peaks and vandalized Rue's Silverado.

"The thing is," Grayson said, "Rue wasn't even that shook up about what happened to his forty-thousand-dollar truck. I couldn't believe it. I took this huge risk to rattle his chain, and it hardly fazed him. That ticked me off. I wanted him to hurt the way he'd made me hurt. After that Baughman lady's dog was poisoned, I got the idea to shoot Montana's dog. I figured *that* would shake Rue up big time, and everyone would think SAGE did it to get even."

Grayson told Bobby how he had planned out every detail. But when the moment finally came and he was holding the rifle, his finger on the trigger, he just couldn't go through with it. He explained how the deer startled him and the rifle discharged accidentally.

"I wanted to die, Bobby. I didn't mean to hurt Montana. I really like that kid. It was a horrible accident."

"Yeah, you felt so bad about it, you just left him there to die."

"No." Grayson shook his head. "I was going to go help him, but his parents were already in the truck racing toward him. There wasn't anything I could do but get out of there. It was the worst day of my life."

"Apparently not bad enough to stop you from burning down the Kesslers' house."

"Whoa! I had nothing to do with that."

"Come on, Grays. It's over. We just nailed the perps who did all the crimes against Baughman and set the fires at the Griffiths' and Everhardt's. They deny any involvement in the vandalism, the shooting, or settin' the fire at the Kesslers'. They have no reason to lie. They're goin' away for a long time."

"Well, I didn't do it. You've got to believe me."

"Why should I? You've told so many lies I doubt you even know what the truth is."

Grayson felt hot all over. He was in enough trouble without getting slapped with arson. He stood up straight and turned to Bobby. "I can describe the guy who did it. I was there. I saw everything."

Flint sat in the interrogation room with Nick and listened to Grayson Knolls confess to vandalizing Rue Kessler's truck and accidentally shooting Montana. He could hardly believe it and wondered how Rue and Elam would react when they got the news, not to mention Grayson's wife and kids. He was glad when it was over with and Grayson was led away and Nick took a late lunch.

Flint made a copy of the artist's sketch of the man that Grayson claimed to have watched set the fire at the Kesslers', then stepped in his office and closed the door. He opened the case file and read over the list of evidence that had been collected by investigators at the scene: plastic cups, soda cans, wrappers, gum, wads of tobacco, cigarette butts, a rusted key, a paperclip, a Xanax tablet.

Flint popped a couple Tums and studied the artist's sketch again. He wanted to be wrong. He laid out the photos taken of the shoe impressions cast at the scene. One was very distinctive and seemed out of place: a size nine-and-a-half Rockport Oxford. Newly manufactured and on the pricey side. Not the kind of shoe a construction worker would wear on the job.

He agonized over what he should do. Was it smart to approach the suspect alone? He doubted that he was armed or that he was a flight risk. Would Nick be angry that he wasn't informed? Probably. Would any of this prove the man's guilt—or just that he'd been at the house? Would Grayson's word that he had witnessed the whole thing mean anything after he had lied repeatedly?

Flint rubbed the back of his neck. What if he was wrong about this? What might the personal repercussions be? There was a lot more at stake than just pursuing a case.

39

GRAYSON SAT IN A ROOM with dull gray walls, his fingers tapping the table. He glanced up when the attractive young woman with dark hair and square glasses came back into the room. Did this court-appointed attorney really care what happened to him? Did she even believe the shooting was an accident?

Jennifer Lyles sat across from him and placed a stack of papers on the table. "Good news. I was able to get you released on a PR, or personal recognizance, bond."

"Released?"

She nodded. "I convinced the judge and the assistant district attorney that you weren't a flight risk and weren't likely to commit new offenses. Also that your financial situation would make it impossible to make bond, no matter how low it was set."

"I can go *home*—just like that?"

"You're required to sign off on this form and swear to pay the bond amount should you decide to jump bail. Which, I might add, would greatly compound your situation." She arched her eyebrows. "Are we clear?"

Grayson nodded. "I've got a wife and four kids. No money saved. And my credit cards are maxed out. Where would I go?"

"It would be nice if you could go back to work and keep things as normal as possible until the trial. But considering the nature of your offenses, that won't be possible."

"So what am I going to do? If I don't have a job, we can't eat. No one's going to hire me now. It would almost be easier to go to jail than stay home and see my family suffer."

"Perhaps you could get a contract labor job on another construction project. You wouldn't have to deal with the paperwork or the questions. And it would give you some income."

Grayson let out an anguished sigh. "Yeah, but nothing even close to what I'm making now. Plus I'll lose my medical insurance. We're already on the verge of bankruptcy and can't scrape up the money to file."

"I'm sorry, Grayson." Jennifer's tone was compassionate, but her eyes seemed to say, *You should have thought of that before you did something so incredibly stupid.*

"Maybe I can work double shifts," he said. "At least between us, Tara and I could cover the essentials: house, food, utilities. But once I go to jail, I don't know how my family will survive…" Grayson let out a sob and then seemed to inhale it. "I can't believe I got myself into this mess."

Flint pulled his squad car in front of the Griffiths' log house and made eye contact with Elam as he came down the steps and got in on the passenger side.

Neither of them spoke.

Flint drove to the end of the private drive, which today seemed miles long instead of two hundred yards, and turned onto Three Peaks Road. He continued on for several miles and then turned north onto the White Top Highway.

He stole a glance at Elam. "How're you doing?"

"I still can't believe that Grayson and…" Elam's voiced cracked. "Anyhow, I've had about all the betrayal I can handle in one day."

"How's Carolyn?"

"She and Ivy were out in the kitchen bawling when I left. Rue was on his way home."

Flint nodded. "I'm really sorry, Elam. You know this hits me hard, too."

"For once I'd rather be standing in your shoes than my own."

Flint slowed the car, exited on Riverview Road, and stopped at the Stop sign, then made a left and an immediate right into the parking lot. He pulled into an empty space and sat for a minute, dreading what he had to do. "You sure you want to handle this?"

"I do."

Flint got out of his squad car and followed Elam to the front door of the Phantom Hollow Veterinary Clinic. He held it open and let his friend go in first. At the moment he would rather be anything but the sheriff.

Elam went up to the receptionist window. "Would you please tell Dr. Griffith his father is here to see him?"

She smiled. "I'll be glad to. Have a seat, if you'd like." The young woman disappeared through a doorway.

Elam turned to him. "You're going to take a lot of heat for this, you know."

"Let me worry about that."

An elderly woman with a Yorkshire terrier on her lap stared at them from across the waiting room.

Elam's silence screamed louder than the words he didn't say, and Flint could only imagine what was going through his mind. A door opened and Rusty Griffith stood in the threshold, looking handsome and professional in his white coat. Flint's mind flashed back to Rusty's high-school days when he worked behind the soda fountain at Dipper's.

"This is a pleasant surprise." Rusty came toward them, his smile wide and genuine. A good indication he had no idea what was going on. "As soon as I take care of Mrs. Dawson's Yorkie, I'll give you a tour of the clinic. I did some remodeling and added state-of-the-art equipment." He moved his eyes from Elam to Flint and back to Elam. His smile faded. "What's wrong? Did something happen to Mom? Jacqueline? The girls?"

Elam tugged at his mustache. "Actually, I think something's happened to *you.*"

Grayson pushed open the side door of the Tanner County Courthouse and jogged down the steps, wishing he could just keep running and never stop.

Bobby got up from a park bench and hurried over to him. "Did they cut you loose on a PR bond?"

Grayson nodded and avoided looking at his brother. "That was a cakewalk compared to what I have to do now. I'd sooner stand in front of firing squad than talk to Tara and the kids. Where do I even begin?"

"I already talked to them," Bobby said. "Like you asked me to. I told them everything—the whole story."

Grayson glanced at him. "I didn't really think you'd do it."

"At least I'm good for somethin'. I doubt they're expectin' you to say a whole lot tonight. I told them you'd be feelin' down and pretty ashamed. But at some point, you're gonna have to find a way to explain yourself."

"Yeah, I know. Thanks for doing the dirty work."

Bobby put his hand on Grayson's shoulder. "So what'd your lawyer say?"

"She thinks the justice of the peace will consider the vandalism as a Class C misdemeanor, and I'll get a fine only, no jail time—not that I have any idea how to come up with money to pay a fine. We'll probably be living on the street by then. As for the shooting, unless she can plea it down, I'm looking at deadly conduct, which is a third-degree felony—two to ten years."

Grayson appreciated his brother's silence in lieu of the lecture he deserved.

"I'm sorry, Bobby. I know I've embarrassed you. You're so well respected down here. Must be really hard."

"Hey, nobody's blamin' me for this. You made your own choices."

Grayson nodded. "You were right to confront me and bring me in. I'm actually relieved, in a weird sort of way. The guilt was eating me up." He blinked the stinging from his eyes. "I'm not sure what I can say to Elam or Rue. But the one I feel a need to talk to is Montana. The kid probably hates me."

"That's the least of your worries now."

"From a legal standpoint. But that little boy is never going to completely get over what happened. He deserves an explanation and an apology."

Flint followed Elam into Rusty's tastefully decorated office and noticed a picture of his wife and daughters on the credenza.

Rusty closed the door and turned around. "What's this about?"

"I thought you should know there was an eyewitness to the arson at Ivy and Rue's house. I brought the artist's sketch Flint e-mailed me." Elam unfolded a piece of paper and handed it to Rusty. "Recognize this man?"

Rusty's eyes grew wide, and his cheeks flushed.

"Were you there, Son?" Elam said. "Did you burn your sister's house?"

"How can you even ask me that? What kind of man do you think I am?"

Elam shrugged. "I honestly don't know anymore. You tell me."

Rusty's eyes welled, and his lips quivered. He brought his fist to his mouth and choked back the emotion, and then finally started talking. "I was there for you and Mom all those years when you didn't know where Ivy was or what she was doing—and even after we found out the disgusting truth. She devastated us. How could you take her back and just shut me out like I didn't matter anymore?" He whisked a tear off his cheek.

"What are you talking about?" Elam said.

"Ever since Ivy came back, you've treated her better than if she had actually done something with her life. In fact, a lot better than you *ever* treated me. You handed everything to her—house, car, job, even a valuable piece of land. It's like you and Mom are totally in denial that Ivy sold herself for drug money and went to jail for covering up Joe Hadley's murder. And it's so obvious that her kid is your favorite—the only *grandson*. You'd have to be in my shoes to see how upside down this is."

Elam folded his arms across his chest. "And you'd have to be in my shoes to see how unforgiving and cruel and heartless *you've* been."

"Someone has to hold Ivy accountable. You and Mom sure aren't."

Elam shook his head from side to side. "For crying out loud, Rusty. Ivy's paid a high price for the things she did. And she's done everything in her power—and God's—to make things right. Who are you to stand as judge and jury over her or your mother and me?"

"It's so unfair that she put us through the wringer and then got off so easily."

"Easily?" Elam's neck and face turned beet red. "Do you know how hard it was for her to kick the drug habit? Or how gut wrenching to leave Montana and serve her jail sentence? The statute of limitations had run. She could've walked. But she *asked* for the maximum. Ivy never tried to sidestep any punishment or consequence. But she's moving forward. And it's about time you knocked that jealous, bitter chip off your shoulder and stepped into the present!"

Father and son stood staring at each other, pin-drop stillness filling the space between them.

Flint decided it was time for him to do what he came to do. "Rusty, you drive a white Lincoln Navigator, right?"

"You know I do."

"And you recently bought a pair of size nine-and-a-half Rockport Oxfords, correct?"

"How'd you know that?"

"You just told me. It just so happens that we cast that exact shoe impression at the scene of the fire."

"I can't be the only man in Tanner County who wears Rockports."

"No, but this particular style has only been on the market for a few weeks," Flint said. "Are you familiar with the prescription drug Xanax?"

"Sure. It's for anxiety, I think. Why?"

"We also found a Xanax tablet lying in the dirt near the place where our witness said the white SUV was parked. The tablet was clean and dry, suggesting it might've fallen out of someone's pocket." Flint's gaze collided with Rusty's. "With all the pressure you've been under lately, I'm betting you have a prescription for Xanax. I could get a warrant and check your medicine cabinet. Or you could just tell me the truth."

Rusty seemed as edgy as a caged cat, and perspiration beads popped out on his forehead. "None of that proves I had anything to do with setting the fire. After I found out Ivy and Rue were building a house, I drove out to look at the place. Is that a crime?"

Elam shoved the artist's sketch in front of Rusty's face. "It is when someone *saw* you burn it. You had two gas cans. You soaked the house inside and out, then made a Molotov cocktail out of a beer bottle and tossed it inside. Son, it's over."

"All right, I did it, okay? I torched her precious house!" Rusty glared at his dad. "Are you happy now?"

Elam's shoulders drooped, his voice suddenly on low volume. "Happy? Rusty, I love you. You think I wanted to see you destroy your life this way?"

"My life's already destroyed."

"Since when?"

Rusty flopped on the couch and buried his face in his hands. "Jacqueline filed for divorce. She wants sole custody of the girls. She says I'm an unfit father…" Rusty's voice cracked. "She said I died inside when Ivy came back. That she's tired of living with a shell." Rusty started to sob. "Dad, help me. I'm so lost. I don't even know how to get out of this pit I've dug myself into."

Grayson lay across the bed, facedown, his head resting on his hands. He heard the door open and close, and then felt someone sit on the bed.

"I'm furious you deceived me," Tara said, "which is really no different than lying. But what you did to Rue and his family is absolutely unconscionable. They'll never be the same. And neither will we—or *our* children. What in the world were you thinking, Grayson?"

The sound of her sniffling tore at his heart.

"Don't expect me to feel sorry for you because you're going to jail," she said. "At least you'll get three squares a day. I'm the one who'll have to put food on the table, keep the home fires burning, and keep these kids in line all by myself. Whatever sentence you get, mine will be worse."

Grayson wondered if she had any idea how ashamed he was or how remorseful. Or if it even mattered. "I guess saying I'm sorry probably wouldn't mean anything."

"It won't *solve* anything, but it would certainly mean something."

He rolled over and took her hand, relieved when she didn't pull it away. "I can't even begin to express my sorrow and regret for what I did. I never meant for things to get out of hand. I was just so jealous of Rue. I hated him for getting the job that should've been mine. I don't think you realize how devastated I really was when I didn't get promoted."

"I knew you were disappointed. I was, too, but it wasn't the end of the world."

"It was to me. I saw it as the only way to get the financial pressure off and free you up to finally quit teaching. I even thought it might make you want me again…" His words trailed off, and he swallowed the emotion that tightened his throat.

Tara's eyes turned to pools. "I've never stopped wanting you, Grayson. You just seemed so angry all the time. So distant."

"Yeah, I know. The financial pressure was so consuming I couldn't think about much else. And it was easier to blame Rue for everything than to admit our bad spending habits early on got us into a mess we couldn't dig out of."

"We would've figured something out."

"I couldn't see how. But that's no excuse for taking my anger out on

Rue. I can't tell you how ashamed I am. Never in a million years would I have anticipated what happened to Montana. Never."

"Had to be horrible."

"Hardest thing I've ever faced." Grayson focused on her eyes and refused to let the image into his mind. "And not just because I knew I was in trouble, but because Montana's a great kid. And no child should have to go through what I put him through. Or his parents."

"I'd hate to guess what they think of you."

Grayson brought her hand to his cheek and held it there. "What's most important is what you and the kids think of me. And if it takes the rest of my life, I'm going to do whatever it takes to earn back your respect."

40

RUE SAT ON THE FRONT STEPS at Elam and Carolyn's, the evening sky a blanket of crimson, and stared at Three Peaks Christian Camp and Conference Center nestled in the pines a couple hundred yards below. It seemed that every nook and cranny of his life had been permeated by the foul odor of Grayson's and Rusty's spiteful actions.

It was disheartening enough that Grayson wanted to hurt him. But Rusty… How would the family reconcile his twisted reprisal against his own flesh and blood?

The door behind him opened, and a few seconds later Ivy sat beside him and hugged her knees.

"Montana's asleep," she said. "The pain pill knocked him out. It's just as well."

"Poor kid has to be confused about what happened."

Ivy wiped a tear off her cheek. "Who isn't?"

"I'm not surprised he seemed more hurt and confused by Grayson's actions than Rusty's. After all, he's never known Rusty to be anything but hateful. Grayson was really nice to him."

Ivy nodded. "He seemed so upset Grayson had planned to shoot Windy that I doubt it matters he supposedly changed his mind at the last second."

"Do you believe that's what happened?"

Ivy shrugged. "Well, I sure can't see Grayson shooting Montana on purpose."

"Your dad believes the rifle fired accidentally."

"And you don't?"

"I'm not gonna give Grayson the satisfaction. As far as I'm concerned, the sheriff can lock him up and throw away the key. Rusty, too."

Ivy linked her arm in his. "Dad asked me to come out and get you. He wants the four of us to talk about this while Montana's out of earshot."

"I'll listen. I already told you how *I* feel."

Ivy let out an anguished sigh. "I just don't understand what they were so jealous of."

Rue stood and pulled Ivy to her feet. "Obviously, they don't think we prodigals are entitled to success and happiness. I wonder if they'll see things differently now that they're the ones stuck in the pigsty?"

Rue sat at the kitchen table, weary of listening to the family rehash the despicable deeds of Grayson and Rusty and the reasons they gave the authorities for having done them.

"Oh," Elam said, "I forgot to tell you. Flint called and said Grayson has a court-appointed attorney and is out on a personal recognizance bond. Rusty made bail and hired Brett Hewitt to represent him. Rue, in case you didn't know, Brett was Ivy's defense lawyer."

Why should he care what kind of legal counsel his wayward brother-in-law obtained? There's no way he was going to get out of this. "Look, I can appreciate how hard this is for you and Carolyn. I know you love Rusty regardless of what he did. But in my mind, neither Rusty nor Grayson deserves this much of my time or attention. And I sure don't feel sorry for them. I just want to get past this and move on."

"We all do," Elam said. "But it's not that simple."

"Seems pretty cut and dried to me." Rue avoided eye contact with Carolyn. "They tried to destroy my family, and each needs to take responsibility for what he did."

"The court will see to that," Elam said. "But I know from experience there's a lot more involved in letting this go than just seeing them punished."

Rue folded his hands on the table. "It's a good start."

The lines on Elam's forehead deepened. "Believe me, I understand how furious you are. I can't begin to tell you how disgusted I am with Rusty and Grayson. I'd like to slap them both upside the head. But frankly, I'm more worried about you and Ivy."

"Why?" Rue said.

"Because I don't want this to come between you the way Ivy's trouble came between Rusty and Jacqueline—or Carolyn and me. I was so bitter when Ivy moved back here that I was suspicious of everything she said and did and wanted nothing to do with Montana. I called him *the boy* for weeks. I wanted to punish her for things she couldn't change. In some ways, my attitude wasn't any better than Rusty's."

"But you worked through it," Ivy said.

Elam's eyes filled. "Because your mother held my feet to the fire. And because I let God change my heart. But it put a strain on our marriage. I came close to losing you. I don't want to lose Rusty. And I don't want to lose hope that you and your brother can be reconciled."

"I doubt Rusty even feels remorse."

"We don't know that," Elam said. "He was as broken as I've ever seen him. Give him time."

Carolyn reached across the table and clutched one of Rue's hands and one of Ivy's, a tear trickling down her cheek. "We all feel betrayed. But the worst thing we can do is let our hearts turn cold like Rusty's. Ultimately, he's lost everything he cares about. In a very real sense, he's been more victimized by his bitterness and jealousy than you two have."

What a crock. Rue pushed back his chair and rose to his feet. "No offense, but I can't listen to this. Rusty *chose* to be a victim. We didn't. I don't hate him. And I don't hate Grayson. But I hope they're both miserable. Maybe they'll get a little taste of what they put us through."

Flint closed the file on his desk and rubbed his eyes. He couldn't even imagine the mood at the Griffiths' house tonight.

Nick strolled through the door and flopped in a chair. "I'm packed up and ready to go. As much as I've enjoyed my stay at the Phantom Hollow Lodge, I'm ready to get home to my wife and kids and some good home cooking."

"Thanks for helping with the case," Flint said. "Your insights were invaluable."

"Let's hope you never need me again. But if you do, you know where to find me. We're a good team, and I can't say that for every sheriff whose turf I've stepped on. How's Lieutenant Knolls doing?"

"Bobby's all right. He knows he did the right thing."

"Well, tell him for me he's a class act. We've had our differences, but he handled the situation with his brother as well as any law-enforcement officer could. He's a good man."

Someone coughed, and Flint saw Bobby standing in the doorway.

"Good timing, eh?" Bobby came over and shook Nick's hand. "Thanks. That means a lot comin' from you. I came by to tell you I appreciated the way you handled my brother. You could've chewed him up and spit him out."

Nick flashed a wry smile. "Once in a while I surprise myself."

"Well, it's been a long day. I'm headin' out. Oh, I almost forgot…" Bobby reached in his pocket, took out a pack of bubblegum, and handed it to Nick. "You really should try this. I haven't had a cigarette in four years."

Nick nodded. "I'll give it a go."

"Be safe on the road," Bobby said. "See you Monday, Sheriff."

Bobby left the office, and Nick rose to his feet.

"Well, Flint. We got the bad guys. Now you can take your family to Disney World without anything major hanging over your head."

"Let's hope that's prophetic." Flint came around the desk and offered Nick a hearty handshake and a pat on the back. "Take care."

"Will do."

Flint popped two Tums, then sat at his desk. He leaned back in his chair, his hands clasped behind his head, and listened to the sound of the special agent's squeaky soles grow faint in the hallway.

Bad guys? What satisfaction was there in adding Bobby's brother and his best friend's son to that list? Making the arrests by anyone's standard was a job well done. But this was not a good day.

Grayson lay in bed facing the hallway, his back to Tara's, and listened to the refrigerator making gurgling noises. All he needed now was for a major appliance to go out.

How was his family going to get by if he went to jail—or if he couldn't find work in the meantime? Jennifer Lyles told him it could be weeks or even months before he got a trial date. Even if he were able to get a contract labor job, his paycheck added to Tara's wouldn't be enough to meet their obligations. And if they got behind on their credit-card payments, they would lose what little cushion they still had. Maybe it was time to forget about the bills and just file for bankruptcy.

He wondered how he was going to face Elam and Rue—or if he even had enough gumption to apologize in person. And what could he possibly say to Montana that would make a difference or lessen the pain he'd caused him?

Even harder to think about was how he was going to explain his actions to his own children, who would also bear his shame.

He heard the sound of bare feet on the hardwood floor and saw Samuel's silhouette in the doorway. The boy came over to the bed and tapped him on the shoulder.

"Daddy, are you awake?" he whispered.

Grayson reached over and stroked his fine hair. "Uh-huh."

"I'm scared. Can I sleep with you?"

"Sure."

Grayson moved over, and Samuel climbed into the bed and curled up in a ball, his back flush against his father's chest.

Grayson relished the closeness, his arm draped over his youngest son, and wondered which of them was more afraid.

41

RUE PULLED INTO the parking lot at Woodlands Community Church and strolled with Ivy and Montana toward the entrance. Before they even reached the door, they were surrounded with well-wishers expressing love and concern and thankfulness to God that Montana had survived the shooting—and that Joel Myers had come home from the hospital.

Rue appreciated the support of his church family but couldn't stay focused on the socializing, the singing, or even the sermon.

As soon as the service ended, he slipped out and meandered through the cemetery to avoid answering questions and rehashing what he'd just as soon forget. His anger was already driving a wedge between him and everyone else. And he didn't know what to do about it.

He stood at the wrought-iron fence, feeling surprisingly blasé about the blue gray mountain range and the cloud puffs that dotted the jagged peaks. It seemed a lifetime ago that he and Ivy had taken Montana on that deli dog picnic at the new house and admired this same view from their unfinished living room.

"There you are."

Brandon Jones came from behind and stood next to him.

"You okay?" Brandon said. "I can't even imagine what kind of week you've had."

"It's been rough. Montana's gonna be all right, though. That's the most important thing."

"Have you talked to Rusty?"

Rue snickered. "No. He's kept his distance, which is fine with me. I know Elam and Carolyn are really hurting. I can't imagine how hard it must be for them, especially after going through such an ordeal with Ivy. Of course, we got a double whammy with Grayson. It's just a lot for us to sort through."

"Are they in jail?"

"No, out on bail. I don't know when they'll get trial dates. I just wish it was over. And that I didn't have such animosity toward them. That's a new thing for me. I don't like it. Any words of wisdom?"

"Time will help."

Rue nudged Brandon with his elbow. "You can do better than that. I know my attitude's wrong, but I'd be a liar if I said I was willing to forgive Grayson or Rusty at this point."

"It's a difficult situation, that's for sure." Brandon put his hands on the fence and seemed deep in thought. Finally, he said, "One of the best pieces of advice I ever got was from a friend in Seaport, Weezie Taylor. She said it's not who we are but Whose we are that really matters. I try to remember that when someone's hurt me. It's hard to do what's right when someone does us wrong, but that's what Christians are called to do."

"You're saying I need to forgive those two losers."

Brandon put his hand on Rue's shoulder. "I'm saying when you realize Whose you are, you can do what seems impossible."

Rue relaxed in the quiet for a few minutes and then glanced at his watch. "You'd better get going. Aren't you supposed to be back at the camp at noon?"

"Yeah, we've got a great group of teens this week. Listen…you have my cell number. I want you to call if you need someone to talk to. Anytime—day or night."

"Thanks, man. I appreciate that."

A second later they were locked in a bear hug, and then Brandon jogged up the hill to the church parking lot, his words still ringing in Rue's mind.

Late that afternoon, the Griffiths and the Kesslers sat out on the front porch, eating the strawberry cheesecake Carolyn had made. Everyone seemed subdued. The only sounds were the clanking of forks and the rustling of the Sunday newspaper in the July breeze.

Rue stared at the graham cracker crumbs on his plate and realized he had eaten his entire slice without savoring a single bite. He kept thinking about the advice he had elicited from Brandon and doubted he would ever be spiritual enough to take the high road when it came to Grayson or Rusty. He decided to go take a nap when Montana slid off the glider, went over to the railing, and craned his neck.

"What are you looking at?" Rue said.

"There's a car coming."

"Oh, I hope it's Pastor Myers." Carolyn hurriedly collected the empty plates. "He said he might stop by after he talked to Rusty."

"I know he did, honey." Elam gently took her arm and held on until she looked at him. "But don't expect too much."

"Hey, it's *Uncle Rusty's* car," Montana said.

"What?" Ivy jumped up. "Why is *he* here?"

Rue stood and spotted the white Navigator coming up the drive. He slipped his arm around Ivy, then pulled Montana over next to them.

"Let's all stay calm," Elam said. "Whatever the purpose for his visit, this is a first. Keep an open mind."

Windy and Sasha raced toward the car, barking protectively.

Rue watched carefully as Rusty pulled into the circle drive, stopped the car in front of the house, and then sat motionless for what seemed an eternity. Finally, he got out of the car and trudged toward them, his hands deep in his pockets, seemingly unaffected by the huskies barking at his heels.

Rue braced himself for an ugly confrontation, but when his brother-in-law stopped at the bottom of the steps, his eyes were red-rimmed and his face blotchy and swollen.

The moment seemed frozen in time. Finally he saw Rusty's lips move.

"I-I should've called first," Rusty said, "but I was afraid I'd chicken out before I got here. I have something to say and would really appreciate it if you'd hear me out. I'm not going to cause trouble."

"All right," Elam said. "Let's go inside."

Rusty climbed the stairs and entered the house. Everyone else followed, one by one, Rue going in last.

They filed into the living room, and Rue sat on the couch with Ivy, Montana between them. He didn't really care what Rusty had to say. What he did was inexcusable.

Rusty stood in front of the fireplace, wringing his hands, the tension in the room almost tangible.

"I-I didn't think I could ever face any of you. But Pastor Myers… he…well, he convinced me you'd want to hear this. I guess I should start by saying how sorry I am that I burned the house…" Rusty paused, his lips quivering. "It was unconscionable, and there's no excuse."

He directed his attention to Ivy. "After all the messes you've been in, I couldn't handle seeing the three of you living happily ever after when my family was falling apart. I worked hard to build a practice and a good life for Jacqueline and the girls. Things were going great—until you came home. After that, nothing I did mattered to Mom and Dad anymore."

Rusty held up his palm. "I realize now that's not true. But it felt that way to me. And then Mom and Dad handed everything to you: house, car, job, land. I went to college and veterinary school and then worked my tail off to get those things, and I resented that you didn't lift a finger.

"I was so eaten up with resentment that Jacqueline finally couldn't take it anymore. She left me the day after you got married…" Rusty's voice trailed off. He whisked a tear off his cheek and then continued. "I didn't come to your wedding because I was angry that you were happy when you didn't deserve to be. I'm sorry. But that's the truth. I'm not proud of it.

"I bought Doc Henley's practice and came back to Jacob's Ear because I couldn't bear to be alone. I thought living close to Mom and

Dad would help. Of course, nothing was the same. That just fueled more anger."

Rusty turned his gaze on Montana. "I'm sorry I was so mean to you at Thanksgiving. I didn't want to like you. But the truth is, you're a neat kid, and your parents should be proud. I used you to hurt your mother, and that was a bad thing. You're the kind of nephew that would make any uncle proud.

"And, Rue…I can't believe how I've shortchanged you. You have such compassion and understanding for what Ivy's been through. I think the dramatic contrast between your attitude and mine was so convicting that I wanted to keep you out of my life. I'm sorry. You obviously care very much about Ivy and Montana and my parents. You would've made a great brother-in-law if I'd given you half a chance."

Rusty paused to gather his composure. "Mom and Dad, I can't tell you how sorry I am for refusing to let go of the past just when you finally could. Not only did I add to your burden, but I judged you wrongly. You never let Ivy get away with anything. You just did what you could to give her a chance at a normal life.

"I've disgraced you worse than she ever did. At least she was addicted to drugs and didn't know what she was doing when she hurt you. I knew exactly what I was doing and did it anyway. I'm so ashamed. I hope you can forgive me."

Rusty buried his face in hands for a few moments and then looked over at Ivy and Rue. "Once you know the total cost of the damage to the house, I'll make sure you get a check to cover the loss. Deal with it however you need to with the insurance company, but I need to do this.

"Brett thinks I'll end up doing jail time, and I've hardly begun to reconcile myself to that fact. I have no one to blame but myself. For the rest of my life, I have to live with the hurt I've caused each of you. I guess I can honestly say that now I know what it is to have"—Rusty's voice trailed off and his words were barely audible—"a broken and contrite heart."

Ivy reached over and squeezed Rue's hand as Rusty struggled not to lose it.

"I've been so far from God I don't deserve to utter His name. I'm not sure what to do with all that. But I need each of you to know how very sorry I am. I think I should leave now. I appreciate your letting me say what I came here to say. I just hope someday you'll be able to forgive me."

Rusty started for the door just as Montana slid off the couch.

"Uncle Rusty, wait…"

Rusty stopped and turned to him.

"*I* forgive you."

No one moved.

Rusty's face turned hot pink, his eyes brimming with tears. He gave a slight nod, then hurried out of the living room and out the front door.

Rue finally exhaled, aware of Ivy sniffling.

"Well, if anybody can top that," Elam said. "Let's hear it."

Rue sat under the stars on the hill next to his in-laws' house, feeling small and insignificant—and depressed that his eight-year-old son was more spiritually mature than he was.

But how could someone that young even begin to fathom the maliciousness behind Rusty's burning down the house? Or understand how much work had been lost? Or what it would take to start over? Or that the dream itself had been destroyed, and no amount of money could buy it back?

Rue sighed. Who was he kidding? Montana had experienced Rusty's wrath in a much more personal way. He had been intimidated and put down and made to feel as if he had no value at all. And still he forgave Rusty without question. Was his young son's willingness to forgive too simplistic—or was his own reluctance to forgive justifiable due to the severity of the offense?

The words of the Lord's Prayer rang in his mind. *Forgive us our debts, as we also have forgiven our debtors.*

That's not what he wanted to hear, but it was hard to get any simpler than that. He was distracted by a form climbing the hill and realized it was Ivy.

She sat down next to him. "I figured I'd find you out here. So what's going on in your head?"

"I think our son is a saint, and his father is…well, *not* so saintly."

Ivy put her hand on his knee. "Don't be too hard on yourself. Montana and I have struggled with Rusty's attitude for over a year. We've already dealt with a lot of the feelings you have now. So have Mom and Dad. We just want this family whole again."

"So do I," Rue said. "But it just seems a little too easy. Rusty deserves to sweat it a while."

"Like he thought I should sweat it because of what I did?" Ivy tilted her head back and seemed to study the night sky. "He was devastated, you know. It nearly killed him when he found out his little sister had sold herself for drug money. And covered up Joe Hadley's murder for ten years. I put them all through unspeakable stress and shame."

"You made amends. You did everything you could to set things right."

Ivy stroked his arm. "Isn't that what Rusty's trying to do now?"

"I don't trust him."

"My dad didn't trust me, either. I had to earn it back."

"I guess I'm not feeling that generous yet."

"I understand. But just remember you can't have it both ways. If you want Rusty to forgive me, you have to be willing to forgive him."

"You didn't burn his house down, Ivy. Your acts weren't malicious. Even he recognizes that."

Ivy started to say something and didn't. Half a minute later she said, "I'm going to go crash. It's so odd, but this might be the first peaceful night's sleep I've had in a long time."

42

THE NEXT DAY, Rue moved his family back to the chalet at Three Peaks and began working twelve- to fourteen-hour days in an effort to keep up with his job, and Grayson's, until Elam could hire a new foreman.

By Friday, he was back in the swing of things and enjoying being able to lose himself in his work. He was almost finished going through his inbox when he heard the front door of the trailer open and heavy footsteps move in his direction.

He lifted his eyes, shocked to see Elam and Grayson standing in the doorway.

"Grayson wants to talk to you," Elam said. "He and I met over breakfast. I think you should hear what he has to say."

Rue's heart hammered. He didn't expect to see Grayson until the trial. "Uh, okay. Come in."

"I'll leave you two by yourselves." Elam walked down the hall to his office and closed the door.

Grayson sat in a vinyl chair, his hands folded between his knees.

"All right," Rue said. "Let's hear it."

"I-I'm really sorry for what I put you and your family through, especially Montana." Grayson swallowed hard. "I'm not here to make excuses. I just wanted to tell you myself how sorry I am. I doubt either one of us will ever get over that day. I'd do anything to go back and do things differently."

"Yeah, well, you can't."

"I'm just glad he's going to be all right. That was the worst day of my life."

"You think you had a bad day? You should've been in *my* shoes."

Grayson stared at his hands. "I can't even imagine what you were feeling. Elam thought it might help you to know what was going on in my head to cause me to do something so awful. It's not an excuse, but it might help you put things in perspective."

"Go on." Rue folded his arms across his chest and listened as Grayson admitted having resented him from the day Elam announced he was going to be project manager.

Grayson explained how he had stolen the Phase One file and then later, when he came to return it, had discovered Rue's note about his aptitude test. He described the chain of events that were set off by his making the assumption he had been lied to, including burning the file, vandalizing Rue's truck, and going out to the Kesslers' property to shoot the dog.

"For crying out loud, Grayson. I told you I'd work with you once I got comfortable with my own job. If you had doubts, why didn't you say so?"

"Everything was coming down around me. I wanted to believe the worst about you and blame you for my money problems. But when you finally told me you and Elam had talked and you were ready to start working me into a better position, I was jolted back to reality. Not only had I read you wrong, but I'd done you wrong."

"Do you think?" Rue rolled his eyes.

"I wouldn't blame you for hating me. I hate me. My life is trashed. My wife is devastated. And my kids won't have a dad while I'm in prison. And the saddest thing of all is that none of this will change what you've suffered." Grayson paused, his lip quivering. "I'm so sorry."

Rue almost felt compassion for the guy but dismissed it. *Why feel sorry for him? He made his own bed.*

"If you ever get to the place where you'll allow it," Grayson said. "I'd really like to talk to Montana. With you there, of course."

"What could you possibly say to him that would help anything? He knows what you told the sheriff."

"I just want to apologize. He deserves an explanation. This thing is going to be with him the rest of his life, too."

Rue paced the front porch at Elam and Carolyn's and glanced at his watch for the umpteenth time. "I must need my head examined to have agreed to this."

"I think it was a good decision," Elam said. "Montana needs closure. And if you don't like the way it's going, you can put an abrupt halt to it."

Rue spotted a car coming up the drive. "That must be Grayson. I'll go get Montana."

"I'll get him." Elam laid his hand on Rue's shoulder. "Lord, we ask You to be present here, to guard Montana's heart, and allow him to hear exactly what You want him to hear. Our desire is that this encounter will bring healing, but use it to Your glory. In Jesus's name we pray." Elam squeezed his shoulder. "I'll be right back."

"Are the dogs in the house?" Rue said.

Elam nodded and went inside.

Rue stood on the porch and watched Grayson's car pull into the circle drive and stop. Why was he so nervous? If Grayson got out of line, he'd run him off.

Montana came outside and stood next to him just as Grayson came up on the porch.

No one said anything. Montana slipped his hand into Rue's and held it tightly.

After what seemed an eternity, Grayson said, "Montana, I won't stay long, but there's something I would like you to know. Should we talk out here or in the house?"

"Out here. I'll sit on the glider, and you can stand over at the railing."

Distance, Rue thought. *Good thinking, Son.*

Grayson leaned against the railing, his arms folded. "I'm going to tell you why I did what I did. And then I want you to ask me anything you want—even if you think it might make me angry. Deal?"

"Deal."

"When I was your age, I didn't have a good relationship with my dad the way you do," Grayson said. "For some reason, nothing I did ever made him proud. When I grew up, my dad made fun of me for taking a construction job instead of going to college or working with him on his job. It really hurt my feelings, you know?"

Montana nodded.

"The reason I'm telling you this is because I never forgave my dad, and my anger just got bigger and heavier, kind of like a snowball when you roll it in wet snow. And I carried it around everywhere. I couldn't get rid of it. I'm not sure if you've ever felt that way, but it's awful."

Montana played with his fingers. "I was *really* angry with my mom when she got high all the time. But Gramma Lu helped me forgive her. Then I wasn't mad anymore."

"That's the right way to do it. But you see, I didn't know that, even as a grownup. And a secret part of me was still hurting because my dad wasn't proud of me. I think that's why I liked working with your grandpa Elam so much. He always told me what a good job I did. But when he gave your dad the job I wanted, I got my feelings hurt and got mad all over again. I was jealous of your dad. Do you know what jealous means?"

Montana's eyes grew wide. "Yeah, it's like when someone gets a video game you're not allowed to have and brags about it, and you just keep wishing and wishing you could have it."

"That's exactly right. I wanted that job so bad. And I was jealous your dad got it, and that he made more money than me. So I got even madder. It's kind of hard to explain, but my mind was so mixed up that I even thought your dad was laughing at me behind my back—just the way my dad did. That wasn't true. But that's what I thought. So I snuck out to the camp and took my anger out on his new truck. I wanted to make him upset, but he didn't even get that angry."

Montana's eyebrows came together. "I don't get why you wanted to shoot Windy."

Grayson swallowed hard. "Because I was still *mad* and wanted to do something that would make your dad really upset. But when I stood there and pointed the rifle at Windy, I couldn't do it. I couldn't shoot her. I knew it was wrong. And unfair to you."

"But a deer made a noise behind you and the rifle went off?" Montana said.

Grayson let out a sob and seemed to inhale it. "Yes…and I saw you lying there on the ground. I was sick inside. I couldn't believe my eyes. I started to come help you when I saw your parents' truck speeding toward you. So I ran. It was the worst day of my life. I'd give anything to go back and change it."

"So you have to go to jail now?"

Grayson nodded. "Maybe for a long time. And that's very sad for my kids. But it's important to me that you know I would never ever have hurt you on purpose. It was an accident."

Montana made a tent with his fingers and seemed to be thinking. "You promise you *weren't* gonna shoot Windy?"

"I promise." Grayson crossed his heart. "I just couldn't do it."

Montana studied Grayson as if he were sizing him up, then slid off the glider and headed for the front door. "I'll be right back."

Rue glanced over at Grayson and shrugged.

Half a minute later, Montana burst through the door carrying the stuffed dog Grayson had given him at the hospital. "Here…" He handed the dog to Grayson. "You take her."

"I understand. You don't want my present anymore. I can't blame you."

Montana shook his head. "No, I want you to give her to your *kids*. You gave her to me so I wouldn't be sad. So now they won't be sad. Get it?"

A tear spilled down Grayson's cheek. "Yeah, I get it. Thanks. I should get going. I appreciate you listening. I'm really sorry I caused you so much pain and sadness."

"I forgive you, though."

Grayson's face went blank, and he seemed trapped in a long pause.

"Son, do you have any questions?" Rue said. "Grayson said you could ask anything you want."

Montana put his finger to his cheek and seemed to be thinking. "Are you still mad at your dad?"

"Yeah, I guess so. But he's dead now."

"Well…why don't you ask Jesus to help you not be mad at him, and maybe you won't get in any more trouble?"

Rue lay in bed, his hands behind his head, and stared at the ceiling fan. How pathetic was it that he found spiritual direction from watching how his young son chose to deal with heartache? Shouldn't it be the other way around?

Ivy rolled over and nestled next to him. "I can almost hear your wheels turning. What are you thinking about?"

"How easily Montana seems to get over things."

"Well, think of all he's been through. If he hadn't learned to forgive, he'd be hard as nails."

"And instead, he's got the most tender heart." Rue sighed. "Do you realize that not once since I found out how Grayson tried to hurt me have I prayed that God would touch his heart? I was too busy licking my wounds."

"It was a huge betrayal."

"But Montana was the real victim, and he's handling it fine. So's everyone else in the family. What's wrong with me?"

"Nothing." Ivy stroked his arm. "You just have to work through it your own way, that's all."

"I couldn't believe it when Montana gave the Windy dog to Grayson for his kids. I honestly don't know where all that compassion comes from."

"Because you never met his gramma Lu. She was a remarkable lady who modeled what real love is all about." Ivy nestled closer. "Lu was a gift—a real treasure. But I've seen a huge change in Montana since he accepted Christ and started going to Joel's Sunday-school class. He's like a little watering can that fills up with all the good things he's learning and then pours them out."

"Well, maybe I need a refill. My watering can is definitely dry."

43

AFTER CHURCH ON SUNDAY, Rue went by himself to take a look at the charred ruins of the dream house he had started for Ivy.

He strolled around the foundation and then sat under the huge cottonwood tree out front. He lifted his gaze to the edge of the woods where Grayson had stood with his hunting rifle. For the first time, he was able to picture what really happened and feel the raw emotion that still clawed at his heart. He hated being consumed by his anger. But no matter how many feeble attempts he made, he couldn't forgive Grayson.

Or Rusty. Though the rest of the family *had*—and Ivy was becoming convinced the best course of action was to sign an affidavit of nonprosecution and ask the DA not to pursue the charges against her brother. She reasoned that since Rusty paid for the damage and expressed deep remorse, it served no purpose for him to do jail time—especially when the only complaining witnesses were his sister and brother-in-law.

Rue picked up a rock and threw it. The pressure to agree with her pressed on his conscience like the cold barrel of a gun. What choice did he really have? If he chose not to sign the affidavit, it would drive a wedge between Ivy and him—and divide the family all over again.

It infuriated him that Rusty should get off so easily. So what if he'd paid for the damage? So what if he was sorry? So what if he finally decided to treat Ivy like a human being? Did any of that erase the pain the guy caused? He couldn't think of one good reason why he should forgive Rusty.

Seventy times seven. The words seemed to shake the valley, though he sensed they resonated only in his mind.

The truth was sobering. He hadn't forgiven him even one time. He wanted Rusty to keep paying for his mistakes the way Rusty wanted Ivy to keep paying for hers. Even God didn't demand that.

Rue leaned his head back against the tree and let his mind wander back through the unlikely events of the past couple years. Were any two people less deserving of mercy than he and Ivy? And yet God had not only forgiven them and cleansed them, He had restored them. And blessed them beyond anything they ever dreamed.

Something Brandon said came back to him. When you realize Whose you are, you can do what seems impossible.

What he needed to do wasn't possible in his own strength. He closed his eyes and withdrew to a private place deep inside himself—the dry, parched desert of his heart—and met with his heavenly Father. He held back nothing and spoke honestly about his anguish over the wrong that had been done to his family and the negative emotions that had hardened his heart. He asked forgiveness for having withheld his own mercy and thanked God for all the ways He had blessed him in spite of his failings.

And then he forgave Rusty. And Grayson. And asked his Father to draw them to Jesus—and restore them, even as he and Ivy had been restored.

He didn't perceive any great transformation taking place or feel any sudden affection for his two enemies. But a sweet peace dispelled the heaviness that had weighed on him just moments before. He rested a long time and allowed himself to experience the newfound freedom.

He came back to the moment when a drop of something fell on his arm. And then another. And another. He opened his eyes and realized a bank of gray clouds had rolled in over the mountains.

He got up and moved out into the open, his arms outstretched, his face tilted toward the sky, and let the summer shower soak him as if it were seeping into every fiber of his being. He opened his mouth and drank it in and then laughed out loud. He wasn't sure what Ivy had meant by a spiritual watering can, but if there was such a thing, his was overflowing.

44

The following Fourth of July

RUE STOOD OUT on the back deck, outfitted in the chef's apron that Jewel Sadler had given him as a housewarming gift, and fiddled with the dials on the new barbecue grill to make sure everything worked according to the directions.

He took a whiff of the pine-scented breeze and was distracted by a mountain bluebird that lit on the branch of a nearby conifer, aware that Windy was barking.

"Grandma and Grandpa are here," Montana announced.

Rue went in the house and out the front door to the driveway, where his in-laws were talking to Ivy. "Welcome."

Carolyn gave him the once-over. "Don't you look festive?"

Elam put one arm around Rue's shoulder and the other around Ivy's. "The place looks great. How does it feel to be moved in?"

Ivy laughed. "Depends on what you mean by *moved in*. We got the last box unpacked around midnight. But we absolutely love it."

"You have to see my room." Montana took Carolyn's hand and pulled her toward the door.

"Come on, Elam," she said. "We're about to get the grand tour."

Montana led his grandparents upstairs, and Rue went out the open sliding glass door to the deck, where Ivy was standing at the table she had set.

"This looks great, honey." Rue pulled her close and kissed her cheek. "Kelsey was right. The stars-and-stripes tablecloth really sets off our white dishes. I'm sorry she and Brandon couldn't make it. Didn't you say his parents were here from Seaport?"

"Uh-huh. And just in time for the big announcement." Ivy eyes twinkled. "Kelsey's expecting."

"*Expecting*? How'd I miss that?"

"She called just before Mom and Dad pulled up. The doctor confirmed it yesterday afternoon. They're absolutely ecstatic."

The doorbell rang and the front door opened.

"Hello? Anybody here?"

"Come in, Rusty!" Rue stepped inside the house and shook his brother-in-law's hand.

"The house looks terrific with furniture in it." Rusty sized up the room. "Really suits you guys. Makes me excited to get ours underway."

"Ours?"

"Yeah. We've got the floor plans picked out."

"We?"

The corners of Rusty's mouth twitched, and then a smile stole his face. "All those weekends traveling back and forth to Albuquerque paid off."

Rue finished his second bowl of homemade cherry ice cream and then pushed away from the table. "What a *feast*."

"May I please be excused?" Montana said. "I wanna go throw the Frisbee."

Ivy nodded. "Stay within whistling distance."

"Wait," Rusty said. "Let me take a look at that arm."

Montana held out his right arm, bent it at the elbow, and flexed it. "I've got strong muscles now. I don't even have to go back to rehab."

Rusty squeezed Montana's bicep in several places, then pulled him into a headlock and started tickling him.

Montana wriggled and giggled, obviously enjoying every second. "Help! Somebody help!"

"Ha ha ha." Rusty let out a ghoulish laugh. "I've got you in my clutches. And I'm not letting go till you say the magic word. Let's hear it... Come on, boy... Spit it out..."

Montana let out a husky laugh and finally hollered, *"Uncle."*

"See how easy that was?" Rusty chuckled and turned him loose.

Montana took a big step backward. As soon as he caught his breath, he cocked his head and wagged his finger. "Big mistake, Uncle Rusty. I'll get you when you're not looking."

"Is that a threat I hear?"

Montana started to go down the steps, then turned around and shot Rusty a grin the size of Texas. "Better watch your back, bucko."

Rusty lunged slightly as if he were going after him, and Montana jogged down the steps lickety-split and disappeared.

"Honestly," Ivy said, "you're more of a handful than any of his friends. So when are you and Jacqueline officially getting back together?"

"She gave her boss two weeks' notice yesterday. So two weekends from now, I'll go get her and the girls and move them here. We'll live in the rental house till our own place is built."

"This is such an answer to prayer," Carolyn said.

"And a whole lot of groveling. But we've had some great heart-to-hearts. I think we're going to be fine now."

Rue leaned forward, his elbows on the table. "So what house plan did you decide on?"

"Something rather unique. I don't want to say anything more until Jacqueline's with me. But it looks like we're all going to be neighbors."

"One big happy family," Elam said. "Something your mother and I dreamed about from the time you and Ivy were kids. Seems almost too good to be true."

Carolyn reached across the table and touched Rusty's hand. "I'm so proud you and Jacqueline didn't give up. You've been through a lot. But you hung in there."

"I'm just amazed she took me back."

"Which reminds me, Dad," Ivy said. "Have you heard lately how Grayson's wife is doing?"

Elam wiped his mouth with a napkin. "Tara's still teaching at the high school, and she and the kids seem to be getting along fine."

"And she's been asking Joel Myers lots of questions," Carolyn added. "She wants to start going to the seeker's class. Isn't that exciting?"

"Seems Joel encouraged Grayson to sit in on one of the prison ministry programs," Elam said. "And he's been asking questions about what it means to be a Christian. Said he still can't believe we forgave him."

Rue moved his eyes from Elam to Carolyn and back to Elam. Why hadn't they ever mentioned this before? "I heard that someone paid off their credit cards and is sending Tara a pretty nice check every month."

"You don't say?" Elam tugged at his mustache and avoided eye contact. "Grayson's up for parole in March. He's been a model prisoner. There's no reason to think he won't get out early."

"You suppose they'll just pick up the pieces and start again?" Ivy said. "I can't picture Grayson in the role of Mr. Mom. And who's going to hire a convicted felon?"

Elam took a sip of iced tea. "Oh, I expect *somebody* in this town will be willing to look past his mistakes and put him to work."

Ivy smiled knowingly at her dad.

"All right..." Rusty brought his palms down on the table. "Who wants to play a little Fourth of July flag football?"

"For heaven's sake," Elam said. "How long has it been since we've done that? I'm game. You may have to haul me out of here on a stretcher."

"Count me in," Carolyn said. "I've got scraps of material in the car that'll make great flags. I'll be right back."

Ivy stood, her chest puffed out, and grinned at her brother. "I can still outrun you any day of the week and twice on Sunday."

"Think so, eh?" Rusty grabbed the football and tossed it to her.

She caught it, tucked it under her arm, and ran down the steps, Rusty in hot pursuit.

Rue went over to the railing and watched with amusement as Rusty attempted to steal the ball from Ivy, who twisted and turned and held on with the tenacity of a pit bull. The sound of her girlish giggling brought an unexpected surge of emotion.

Carolyn stood beside him, strips of red cloth in her hand. "You're going to play, aren't you?"

"In a minute." Rue blinked the stinging from his eyes. "I'm just taking in a whole new side of Ivy. It's exciting to see this part of her come back to life."

"Truthfully, I wondered if I'd live long enough to see the spirited side of those two again. It's been a long, hard road."

"It's absolutely astonishing to me what's happened to this family in the past couple years."

Well," Carolyn stroked his back, "we have an astonishing God."

Rue folded his arms on the railing and relished for a moment the sights and sounds of his wife and son and brother-in-law—laughing, loving, *living*. Beyond them, the blue gray peaks of the San Juans stood glorious in the afternoon sun.

He lost himself in this little slice of heaven and let the laughter infuse him with joy and hope. For the first time in his life, he knew to the depths of his soul that absolutely nothing is impossible with God. And that in the Grand Scheme, all things do work together for good— even the pain we would never choose.

AFTERWORD

Bear with each other and forgive
whatever grievances you may
have against one another. Forgive
as the Lord forgave you.

COLOSSIANS 3:13

Dear friends,

I loved being able to end this series with a happily-ever-after, especially after having put the Kesslers and the Griffiths through an intense saga of mistakes and consequences. Our God truly is a God of victory. But that victory doesn't come without sacrifice.

I was so proud of Rue for realizing that his unwillingness to forgive or show mercy to Grayson and Rusty was the antithesis of what God had done in his life and Ivy's—and would only breed unhappiness for himself.

Oh, but the pain he and his family suffered as a result of Grayson's and Rusty's jealousy. James 3:16 tell us, "For when you have envy and selfish ambition, there you find disorder and every evil practice." This was certainly evidenced by the duo's unconscionable actions in this story.

Envy, like a deadly virus, is neutral until it finds a host. But when our defenses are down and we become infected, it can quickly overtake us. While believers are not *immune* to envy or the symptoms that accompany it, our strongest defense is a steady diet of God's Word, which promises that lasting satisfaction is found in Christ alone.

Life isn't fair. And our human minds will never understand all the inequities this side of heaven. Only when we learn to be content and confident in the person God is shaping us to be can we hope to stop comparing ourselves with others and cease to feel cheated when this world disappoints us.

Let's not forget that when His glorious, divine plan is played out to the fullest, all believers will dwell for eternity in joy unspeakable. What happens here is just a blink in time.

I have so enjoyed bringing the characters of Phantom Hollow to life on these pages. I hope they'll remain in your heart, as they will in mine.

I would love to hear from you. Feel free to contact me through my publisher at WaterBrook Multnomah Publishing Group, 12265 Oracle Boulevard, Suite 200, Colorado Springs, CO 80921, or drop by my website at www.kathyherman.com and leave your comments on my guest book. I read and respond to every e-mail and greatly value your input.

In His love,

Kathy Herman

DISCUSSION GUIDE

1. Explain what you think is meant by James 3:16, "For where you have envy and selfish ambition, there you find disorder and every evil practice."

2. Why do think envy is often referred to as one of the seven deadly sins? How widespread do you think envy is in our culture? in the church? in business? in school?

3. What does Proverbs 27:4 mean to you? "Anger is cruel and fury overwhelming, but who can stand before jealousy?" Have you ever been victimized by someone's envy? How did you respond? Did it lead to other sinful behavior? Was it ever resolved?

4. What kinds of things might a person do that might incite feelings of jealousy in someone else? Has anyone ever tried to deliberately make you jealous? Have you ever deliberately sought to make someone else jealous? If so, can you identify the motivating factor for such behavior?

5. Do you think people sometimes deliberately divulge information that would cause others to be envious of them? Why do you think someone would do that? Have ever you been guilty of doing that?

6. Do you think that publicly giving God the glory for our talents, accomplishments, possessions, good fortune, or any other blessing is an effective way to avoid making others jealous? Can this sometimes come across as false humility? If so, explain how.

7. Do believers bear any responsibility for the way they talk about how God is blessing them? Is there a right and a wrong way to share? Explain your answer.

8. If you were to discover that someone was jealous of you, what (if anything) would you do to diffuse the situation? If you were feeling envious of someone else or his/her good fortune, what do you think God would have you do about it? Do you think it's helpful to confront a person and admit your feelings? Is it sometimes better to just confess it to God, or to God and a trusted friend?

9. Do you think praying for the person you're jealous of would have any effect on the way you feel about him or her? Why or why not?

10. Is there anything flattering about someone envying you? Should there be? Is it possible that jealousy leveled at you could actually cause you to feel proud? feel superior?

11. Do you think envy and anger go hand-in-hand? Which came first with Grayson? Which with Rusty? What about in your own life—which tends to come first?

12. Have you ever been guilty of professional envy for a colleague or boss? Could you relate to Grayson's feelings in the story? Do you think Rue and/or Elam could have been more sensitive about Grayson's bruised ego? Should they have been? If so, what would you have done differently?

13. Even if you've never had to deal with drug abuse in your family, could you relate to Rusty's feelings toward Ivy? Have you ever felt jealous of a sibling? Have you ever resented your parents for paying more attention or giving out more praise to a sibling,

especially an undeserving one? Do you think families can be a breeding ground for envy? Is there a way to guard against it?

14. Who was your favorite character in this story? If you could meet that person, what would you like to say to him or her? Did God speak to your heart through this story? Was there a particular thought or principle you took away?

15. Fill in the blank: If there's one thing I won't forget about envy, it's_____.

Twenty-eight year old Ivy Griffith is back in her hometown of Jacob's Ear—still carrying a secret that could destroy her. But after disaster strikes at her high school reunion, she's the only one left alive who witnessed that fatefull night so long ago...or is she?

After serving time, Ivy Griffith has paid her debt to society, kicked her drug habit, and she's making a fresh start. But is something bigger at play here—something orchestrated outside of her control that's about to bring down the curtain on everything, including her past?

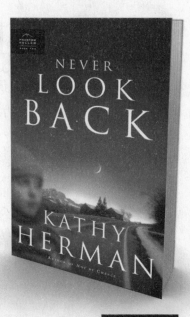

www.KathyHerman.com

A SEAPORT SUSPENSE

A Quiet Little Seaport Town...
So You Think!

A Shred of Evidence, Book 1

Ellen Jones stumbles onto information too alarming to keep to herself. Will she become enmeshed in speculation and gossip—or can she become a catalyst for truth and healing?

Eye of the Beholder, Book 2

Guy Jones becomes enamored with his newfound status in a prestigious law firm and grows increasingly embarrassed by Ellen's needy friends. Their marriage is on the rocks, and Guy's integrity on the line!

All Things Hidden, Book 3

How do you let go of a past that won't let go of you? That's what Ellen Jones would like to know. The consequences of past mistakes don't just disappear...

Not by Chance, Book 4

Thirty-year-old Brandon Jones arrives at his parents' house burned out, jobless, and now fiancée-less. As he struggles to find his life's purpose, he discovers the pieces of his life are not by chance.

www.KathyHerman.com